79A

by

Chris Gleeson

To Cathy,

Love and best wishes

Chris.

Copyright © 2018 Chris Gleeson

ISBN: 978-0-244-98310-9

All rights reserved, including the right to reproduce this book, or portions thereof in any form. No part of this text may be reproduced, transmitted, downloaded, decompiled, reverse engineered, or stored, in any form or introduced into any information storage and retrieval system, in any form or by any means, whether electronic or mechanical without the express written permission of the author.

This is a work of fiction. Names and characters are the product of the author's imagination and any resemblance to actual persons, living or dead, is entirely coincidental.

PublishNation
www.publishnation.co.uk

For
Cole
Our beautiful boy

INTRODUCTION

On August 24th, 79AD, Mount Vesuvius in Italy erupted. The volcano spewed forth a deadly cloud of molten rock, pulverised pumice and hot ash at a rate of 1.5 million tons per second, ultimately releasing a hundred-thousand times the thermal energy of the Hiroshima and Nagasaki bombings combined. No one knew what a volcano was at that time.

The ancient world had entered the geological age.

On July 16th, 1945, at Trinity site, near Alamogordo, New Mexico, scientists of the Manhattan project readied themselves to watch the detonation of the world's first atomic bomb. The device was affixed to a one-hundred foot tower and discharged just before dawn. No one was properly prepared for the result.

The modern world had entered the nuclear age.

PREFACE

In this novel I have tried to be accurate to the facts of both the ancient world and the modern world; although, for the sake of the plot and continuity, some details have been 'reformed' to suit the artistic licence that fictional stories of this genre require. I have also thrown in some concepts of my own that may or may not be accurate but, nevertheless, add some weight to the novel.

1

TUESDAY, AUGUST 26TH 79 AD:

News of the disaster at Pompeii and Herculaneum spread like wildfire throughout the streets of Rome. People stopped and questioned the messengers vigorously. Some were desperately worried for word of their relatives whilst others had business interests to be concerned about. The exhausted messengers, who had galloped on horseback for two days, told a harrowing tale that was hard for the people to fathom.

Daccus Atholos, a grain store accountant, whose family had immigrated to Rome from Greece, felt bemused by what snippets of news he could catch upon the air as he stood by his office window. Apparently, the deities of the underworld had unleashed their fiery temper from beneath Mount Vesuvius killing thousands at Pompeii and Herculaneum. Daccus knew that the emperor's enemies would use this news from Campania to their advantage. It was always the way in Rome. Disasters of any kind were seen as a chance for political point-scoring by all parties. But politics was not Daccus' concern right now.

Moving from the window, he sat down at his table, picked up a stylus and twiddled it impatiently between his fingers and thumb whilst he waited for his young assistant, Letticus, to return. Priming his ears as he sat back, he could hear the cries of many anxious citizens reverberating through the narrow streets but he did not have long to wait. Letticus came running in with eyes wide open and perspiring profusely from the oppressive heat. He looked scared out of his wits and was clenching a small stone charm of Jupiter tight in his fist for comfort. Daccus laid the stylus down gently upon the marble desk and folded his arms in anticipation of the boy's report.

'It is true,' said Letticus in an agitated tone as he walked across the room and proceeded to gulp a mouthful of water straight from the clay jug that was sitting upon a low shelf. After he finished, he placed the jug down upon the shelf and spoke in a quivering tone.

'The gods under Vesuvius have woken and their stirrings have destroyed the area for miles around. The messengers say that there are survivors who speak of day turning to night with fire and ash raining down from out of the mouth of the mountain. They say the gods of the underworld are coming to kill us all.'

Fourteen year old Letticus looked positively terrified and seemed to be sweating more out of pure fear rather than the heat. But Daccus stayed calm knowing that such stories from afar can be grossly exaggerated. Messengers often added their own interpretations to garner a more dramatic response, especially when military action was needed to quell some disorder at a far-flung outpost. But he suspected that this news was uniquely different. There had been rumours that Mount Vesuvius was acting strangely of late. Talk of funny smells and earth tremors were rife in the region of Campania but his quick mind struggled with this latest report. One thing he certainly didn't believe in was that the gods of the underworld had something to do with it. He was a supporter of Greek free-thinking which had blossomed through the life and works of Aristarchus, Aristotle, Pythagoras of Samos and Archimedes and in the light of their brilliant minds he knew that something else, other than the gods, was at work underneath Vesuvius - but what?

Daccus allowed Letticus to go to his family telling him not to worry too much about the gods. The terrified boy was gone in a flash.

After a few moments of deliberating, Daccus stood and walked to the far wall of his office, washed his hands and face in a bowl of scented water, dried himself then returned to his desk, opened up a new wax tablet and began to copy down the sum total of his day's work. When he had finished he closed the tablet, tucked it under his arm and quickly exited the building, locking the door behind him.

The sun was high in the sky and the city heat was confined within the claustrophobic surroundings of the narrow street, trapping in an atmosphere filled with an air of dread and foreboding. He turned left down the rickety, cobbled pathway and made his way to the Tri-via. The three streets which intersected at the bottom of the hill were thronging with people wanting to know more about the news from Pompeii. A man was nailing a wooden placard to a post outside Dio's tavern and a crowd had gravitated towards it. But Daccus ignored the commotion, knowing that the hastily prepared notice would be an order by the local magistrate appealing for calm.

When he reached the junction he turned right and headed uphill towards Fario's home. His friend and confidant would be at rest, convalescing from his fall - he had foolishly tried to repair a dislodged tile from the roof of his sister's villa and slipped. The broken leg would keep him out of action for months.

Daccus began to labour as the incline grew steeper with every step but he could see his friend's home a good few paces onwards. Its white front, adorned with hanging baskets filled with flowers of all descriptions, stood out amongst the rows of shoddily assembled drab, brick buildings belonging to Fario's lesser house-proud neighbours.

Daccus was thirty-one years of age and growing a bit of a spread around his mid-riff. His black, curly hair and straight nose dissected by even blacker, thick-set eye brows made him look at home amongst his Roman compatriots but he felt Greek; spoke Greek when he needed to and was fiercely proud of his lineage. Fario, on the other hand, was an Etruscan; loud, volatile and fiery of temper, though his fall had somewhat softened him up a little as of late.

After another few laborious steps a puffing and panting Daccus came to Fario's front door and rattled his knuckles hard against the pine framework. The door swung in silently and a black face stared out at him from within. It was Mumi - Fario's slave girl, which he had purchased from an African slave market. She stepped aside to allow Daccus to enter the vestibule; the whites of her big, brown eyes was all he could see from within the interior as he waited for his eyes to adjust to the dim light. He took this moment to recall her lithe, ebony body and the touch of her oiled skin as she obeyed his every command. He would never know whether she enjoyed his pleasure or not; he didn't care. Mumi had been offered to him by Fario at a party to celebrate the feast of Saturnalia and he took full advantage of it. The feast of Saturnalia was an annual role-reversal played out every December, where the master of the home would bring food and presents to the table for his or her slaves and there would be much frolicking and jollity. The party was a grand affair and Fario did not disappoint his guests. Daccus could not wait until this year's celebrations when Fario had hinted that his next one would be even better than the last.

Soon his eyes adjusted to the lighting and he stepped through into the hallway whilst Mumi scurried off to the garden to alert her master. Whilst he waited he took the moment to look around at Fario's amazing collection of artefacts gathered from around the known world. He never grew tired of eyeing up the fascinating array that his friend had amassed over the years. There were no spoils of war or shields and swords adorning these walls. Fario was an avid collector of items from many and varied cultures. He collected wood carvings from far-off lands depicting animals and birds, some of which no one could recognise. Stone tools, stone carvings and stone cooking pots. He even had a collection of human skin which was tanned and made into pouches and head garments.

Eventually, Daccus made his way over to a large table were a mixed variety of jewellery sat. But then one item caught Daccus' eye in particular, one he had not seen before. It was a dark, wooden box which was set back from the rest of the collection and was half-hidden under a finely woven cloth. He pulled the cloth aside, guessing that this must be Fario's new acquisition from Gaul, the one he had heard whispers of. He looked down at the square box with open curiosity. It was about the same size as a money case, the same kind that tax collectors used. Upon the lid was a depiction of a wheel with four spokes carved deep into its black wood and between the spaces of each spoke were images of the sun, a full moon, a half moon and a crescent moon, respectively. Beneath were letterings that were indecipherable to Daccus.

He wondered what the strange words meant. Even stranger were the two iron bands wrapped tightly around the box and both sealed by a blacksmith's join. It seemed to Daccus that whatever was inside the casket was meant to remain there. He shook his head and smiled wryly to himself.

Mumi returned, bowed and pointed in the direction of the garden. The slave could not speak. She had been dumb from birth, which was convenient for she could not complain every time she was being abused. Strangely, Daccus had always felt a sense of pity for her but he had to dispel such thoughts for he was a Roman citizen and she was a lowly slave girl. Though he found her exquisite beauty most perturbing and yet satisfying, deep down, he hated slavery but was unwilling to show contempt for it for his Greek ancestors were also guilty of such inhumane practises.

Moments later he found himself in the small but grand surroundings of Fario's garden. His friend was seated in the shade at a table on the far end with his walking stick propped up against his chair. His face was as dark as a thunder cloud.

'Whatever is the matter my friend?' asked an inquisitive Daccus as he strode purposely towards him, 'have you broken your other leg?'

'Is the news from Pompeii true?' asked Fario in his rough, Etruscan accent.

'It seems so. Vesuvius has disgorged itself upon Pompeii and Herculaneum. I hear many have been killed.' Daccus let his sentence hang in the air and scanned his friend's face for a sign of a response but Fario sat stone-faced, grimacing in deep thought. Daccus took a seat and sat down at the table then continued:

'The people of Rome are frightened. They think their gods are going to kill them.'

Fario raised a cursory eyebrow and leaned back in his chair. He was fifty years of age, slim, wiry and rich. Not as rich as the aristocracy and certain members of the senate but rich enough to own several slaves and a second house in Rome. His first home was a villa which rested in the hills of Isernia. The property was previously owned by the late Pontius Pilate. He had bought the run down property off Pilate's family at a snip and renovated it to an exquisite standard. He had made his money in gold and silver and traded them very successfully around the Mediterranean, successfully enough for him to be able to retire at the grand old age of forty-one. Amongst his many business interests he also made a tidy profit from his olive groves that surrounded the grounds of his villa in Isernia.

'The gods!' laughed Fario with a hint of cynicism in his voice. 'Those stupid Roman bastards are running around in fear of their own arseholes never mind their gods.'

Daccus chuckled under his breath knowing exactly what Fario meant. Like Daccus, Fario was also an advocate of Greek free-thinking. That was why he had founded the secret society of Apollo. He chose Apollo who was the Greek god of music and healing, the god of light and the god of truth as a deliberate cover to keep the eye of suspicion trained elsewhere. But the Apollonians - as the society members liked to call themselves - were not in the business of adoring such deities. Their beliefs in democracy and free will stemmed from a natural curiosity of the real world where nature can be interrogated, examined and revealed in ways that did not require the input of a god or gods. They wanted Rome to turn away from superstition and mysticism and awaken to the call of a grander truth where people can live without fear and ignorance.

'I shall call a meeting. The day after tomorrow will do,' said Fario as his eyes strayed towards the clear, blue sky. 'I fear the emperor and his friends in the senate will have to blame someone for the disaster at Pompeii and if we Apollonians were ever found out we would be easy fodder.'

'Let's hope he blames the Jewish slaves who are finishing off the gleaming new Flavian Ampitheatre; Titus will have to find a way to get rid of them somehow or other,' replied Daccus.

'I hear the locals are calling the Ampitheatre the Coliseum in memory of Nero's statue. It seems they still hanker after the vile wretch. As for the Jews, Titus will probably auction them off or have some use for them in the inaugural games.' Fario clapped his hands and a servant boy came running to his table. 'Fetch me some wine and toasted bread,' he ordered. The boy scurried off obediently.

Daccus shifted his growing bulk upon a high backed chair and sighed under his breath. 'So, my friend, what do you say caused Vesuvius to wreak such devastation?'

Fario scratched at his slowly healing leg and pondered upon the question. He seemed to be digging for something in the recesses of his considerable mind. The slave came back with a jug of wine and a rack of toasted bread laced with a thin coating of honey, laid them out on the table and stood back. The two men began to eat and drink at ease whilst the boy stayed where he stood, staring longingly at the fare on offer. An annoyed Fario slapped his palm down hard upon the table and the boy jumped. Then Fario reached for his walking stick and raised it towards him threateningly. The slave, who was all but ten years of age, turned reluctantly and strode off back into the house.

'The youth of today, no respect,' Fario muttered as he sipped at his wine and replaced the stick.

After a short pause, Fario stared hard at Daccus and spoke in a distant tone:

'Some of the great minds of the library of Alexandria said that mountains are the earth's pores just like we have pores on our skin that help us sweat and that they help the earth to stay cool. Others said that there is great pressure within the earth from all the weight of the mountains pressing down upon it and that the pressure must be released from time-to-time.'

'By what means is the pressure released, Fario?' asked an inquisitive Daccus who was forever fascinated by his friend's explanations.

'Heat,' he replied. 'The name of the great mind who suggested such a thing is lost to us but some texts and word of mouth have come down through time. I will ask my good friend, Attuso of Crete. He will expand upon it at the meeting. He is very knowledgeable in such matters.'

Daccus was fascinated by Fario's answer and would not miss the meeting of the society for anything. Then he remembered the wax tablet he had brought with him. He placed it down upon the table.

'Ah, my monthly accounts?' asked Fario.

'Yes. You are a very rich man,' said Daccus.

'Only rich because you keep the eyes of the tax collectors fixed elsewhere.'

'Oh, I make sure you pay enough to make them think they're ripping you off.'

'Ha, ha!' laughed Fario as he raised a glass to propose a toast. 'You may stay the night as my honoured guest and let's drink to Apollo?'

Daccus gave Fario a grateful nod and drank the toast but he was not laughing knowing that the danger of such clandestine meetings was very real. If the magistrate found out what the Apollonians were discussing at their meetings they would be arrested immediately and found guilty of subversion and whatever else the senate could throw at them. Although religious tolerance was observed within certain boundaries throughout the empire, free thinking and dangerous political ideas that contradicted the established order was suppressed by the Romans on pain of death. Then Daccus remembered the strange box that Fario had brought from Gaul and asked him about it.

Fario's face immediately went ashen and he stirred uncomfortably in his chair. He looked down long and hard at his wine glass then he looked up with that mischievous stare of his and grinned:

'I will reveal my latest acquisition at the meeting,' was all he said.

2

SATURDAY, AUGUST 29ᵀᴴ PRESENT DAY:

Archaeologist Carl Allen shoved the tip of his spade into the earth at the base of the plastered wall and pulled it out quickly. In eager anticipation he raised it slowly to his face to examine the damp soil which, upon close inspection, confirmed his suspicions. The speckles of silver dust glinting in the spotlight made his vision blur for a split second, but it was there nonetheless; silver mixed with gold! His heart skipped a beat and he sat down upon the ground to wipe his sweated brow.

'Lana, come over here!' he called triumphantly, 'you gotta see this.'

Lana Evans came running over to the plot and looked down into it. Carl was sitting in the remains of the cellar of a wealthy home that had probably belonged to a councillor or a successful businessman. Carl raised the spade up for Lana to see. It was glinting brightly, like tinsel.

'Is that what I think it is?' she asked incredulously.

'It seems we have found something of great interest,' said Carl.

'No, 'you' have found something of great interest,' replied Lana. 'Wait, I'll get my camera.'

Carl Allen watched as she headed off to the field tent then he stood up and faced the plastered wall which was covered in bits of dry grit and soil. He began to remove the dirt carefully with a stiff-bristled hand brush. Immediately, a face appeared; the black face of a young African woman. He brushed more dirt off the wall and saw by her attire that she was a slave girl, dressed in a rough linen tunic, tied at the waist by a thick cord.

Lana Evans soon returned with her camera in hand and jumped down into the plot without using the ladder. Her athleticism always surprised Carl for she was no spring chicken. Thirty-eight years of age, six foot tall and endowed with the most spectacular figure, she was every field-trip male's 'perk'. She wore a sky blue T-shirt with a picture of Jimi Hendrix emblazoned upon it, playing his guitar with a large reefer sticking out of his mouth. The T-shirt was stretched tightly over her perfectly shaped breasts which were the dominant feature of her physique. Her very short cut-off denims revealed a set of perfectly, bronzed pins that any catwalk queen half her age would die for. Out of professional courtesy, Carl Allen quickly forced his gaze from her legs and turned his attention to the work at hand.

'Oh my god,' said Lana as she brushed aside a lock of jet-black hair and began clicking away with the Nikon P520. 'She's beautiful.'

'Yeah, not bad for a slave,' replied Carl as he stepped forward and continued to brush away at more grit. 'It seems the owner adorned his house aplenty, even down here in the cellar.'

'It seems this owner was careless with his silver and gold collection,' said Lana in between snaps.

'Well, as you know, rich owners often kept their wealth beneath the grounds of their homes but looters and opportunist alike knew this, so I assume a few bags or pots of gold and silver were accidently spilled during the robbery.'

'Fascinating,' said Lana as she clicked away on her camera. 'Do you think we'll find a full pot?'

'Not a chance. Treasure hunters in those days were very efficient. Nothing much was left behind.'

After almost an hour, Carl had removed enough grit to reveal all of the figures painted on the wall. The fresco showed a gathering of men - he counted eleven in all - dressed in togas, the attire of Roman citizenship. One of the men was holding a placard depicting the Greek god Apollo. Carl pondered for a short while and Lana picked up on it.

'What's bothering you, Carl?' she asked as she lowered her camera.

'I'm wondering why a fresco of this quality is down here of all places?'

'Maybe Professor Barnes will throw some light on it.'

'Yes, I guess he would,' replied Carl. Just then a bell rang out and a shout from the headquarters went up; the dig was over for the day. Carl looked to Lana and sighed. She nodded and let out a sigh of her own.

'It's going to be dark soon and you look like shit,' she said as she turned her camera off, replaced the lens cap and closed the leather cover around it.

'Thanks,' said Carl as he laid down the brush and stretched his aching arms 'I can never say that about you!'

Lana rolled her eyes and shook her head.

Carl Allen was forty-one years of age, six foot two, blue-eyed and grey-haired. His slim body was in relatively good condition but he endured minor aches and pains that were acquired after many years of digging in the field of archaeology. His home was in Livingston, Montana in the beautiful foothills of Yellowstone national park. Harvard educated and the second son of an industrialist, he bucked the family trend and found his vocation in studying the antiquities rather than a life of endless boardroom meetings and presentations. His father disapproved, of course, but he never stood in his way and even funded Carl's first dig in Libya. Now, twenty-one years later, he was in Rome in charge of his thirteenth dig. His team were the best in the business, a good mixture of old and new, experience and enthusiasm, not a bad blend as he would often say.

This latest dig was situated near the outskirts of Rome which in ancient times was populated mostly by Plebeians, the poorest of citizen, but secluded areas were occupied by wealthier people who needed to be in the city to keep their eyes on their business. The ruin of the building he now stood in was just such a place.

Taking a final glance around at his handy work, he made his way up the six foot ladder and out across the dig site with Lana in tow. The field lights were soon switched off and the area was immediately plunged into semi-darkness illuminated only by the lights of the surrounding buildings of modern day Rome. The subterranean site was roughly two acres in size which required many hands to excavate. To Carl it seemed an eerie place which echoed to the sound of the Roman life that was not in the history books. The everyday going's on of the everyday people and slaves in the largest city in the world, at that point, seemed very real. He had been to many digs all over Europe and the middle east but with this one he somehow felt more connected to; more 'vibes' as Lana would say.

As he progressed he could hear from up ahead the conversations from within the large canvas marquee that served both as the canteen and headquarters. The booming voice of Professor Terence Barnes rang out the loudest, no doubt spouting his considerable knowledge around the table to all within earshot. When Carl and Lana entered the canteen all eyes turned. Most male eyes latched onto Lana whilst the rest watched Carl, expecting him to be carrying a tray of new artefacts. When they saw nothing, the conversation and the eating resumed as before.

Dinner was functional but fulfilling as usual and the banter was the same as the night before but Carl had decided that he would say nothing about his dig until the morning. He was glad when Professor Barnes roped him in to a debate about whether the early Roman republic made a fatal error in invoking the office of dictator to one man in times of crisis and whether this act opened the door to greedier men who saw it as a way to further their ambitions – hence the rise of Sulla and Julius Caesar which eventually led to a succession of emperors. Carl humoured the professor by saying that 'if all the emperors of Rome thought like the first dictator, Cincinnatus, who gave up the honour to return to farming his fields, there wouldn't be much for the classical writers of the day to write about'.

Carl was glad that Lana was staying obediently quiet throughout but he could tell that she was bursting to share the news of the find with the others. More questions were bounded about and Carl answered them with regulation answers, keeping his sentences short and to the point. Eventually, he excused himself saying that he was tired and would be retiring to bed early. But Lana was full of energy and was already opening her third bottle of Budweiser along with the three male French graduates who were drooling over her immaculate figure. He knew she could out-drink, out-smoke and out-party them all. He'd seen it so many times before with students and tonight was going to be no different.

As he made his way out, he picked up his torch and Lana's camera and headed for the exit. 'I'll look after it for you,' he said to her with a knowing wink. She nodded back and took a long gulp from her bottle as the goggle-eyed graduates stared longingly at her fabulous tits. Carl laughed to himself. She was a real all-rounder!

Lana Evans was educated in archaeology by her father, Professor Martin Evans who was chief lecturer at Oxford University. Although American by birth and an only child she was brought up in England until she was twenty-two years of age and then moved back to California after her father had died of a sudden heart attack. In California she spent the rest of her twenties wasting her inheritance money on beach parties and fun in the sun. She was burning up the one and a half million dollars of her father's will at a frantic rate and it was obvious to all that she was running away from the loss of the only family she had. Her mother had died of pneumonia when she was only three and her father had brought Lana up by himself. He never re-married but, instead, concentrated all his efforts on his daughter and his work. In California, on the day of her twenty-eighth birthday, she met Dennis Moreno at her birthday bash and everything changed. Within a year she was married to the dashing thirty year old popular surfing champion from Big Sur and the couple were constantly in the public eye but within six months Dennis was dead; killed by a big wave off Waikiki. Lana was devastated. But Dennis had gone to the big Kahuna in the sky leaving a trail of debt amounting to a total of three million and seven-hundred thousand dollars. He had no insurance to cover the debts leaving Lana on the brink of bankruptcy. She was forced to sell their Malibu beach house; sold on their beautiful yacht; sold Dennis's prized collection of vintage cars including a Plymouth Barracuda which was his favourite and auctioned off his medals and trophies. The remaining thirty-thousand dollars of the debt she paid off with what was left of her inheritance leaving her with the famously princely sum of nine hundred and ninety nine dollars and ninety nine scents which the publishers of the national celebrity magazines of the day were eager to quote.

Instead of putting a gun to her head Lana re-invented herself. She ditched her marriage name by deed poll, took back her family name of Evans and re-entered the world of archaeology. She re-studied in her field vigorously for two years to sharpen up on her skills and graduated on her thirty-first birthday. She was an expert in classical Greek and Roman history and within a year she was digging the dirt in Caesarea in old Judea which is now modern Israel. Her command of ancient Greek, Latin and extinct European languages was second to none and she was also an accomplished symbolist. Carl had a lot of professional respect for her after all she'd been through knowing that by throwing all her efforts into archaeology it must have helped her to forget so much pain.

On this night Carl chose to sleep in his field tent. He couldn't care to walk the five hundred yards up the hill to the Coppola Inn. The air conditioning of the Inn dried the back of his throat and he found it irritating to say the least. He switched on the torch then strolled back to the dig site in deep thought. As he made his way back he suddenly found that the atmosphere felt decidedly different from before. He had an overwhelming feeling that he was being watched and he absentmindedly looked about but there was no one around.

Before retiring to his tent he strode over towards the pit and shone the torchlight down into it. It was the same as he had left it; the faces upon the fresco stared out into the night like sentinels guarding his prize. Then something caught his eye. In the dirt lay a half-buried gold coin. He immediately scurried down the ladders and bent down to retrieve it. He was surprised to find that it was larger than the average coin and heavier too. After he held it in his hand for a while he carefully rubbed the dirt away with his thumb to reveal an intricate carving of exquisite design that seemed as if it was carved only yesterday. He saw that the coin had an eyelet for a chain or cord attached to the top and he knew now that it was, in fact, an amulet. Closer inspection of the detail on the amulet revealed images that meant nothing to him. In the centre sat a gemstone dulled by years in the dirt. Then he noticed that the eyelet at the top was cracked open as if it had been yanked violently from the wearer's neck. He stood and pondered for long moments. Then suddenly, almost imperceptibly, the air around him dropped in temperature. He looked up at the sky and saw a thin whisper of smoke, or was it a cloud, slowly spiralling hundreds of feet above him, like a miniature tornado. Inside the cloud there seemed to be a glowing, bright light. He smiled to himself and shook his head wearily. *Tiredness plays tricks on the mind,* he thought.

He quickly clambered back up the ladders, entered his tent, took off his boots and lay himself down on top of his sleeping bag, fully clothed. He felt exhausted and sleep was only seconds away. Putting the amulet aside, he took out his cell phone from his pocket and saw that it had two text messages; one from his brother and the other from Ted Brooks of the National Geographic. Too tired to be bothered to read them he turned off the phone and put both it and Lana's camera to one side; the messages and the snap-shots can wait until the morning, he thought. After a while, he picked up the amulet once more and held it up in the torchlight. The light from the torch suddenly dimmed which was shortly followed by a crackling sound outside the tent. He immediately clambered out of the tent and looked up at the night sky. The spiral of smoke or cloud had not moved but stayed where it was, only turning faster this time. Rubbing his sleepy eyes, he decided to make his way back to the edge of pit, feeling drawn to the fresco for some reason; why, he didn't know, but it felt like something was wrong. The cold, unfeeling stares from the surface of the fresco sent a shiver down his spine.

After a short while, he made his way back to his tent, turned off the torch and flopped onto his back, puzzled and confused. He stuffed the amulet under his sleeping bag and lay still, deciding that the odd events of the evening were a result of him working too hard as thoughts of a well-earned vacation crossed his mind.

He was glad to be resting his aching limbs after a long dig in the heat. Crickets sounded in the distance and the faint roar of a jumbo jet arching over the eternal city back-dropped the din. He left the canvas flap of the entrance open to allow some air to drift through, finding it preferable to the artificial air of the Inn. Looking out through the open flap at the moonless sky, he saw the planet Venus and he watched it shimmer in the haze.

How many Roman philosophers, poets, magistrates, soldiers, generals and slaves had looked up at her and wondered at her beauty, he thought. Little did they know that Venus was a planet-sized version of hell!

Within minutes he had drifted off to sleep but it felt like he had only blinked for a fraction of a second and was instantly surprised to discover the odour of stale alcohol and cigarettes wafting over him. Then heavy breathing next to his left ear jolted him out of his stupor and he sat upright. In the dull light of his one-man tent he could make out the figure of Lana Evans lying on her back next to him, fully clothed and completely unconscious – and drunk of course; a throwback to her California days. He hesitated in trying to wake her up for he knew it would be futile so he laid himself back down and couldn't help but allow his eyes to wander over the outline of her awesome body. His loins were instantly on fire but it felt like torture. Out of professional respect he wouldn't try it on but he couldn't resist kissing her gently upon the cheek and whispering her good night. She never budged.

Now he felt restless so he flipped open his phone and opened his brother's text. It read: *Great news Bro', we're pregnant again. Baby's due in late April. Catch you when you get back.* Carl immediately called Sam to congratulate him. The phone rang for several moments then Sam answered.

'Hi Carl were just going to bed after a night out at Calino's to celebrate. Wish you had been there kiddo.'

'Congratulations bro',' replied Carl, suddenly feeling homesick. 'You owe me a lunch, remember?'

'I do too. When are you back home?

Then suddenly, from out of nowhere, a bright light blinded Carl from all directions, penetrating through the canvas sheeting of the tent. Then a terrible sense of falling from a high jolted him upright and shouts and calls from afar rang in his ears. Sam's voice crackled in the speaker and faded. A sudden blast of freezing cold air tore through the entrance of the tent and then, silence.

The next instant he could hear voices in the distance, like mutterings in the dark. He looked down at his phone, which was glowing white. He put the phone back to his ear but Sam's voice was barely perceptible. Carl raised the volume on his phone to peak level but, by now, Sam's voice was gone, even though the line was open and registering five bars. He turned to Lana. She was lying on her side this time, curled up and facing away from him. Her fabulous arse filled her denim shorts to bursting point and the lower cheeks of her backside protruded ever so invitingly out of the cut-off line. Then suddenly, his phone went dead. The screen registered no signal. The connection to his brother was cut. From nowhere a shout came through the night air. It seemed as if it was directed at his tent but what was strange about it was that the words were spoken in Latin.

'Hey, who's in there?' come the Latin dialect once again.

In the next instant a bearded face peeked through the flap and out again. Then the orange glow of a flickering flame danced across the canvasing and two heads popped in, lit by the flaming torch. The faces of a young boy and an old man stared wide-eyed at Carl, seemingly dumbfounded by his appearance. Then the man brought the flaming torch further into the tent and his eyes settled upon the sleeping form of Lana. He immediately exited at once, followed quickly by the boy.

'Master, master,' called out the man as his cries faded in the distance.

Carl flipped his phone closed and shoved it into his pocket then was out of the tent in one bound. The view that greeted him totally blew him away. Incredibly, he found himself standing in a neatly kept garden surrounded by hanging baskets full of flowers and plants. A miniature pond, rimmed by a low circular wall, sat in the centre of the garden and beyond that, sat a table and four high-backed chairs. He looked up at the sky and noticed that there was now a full moon. Then he was distracted by the sound of a large door creaking open which was followed by agitated voices from behind it sounding out across the peaceful surroundings.

'Who are you?' someone cried out in Latin. 'The master has been woken and will be most displeased. Go away and take that wench with you.'

Carl scratched his head thinking that this dream was much too real.

Wench? Lana will want to speak to that individual.

'Why are you speaking in Latin?' was all Carl could say in English as his brain slowly began to unscramble. 'Is this some kind of trick by the students of the Vatican, up to mischief once again? Monsignor Vincetti will hear of this!'

Silence followed and Carl thought about waking Lana when all of sudden the large door creaked open and out stepped a man who was leaning heavily upon a walking stick. He was being informed by the old man and the boy and fingers were being pointed in Carl's direction. Soon, the old man and the boy began to light up all of the torches that were attached to the surrounding

~ 18 ~

walls. Then the man with the walking stick, who was dressed in a toga, made his way towards him. Carl thought for one moment that he had strayed into a fancy dress party or some gathering of a weirdo sect as he looked on at the approaching man. His progress was slow and painful but his sleep-filled eyes had a steely look in them and he felt that this individual would have an even more steely tongue. After several moments the man, who looked about the same age as Carl, came up close and glared at him angrily. It was then that Carl felt a flash of recognition crossing his thoughts. He knew he had seen this face before but couldn't quite place it.

'This is an outrage,' said the man in Latin. 'How dare you pitch your tent in my garden? I will have you arrested for this!'

There goes that Latin bullshit again, thought Carl as he now felt fully awake and thoroughly pissed off.

'What the hell have you and your people done to our site?' he replied in English.

The man stared back at him as if Carl was talking out of his arse.

'What part of the empire are you from?' asked the man in Latin once more.

'Cut the crap!' replied Carl feeling most agitated. 'I'm not going to have a conversation with you in Latin. Speak English or I will call the police!'

The man looked dumbfounded by Carl's strange words and shrugged his shoulders. Then he spoke in a softer tone but once again in Latin:

'I have travelled the four corners of the Empire and never have I heard such a language. By the looks of you I would say you have come from a far-off land.'

'Why are you trying to wind me up? Have you been smoking something all night, mister?' questioned Carl in English.

The man turned when he suddenly heard a loud groan coming from within the tent which was quickly followed by rough, chesty coughing.

'Is that the wench my slaves have been talking about?' he asked.

Slaves, Carl thought incredulously. *This man is nuts.*

Lana's head suddenly peeked out from the doorway of the tent. She looked around wearily.

'Where are we?' she asked as she clamoured awkwardly out onto the lawn and stood stretching her immaculate figure whilst yawning loudly in the process.

'I think we're inside the grounds of a lunatic asylum,' replied Carl frustratingly as he moved his eyes in the direction of the man who was busy staring Lana up and down. With his jaw agape and his walking stick wavering under his weight it seemed to Carl that he was about to collapse. Then, from across the lawn, came running a lithe and spritely looking black girl carrying a flaming torch. She was dressed in a coarse, off-white tunic tied at the waist with a thick cord. Suddenly, a shocking thought struck Carl from out of the blue; a recognition that was absurdly impossible to comprehend, yet here she was in full realisation. It was the girl in the fresco – the slave girl!

No!

Within seconds she was at the man's side, holding him up from falling and indicating for him to sit at the table. She helped him limp the twenty feet or so across the lawn to the waiting chairs whilst giving Carl and Lana a warning glance as she went. Then the full realisation hit Carl hard.

'What the fuck…?' asked Lana.

'… I know,' answered Carl to Lana's half-asked question as he watched the struggling man and girl go, 'I recognise their faces from the fresco.' He put his hands on his hips in resignation as he and Lana both looked to each other in utter astonishment.

3

Fario slumped heavily into his chair and immediately ordered Mumi to wake up Daccus. Mumi made her way quickly through the heavy wooden door leaving her master to face the imposters alone.

Fario stared at the two intruders with both fear and fascination coursing through his mind. They looked like none he had seen before. Their clothes were of a strange cut, especially the woman's. Whatever she was wearing around her private parts looked, to all intents and purposes, to be a most uncomfortable, torturous garment indeed. And the garment adorning her torso had upon it the face of an African man with a burning stick protruding from his mouth and he was holding some kind of weapon. Fario was amazed at the accuracy of the painting on the cloth and guessed he must be a deity of some kind. Then he turned his attention to the man who had just finished putting on some odd-looking footwear. When the man eventually stood up he reached inside a pouch at the side of his hip, pulled out a small object and began to busy himself with the item by holding it to his ear and talking into it.

'What incantations are you speaking there stranger?' called out Fario, fearful that the imposter was up to no good but the man stood where he was, seemingly preoccupied with the object.

Fario's leg ached incessantly throughout, reminding him of his incapacity which only served to stir the anger rising from within.

'Mumi, where's Daccus?' he called out loudly.

His frustration deepened when the man turned and began to approach. The thing he was holding to his ear glowed blue as he walked across the lawn. Then the glow stopped and he put it back into the pouch at his hip that was sewn into the right hand side of his garment. Fario reached for his walking stick and called to his slaves for help but an old man and a boy would be no match for the tall stranger. Then Daccus appeared from behind the door dressed in his toga. He seemed groggy from too much wine.

'What's the problem Fario?' he asked in annoyance.

'We have intruders,' he replied.

Daccus turned and quickly stepped in between the two men. 'What abomination is this, stranger?'

'There goes that Latin crap again,' said Carl under his breath as he stopped just three feet away from the burly looking man. 'What the hell is going on here?' he decided to reply in Latin.

'You are in the villa of my friend, Fario Ardenia. He wishes for you to leave these premises at once. If you don't we shall be forced to inform the authorities and have you removed,' replied Daccus.

Carl shook his head as it suddenly dawned on him that the chubby looking man was also featured in the fresco. He tried his best to clear his mind from the persistent nightmare that was beginning to annoy him to the point of doing something he might regret. Then Lana came up and stood next to him looking flustered and a little perplexed.

'What the fuck is going on here?' she demanded in English but Carl raised his hand and spoke to her calmly.

'It seems these fools insist that we speak to them in Latin,' he said sarcastically.

'It's about four in the morning and my head is banging,' protested Lana to the man in perfect Latin. 'How did you manage to move our tent from the dig site and what's with the togas?'

Daccus stared in amazement at the woman standing before him. She was dressed in the strangest of clothes but her figure was exceptional underneath her tight-fitting garments which exaggerated her immaculate body. He turned to Fario for some enlightenment but Fario simply looked on in fascination. Daccus took a deep breath and decided the situation needed to be calmed down. He raised both his hands in a peaceful gesture and spoke softly to the two strangers:

'It seems a little explaining is required here,' he said delicately. 'First of all, my name is Daccus Atholos. I am an accountant and this is my friend Fario Ardenia. He is a merchant and the owner of this home. We are peaceful people and carry no weapons.'

Carl and Lana stood open-mouthed at the man who was still speaking in Latin as if it was his native tongue. The one called Fario stirred in his chair and seemed to suddenly change his mood to a friendly attitude.

'You both look as if you could do with some refreshments. Will you accept my hospitality and join me at my table?' he asked.

'Maybe it will help clear up this mess,' said Carl in Latin. 'This ladies' name is Lana Evans and my name is Carl Allen.' He decided not to elaborate any further.

The man clapped his hands and within minutes two extra chairs were brought out by the young African girl. It was uncanny in the extreme but she was definitely the girl in the fresco and it seemed to Carl that she was a servant of some kind.

Soon, he and Lana were seated around a table with the two curious men who stared back in fascination at them. Then the old man and the boy appeared carrying a huge jug and wooden beakers between them which they placed upon the table. The old man poured out a sweet smelling, light green liquid from the jug into all the beakers and stood back with his head bowed. The man named Fario clapped his hands once again and all three servants made their way back into the villa, via the wooden door. Carl and Lana looked to each other with a strained curiosity.

'Please drink… drink!' ordered the owner as he proceeded to gulp a mouthful down proving that the liquid wasn't poisoned.

Carl picked up his drink and sniffed at it first. It smelt like lime mixed with pomegranate and he took a tentative sip. When his eyebrows rose up in surprise at the satisfying taste the two men opposite gave a short chuckle and raised their beakers.

'Cio,' said the older man. 'It is a drink I discovered whilst on my travels in Lusitania, refreshing, yes?'

Carl looked to Lana in puzzlement - Lusitania was the ancient name for Portugal.

'Well?' asked the old man.

'Not bad,' Carl replied in Latin and nodded to Lana.

Lana quickly drank the whole lot down in one go, licked her lips and smiled back at the two men.

'Yeah, great but it's not the hair of the dog?' she replied in Latin.

'I assure you the recipe does not include dog hairs,' said Fario.

Lana shook her head and sighed then she spoke:

'So what has happened here? First, I get wasted and crash out in my friend's tent and in the next moment I'm sitting at a table in a roman garden drinking bat's piss with two psycho's who are trying their utmost to show off their command of the Latin language like it's a sketch from a Monty Python show.'

'You use a strange choice of words woman,' replied Fario whilst trying to remain calm. 'I can see you're a little upset but my version of this morning's events is quite different from yours. You see, I was fast asleep when I was woken by Tucus, my slave boy. He said he was startled by the glow of a white light that seemed to come from out of thin air and then disappear leaving your tent standing in my garden. I didn't believe him at first but… here you both are!'

Carl grinned and looked down into his empty beaker feeling a sense of foreboding wash over him. Without thinking, he asked Fario what date it was. Fario replied that it was the morning of the twenty-seventh in the month of Sextilis. Carl knew that Sextilis was the Roman name for the month of August. He looked up at the two Romans who were staring at him with strained curiosity.

'What year is it?' he asked.

'What do you mean 'what year'?' butt-in Lana in amazement. 'What's wrong with you?'

Carl raised a calming hand and repeated his question.

Fario stared back as if Carl had taken leave of his senses.

'Why... it's the one-hundred and sixth year of the reign of the Caesars,' he replied.

'Oh shut up!' said Lana to the Fario. She felt very intimidated by the man's stupid announcement. 'Carl, I'm not staying here to listen to this crap all night. Take me back to the site please.'

Carl shrugged his shoulders and stared even harder into his beaker.

This sucks, he thought. *The men in front of me are making a good job of fooling us.*

With simple mental arithmetic he toted up the dates of the Caesars then he looked up and smiled sarcastically back at Fario:

'I suppose you'll tell me next that Titus is your emperor?'

'Well of course he is,' replied Fario with sincerity in his voice.

'What the fuck are you saying you freak?' questioned Lana to Fario who jumped back in surprise at her outburst. 'Don't buy it Carl. He's getting off on this.'

But Carl seemed to be mulling over something in his head. Lana fell silent fearing what he was thinking. Carl looked up curiously at the night sky then he spoke:

'It's beginning to make sense now,' he said in resignation while talking in English. 'Something strange has happened tonight. Before I retired for bed, I noticed that there was no full moon, now look!'

Lana glanced up at the night sky to see the familiar face of the moon in full glow.

'So, what are you implying, Carl?'

'I also felt an atmosphere descend over the dig site,' he continued. 'It was like... I was being watched from afar but not by eyes that see like you and I see but by eyes that were reaching out from somewhere otherworldly... in space and time.'

'Stop it Carl, you're frightening me. Let's just leave these fools to their roll-playing and walk back to the site. I won't report them to anyone if you don't.'

In an attempt to stay as calm as he could he tried to think hard and then he remembered something he had noticed only moments after exiting the tent. He turned to Lana and spoke:

'Listen Lana, what do you hear?'

Lana sighed and cocked her head in compliance. After a while she said she could hear nothing.

'Precisely,' said Carl as both he and Lana continued to talk in English much to the annoyance of their guests. 'You know the sound of Rome at night. Where's the background hum of the traffic. And music, there's always music playing somewhere in this city even at this hour. And look, I can't see the glow of the street lamps.'

Lana wrapped her arms around herself not from a chill but out of fear of what Carl was suggesting.

It cannot be!

'What kind of talk is this?' asked the one called Daccus. 'Speak Latin!'

Carl felt the need to test his instincts and his historical knowledge and pressed on with another question. He looked Daccus straight in the eye and spoke.

'Do you know of a mountain called Vesuvius?'

'I do,' said Daccus protectively.

'And has this... mountain... caused any trouble of late?'

At once two men looked to each other with suspicion etched upon their faces. Then Fario spoke:

'Do you two have something to do with...?'

'... No, no, no?' said Carl in quick response. 'It's just that we know of the disaster at Pompeii from our history lessons.'

'What do you mean history lessons?' asked Daccus. 'The mountain disgorged its self only three days ago...'

Daccus was silenced in mid-sentence by the calming hand of Fario.

'What have you heard from Pompeii?' Fario asked, suspiciously.

Lana was beside herself with disbelief. 'No, this cannot be happening... no!' she cried out.

Carl placed his left hand on Lana's thigh to calm her down. He didn't want to believe it himself but somehow he and Lana had been sent back in time to the reign of Titus, who lived almost two-thousand years ago. He cleared his head and steadied himself whilst trying his best not to ponder too much upon the implications of the situation.

'Pompeii has been buried under many feet of ash,' replied Carl. 'Hundreds have been killed, including Pliny the Elder!'

'Pliny the Elder - killed?' asked Fario in surprise. 'How do you know of this so soon after the event?'

Carl scratched his head irritatingly and looked to Lana to gage her mood but she seemed to have withdrawn into herself whilst she sat contemplating their fate. Without wanting to give too much credence to his thoughts he decided to say what his conclusion was, incredible though it seemed.

'It seems that Lana and I have come here from the future.'

He let his words hang in the warm, still air for a moment. The look upon the faces of the two Romans forced him to carry on.

'We are archaeologists who have been digging in the ruins of this home.'

Again the expressions upon Fario's and Daccus' faces were as blank as a sheet of A4 paper.

'In the cellar of this building,' pressed Carl, 'is a fresco depicting the figures of eleven men and one woman. That woman is your... servant girl and one of the men is holding a placard with an image of Apollo painted upon it. That man is you, Fario. And you are also on the fresco,' pointed Carl to Daccus who glared back at him with suspicion. 'Am I correct?'

'You are a spy!' cried Daccus, 'sent by the magistrate to check on us...'

Fario rose to his feet painfully and placed a hand on his friend's shoulder to silence him. Daccus immediately felt that he had revealed too much. Fario hobbled a little distance away from the table and turned his back on his guests in deep thought.

'Who are you working for?' he asked without turning.

Carl could tell from the tone in his voice that he was very serious.

'We work for the National Geographic,' Carl answered, deciding that honesty was his best policy right now. Reaching into his pocket he pulled out his cell phone and held it up. Fario turned and glared at the object. Carl continued: 'If I was back in my time I would be able to ring my boss to confirm it.'

The two Romans looked curiously at his phone and Carl decided to choose this moment to quickly take a photo of them. The flash made the two men jump then Carl placed the phone down upon the table and sat back. The phone glowed bright blue and the two men's brows furrowed with curiosity and surprise all at once. Carl was disappointed when he noticed that there was no signal showing on the screen; not even one bar. It served only to add to his suspicion that they were, indeed, two-thousand years adrift in time. Daccus stood up next to his friend and pointed a finger at the phone:

'What contraption is this?' he asked.

'It's called a cell phone. It enables me to speak to anyone around the world who has another one just like it.'

'What was that flash of light?' asked Fario, sounding fearful.

'I took your photograph,' replied Carl. 'Look!'

The two Romans leaned forward curiously as Carl showed them their picture. Daccus recoiled with fright from the image and put his hand over his mouth to hold in a cry of astonishment but Fario sat back down slowly and looked up in amazement at Lana and Carl. He seemed to want to believe that they were from another time and place but he was clearly struggling with the thought of it. Then he turned to Daccus and spoke in a calm manner:

'I think we have a lot to discuss with our new-found friends from another world, don't you think?'

'I don't know, Fario,' replied Daccus without taking his eyes off the phone. 'May I?' he asked Carl as he reached out.

'Be my guest,' said Carl who was now finding the situation fascinating.

Daccus picked up the phone in a slightly trembling right hand and stared at it like a toddler would with a Rubik's cube. He looked underneath it and shook it to try to find the source of the light and then he accidentally pressed a few buttons at random and suddenly the ring tone went off. Travelin' Band by Creedence Clearwater Revival filled the night air. Immediately Daccus dropped the phone to the table and stood up rigid with fear.

'What is that terrible noise?' he screamed.

Carl quickly pressed the off button and glanced towards Lana. She seemed utterly deflated.

Fario leaned forward and spoke in a calm manner:

'If it's true that you are from the future then we have many questions to ask you.'

'You may ask as many as you like,' said Carl. He glanced once more at Lana who was still sitting stone-faced and looking as though the weight of it was all too much to bear.

After a long pause, Fario spoke in a hushed tone but his eyes were lighting up with a curiosity fuelled by what Carl could tell was a bright and inquiring mind.

'What processes caused Vesuvius to wreak such devastation?'

After a short pause Carl spoke:

'Mount Vesuvius is not a mountain in the true sense of the word but is in fact, what we call a volcano,' he replied as if he was giving a lecture to his students. 'It is the tip of a large crack in the earth that goes deep underground where a melting pot of lava, which is basically boiling rock, sits there and builds up pressure over hundreds or even thousands of years. When the pressure from the trapped heat gets too great the lava is forced up the crack and erupts out of the volcano sending hot ash and gasses all over the land around it killing every living thing in its path.'

Silence followed for long moments as Fario and Daccus tried their best to digest the stranger's words. But instead of reacting in the way that Carl was expecting them to – by bursting into raucous bouts of laughter – they seemed to be thinking it through with some measure of intelligence.

Lana stirred next to Carl and whispered erratically to him in English.

'This can't be true... it must be some kind of joke... we've been bamboozled... are we on candid camera or something?'

Carl said nothing but stared back at his hosts who were still puzzling over his explanation of the volcano. Eventually, Fario leaned forward and placed his hands flat down upon the table.

'Where are you from?' he asked.

'We are both from a country called America,' said Carl knowing that the two men would not have heard of it. 'It is known as the land of the free.'

'I have never heard of this land of the free,' said Fario sounding rather disappointed. 'But what you say fascinates me. How far away is this, Americus?'

'America,' corrected Carl. 'It is a place far, far to the west of Rome, four thousand miles to be precise.'

Fario leaned back in his chair and formed his fingers into a steeple in the manner of someone contemplating much. But Daccus was shaking his head.

'Are you saying that you come from beyond the edge of the world?' he asked, despairingly. 'But there is nothing beyond the edge of the world?'

Fario coughed for attention and Carl could see that he seemed excited and yet a little apprehensive. He could tell that he was definitely a very intelligent man who seemed to be brimming over with curiosity, a curiosity that probably got him into many scrapes with many people.

'Daccus, my friend,' said Fario as he slapped a hand down upon the table making the increasingly fragile Lana jump out of her skin. 'I think our new guests will be a most welcome addition to tomorrow night's meeting, don't you?'

4

Lana purposely kept her back to Carl as she stared out of the window at the full moon; her arguments long since dried up. Carl had accepted Fario's offer for them to stay the night, and in the circumstances it was the right thing to do. The events of the past few hours had been mind-numbingly stupefying. It was hard to accept that she was back in the days of the Roman Empire. By what means had they gotten here? What force of nature had done this? The questions piled up and her head began to ache from it. To further confuse the situation, Daccus, wishing to prove that she and Carl were in ancient Rome, had taken them both outside the walls of the villa to show them the narrow street which he had walked up the previous day. Down the bottom of the hill was a Tri-via where three roads intersected. A few people, dressed in togas and holding aloft flaming torches, were gathered in deep conversation and Lana recalled that this was how the word 'trivia' (Tri-via) had come down to the modern day where trivial information was passed around at such meeting points. The people were speaking in Latin and it only served to confirm the unthinkable; here she was; a guest of a Roman businessman in a real Roman home, in real time; the time of the emperor Titus who was the son of Vespasian who had commissioned the Coliseum or the Flavian Ampitheatre as it was officially titled. As an archaeologist her heart raced with excitement at the prospect of seeing the Coliseum in all its glory but the fear of it actually being true rested heavily on her mind. How had this come to pass?

'Come to bed,' she heard Carl saying from behind her but she shunned him. Sleep was the last thought on her mind although her body craved for rest. The effects of her drinking session had still not worn off but she was determined to think; think through the cloud of uncertainty and dismay. She knew these ancient times were brutal and unforgiving. What will become of the two of them? What did Fario and his chubby friend have in store for them? They seemed reasonable folk but she knew the clash of cultures brought about by the enormous gulf in time would cause problems untold and then there are the paradoxes. They would have to be careful not to interfere with the course of history. They would have to be careful what they say and do...

She began to tremble with fear as tears rolled down her cheeks. She eventually turned to Carl for solace but he had fallen fast asleep.

Dad, what would you do in these circumstances? What would you expect of me?

Lana wiped the tears from her eyes, turned away from the window and sat upon a low stool and looked about the room which was lit by the glow of moonlight. It was sparse, to say the least. The room was about twelve foot by twelve foot square with one brick wall completely free of plaster. The other three plastered walls were coloured in a reddish die that showed signs of water damage, probably from a leaky roof. The bed Carl was sleeping on was about four inches clear of the floor and was made from a crudely constructed timbre framework. A lumpy mattress filled with straw topped the bed but there was no pillow. Carl snored away contentedly enough, no doubt dreaming of seeing the magnificence of Rome, first hand – ever the archaeologist, she thought. In one corner of the room sat a low table with a clay statuette of the goddess Venus placed in the centre. Next to Venus sat a bowl and a neatly folded cloth. On the other side of her was a small oil lamp. Without thinking Lana reached inside her back pocket and pulled out her cigarette lighter. She went over to the lamp and ignited the lighter. Immediately, the shuffling of footsteps from an unseen person sounded from close behind her and she jumped, dropping the lighter to the floor.

'Who the fuck?' she said aloud as she spun around.

The eyes of the black girl in the fresco blinked back at her as she took a step back.

'Hello,' Lana found herself saying, absentmindedly, but the girl didn't reply. Instead she reached down and picked up the lighter and offered it up.

'Thanks,' said Lana who suddenly remembered that she had no cigarettes left and immediately began to 'psychologically' gasp for one. 'Got any smokes?'

The girl frowned not knowing what she meant by that question then indicated with hand signals that she was dumb and tried to force a friendly smile back but Lana could see that there was sadness in her big, brown eyes. Then it suddenly dawned on her that the girl was actually a woman, undernourished and stunted by years of neglect. She gauged that she must be in her mid-twenties, at least, and by the looks of her sorry state she must have endured a life of hardship.

Slavery, Lana concluded disappointingly. *The cancer of the ancient world!*

Her heart sank to a new low. This was yet more proof of their predicament.

'So, you are a slave?' asked Lana in Latin still feeling rather put out at having to speak the words of a dead language.

The woman nodded slowly and then reached out a hand and touched the hem of Lana's T-shirt. She then pointed at the image printed on it and made a questioning gesture with her eyes.

'This is Jimi Hendrix,' said Lana.

The woman bowed to the T-shirt.

Oh shit. She thinks he's a god!

'Well, some people think he's a god of sorts, I suppose,' said Lana out of hand.

She instantly regretted her remarks and felt that she was digging herself into a hole. She understood that the slave was connected to the image because he was a black African but this was proving tricky. She turned and lit the oil lamp with her lighter, filling the room with a warm glow. The slave looked on in wide-eyed wonderment at the lighter then went over to the window and drew a light, hessian blind across it. Lana had the presence of mind not to make too much of the lighter and she shoved it quickly back into her pocket.

'Why have you come to our room?' asked Lana, as she looked the woman up and down. Within the glow of the lamplight Lana could see that the woman was stunningly beautiful and with a little bit of tender loving care she would not look out of place on a catwalk.

In response to the question the slave then began to slowly undress herself but Lana got the picture straight away and raised a hand to stop her. It was clear that she had been sent by her master to 'please' his guests but Lana felt nothing but pity for her. She grasped the slave's hands in hers and couldn't help the tears from welling up in her eyes.

'No, no,' she said, 'cover yourself up, my dear. We do not need you for such a thing.'

Lana was shocked at how rough and calloused the woman's hands were. She turned them over and could see a history of untreated wounds and lesions in her palms. Her tears fell onto the woman's hands and she wished, for all intents and purposes, that they would wash away the scars.

The slave looked surprised at Lana's show of emotion and quickly pulled up her tunic, re-tied the rope around her waist and stood there looking like a picture of innocence.

Lana could feel her heart sinking in her chest. She knew that from this moment on she would have to steal herself in preparation for the way the socially unfortunate of these times were treated and there will be shocks ahead.

'Go back to your quarters, my love. I'm going to sleep now,' said Lana as she wiped the tears from her eyes once more.

The slave bowed and left the room as quietly as a phantom in the night.

It took Lana a tremendous leap of faith to finally admit to herself that she was back in the time of the Roman Empire; a time where human beings were treated like property, where nearly all women were third-class citizens and children were virtually none-existent in the collective psyche of the populace.

Shit, not too dissimilar to modern times!' she thought, *'except in our times we are a bit more subtle about it.'*

Feeling desperately tired and a little sick from the trauma, Lana blew out the lamp, laid down next to Carl and was asleep within seconds.

The sound of a cockerel woke Carl with a start and he jumped up out of bed. Immediately his head began to pound and his neck felt as stiff as a board. He stretched to his full height of six-foot two inches and yawned.

'Shit,' he called out disappointingly as the memory of the previous night came flooding back. But before he could clear his mind the door behind him swung inwards and in entered the slave girl. She was carrying a large jug of water and a few folded towels over her arm which she took straight over to the table and plonked down next to the statuette of Venus. She then made her way to the window, pushed aside the crudely made blind and the room was instantly filled with light. Carl clamped his eyes shut and turned away from the window.

'Damn it woman,' he said in English, 'you could have warned me.'

When his eyes finally adjusted to the light he looked about for the slave but she was gone, the door closing behind her. He scanned the sparse, musky room and felt disappointed that his host would put them up in such a shit hole. He looked to Lana who was asleep upon the lumpy, uncomfortable bed but he didn't care to admire her physique this time, instead, he shook her gently awake by the shoulder. She groaned and opened her eyes, squinting from the sunlight.

'Good morning,' said Carl knowing that it was not a good morning at all.

'Hi,' replied Lana sounding distant and afraid.

'I'm hoping that all this is a mistake and that we've been abducted by some weird sect that wants to protect the ruins of the dig site by using us as hostages.'

'No it's real all right,' said Lana remembering her encounter with the slave. She sat up and groaned. 'I must reek. I haven't had a shower for two days!'

'Or two-thousand years!' replied Carl.

'Damn it Carl that's not funny.'

The sound of shuffling feet outside the door made Lana jump out of bed and Carl came towards her to put a comforting arm around her shoulder. Lana allowed him the honour. He vowed in that moment that he will be her protector whatever befalls them.

The door swung inwards and in entered the old slave who Fario had introduced as Lucius. He looked to be in his sixties but he was probably younger. The old man stared the two of them up and down and spoke in a croaky voice:

'The master awaits you in the garden. The table is set. Now you both must wash,' he said mechanically.

'I need a shower – hot water!' pronounced Lana.

'A shower?' questioned the slave. It suddenly dawned on Carl that the man was a bit simple-minded. He seemed very intimidated by Lana and looked set to bolt out of the door at any moment.

Lana buried her head in her hands and began to moan aloud.

'We will be along shortly,' said Carl to the man who quickly nodded with relief and exited at once.

'Jesus Christ! This situation is going to get worse Carl,' said Lana as she strolled over to the large jug and poured out some water into the bowl.

'I think our host won't mind us setting up a crude shower,' Carl suggested.

'I'd love to,' said Lana, 'but we can't bring technology into these times no matter how simple, you know that.'

'Of course,' replied Carl. 'Shit. We'll have to hide the phone, the camera and my watch.'

'Exactly, now turn around while I wash myself down.'

Carl did what he was told and sat down on the bed with his back turned to wait his turn to wash. He knew he was going to have to be strong for Lana. She will be treated less favourably than him and her great beauty will either be a blessing or a burden. He feared the latter. Without thinking he reached inside his pocket and took out his cell phone and flipped it open. The battery was still full but there was no signal. He tried phoning his brother anyway – dead! Then he decided to read the second text message that he had received the previous night. The last one was from Ted Brooks of the National Geographic, it read:

How's the dig going? Hope you can speed up the processes. Our creditors want to cut back on funding. You might have two months left but I will see what I can do from this end.

'Shit,' said Carl out aloud.

'What's wrong?' asked Lana.

'The big wigs at Nat Geo want to cut back.'

'What's new?'

'Yeah right,' he replied.

Then he quickly opened his brother's text and read it again:

Great news bro', we're pregnant again. Baby's due late April. Catch you when you get back.

The last sentence of the text hit Carl hard. He closed the phone and put it back in his pocket.

'I'm done,' said Lana as she finished dressing herself, 'now all I need is a change of clothes.'

Carl didn't reply but simply stood up and quickly washed his face and hands.

I must be strong for both our sakes, he thought as he dried himself then turned and exited the room with Lana by his side.

They walked down a narrow, covered pathway following the sunlight out into the garden. Immediately their nostrils were filled with the aroma of flowers which were blossoming in the warming air powered by an already hot sun. By the angle of the sun in the sky Carl guessed it to be around ten o'clock. Then he noticed his tent was missing.

The camera!
'Good day to you both,' came a loud voice from behind them. Carl spun and saw Fario standing in the doorway. 'Shall we eat?' he asked.

'What have you done with my tent?' asked Carl.

'It's all right,' replied Fario, 'it's in a safe place. Maybe what you're looking for is on the table.'

Carl glanced over at the table and noticed, in amongst the plates of food, were his field notebook and pens and Lana's camera - all safe. The camera was still enclosed in its leather casing. He went over to the table and picked up the expensive Nikon.

'I found Tucus, my young slave boy, playing with that,' explained Fario as he crept his way gingerly around the table and sat down. 'It's lucky I caught him in time, he was shaking it wildly. I didn't want him to break it but don't worry I've had him punished for his transgression.'

'What did you do to him?' asked Lana, dreading the answer.

'I had Lucius whip his hide with a cane.'

Her stomach turned but she decided to say nothing.

'Now let's eat shall we,' said Fario without the slightest thought to what he had just said.

Carl nodded to Lana that they should eat and they sat down. Carl placed the camera back upon the table.

'What is that artefact anyway?' asked Fario eyeing the camera whilst he eagerly tucked into his breakfast.

Lana gave Carl a warning glance and he had to pause for thought.

'It's a... a box,' was all he could say.

'I can see that but what's inside it?'

'The ashes of my ancestors,' said Carl making the subject immediately personal.

Fario stopped chewing on a piece of pork and seemed to have the look of someone who didn't like being lied to. After a while he began chewing again and took a sip of water from a wooden beaker. After placing the beaker down he stared at Carl and a thin smile formed upon his lips.

'If you say so,' he said nonchalantly. 'Now please, eat!'

The food on offer was a variety of pork, fish, fruit and bread. Lana took a little nibble of everything but not nearly enough to sustain her. Carl made the most of it and he found the food to be surprisingly tasty although the bread was a bit coarse and grainy.

'So,' announced Fario to Carl. 'After this meal would you like to be shown around our glorious city?'

'I would like that very much,' said Carl with much excitement but Lana recoiled from the offer; fearful as to what Fario's intentions might be. She was also acutely aware that Fario was not paying her much attention, which was something she had never experienced back home, and that all his conversations were directed towards Carl. Her historical knowledge informed her that for a female stranger to be seated at the table of the head of the household was not something her host was used to. Again she decided that she would not point it out – she could not – she was a woman!

When the meal was done Fario clapped his hands and the three slaves appeared. Lana was shocked when she saw the slave boy walking very gingerly. She could tell that he had been crying and that he was in much discomfort. She looked to Carl pleadingly but Carl shook his head ever so slightly. Lana was boiling inside. She felt like kicking Fario in his broken leg and smashing his walking stick over his head. It was all too much. She leapt from her chair and ran back into the house.

'What's wrong with her?' asked Fario looking not in the least bit concerned.

'Well, under the present circumstances, I think she's missing home somewhat,' replied Carl.

'Home,' said Fario dismissively. 'There is a saying throughout the empire that Rome is everybody's home.'

'But our home is beyond your borders,' replied Carl as he took a sip from his beaker.

'Yes,' replied Fario sounding unconvinced, 'so you've said. We have much to discuss but not until Daccus has taken you both on a tour of the city. I will provide adequate clothing so you don't stand out in the crowd.'

'Where is… Daccus?' asked Carl.

'He left early this morning. He had some unfinished business at the grain store. He'll be back at mid-day. Now tell me what these other things are?' Fario was pointing at a biro and a small notepad.

Carl couldn't disguise what they were so he explained them to Fario. The Roman's eyes lit up when Carl eventually wrote out Fario's name. He stared in wonderment at the pen as the letters flowed freely across the page in black ink.

'You use these in the land of the free?'

'All the time,' said Carl. 'Now if you'll excuse me I will go and check on Lana.'

Fario immediately reached out for the pen and Carl allowed him to take it and the notepad.

'Just write like you would with a stylus on wax and see the difference,' he said as he turned and picked up the camera.

'Wait one moment,' said Fario casually. Carl turned back and saw that Fario had replaced the pen and began reaching for something inside his toga. 'How did you come to possess this?'

Fario produced a golden amulet and set it down gently upon the table then leaned back in his chair to await a response. Carl chided himself for forgetting about it. The amulet shone brightly in the morning sunlight and then he noticed that the eyelet was unbroken and a chain was threaded through it. In fact, it looked brand new. Once again he decided that honesty was his best policy right now.

'I found it buried outside my tent at the dig site last night but… but…'

'But what?' asked Fario, sounding a little angered by Carl's reply.

'It looks brand new,' said Carl accepting it as yet more evidence of his predicament.

'I assure you that this amulet is at least three-hundred years old. It is part of my collection and I find it most disturbing that it was found in your tent.'

'As I have said, I dug it up from the ruins of this villa two-thousand years from now.'

Fario stared Carl hard in the eyes unsure what to say to that statement.

'Where did you get it?' asked Carl moving the conversation along though feeling just as confused as Fario looked.

'I bought it from a trader,' said Fario as he picked up the amulet and hung it around his neck. 'Your woman, I can hear her crying.'

Carl cocked his head and could hear Lana's sobs coming from their room. He turned without saying anything to Fario as the Roman picked up the pen out of curiosity and began writing.

Carl shouldered the camera and quickly walked back to the house as his mind raced. It was incredible how the amulet looked so new but now he knew why. It was back in its own time and he had brought it back, but how?

Just as he approached the door of his room a loud hammering by someone heavy-fisted rattled the front door. Immediately the black girl appeared and made her way towards it. Beyond, a loud voice cried out:

'Hurry, hurry we haven't got all day!'

Carl quickly snuck in behind the door, threw the camera on the bed and watched proceedings unfold. The slave girl opened the front door and in stepped three Roman soldiers dressed in leather uniforms. Two of them wore red robes whilst the other, a stocky, bearded man, wore a white robe. They looked surprisingly small for soldiers which gave credence to the theory that most soldiers of the ancient times were small in stature. They were also armed. The bearded one spoke to the slave and she turned and gestured for them to follow her out to the garden. Carl was amazed at how accurate Hollywood had portrayed the soldiery. He could have been on a film set and it wouldn't look out of place if Sir Lawrence Olivier appeared at any moment.

'What's wrong, Carl?' said an emotional Lana from behind him.

Carl quickly put his fingers to his lips and whispered; 'soldiers!'

With ears strained to the limit they both listened to the sound of proceedings coming from the garden. It seemed the soldiers were summoning Fario to the magistrate's office. It had something to do with the disaster at Pompeii and they were demanding that he offer up money for the emperor's relief funds. Fario was resisting; saying that all his money was tied up in property and business but the soldiers seemed undeterred and soon the sound of a scuffle broke out. Fario sounded outraged and began calling the local magistrate a thug and that the soldiers were doing the work of a tyrant. In the next instant it all went quiet then a few moments later the soldiers appeared; two of them were carrying an unconscious Fario between them; he had been bound and gagged. Then Carl noticed that his damaged leg was bleeding. The soldiers had re-broken it!

'We'll teach this bastard a lesson or two,' said the officer in the white cloak to his other men. 'The magistrate has always suspected that he is no friend of the empire.' His men nodded and struggled onwards with their prisoner.

A shocked Carl watched the soldiers take Fario out the front door and off to who knows where? His only friend in this alien world was gone. He turned to Lana who had the look of absolute fear etched across her face.

'My god Carl, we're dead!'

5

Daccus walked the short distance from his office towards the Tri-via where a large gathering of people had formed. A soldier had just finished addressing the crowd whilst another was holding aloft a placard for all to read. He made his way towards the placard and stared up at it; it was a decree from Titus ordering that - *'all able-bodied men must report to the commanding officer at their local barracks in case they will be needed to help in the rescue of the unfortunates at Pompeii, Herculaneum and the surrounding areas. Failure to report will mean imprisonment or a fine'*.

Beads of sweat formed on his forehead as he walked on – his only thought was of the meeting tonight and the strangers from the future.

Damn it! Why doesn't Titus use slaves? Damn him!

Daccus knew it would be futile to disobey the emperor's orders so he decided that he will make the slight detour to the barracks on his way back to Fario's place. It would not take long. He had registered at the barracks a few years earlier when Titus' father, Vespasian, had ordered civilian men to aid his soldiers in rounding up a band of Jewish slaves who had rebelled during the construction of the Flavian Ampitheatre. Although Daccus was not called upon at the time he remembered that all seventy-one slaves were captured and burned alive in front of their colleagues as an example.

He quickly made his way along the Via Toribus and down the steep decline towards the Macabus barracks where a few guards were busy organising a queue outside the rather grand looking Marcus Licinius Crassus memorial gates.

'Form a line, form a line!' ordered one of the guards to twelve, very under-eager men. Daccus soon became the thirteenth. He looked along the line and quickly spotted Paxus who was one of his Apollonian comrades. He called to his friend who turned and nodded back at him.

In no time the line was on the move. The men had to give their name, status and age which was taken down by a scribe as another man issued each one with a numbered wooden token. If the call went out you were to hand in your token before being given your orders. Daccus did his duty and had soon put his token inside his pouch then raced onwards to catch up with Paxus.

Paxus Strupalo was a Roman through-and-through and he was one of the brightest of the Apollonians. A tall, muscular man who managed to look very athletic under his toga strode along at a fair pace looking somewhat annoyed at being ordered to report to the barracks. He was a politician but not yet a statesman, he was one of a new breed of the lower class members in the senatorial juniors whose duties were mainly secretarial but he showed great promise and had been recommended for office on no fewer than six occasions; each time falling short by only a few votes. It was generally accepted amongst the juniors that it was his friendship with his Greek counterparts which was hindering his progress. Prejudice ran deep within the hallowed halls of the Roman senate but he also knew that time was on his side. Paxus knew that the elder statesmen, who were so set in their ways, and had consistently voted against him, will eventually die out and it was then that his patience will be rewarded.

'Slow down Paxus!' cried Daccus as he approached him from behind.

'You sound out of breath, my friend,' said Paxus in his familiar, gravelly voice. 'You need to cut down on your consumption of wine.'

'I'm all right, Pax, it's just my age.'

'I hear there's a meeting tonight.'

'Yes. Fario has a surprise in stall.'

'Oh, what surprise?'

Daccus couldn't contain himself and spoke in a whisper:

'Two strangers arrived at Fario's home the other night. They say they are from a place called America; they call it the land of the free.'

'America?' asked Paxus. He stopped in his tracks and folded his arms to await further information. 'Is there any more?'

'Only that they claim to be from the future but that's crazy, right?'

Paxus raised a curious eyebrow and then frowned, seemingly unimpressed, but Daccus could tell that his friend was puzzling over some other matter entirely. Paxus looked up and spoke cautiously:

'I don't know what Fario has been up to lately but ever since he brought the black box back from Gaul; the one that he's been harping on about, things haven't been the same; the broken leg, the raised suspicions from the magistrate and he's been spending a lot of his wealth sucking up to certain members of the senate to boot. He needs to learn to keep his mouth shut.'

'Yes I know, Pax. He seems to have changed lately.'

'Have you seen the box?'

'Yes,' replied Daccus.

'Fario must keep it safe.'

'But why, Pax?' asked Daccus.

'I... I ... don't know. Just make sure it stays safe.'

Daccus stalled for a brief moment feeling that his friend was hiding something from him but then he dismissed it and spoke up:

'Anyway, Fario said he will reveal all tonight, are you coming?'

'Sure, I'll be there,' replied Paxus.

Just then the sound of booted feet came around the corner and three soldiers appeared marching quickly towards the barracks. One of them was carrying someone over his shoulder. When Daccus and Paxus stood aside to allow the soldiers to pass they went cold. At once they recognised the limp form of Fario. He was unconscious and his broken leg was bleeding profusely. Daccus moved to question the soldiers but a hand clamped firmly around his forearm.

'Leave it be,' whispered Paxus from behind him. 'Something's afoot!'

The two men watched on helplessly as the soldiers entered the barracks and disappeared inside.

'What the hell has he done?' asked Daccus.

'Damn it!' cursed Paxus. 'You see, I told you he's been talking too much, now look what's happened. Those soldiers were Drexa Vitanian's men, our 'beloved' magistrate. He will interrogate Fario now. We must cancel the meeting. I will send out messengers to inform the others until we find out more.'

Daccus shook his head and feared the worst. His heart was pounding loudly in his chest as the two Apollonians spoke for a while longer then quickly went their separate ways.

To avoid bumping into more soldiers, Daccus decided to take the longer way around to Fario's home hoping that the strangers from the future had not been arrested too.

The noon-day sun beat down relentlessly as Daccus wound his way through the narrow streets. The usual smells of rotting things and human waste filled his nostrils and he was forced to cover his nose with his hand. This part of the city was crammed with people and animals which thronged with market stalls selling the left-overs from the richer households. Vegetables and fruit, which had seen better days, were being openly resold to desperate people in defiance of the law. He passed the emaciated and half-eaten body of a dog and nearly puked from the rancid smell of it. This was the ugly side of Rome. There was no glory here, but still, people came from all corners of the empire in search of a better life, but there were beggars everywhere he cared to look. Children with disfigured limbs who had been deliberately made that way by their parents so they could beg for more money were staring up at him as he passed; a lost generation whose only relief from their hellish existence would be the sanctuary of death. This was Titus's Rome; the power and the glory stunk of death.

He cleared his mind as he concentrated his thoughts on Fario's place. After several minutes the Tri-via appeared and the relief from the smell of the streets behind him was welcome indeed. Ignoring the crowd, he turned left up the hill towards the house. To his surprise there were no guards posted and within seconds he was knocking at the door. A tearful Mumi answered and let him in. She was terribly distressed and immediately led him towards the guest room. He noticed the door to the room was ajar and he could hear the two strangers talking heatedly in their own, strange language.

Daccus knocked and pushed aside the door. The two guests looked scared out of their wits. He entered the room and raised his arms to try to calm them.

'Thank goodness you are safe,' he said with relief. 'Come, come. I will see that you get out of your attire and into more civilised clothing. I'm going to have to get you both away from here.'

'Soldiers came and took Fario,' explained Carl, excitedly.

'I know... Carl, I saw him being taken into the barracks. What did the soldiers want?'

'They wanted money off him to help them pay for the rescue of the people at Pompeii,' replied Carl.

Daccus breathed a sigh of relief. The Apollonians were safe, for now, but he feared the soldiers will be back.

'They said that the magistrate suspected that he's no friend of the empire.' Carl didn't mention the pen and notepad. He had burnt them immediately, glad that the soldiers hadn't taken them.

'The magistrate's name is Drexa Vitanian,' said Daccus. 'He is the emperor's eyes and ears; always suspicious of anything out of the ordinary and believe me, you two are very out of the ordinary.'

Without a second's pause, Daccus led Carl and Lana up a small flight of stairs and into a grand looking room, full of light and colour. The most striking object in the room was a marble bust of Caesar Augustus which stood proudly upon a plinth in one corner. In the centre of the room sat an overly large bed ordained with silks and cushions of many varied colours.

'Enter through those doors and you will find a variety of togas to wear,' said Daccus whilst pointing towards two, white latticework doors. 'I will send Mumi up to help you both. Let her dress you, she knows what to do. I will be back in a few moments.'

He quickly exited the room calling for Mumi as he went, leaving Carl and Lana standing alone. Lana immediately opened the two doors that Daccus had shown them and was amazed to find racks of shelving stocked full with folded cloth.

'Phew,' said Lana as she stared around the room, 'how the other half live, eh?'

After issuing Mumi her orders, Daccus went to the table where he had last seen the black box. It was gone! He quickly scanned the rest of the room. It looked the same as usual but no black box. He looked on top of shelves and under chairs and looked inside a few wooden crates but no sign of the box.

Where the hell ... The cellar!

He raced back up to the master bedroom and strode across the floor towards the bust of Augustus, not caring to even glance at the guests who were trying on various coloured togas. He carefully tipped up the bust to reveal a large key that was sitting in a recess dug into the surface of the plinth. He grabbed it and sat the bust down gently then walked towards the door but Carl stopped him and offered up a glass vial sealed with a wooden cap. Inside was a wound up piece of cloth. He looked to Carl quizzically.

'It's a note, a message in a bottle if you like… to my people in the future. Could you leave it in the cellar for me, please?'

Daccus took the vial without thinking. He didn't have time to discuss such a ridiculous request but he would do what Carl asked.

~ 48 ~

He made his way to the lower level as fast as he could, down a long corridor that led underneath the garden. At the end of the corridor he found a flint and stone set aside in a wall and quickly sparked life into a torch that was resting in its bracket. Placing the torch in the bracket he reached down and lifted up a large piece of mosaic flooring. Underneath the mosaic piece was a metal ring recessed into the floor. He pulled hard on the ring and a patch of the floor rose up upon a pair of hinges. Beneath the floor was a set of nine stone steps. Securing the false floor with a wooden pin he reached for the torch and made his way cautiously down the steps and came to a heavy, wooden door. He put the key into the lock and turned it. The lock clicked loudly then he lifted the latch and quickly entered.

The Apollonian's secret meeting room was a cellar which was about forty feet square and was stuffed with an assemblage of yet more artefacts from around the world. Twenty-two, man-sized vases filled to the brim with gold and silver dust stood up against the right-hand wall, like sentinels guarding the room. On the wall to his left the faces of the eleven founders of the Apollonian society stared out at him. Daccus and Fario's faces stared back in cold indifference. Cleverly, the beautiful figure of Mumi was painted in 'to offset any imperial suspicions' as Fario had once put it. He bent down and scratched away at the soil at the base of the fresco and placed Carl's glass vial in a small hollow then covered it up. He smiled at the absurdity of the request.

He stood and panned the torch around the room, quickly spotting Carl and Lana's tent which was rolled up and shoved under a table. Fario's appetite for collecting things was never ending, he thought. As he panned the flaming torch further around the musky room he spotted something unfamiliar upon a table that was covered in a dust-free cloth. He threw back the cloth and there sat the box, untouched and looking just as it was the other day. He quickly re-covered the box with the cloth, hefted it under his free arm then grabbed the tent and exited the cellar, dragging the tent behind him as he went. Locking the door behind him he climbed the steps and lowered the false floor.

Dousing the torch and replacing it in the bracket, he made his way up and out into the garden and set down the tent upon a patch of gravel at the far side. Then he made his way back to Carl and his woman with a burning curiosity flooding his thoughts.

Carl and Lana stood facing each other admiring their new attire. Mumi had dressed them in standard white togas which had intricate black edging all around the outsides. Carl had to make do with a pair of undersized sandals for now but Lana's sandals fitted her perfectly and she looked stunning in her toga. The fit emphasized her wonderful figure even more so than her modern day clothes. Her magnificent breasts looked amazing without her bra; Mumi had insisted she remove it and to Lana it was no problem. She had hardly ever worn a bra during her time in California and those endless beach parties. In that moment Carl knew that he loved her. He had always loved her but his professionalism and his work had gotten in the way. He knew that Lana liked him but it was purely on a working level. She had been his pal, comrade and workmate off and on for almost ten years but he knew her taste in younger men was unwavering; perhaps the memory of Dennis, her surfer husband who was taken from her at a tender age, was still fresh in her mind.

'Oh my, I never thought I'd be dressed in a real toga,' said Lana looking rather embarrassed.

'You look absolutely beautiful,' said Carl without thinking and he noted that Lana recoiled from his words a little.

'That's the first time you've ever paid me a sincere complement,' she replied, coyly.

Carl felt embarrassed and a little ashamed that it had taken him all these years to say something to her that came from the heart.

The moment was disrupted when Mumi signalled for Lana to be seated. She quickly obliged and Mumi immediately set to work on her hair. She raised her long, black locks up into a bun and began to pin it all together. Once again Carl was taken aback at her beauty. He had never seen Lana with her hair up before. Her long, elegant neck gave the appearance of someone of royal stature; of a privileged line. When Mumi had finished Lana looked completely transformed by such a simple thing as having her hair pinned up.

'My god,' he found himself saying, 'you look like a goddess.'

Before Lana could reply, Daccus entered the room looking hot and flustered. He was carrying something bulky under his arm which was wrapped in a cloth.

'We must leave!' he announced. 'I have told Lucius and the boy that the soldiers will return and ordered them to leave so it's up to them if they want to. I am taking both of you to my friend's home. Come quickly!'

Mumi immediately ran back into the wardrobe and brought out a large sack. She began stuffing it with Carl and Lana's discarded clothes, including their boots. When she picked up the Jimi Hendrix T-shirt she looked pleadingly to Lana but Daccus was shaking his head.

'Put it in the sack, Mumi!' he ordered. 'We will go into the garden and burn them. I don't want to leave anything behind for the magistrate.'

Mumi reluctantly shoved the T-shirt into the sack and stood back with arms folded. Carl placed his mobile phone, his watch and the camera inside a smaller sack that Mumi had provided earlier and spoke to Daccus in a serious tone:

'I will take these with me,' he said to Daccus.

'If you must,' replied Daccus, 'but keep them with you at all times. Now let's go.'

'Mumi comes with us!' announced Lana. 'I won't leave her.'

Daccus turned and looked Lana up and down.

'Bring her, but she's your responsibility until Fario decides otherwise.'

Daccus turned and left the room in a hurry with Carl, Lana and Mumi in tow. He made his way to the garden where he ordered Carl to throw the sack of clothes onto the tent. The old slave, Lucius and the young boy were waiting. Carl obliged then Lucius poured olive oil onto the heap and set it alight with a flaming torch. Daccus asked the two slaves to leave as soon as the fire burns itself out but the two seemed dumbfounded by his request. Without further ado they left the slaves to watch over the fire.

The streets of Rome took Carl and Lana completely by surprise. The first thing they noticed in the afternoon heat was the smell; a light odour laden with the stench of raw sewage hung in the air mixed with the smell of burning wood. The second thing was the dilapidated look of the buildings; shoddily built and in a state of disrepair. The both looked to each other in astonishment as the small entourage headed down the road towards the Tri-via. Once again the crossroads was thronging with people anxious for news from Pompeii. Daccus' pace increased as he led them around the crowd. Happily, no one paid much attention to them and within no time they were heading west into an even rougher looking district. Carl's hope of seeing the glory of Rome had gotten off to a bad start. He felt the gulf in time growing in his heart and it deflated him, but as an archaeologist he found himself taking in the surroundings.

'My friend's name is Paxus,' said Daccus absently. 'We are not far from his place. He'll keep you both safe while I go and see how long Drexa Vitanian, the magistrate, intends to keep Fario.'

'Is Fario's life in danger?' asked Carl, sounding most sincere.

'It could well be,' replied Daccus. 'It depends on what charge Drexa will throw at him.'

When they turned into another dismal looking street a band of tough looking characters suddenly appeared from around a corner. The six, unkempt and dirty-faced strangers stopped and stared at Daccus' troop with a less than friendly look upon their faces. Carl strained his eyes to look up and down the street but there was no one else; they were on their own.

'Hey, fatty what you got tucked under your arm?' said one of the men to Daccus.

Daccus stood where he was without replying. Another, smaller man stepped forward and spoke aloud:

'Didn't you hear what he said, what have you got there – fatty?'

Daccus took a step backwards and stuttered a reply:

'Now... listen here gentlemen, I... have people in high places and they wouldn't want to hear of any mishap befalling me or my friends.'

'Fuck them!' said the first man, 'what have you got there?'

'Hey dickhead, watch you're saying.'

A stunned silence immediately descended upon all the gathered men as they stood in disbelief at the sound of a female voice. Carl immediately felt his blood turn cold.

'What did you say, wench?' said the first man who looked the toughest of the lot.

Lana stepped forward and stared the man out.

'I said watch what you're saying, cloth ears.'

Carl felt like throttling Lana for virtually guaranteeing their deaths but he was taken by surprise when she suddenly made the classic martial arts stance; yet another off-shoot from her time in California, no doubt.

A collective chorus of laughter came from the six men as they quickly surrounded Lana in a tight circle. Carl felt his arsehole begin to loosen and his throat immediately turn dry but then a loud whistling sound came zipping through the air followed by a wet thud. Carl jumped back in surprise as one of the villains fell to the floor at his feet with an arrow sticking out of his neck. He found he had to blink twice to make sure he wasn't seeing things but it was true; a man lay dying at his feet!

Within seconds the other men had scampered away and disappeared down the side streets without a trace. The dying man breathed his last as a pool of blood grew around him, staining the street crimson.

'This city is full of scum,' said a gravelly voice from behind Carl.

'Paxus!' said Daccus with relief as Carl turned to see a tall man striding towards them. He was accompanied by two similarly tall strangers.

'You and your men are a most welcome sight, my friend,' said Daccus.

'We must get off the streets. The plebeians will be back,' replied the tall man. He bent down and yanked the arrow from the dead man's neck. 'Tacus, Anabus dispose of the body before any soldiers arrive!' he ordered as he handed the bow and arrow to one of them.

Within seconds the party were on the move. They were led by Paxus down a narrow alleyway and into a small house that reeked of the smell of sewers. From there they were taken outside through a doorway at the back of the house and down a long flight of stone steps. Paxus called a halt when they reached a wall and he turned and spoke:

'Are these your friends from the other night, Daccus?'

'Can you keep them in hiding for a while until I find out what's going to happen to Fario?'

Paxus stared Carl and Lana up and down for a brief moment. His expression left a lot to be desired.

'They look scared shitless,' he said offhandedly.

'Well I did tell you these two are not from our time.'

'Yeah right,' said Paxus, sounding completely unconvinced. 'I will keep them and the slave girl for the rest of the day and tonight only but then you must come and get them. I can't have the magistrate and his men grow suspicious of my activities. My career is on the line as it is.'

With that Daccus shook arms with Paxus in the usual Roman manner then he gave him the black box asking that he take care of it for a while. Paxus hefted Fario's box in his arms looking pleased to be in possession of it.

'So this is the box Fario has been so animated about?'

Daccus gave a reassuring nod to Paxus noting that the tall politician knew more about the box than he was letting on. He reluctantly turned and went back up the steps without another word.

Carl stared after Daccus then turned to face Paxus. The look upon the tall man's face instantly turned darker as he examined the box.

'So you two are from the future?' he asked, without taking his eyes of the box.

'It... seems so,' Carl replied, reluctantly. He felt an instant dislike towards the man. He seemed to Carl to be someone who would slit your throat first and ask questions later.

'Where are you taking us?' asked Lana sounding completely unnerved.

Paxus lowered the box and raised his eyebrows, seemingly surprised that a woman would speak to him first, reminding her, yet again, about women's place in this brutish society.

'I am taking you to my father's tavern,' said Paxus directly to Carl whilst completely ignoring Lana. 'You will do what I say and do not leave the premises without my say so.'

With that, Paxus tucked the box under one arm and led the three of them down along the wall until they reached a door. He unlatched the door and showed them through into a small, tiled courtyard which was surrounded on three sides by the rear end of tall buildings. Carl guessed them to be at least five storeys high. Attached to the buildings was a network of wooden stairs. They looked solidly constructed and led to many doorways.

'Follow me!' ordered Paxus.

Carl, Lana and Mumi, were taken up one flight of stairs and shown in through the rear of a building that reeked of burning wood. All three coughed from the chocking atmosphere but they followed the big man doggedly through a maze of hallways and turns and rooms that seemed to go on forever. Eventually, they came to a sunlit and smoke-free room. Carl guessed they were now at the front of the building and could see a large window through his smoke-filled eyes. He strained his ears to hear the sound of people calling out – in Latin - across what sounded like a wide open area beyond the window.

'You must stay here and don't show yourselves at this window for too long,' ordered Paxus. 'I will have food and water sent up in a while. Don't speak to anyone other than me.'

Without a moment's pause, Paxus turned and exited the room taking the box with him. The sound of a key turning in the lock confirmed that he meant what he said.

'I don't like him,' announced Lana as she plonked herself down upon a stool and sighed heavily. Mumi came over and put an arm around Lana for comfort.

The two women looked insignificant to Carl and his heart reached out to both for differing reasons. But he was pleased to be out of the oppressive heat and he sauntered casually over to the far side of the room to peer out of the window. The sight he beheld briefly lifted his archaeological instincts as he found himself staring across the river Tiber. Various sail boats lay moored along the banks on either side of the river and a few rowing boats were plying their way up and down, carrying people and goods. But the scene eventually brought it all home to him. Without a doubt, he and Lana were two-thousand years adrift in time, lost and alone. Carl's heart sunk in despair but he found he couldn't take his eyes off the fascinating sight before him.

He looked up and down the entire stretch of the river as far as the window frame would allow and saw no recognisable buildings along the banks that he would have known from his studies. There was no St Peter's basilica, of course. Construction of the famous building would not start until 1506; a mere 1,427 years from now. He felt disappointed but quickly turned his attention to the people going about their business. On the nearest bank, he saw toga-clad Romans milling about the tiled walkway as if they were out on a Sunday stroll. There were also people talking in groups and gesticulating to one another, no doubt talking about the main topic of the day. Carl was struck by how picturesque the scene looked with tree-lined pathways and highly decorated water fonts spouting fresh water at every fifty or so paces. This would be a stretch of the river where the well-to-do of Roman society resided. It was the same for the opposite bank. The buildings were lined along the bank like rows of apartments and decorated in the grand Roman tradition usually associated with country villas. Then further along the bank his eyes focused upon a metal grill that straddled the width of the pathway. It was a demarcation line separating the classes. Beyond the grill he could make out the ramshackle dwellings of the less fortunate. There was no tiled walkway here or trees lining the bank, only a dirt track full of litter and waste of all kinds. He could make out beggars and cheap street merchants offering their poorly made wares for sale to the rich through the bars of the grill, more in hope than anything else. A group of naked and undernourished children, who looked to be between the ages of six and ten, respectively, were jumping off a dilapidated jetty into the river and swimming with the current until they reached a half-sunken wreck. When they reached it they clambered up onto the wreck and back onto the bank, running as fast as they could to take their turn in the queue.

    He knew that these poor kids would never have the chance of an education, never be inoculated against diseases, never fed properly and never have the chance to work for a living. Most of them would be dead by the time they reached puberty. The ones who survive will almost certainly become slaves or beggars or, even worse; murdered and sold to the butchers for meat in desperate times. He knew that this generation was simply the next in line of children who were born bastards. Their unknown fathers - most likely returning soldiers desperate for the pleasures of a woman - would quickly be off on another mission to expand the empire; most never returning. Empire building required sacrifices and many of those sacrifices rested upon very small shoulders. Carl felt a longing for home overwhelm him completely and he found himself choking back tears. Then he heard Lana's footsteps approach and he quickly wiped his eyes upon his toga.

    'Carl,' whispered Lana from behind. 'I need a hug.'

6

Daccus twiddled his thumbs idly whilst he waited patiently in the jailor's lodge. Casual glances towards the single guard sitting behind a large table did little to relieve the boredom but at least the shade and cool breeze wafting through the open window was a welcome relief from the burning, noonday sun. Whilst seated upon a low, wooden bench he could hear cries of anguish coming from prisoners in the cells below; all kept at the pleasure of the magistrate. And pleasure is what this particular magistrate wallowed in. Being Titus's pet, Drexa Vitanian was given free licence to exercise his authority with impunity. Daccus had met him on a few occasions and remembered him as a fat and sickly looking character; quick-minded and sharp of tongue but his overriding feature was his black eyes; they pierced you through to the heart and kept on going until they reached your soul. Daccus remembered those eyes, so filled with malice and hatred of everything that was good in the world, it almost made him wretch just thinking about them.

A cough from the guard alerted Daccus as the muffled sound of shuffling feet from below sounded through the floorboards. He got up immediately and stood shaking in his sandals. Almost at once his throat dried and his tongue began to swell. The jug of water upon the guard's table looked most inviting but he stood his ground. Soon the rattle of a key in a lock sounded and the large wooden door to the cells directly in front of him creaked open and into the room stepped the jailor, a certain Vesti Barrius who was big and broad of shoulder. He was carrying a bunch of keys in one hand and a bloodied whip in the other. It was well known that the tall and brutish looking Etruscan had a reputation with the whip and quite clearly he had been getting in a little practice upon yet another wretched soul. The jailor met him square on which made Daccus want to bolt for the door. Vesti's sweat-soaked body was covered in scars and lesions that he had acquired on the battlefield but an injury to his right knee had forced the thirty-eight year old soldier to retire from his legion and take the job as head jailor for Drexa Vitanian - a post he revelled in. Vesti Barrius looked Daccus up and down for a short while then he tossed the blood-soaked whip on to the table where the guard was seated at. Specks of blood from the whip spattered the guard's face and he reeled backwards from the cold touch of it.

'Ha,' laughed Vesti sarcastically at the guard, 'you lily-livered city soldiers are a bunch of shithbags. Haven't you seen the sight of blood before?'

The guard stood up and wiped his face clean with his hand then announced that Daccus had come to see the prisoner, Fario.

'Oh, that fucking turd,' said Vesti with scant disregard, 'he's got enough money to buy his way out of my jail any day but unfortunately for me the magistrate has him.'

'Where is he?' asked Daccus ignoring the insult to Fario.

Vesti sauntered lazily over to the table and plonked the bunch of keys down onto it with a loud clatter. He picked up the jug from the table and drank straight from it allowing most of the water to run down his chest. When he finished drinking he turned to Daccus and sat down on the corner of the table, eyeing him up and down with much curiosity. Daccus felt uneasy and his throat dried up even more.

'He is in the infirmary, something to do with his leg,' said Vesti offhandedly.

'Can I see him?'

'No. You will have to wait, now get out of here!'

Summoning up as much courage as he could muster, Daccus stood his ground and spoke in a quivering but determined voice:

'Do you know who I am?' he said.

'I don't give two shits who you are; fuck off!' bawled Vesti as he laughed raucously to himself.

'I am the son of a politician and I demand that you take me to Fario.' Daccus was visibly shaking now.

The jailor raised his eyebrows and rose to his feet in a threatening posture. He reached backwards and laid a palm upon the handle of his whip making sure Daccus could see it clearly.

'I have told you once don't make me say it again…'

'… I will pay you for information then,' butt-in Daccus knowing that a few pieces of silver would loosen the jailor's tongue. He took out several denarii from his pouch and jiggled them about in his hand. The jailor's brown eyes widened with pleasure. He turned to his guard and the soldier left the building without a word spoken. Jailors were often bribed for many reasons including the murder of their prisoners when someone was willing to pay enough to have them silenced.

'What's so important about the trader that makes you want to part with your cash?'

'I need to know if he will survive the injury to his leg?' asked Daccus.

'They amputated it above the knee just an hour ago.'

Daccus felt a surge of nausea swell in his stomach and he wretched.

'Here. Have some water,' said the jailor offering up the jug. Daccus gratefully accepted and gulped it down not caring that most of it spilled over the rim and down his toga.

'From what I hear he screamed like a girl and begged for his mother,' said the jailor as he held out the palm of his hand expectantly. The coins were dropped in to his beefy hand and he stood aside to show Daccus out of the door, then he spoke again. 'I doubt your friend will survive the butchery of Vitanian's surgeons so don't expect to hope.'

Daccus turned and left as quickly as he could.

As he exited, he heard the jailor utter something further more derogatory about Fario under his breath but Daccus was beyond caring. He felt deflated and utterly distraught as he followed the guard the four-hundred feet or so to the barrack gates. Poor Fario, he thought. He wasn't sure if his friend would have the strength to survive such an ordeal. If he were to die, what would happen to his property and his expensive collection? Then he remembered something with horror. Drexa Vitanian would order Fario's family to be murdered leaving him free to claim the wealth of his estate for himself. It was common practise amongst the upper echelons of Roman society and it was carried out in secrecy. When entire families are obliterated who was left to oppose the offenders?

Daccus knew what he must do next but it meant having to take a risk. Then another thought struck him even harder; what would become of the Apollonians if Fario was to die? Would it give Drexa a chance to discover them? Or worse still, has Fario talked? He felt his heart begin to race at the thought of what torture and punishment the evil magistrate would have in stall for them.

Fario must pull through. He must!

On his way to the gates he noticed that the barracks was a hive of activity. Many carts loaded with timbre, tools, food and blankets were lined up and ready to leave for Pompeii. The relief was well under way and remembering that he could be called up at any moment, he quickened his pace out of the gates.

Carl and Lana had kissed. It was a moment that was as brief as a spark and had died like an ember. A second was all it took; within the space of a heartbeat their world had changed. Nothing will ever be the same again. Was it love? Of course it was!

A loud rattle at the door and a turn of a key in the lock shook the two Americans awake from their romantic embrace and in walked a young boy, no older than eleven years of age, holding a tray of food. He promptly placed the tray upon the table then turned and ran out of the room. Someone else closed the door and locked it behind him.

'Are you hungry, Carl?' asked Lana as she walked over to the table to examine the fare on offer.

'Starving,' Carl replied whilst trying his best to control his emotions.

Why hadn't this happened back home? Why did he wait until he was two thousand years lost in time to finally kiss her?

All he could think of was his home in Montana and his big, comfortable bed. His thoughts raced as he imagined making love to Lana. It was a thought that excited him to the core.

His hopes were raised further as he watched Lana tuck into to a large apple. She also picked up a bunch of grapes and strolled over to the window to look out over the river Tiber. At last, she was finally eating something! He watched Mumi tuck in to some boiled eggs and some kind of biscuit whilst he grabbed a bread roll and a block of cheese and came to stand by Lana. The bread was course and grainy, as he expected, but the cheese was very strong and aromatic, just the way he liked it.

'It looks busy out there on the river,' she said in between bites.

'It looks very different,' said Carl knowing that they were both making small talk.

'I wonder what's going to happen to us Carl. I'm missing home.'

'I'm missing the cool, fresh air of Montana and the rolling hills of Granite peak in Yellowstone,' he replied, feeling strangely insignificant.

Just at the point, where they fell into private thoughts of happier times, the door to their room was unlocked once again and in strolled Paxus, this time without Daccus' box in his possession. He looked flustered and impatient with his thoughts.

'Bring your food with you if you want but we must leave now,' he said.

'Where are we going?' asked Lana.

Once again she got that look of indifference – a woman speaking first!

Paxus' gaze shifted to Carl but Lana stepped forward and spoke aloud:

'I asked you a question,' she said aloud. 'Where are you taking us?'

Paxus looked to be annoyed at her persistence and he didn't know where to put his eyes.

'Look, let's get something straight Buster,' said Lana, defiantly, 'where I come from women are free to speak their mind, free to work, free to make decisions on their own, free to do what they please, so stop this sexist bullshit and treat me like a human being.'

Paxus recoiled from her stinging tongue and though confused by Lana's choice of words he seemed to get the picture. Carl was very impressed by her strength and felt closer to her now more than ever.

'So, I will ask you again,' continued Lana in a calmer tone, 'where are we going?'

'I am taking you to the Flavian Ampitheatre.'

Daccus was growing increasingly impatient as he stood in the observatory zone; a large raised platform which was marked off by a low, semi-circular, wooden fence. This area was where the general public were allowed to gather by the side of Via Truna and watch how the construction of the Ampitheatre was coming along. Most of the one-hundred or so citizens were watching the progress of the building purely to enhance their pride at the superiority of Roman society over the other races. They were eating and drinking titbits from a stall but Daccus was not indulging, he had been waiting for Paxus for far too long. Had something happened? Had the magistrate tortured Fario enough to glean the whereabouts of Paxus' hideout? No sooner had the last thought struck home he spied the wagon trundling along the Via Truna. Paxus was seated next to Munos, the driver and owner of the large horse-drawn contraption. Behind them sat Carl and his woman along with Mumi. The two strangers to his city sat wide-eyed in wonderment at the construction work going on behind him. Hundreds of slaves were toiling over the upper parts of the Ampitheatre; getting it ready for the inaugural games which were set to be in a year from now. The emperor Titus had been a daily visitor to the site now that it was nearing construction but Daccus had gleaned from an eager onlooker that Titus had recently left the city to oversee the tragedy at Pompeii.

He made his way quickly down the wooden steps and approached the wagon as it neared the site.

'My friend,' said Daccus with relief to Paxus as the wagon approached. 'How are they faring?'

'You sent a message for me to bring them and I have done so. They are your charge now.'

'Have you brought the box?'

Carl and Lana barely noticed as Paxus jumped down from the wagon and took Daccus aside. He spoke for long moments with him in a heated discussion and with much gesticulating. Then the conversation ended and a hot and flustered looking Daccus climbed up onto to the wagon with no box. Paxus turned and strode off seemingly relieved of his charge.

'Welcome,' said Daccus to his two dumbstruck friends as he climbed aboard. He noticed that both their jaws were agape as they gazed up at the Coliseum. Its network of wooden scaffolding could not hide the grandeur of its construction and he allowed them a moment to stare in wonderment at Rome's latest architectural marvel. Then he was struck by the sight of tears flowing freely down both their faces as they clasped each other's hands like excited school children. Daccus was taken aback by the show of emotion.

'My friends,' he said with pride, 'I give you the Flavian Ampitheatre.'

Carl looked visibly shaken as Lana clung onto him for dear life. They wiped the tears from each other's eyes and stared in silence for a long time.

'My god, Lana,' said Carl in English, 'it's a work of art!'

Lana did not reply. She was impressed by the building but her eyes were soon drawn towards the semi-naked slaves toiling away in the heat of the day under the gaze of their brutal looking guards. She knew that they were all Jews, captured by Titus during the fall of Jerusalem. It reminded her of the news reels of the Nazi death camps where thousands of Jews were worked to

'What are you doing?' asked a curious Daccus.

'Just one moment,' came the reply.

'Carl?' asked Lana in puzzlement.

To Lana's surprise Carl had pulled out the camera and began opening up the leather cover.

'I can't let this moment pass by,' he said with a grin.

Within seconds he had quickly reeled off a dozen shots of the Coliseum with the rapid fire shutter on the Nikon, being careful not to reveal it to prying eyes. Satisfied, he quickly stuffed the camera back into the sack and sat back with a wry smile upon his face.

'National Geographic are going to love you,' said Lana, wryly.

Within the hour Carl, Lana and Mumi found themselves out of Rome and heading into the country. The two horses pulling the wagon ambled along the gravel road at a leisurely five miles per hour whilst the riders sat in silence in the back of the wagon upon sacks of supplies, staring forlornly at the receding city. Clouds of smoke from the many open fires and rising thermals generated by the heat of suburbia distorted the view of the city making the image look to Carl as something not too dissimilar to the industrial skyline of Pittsburgh.

Mumi sat in stone-faced silence and fear whilst Lana couldn't shake the image from her mind of the wretched souls working away at the Coliseum. Daccus sat at the rear end of the wagon looking withdrawn and deep in thought.

Previously, at the gates of Rome, they had been requested by Munos to hide in the back of the wagon under canvas sheeting as a precaution against a random check by meticulous guards but they were allowed through without a hint of curiosity from the bored men on duty.

Carl's gaze finally fell upon Daccus and he decided it was time for him to speak up.

'We are ready for your explanation,' he said in a calm tone.

death. She could see that they were covered in stone and marble dust along with bits of dried-out concrete that was stuck to their emaciated bodies like limpets. The whole building site was a hive of activity which seemed a disorganised mess and she wondered how on earth such a magnificent building could come from such chaos.

'Look at those poor people, Carl,' said Lana. 'My heart is breaking for them.'

'Please do not speak in your own tongue,' insisted Daccus in a low whisper.

Lana shunned him and looked around at the faces of the gathered crowd. They seemed completely indifferent to the suffering of the slaves and she found it disgusting to say the least. Then she felt a firm grip on her forearm. Carl shook his head pleadingly.

'Don't allow your emotions to cloud your thoughts, Lana,' he said in Latin. 'It is how it was in these times. You will not be able to change their minds.'

'I can't watch this Carl. I… I feel like I'm going to puke.' She looked to Daccus and questioned him in Latin: 'Why have we been brought here?'

'Munos here will be taking us to Isernia. This road leads out of the city.'

'Why are we leaving?' asked Lana.

'It is not safe for you both to be here. There are too many prying eyes. Munos will be more than happy to welcome you into his home.'

The driver turned around and smiled a kindly smile and nodded to the strangers; 'My wife makes the finest dishes this side of the Alps and my slaves are the happiest slaves in the whole of the empire.'

'Why are you going to such lengths to protect us?' pressed Carl.

'I will explain along the way. Now we must go.'

In the next instant, Carl reached into the sack at his feet and began rummaging through the contents.

Daccus blinked and sighed. He seemed to be unwilling to reveal all but, nevertheless, he eventually sat himself upright and folded his arms.

'Rome,' he announced as a statement; 'she is like a woman; you either love her or loath her; she is both loving and caring but your best will never be good enough for her!'

Carl glanced back at the city. The first metropolis in human history would most certainly leave an indelible impression on the mind of a first century traveller.

'Continue,' said Carl not willing to let Daccus ponder too much upon the attributes of Rome. Daccus' face suddenly went dark and his brown eyes pierced Carl's to the core.

'I am of Greek descent and I am part of a secret society calling themselves the Apollonians, after the god, Apollo, though this is a decoy to prevent suspicion from the authorities,' said Daccus with some detachment. 'Every fourteen days we meet in the cellar of Fario's villa. The purpose of our meetings is to continue the work of the great Greek politicians, philosophers and scientists of antiquity. We are a political movement that wish to overthrow the dictatorship of the ruling class and long to see Rome as a true democracy. We do not believe in gods or soothsayers and the mysticism that underlies all aspects of Roman society and for our beliefs we live in fear of our lives.'

'Is that why Fario's life is in danger?'

'Anyone's life is in danger when they are in the hands of Drexa Vitanian; our dear magistrate and protector,' said Daccus, sarcastically. 'The soldiers who took Fario deliberately broke his bad leg under orders from Vitanian. Now I hear that they have amputated it!'

Carl and Lana gasped in astonishment.

'Its bad news,' continued Daccus. 'I fear he will not survive the treatment, but worse, I am certain Vitanian means him not to.'

'But why?' asked Lana.

'Oh, it's his way of murdering him without it looking like murder but the real purpose of it all is to get his fat, greedy paws on Fario's wealth.'

'What an evil man,' said Lana.

'And it gets worse. He will have to murder Fario's family so they cannot lay claim to his property. That is why we must get to Isernia and warn them.'

The brutality of the times hit home hard and Carl could feel Daccus' pain ten-fold.

'The other great fear is that Vitanian could learn the truth about the Apollonians,' continued Daccus, 'and then there will be many deaths to follow.'

'Then you must kill Vitanian,' said Lana. 'Get rid of him somehow.'

Carl sat up in shock.

'Hire an assassin,' pressed Lana, 'someone - anyone who will do it.'

'Lana! What are you saying?' asked a shocked Carl.

Daccus raised a hand for silence.

'If we did such a thing the retributions would be terrible,' announced Daccus. 'Vitanian is the emperor's pet; he is the eyes and ears of Titus; he reports everything and everyone on a whim and without mercy.'

Just as he finished speaking a loud rumbling of many hooved feet sounded out over the rise behind them.

'Soldiers,' said Munos the driver, 'what do they want?'

Soon a column of forty or so soldiers on horseback come racing up to the wagon. A call from one of the soldiers ordered Munos to stop. He jolted the wagon to a standstill and stood up from his seated position.

'What is the meaning of this?' he demanded angrily.

'We are commandeering all civilian wagons for the relief at Pompeii, by order of the emperor,' said the soldier. 'Turn around and we will escort you to the barracks.'

Carl glanced at Daccus who had the look of dread upon his face.

'Shit,' Daccus whispered under his breath, 'Fario's family are dead.'

*

The bulky wagon took an age to turn around on the narrow road but before they knew it, they were on their way back to Rome. Four soldiers were left to escort them back whilst the rest headed off along the road, no doubt to commandeer more civilian transport.

'The almighty Titus is trying damned hard to impress the public with his generosity towards the unfortunates at Pompeii,' said Munos to Carl under his breath. 'He's desperate to outdo his father in all aspects of his stewardship of Rome!'

'What about Fario's family?'

Munos shrugged his shoulders in reply to Carl's question and stared ahead at the road in silence.

Carl was struck by Munos's sudden acceptance of the change of circumstances. It seemed the iron fist rule of the emperor was never to be questioned. He glanced towards Daccus who simply stared back with a look of resignation upon his face.

'Jesus Carl,' said Lana in English, 'just like that eh?'

After several moments of silence Daccus looked at Carl and Lana in turn and spoke softly:

'So who is the emperor of Rome two-thousand years from now?' he asked like it was a throw away question.

Carl and Lana looked to each other in stunned silence. Neither could think of how to put it to him. Daccus rolled his eyes as he readied himself for bad news.

'Tell me, please,' he begged.

Carl coughed to clear his throat then sat up from his slumped position.

'The Roman Empire, as you know it, ceased to exist some four-hundred years from now.'

Daccus' face went as white as a sheet. He seemed disappointed in something else other than the news of Rome's demise.

'Rome became too big for its own good and had too many enemies to quell,' continued Carl, 'the empire couldn't defend its borders and was overrun by what you call Barbarians, including the many Germanic tribes from the north. The city of Rome was all but abandoned and became a shadow of its former self for centuries after.'

Lana could see that Daccus was taking Carl's history lesson quite well, all considering. Carl pressed on:

'Five hundred years before Lana and I were born, in a time we called the Renaissance, scholars and historians began to rediscover the ancient histories of Greece, Egypt and Rome. Texts and scrolls and manuscripts were read and scrutinised until the time of our day where we know so much and yet so little.'

Daccus raised a hand for silence. 'Enough of these times' he said looking somewhat downhearted, 'now tell me now about your world?'

A long pause followed as Carl pondered upon his thoughts. He looked to Lana and she shrugged and rolled her eyes.

'Go on, dazzle him,' she said in resignation.

'In our time, slavery has been abolished,' he said matter-of-factly. 'We have machines that do most of the work of slaves.' Daccus sat stone-faced with arms crossed. 'We have flying machines that can carry hundreds of people thousands of feet up in the sky and off to foreign lands in just a few hours.'

Carl began to feel a little silly at what he was saying, like he was talking to a two-year old but he continued on regardless.

'We have things called televisions that have moving pictures and sounds; we've discovered medicines that can cure illnesses and stop infections. We have put men on the moon and we have weapons of war that can kill thousands of people in the blink of an eye…'

Carl paused and stared at Lana. They both assumed that Daccus thought Carl was talking gibberish so they sat and waited for his response. They did not have long to wait.

'Fario has told me many strange tales from his travels over the years but never have I heard such stranger than this.'

Lana raised her hands up and spoke:

'We do not expect you to understand, Daccus, but we are not lying to you.'

'I find your words hard to believe,' he replied. 'How can you live in such a world without slaves? How do you ever get anything done?'

Prophetic as his words were Lana could not supress the urge to counter his question.

'How can you live in this world where slaves are treated like animals and human life means so little to you? How can you treat women like property and belittle them so-much-so that they feel worthless? How can you have an emperor with so much power, able to wield such tyranny with absolute impunity?

Daccus stirred uncomfortably from his seated position and rose to his feet. He seemed in deep thought and a little perturbed by Lana's angry outburst. He turned to Carl and spoke in a trembling voice.

'I am struggling with the concept of what you have told me. I will sit up front with Munos for a while to discuss politics. In the meantime, you and Lana had better get used to life in these times.'

7

It took several hours for Fario to die. The surgeons had made the amputation look professional enough but they had used the bluntest of instruments and made sure the stitching was not adequate enough to stem the flow of blood. Drexa Vitanian had greeted the news gleefully and paid the surgeons handsomely for their work. He was now free to make his move. His first act was to send six of his men to Isernia to kill Fario's wife and his two sons. The next step now was to find the black box that Titus so urgently wanted, but Drexa had devised a plan of his own.

'Bastia,' he cried out to his valet as he stared out across the city. 'I shall eat now.'

Bastia clapped his hands and in no time several slaves came into the opulent looking room with plates of hot food and placed them down at one end of a long table. Drexa turned away from the open window which looked out over the entrance to the Forum and sat down in front of the food. Bastia clapped his hands once again and the slaves returned to their never-ending chores.

'Today is a good day don't you think, my friend?' said Drexa as he tucked into a plate of stewed mice stuffed with dried grapes and herbs.

Bastia paused in his reply not knowing just exactly what his master meant but he was smart enough to humour him.

'The gods have blessed this house and its master most generously.'

Drexa did not reply, but instead, he proceeded to guzzle his food down just like he always did and drank lots of wine in the process. The fare on offer seemed wholly inadequate to satisfy his considerable bulk but Bastia had made sure that the slaves had prepared a second helping should his master be in the mood for more.

'I am going into the Plebeian quarter of the city soon!' announced Drexa followed by a loud burp, 'so make the necessary preparations will you!'

Bastia bowed and scuttled off to the guardhouse at once.

Thirty-five years of age, five feet-ten inches tall, thin but strong looking, the black haired and lightly bearded Bastia had been a slave for as long as he could remember. He had been informed that he was from Gaul and was a son of the Arverni tribe. He was captured at the age of six along with the rest of his family. The family were sold into slavery but he had no recollection of his mother or father or any sisters and brothers, for that matter. His long life of servitude began at the home of a wealthy pimp who owned several whore houses in Pompeii and Herculaneum and in many smaller towns along the coastline of Campania on the south western side of Italy. By the time Bastia was thirteen years of age his master had died of syphilis and from there he was sold on to Borus Axia, a wine merchant who had vineyards centred round Tusculum, ten miles south of Rome. The merchant was a brutal paedophile who had many slave-boy lovers and Bastia was one of them. He still had nightmares about his time with Borus; a time when he longed for his life to end but then, several years' later, fortune intervened when the emperor Caligula came to the vineyards to sample Borus's new batch of wines. Later that evening, after downing copious amounts of wine, the emperor became ill and accused Borus of trying to poison him. Caligula had him strangled to death and his wife flogged to within an inch of her life. The vineyards and the house became the property of the emperor. Borus's estate was confiscated and distributed amongst Caligula's loyal officers.

At twenty years of age Bastia then became the property of Centoria Millenius, the wife of Astrus Millenius, a high ranking officer in Caligula's praetorian guards. Centoria was a kept woman who wallowed in the trappings of the richness that her husband provided but she was also the unhappiest person Bastia had ever known. She was quite a beauty at the age of thirty-six; often left alone for many months at a time while her husband was away with Caligula on his escapades around the empire. It was little wonder that Centoria seduced the twenty year old Bastia at her pleasure. Her body was exquisite and she knew every trick in the book. She would often invite her elder sister, Agromina around for threesomes which was exciting for the young and virile Bastia but he still felt used; still a slave; an item of idle, lustful interest to the sisters. Before long Centoria's taste for younger men grew and she threw wild parties with much frolicking and debauchery but within a year she was divorced and made penniless by her angry husband. Bastia was finally given to Drexa Vitanian as a gift from Astrus Millenius for 'political favours' just at the time when the young and ambitious Drexa had begun his meteoric rise in politics.

Today, Bastia was going to escape. He had been formulating his plan for the last seventy-two hours since his last meeting with a certain Paxus Strupalo who was, apparently an up and coming politician. Paxus had informed him about the Apollonians and what their political agenda was and he insisted Bastia join the movement. Bastia wanted in and he would do anything to be part of a political movement that could undermine the dictatorship of Rome and free him from slavery. His plan was simple; when Drexa left his home he would change into the attire of a Roman citizen then make his way to rendezvous with Paxus at the pre-arranged meeting place by the banks of the Tiber. He knew it was bad news for any of the slaves if they stayed behind because upon discovering that he had become a runaway, Drexa would have the entire household of slaves burnt alive and their ashes scattered to the wind but Bastia couldn't care less for his comrades. It was time for him to move on and be the master of his own destiny.

After informing Drexa's bodyguards of their masters' intentions, Bastia made his way to the stables to oversee the wagon being readied. All he could think of was freedom. The Apollonian had given him hope and a purpose and he wasn't about to give up on the chance lightly.

Two hours later, as the sun's intense heat began to wane Drexa Vitanian appeared along with his entourage. His gay lover, Quintus walked beside him along with his scribe, Aramus and his lawyer, Sila followed by the usual escort of heavily armed and mounted soldiers. Drexa had a look of eagerness in his eye and he spoke to the two slaves with impatience as they struggled with the horse's bridles, snapping at them with a bitter tongue. After the fuss was over he turned to Bastia and spoke:

'I shall be gone for the rest of the day and… maybe tomorrow,' he said as he hefted his bulk up onto the wagon and sat himself down heavily upon the seat alongside Quintus who had taken up the reins, 'do the usual will you and keep the slaves on their toes.'

Bastia knew what 'the usual' meant. It was his responsibility to run the household in the absence of his master, keeping it clean and tidy though he always relaxed the discipline to allow a little respite for the slaves.

'May your day be untroubled master,' Bastia lied as he bowed courteously, hoping that the fat bastard would be robbed by a band of thieves somewhere in the city and beaten to death. With an anxious impatience growing inside him he watched the entourage disappear out of the gates. It was time!

Within the hour Bastia was on the streets of Rome, heading towards the Tiber and freedom. In the cooling air of the early evening he hastened his pace as he passed the Praetorian barracks guarded by a single sentry. He felt uncomfortable dressed in the loose-fitting toga which he had taken from Vitanian's wardrobe. There was room enough for three people in this garment, he thought whilst trying his best to look at ease in the outfit. The stolen sandals were not helping either. They were two sizes too small and he began to feel the aches increase with every step. He couldn't care though. He was on his way to the meeting point in a hurry. He had figured out that it was only a twenty minute walk away.

As he went, he pondered upon Paxus' eagerness to have him join the Apollonians. The young politician showed an unusual interest in him. They had first met three weeks ago at one of the public baths when Bastia had been busily massaging Drexa Vitanian's repulsive flesh. At first he had thought Paxus was attracted to his naked body but he had been taken quietly aside during a break and all was explained to him about the Apollonians. Bastia quickly saw the opportunity with the promise of freedom and was his only thought ever since the chance encounter. Paxus obviously had his reasons for revealing himself to a lowly slave but Bastia was left uninformed why. But still, he was keen enough to go through with his dangerous plan. As the great slave hero, Spartacus once said; 'It's is better to die on your feet than to die on your knees.'

Soon, the smell of the Tiber tinged the air about him; sewage and all. Bastia hastened his pace and followed the pong down a narrow street past a throng of people who were gathered at a stall selling the carcases of rats, mice, squirrels and lizards. A troop of soldiers were gathered at the end of the street waiting for something or someone. Bastia's heart immediately began to pound. He still had a fair distance to go but he dared not slow his approach or show any sign of intimidation; Roman soldiers were trained to detect such signs and react accordingly. He kept his pace steady and focused only on his next step, keeping his eyes fixed straight ahead. As he got to within forty paces of the soldiers, one of them turned and looked him straight in the eye. But to his relief the soldier's gaze passed him by and he seemed to be focusing on something else behind him.

'Stop!' he suddenly shouted and withdrew his sword. His comrades immediately did the same and all six ran past him towards their intended target. Bastia stopped and turned to see what the commotion was all about. The soldiers had surrounded a large man and set about grappling him to the ground. The man was screaming his innocence of some crime he was suspected of.

Bastia sighed with relief then a tap on his shoulder from behind made him almost jump out of his skin.

'Come this way!'

It was Paxus. He bore the face of a very worried man.

Bastia hurried along after the long, loping strides of the tall politician. He quickly matched his stride and allowed the Apollonian to guide him towards the Tiber. As he went, his mind raced. Paxus had actively sought him out. It seemed there was trouble brewing and that he was about to be embroiled in it from the off. The sky was growing darker by the minute and so was Bastia's mood as the two men disappeared down the side streets.

Ten minutes later, he found himself standing at a large, circular table opposite five ageing men who were staring back at him with a collective curiosity that he found to be a little disconcerting. He was asked to sit and was glad that he could finally kick off the excruciating sandals he had stolen from Vitanian's wardrobe. From his seated position he looked about at his surroundings. The large, lamp-lit storage room was full of the odours of spices and herbs, fruit and vegetables. Outside of the open window he could hear the sounds of the traffic on the Tiber as the people went by their business. Standing tall and foreboding above the table was Paxus, arms folded and scanning the faces of his comrades. The eldest looking man, who was seated directly opposite Bastia, spoke first:

'Pax, the window!' he said in a gruff voice.

Paxus turned, closed the window and drew the blinds. At once Bastia felt the atmosphere in the room become claustrophobic. He tried his best to put on a brave face but the gloomy looks from the men around the table left little hope for him to raise his spirits.

'You are from Gaul?' asked the old man who had spoken first.

'I was born in Gaul,' Bastia replied, defensively. 'I have been told I am a son the Arverni tribe.'

The old man glanced around at the other men and stared back hard at Bastia. 'The Arverni have been suppressed and pacified by the Romans for a long time now,' he said apathetically. 'Most of the Arverni in Rome today are slaves, just like you!'

The grim picture the old man painted didn't sit too uncomfortably on Bastia's mind. He knew that many tribes across Europe were assimilated into the Roman Empire, whether by choice or by force and the Arverni were no exception. He felt no affiliation towards his tribe or towards Rome for that matter. As far as he was concerned he was a lone slave with nowhere to call 'home'.

'I am glad to be free of my master,' he said, trying to change the subject, 'even if it's only for one day for I would rather die on my feet than die on my knees.'

'A noble gesture but do you know why you have been chosen?'

Chosen?

'I see you are puzzled by my question?' said the old man who suddenly smiled a broad smile as he leaned back in his chair and glanced around approvingly at his companions. To Bastia the man looked to be a few breaths away from the grave but he seemed to carry an inner strength tinged with an aura of authority.

Bastia answered no to the question and began to feel that he may have made a bad choice. The exit to the room was closed and guarded by another man so a quick bolt out of the door was not an option.

'Let me introduce myself,' said the old man. 'I am Sacria, to my left is Bax; Amnia is to my right, further to my right is Casiopa and nearest to you is Fustian.'

Bastia looked the old men over one-by-one. They didn't look too dissimilar to a sitting of the senate at the Curia Julia within the Forum which he had seen many times whilst escorting Drexa Vitanian. They all wore forced smiles upon their faces and were now trying their best to be genuinely friendly.

'Why am I here?' asked Bastia with as much restraint as he could muster.

The old man calling himself Sacria reached forward and picked up a jug that was sitting in the centre of the table and poured out a light brown liquid into a vial. He pushed forward the vial and leaned back.

'Drink this,' he said calmly, 'it will help to clear your head.'
Bastia stared questioningly at the liquid in the glass.
'Drink it, please!' asked the man.

Whether it was because he had a lifetime of being told what to do or there was something in the man's voice that made him react, Bastia felt compelled to drink it. It tasted slightly salty and bitter with a hint of pleasant fruitiness to it. When he finished he placed the vial down and waited for a reaction - there was nothing.

Then Paxus leaned forward and put both palms of his hands down upon the table.

'The other day at the public baths when you were massaging Drexa Vitanian's body, I noticed a tattoo on your back.'

'Oh,' Bastia said in surprise. 'What of it?'

'How did you get it?'

'I don't know... I've always had it.'

The room fell silent for long moments as the men cast knowing glances at one another.

Then Bastia began to feel a little light headed and the tenseness in his muscles began to relax.

'The tattoo on your back means that you bear the mark of a king!' said Paxus.

Bastia's jaw dropped a little.

'You are the rightful heir and only son of King Banax of the Arverni,' said Paxus with a serious intent.

Bastia managed a sarcastic chuckle and a wave of his right arm in the air dismissing Paxus' words as if they were a mere trifle. But then Paxus reached up to a row of shelves behind him and took a cloth covered object down from the middle shelf. He placed it carefully upon the table and removed the cover.

'There is a coincidence between the tattoo on your back and the engraving upon this wooden box that was bought off a trader in Gaul by one of my friends,' said Paxus. 'According to Celtic tradition, the engraving of a wheel with the sun and the moon's phases signifies the passage of time but it also signifies the gold of the Celtic tribes of the north and whoever bares this mark is of royal blood.' Paxus paused allowing his statement to linger in the air between himself and Bastia, 'though the strange writings beneath are not understood.' He then placed his hands gently upon the lid of the box and whispered. 'This box contains a key, a key to the great treasure of the Celtic tribes of Gaul.'

After several silent moments, Bastia leaned forward to examine the box. Upon the lid was, indeed, the same marks that he bore upon his back; a wheel with the same celestial images between the gaps of each spoke and beneath were letterings that he could not read. He slumped back in his seat and spoke up with both palms raised in resignation:

'I am the king of a dead tribe!' he pronounced with irony.

His joke was met with a deathly silence.

A grim-faced Sacria leaned forward and spoke in a calming voice:

'May we see the tattoo?'

Bastia glanced around the table at the inquisitive faces staring back at him. Without further ado, he stood and dropped his toga down to waist level then turned around. A collective gasp from the men followed and whispered mutterings beyond earshot filled the room. After several moments, Bastia pulled up his robe and sat down. Then Sacria waved a hand in front of Bastia's face and spoke in a serious tone:

'Do you remember anything about your time as a boy amongst the Arverni?'

Immediately, Bastia began to recall memories that he thought he never owned. Flashes of images began to build up; there was the gentle voice of a woman singing softly close to his ear. There was an animal kill with men gathered around the carcase and butchering it. There were images of children playing and running in fields of tall grass; laughter, rain, snow, campfires, singing, dancing and frolicking. Bastia shook his head to clear it.

'What concoction have you given me?'

'Never mind,' said Sacria, 'Now tell me the last memory that you have of the Arverni?'

Bastia thought hard through the mists of confusion and time then, like a flash, it was there, as clear as daylight.

'I can remember my people being captured by soldiers.'

'Roman soldiers?' asked Sacria.'

'Yes. The men of the tribe were separated from us.'

'What happened?' butt-in Paxus, his eyes burning brightly with curiosity.

'The soldiers started digging. They seemed to be looking for something and they were shouting questions at... at... my father.' The memory of his father being tied up and beaten suddenly came flooding back. Bastia was surprised at how vivid the scene looked to him. He paused for long moments whilst he contemplated.

'Is there anymore, Bastia?' asked Sacria, calmly.

'I can remember that the soldiers kept us captive for many days whilst they carried on digging in and around our village. They grew angrier by the day and began to execute the younger men in front of the elders.' Bastia found it hard to explain what he was visualising now. The images seemed all too real but he was more surprised by the fact that it was affecting him so much.

The men around the table obviously felt for Bastia and allowed him a long period of reflection. Then the one called Casiopa quietly spoke up:

'It fits!' he pronounced to the others who nodded in agreement.

'What fits?' asked Bastia.

Paxus quickly pulled up a chair and sat at the table. He stared hard at Bastia and spoke in a distant tone:

'During the reign of Claudius, in the springtime of his second year as emperor, the soldiers of the ninth legion began hearing fables from Gaul of a vast treasure trove which belonged to the Celtic tribes. Upon hearing the news, Claudius immediately ordered the legion to besiege the Arverni stronghold of Gergovia, your hometown. During the following days the soldiers began to dig, in and around the area in search of the treasure – a treasure that was said to be worth double the value of the entire Roman Empire. When the soldiers failed to find it, they tortured your father but he would not reveal the treasure's location. He eventually succumbed to the torture and died of his wounds. An angry Claudius ordered the tribal elders and their families to be brought to Rome. The elders were then subjected to the worst possible treatment at the hands of the most brutal torturers that Claudius could muster. Eventually, they too succumbed to their torturers' deeds and paid with their lives but not one of them could reveal the whereabouts of the treasure for they were wholly ignorant of its location and a disappointed Claudius feared the treasure was lost forever.'

Bastia felt his stomach crawl. He could think only of his father as his hatred for the Romans grew deeper with every word spoken. The tall politician continued:

'After the torturers had finished their work, the remainder of the elder's families were sold into slavery, including you. Claudius returned to his imperial duties a bitterly disappointed man. But then, a year later, a stranger came to Rome seeking an audience with him. The stranger recited Claudius an account which tells of the time when Julius Caesar was at war with the Celtic tribes of Gaul. He told him that Vercingetorix, the Celts chosen leader, had ordered the entire hoard of treasure from the great tribes of Gaul be brought together within his stronghold out of fear that their wealth would end up in Roman hands. The elders of all the tribes agreed, but on one condition; that once the treasure had been collected it must be taken to a far-off land for safekeeping. The choice for the site of the burial of the treasure was decided upon by four men; your father; a Britannic king, whose name has not come down to us and two druid priests. Their names were Velen and Ulnur. They had chosen Britannia for it was an unchartered and unfamiliar land for the Romans. The stranger also informed Claudius of the existence of a box that held a key to an underground vault where the treasure was interred. Claudius paid the man in gold for his troubles and had many sleepless nights thereafter.'

Bastia sat open-mouthed at such an incredible tale. For the first time in his life he felt a belonging; an urge to know more about his origins.

Then Sacria leaned forward and spoke:

'Acting upon this information alone, Claudius eventually began his campaign to conquer Britannia; not for the expansion of the empire's borders and for the glory of Rome, may I add, but to seek and find the Celtic treasure and the illusive key which had yet to be found.' Sacria's eyes strayed to the box and then back to Bastia with an air of expectancy.

After all he had heard Bastia remained puzzled as to why he had been 'chosen'.

'What part have I got to play in all this?' he asked, fearing the worst.

'We know the symbols inside the spokes of the wheel upon this box indicate your lineage and the passage of time but the ten strange words beneath the wheel are the secret as to the whereabouts of the Celtic treasure,' said Sacria. 'Unfortunately, not long after the box was made, it went missing. We believe it was stolen by a traitor to the Celts whose motive remains unclear. But alas, after Vercingetorix's defeat at the hands of Julius Caesar, your father, a young man at that time, who was custodian of the inscriptions, decided to have them tattooed on you. He made this extraordinary decision, knowing that the Romans would never have questioned the markings on the back of a six year old boy for many boys from Gaul were tattooed. But unfortunately for us the writings upon you are written in an ancient Britannic language which can only be read by a druid priest.'

Bastia squirmed in his seat feeling ever more embroiled in the story. He felt confused and very apprehensive but the men in the room seemed deadly serious and he was inclined to think that they knew what they were talking about.

'How do you know all of this?' he asked inquisitively.

Paxus took his turn to speak as he leaned back in his chair and pointed at each man in turn:

'These men are free men but they are also Arverni tribesmen; your loyal subjects!'

As one, the men stood and bowed their heads to Bastia. He immediately wished the earth would open up and swallow him. The weight of his lineage suddenly felt real and he cringed with embarrassment. Eventually the men sat down and Sacria smiled back a warm smile which seemed genuine.

'I was once your father's friend,' he said in a warm tone. 'Banax and I were as close as brothers in our younger days but, alas, we fell out over the love of your mother. She was such a beauty. Her name was Sirene. You have her eyes but your father's looks.' The men nodded in agreement.

Bastia sat open-mouthed in fascination at Sacria's words. The old man continued:

'I don't remember you being born for I was a hunter, often gone for weeks or months with my men into the forests and hills, but I do remember one occasion when you were being taught how to ride a horse by your father. You were only hip-high then. It was the funniest thing I have ever seen. You kept falling off the horse into your father's arms and crying that you didn't want to ride but he kept putting you back on the horse and then you started to deliberately jump off into his arms time and time again until you both burst into laughter and the watching villagers laughed along with their king and his son.' Sacria's eyes were bright with happy memories but then his eyes darkened as a thought crossed his mind; 'Only a few months later, the ninth legion arrived.'

A silence filled the room once again as the men collectively fell into their private thoughts. Bastia stirred uncomfortably in his seat. It was strange to hear such a moving tale from his former life but he had been a slave for most of it and being a slave had tempered his soul until it was as tough as old leather. Sentiment was a stranger to the emotions of a slave. After several long moments he felt he must speak up.

'So the treasure is buried in a land far to the north?' he asked without thinking.

Paxus slowly rose from his seated position, lifted the box off the table and tucked it under his arm. 'Fortunately for us the Romans are unaware that we know of the treasure and that we are on a mission to find it before they do. But first we must see Jesaphine, the blacksmith, who will open this box which we believe contains the key to the vault. It is now your destiny to help us find the treasure and rid the world of Roman tyranny.'

Bastia felt he had no other choice. His charge was much more preferable to a life of servitude so he accepted it without hesitation. The Arverni men shook arms with Bastia and wished him well. They dressed him in more fitting clothes then, in no time at all, he was following Paxus out of the door.

The following hour or so passed by in a blur. Whilst struggling to shake off the lingering effects of the concoction he had drunk, he found himself following a glowing torchlight through a dark and damp subterranean passageway for what seemed like an eternity. Eventually he found himself at the foot of a long flight of stairs where he was led up the stone steps through a doorway and into a large, draughty building. In the torchlight he could see that the building was an empty warehouse. Spilled sacks of grain lay rotting in one corner and a broken cart, far beyond repair, sat idly in the centre of the floor.

Paxus doused the torch and approached the cart. He pushed against the rear of the wreck with his shoulder and it rolled forward creakingly by a few feet. He bent down and tapped three times on the floor. Immediately a hatch in the floor opened outwards and a head popped up.

'Hello Daccus,' said Paxus without much ceremony, 'I'm glad you got my message. We need to talk.'

8

Carl and Lana clasped hands tightly as they stepped back from sight of Paxus descending the steps. The tall politician was quickly followed by a smaller man who bore the look of a lost soul. Paxus went straight to Daccus and handed Fario's black box to him. He then proceeded to inform him about the latest developments in hushed tones.

In the secluded cell, lit only by a single oil lamp, Carl and Lana listened intently to every word he was saying. There was the mention of Gaul and treasure and kings and Britannia. Then Daccus broke the news of Fario's death to Paxus and that they must assume that Vitanian knows about the black box. The politician seemed genuinely upset about Fario's demise and needed a moment of respite to think through the implications of the death of their leader.

Earlier, Daccus had been informed of Fario's death by one of the Apollonians upon his return to Rome after their failed attempt to leave the city. The Apollonian had also told Daccus that Vitanian was seen making his way to Fario's place with his henchmen in tow. Carl and Lana guessed that things were about to take a turn for the worse when Paxus ordered them all to follow him.

Carl, Lana, Mumi, Daccus and Munos were whisked away in the night through underground passageways and tunnels that passed by in a flash. After approximately half an hour they found themselves in a large cave filled with ironworks of all shapes and sizes. A big man was busily working at an anvil. Around him were flaming braziers, weapons, armoury and many other familiar items. Daccus informed Carl that Roman ironmongery went on for all hours of the day, none-stop, for every day of the year. The little group found the heat and humidity uncomfortable as well as the smell and the taste of metal in the air. Without further ado, Paxus and Daccus approached the very obese looking blacksmith who had stopped working and was standing by the anvil with arms folded. They took him to one side and spoke to him. The box was offered up and he held it tentatively in his beefy hands, turning it over, inspecting it closely with an expert eye. Carl and Lana stood at a distance with the others, patiently waiting.

'He must be the blacksmith!' said Carl as an understatement.

'You don't say?' answered the stranger that Paxus had brought with him. Carl turned and looked him up and down and could tell that he was not Roman, nor did he seem comfortable with the present company he was with.

'My name is Bastia,' said the stranger out of common courtesy, 'I have been brought along by Paxus because, apparently, I am the king of the Arverni!'

A long silence followed as the others turned towards the stranger.

Carl knew about the Arverni. Their legendary leader, Vercingetorix, who had fought bravely against Julius Caesar and was ultimately defeated, is still celebrated in modern day France as a national hero.

'I know of the Arverni but you don't look like a king,' replied Carl without thinking.

'Oh, and what am I to look like?'

'I… I don't know…'

Just then Daccus returned and told them that they were going to be a while then promptly walked back to watch the blacksmith begin working on the heavy iron bands. The others found various barrels and crates to seat themselves down upon and wait.

'I wonder what's inside the box?' said Munos, breaking the silence.

'A key,' replied the man called Bastia.

After puzzled glances came his way once more, Bastia felt obliged to explain what had transpired during the last few hours. The rest sat in wonder at what he was telling them...

'... So you see I am on a quest to find the lost treasure of the Celts. Never in my wildest dreams would I have foreseen this.'

'You were a slave now you are a king.' said Munos sarcastically. 'That's one mighty story you're telling us, my friend.'

'Firstly, I am not your friend,' replied Bastia, sharply, 'nor am I a true king. My tribe are no more and my people are enslaved. Just treat me like you would any stranger and let's keep it at that shall we.'

Munos frowned but did not reply.

Paxus and Daccus stood over Jesaphine as he busied himself with various implements. As the seconds ticked by the tension was becoming unbearable. Jesaphine eventually settled on a thick metal bar that was flattened to a thin edge at one end and proceeded to wedge it between one of the metal bands and the box. He pushed upwards with all his might until the iron band buckled, coming away from the box with a loud crack. But for all his efforts he managed only to prize open a small gap, about an inch wide. He looked up at the two men and frowned.

'This is tough iron,' he said with a shake of his head. 'The Gaul's are just as clever with their hands as they are with their heads. Damn tough!'

'Can you break it?' asked Paxus.

Jesaphine scratched his bald head and frowned. 'It could take up to an hour or so. That's if you don't want me to damage the box.'

'We must be careful,' said Daccus, stepping forward, 'we don't want to destroy what's inside it.'

'Then you must be patient. This iron is as hard as diamonds,' replied Jesaphine. 'I have tools that can do the job but I can't guarantee the condition of the box after I am done.'

Paxus laid a palm on Jesaphine's shoulder and spoke in a soft tone:

'Take your time, my friend. We will be waiting over there with our company.' He pointed in the direction of Carl and the others.

Jesaphine peered over inquisitively at the group. 'They look like a right bunch of shit-bags!'

'You don't know the half of it Jes,' replied Paxus in a darker tone. 'Come Daccus.'

Paxus and Daccus approached the gathering and sat themselves down next to Bastia. They quickly explained the situation to them as the sound of the blacksmith's work reverberated around the cave walls. After several long moments of silence Paxus looked up and stared Carl hard in the eyes.

'Perhaps now is the right time to explain how you came here from… the future.'

Carl felt that Paxus was scorning him in front of the others; a typical tactic by a politician, but he was not going to be intimidated. Then Lana stole his thunder when she leaned forward and spoke:

'We do not know how it happened but we are here in this shithole, nevertheless.'

Paxus' face suddenly grew dark as he stood up and drew out his sword, pointing it at Lana in a threatening manner.

'Now you listen hear bitch and listen well. No longer am I going to put up with your crass remarks and ill-informed statements. When I wish you to speak I will ask you directly or you will feel the edge of this sword cut into you – do you hear me?'

Lana immediately cowered behind Carl.

Carl stood as tall as he could in front of Paxus and announced that the lady will obey. Upon hearing Carl's words Lana felt betrayed. His cowardly promise crushed her already frail confidence and left her bereft of any hope of returning home.

Mumi did the best she could to comfort Lana by stroking her hands and forehead and after a short while Lana regained her composure but chose to turn her back upon the others.

'Good,' said Paxus with relief, 'now we can continue.'

Carl was prompted by Paxus to explain how they ended up in Rome so he quickly retold his version of events as best as he could. He told them that he and Lana were archaeologists, explaining the meanings and techniques of their work and that they were working in the ruins of Fario's home. This caused surprised glances amongst the gathered men who looked to each other in turn but they said nothing. Carl went on to explain that he and Lana were from a place called America; far from Rome and far in the future. Mouths began to drop open now and he could see that their attention was beginning to wane. Daccus, who had heard it all before, sat in silence.

'What's in this land of the future?' asked Bastia. His question sounded sincere enough but Carl felt that whatever his reply would be he may as well be talking to a brick wall. He turned to Lana and asked her to contribute, much to Paxus' chagrin. After a short while Lana turned around and stood up proudly. She strode into the centre of the semi-circle and glared back at the cynical stares of the men around her then she spoke openly from the heart.

'I come from a town called Malibu which is by an ocean we call the Pacific. I lived in a house by the beach. It had three floors, two swimming pools, a double garage, six bedrooms, four fifty-inch widescreen TV's, a multi-surround sound Sony hi-fi system and a kitchen to die for. I would often throw barbecue parties on the beach drinking plenty of bottles of Budweiser where we sang along to Beatles and Beach Boys songs until all hours of the morning. I'd go shopping with my friends to the local Mall to buy Gucci or Versace and we'd eat at McDonalds just to be daring. At weekends Dennis and I would take a drive up to Big Sur in his Plymouth Barracuda soft-top where we'd spend time together and not see a single soul the whole of the time.'

Lana paused and stared in defiance at the men. Then she silently stared at the ground remembering her times with Dennis and the good life she once had.

Carl glanced at the faces of the men and could see, reflected in their eyes, the utter ignorance of almost every word she had spoken. Then, as one, Bastia and Munos burst into raptures of laughter, apart from Daccus, who cast a glance towards Paxus. Paxus wasn't laughing. He slowly sat down and spun the tip of his sword idly in the dirt between both hands in contemplation. When the mocking had stopped all eyes turned towards him. He eventually looked up and pointed an accusing finger at Lana.

'If this woman uttered those words in the Curia Julia, the senate would accuse her of witchcraft!'

Lana spun on the spot and faced Paxus down because she knew what the ramifications of what he was saying would be. Daccus and Carl jumped to their feet together and confronted the politician. Daccus spoke up in defence of his friends.

'I'm telling you they are from the future. They can prove it.'

'Show me,' said Paxus as he stayed seated.

A quick glance from Daccus and Carl knew exactly what to do. Without hesitation he whipped out the Nikon camera from his sack, undid the leather cover and fired away with the continuous drive function, taking his time to pan around at the curious onlookers who recoiled from the harmless flashes. When he finished, he punched in the playback mode, put it on pause and asked the men to gather around him. When they obliged he let the camera roll. All the men's faces had the look of shock at what they were observing. The show lasted several seconds before the screen finally went blank. Quickly, Carl remembered the snapshots he had taken of the Coliseum and played them back. The men reeled from the images and stared at Carl with dubious eyes.

'Witchcraft… witchcraft!' cried Bastia who growled angrily at Carl.

'Now listen here,' said Daccus pleadingly. 'I am not willing to abandon the Apollonian values which Paxus and I cherish so much? Pax, please, you of all people should know.'

Paxus returned to his seat and began spinning his sword tip in the dirt once more, a well-used technique to help him think things through.

'I dare say the Apollonians would be at a loss what to do with these two,' he said without raising his eyes.

'Then in the name of Fario's memory Pax, let them prove themselves and let's not have a trial.'

'A trial?' asked Paxus angrily as he glared back at Daccus. 'Ever since you introduced me to them they have been on trial.'

In desperation Carl stepped in between the two Romans and made a bold statement from memory.

'On the 13th of Septem or, as we call, the month of September, next year the emperor, Titus, will die. His brother, Domitian will take his place. There is also a great plague coming that will ravage the empire, killing thousands.' Paxus and Daccus stood in silence. 'Now ask me how do I know that?'

'You see Pax,' said Daccus. 'Give them time.'

Paxus pondered for a long period. His thoughts were racing around in his head. He seemed to be in two minds; firstly, with his Apollonian beliefs and secondly with the typical mystical beliefs of the day. Carl couldn't blame him. The revelations were mind-blowing in the extreme. It's not every day that a politician is asked to make a decision on the lives of time travellers. After what seemed like an eternity, Paxus reluctantly sheathed his sword and looked Carl in the eye.

'Will our quest be successful?' he asked, cynically.

'I know only of what has come down to us through the writings of contemporary scholars,' replied Carl. 'There is nothing about the finding of a large hoard of Celtic treasure, nor any mention of you for that matter.'

Paxus frowned but looked resolute. He stared Carl up and down with contempt. Then, with a wry smile forming upon his lips he spoke in a sarcastic tone:

'Tell me what life is like in your time.'

Lana had heard it all before so she chose to move further away from the circle of men with Mumi following behind. Both women sat in a dark corner upon a pile of wood chippings which was used to fire the blacksmith's furnaces. She could hear Carl dictating the future of the empire to his encapsulated audience. His lecture was restricted to the big stories of course. The petty, everyday lives of the ordinary people and the slaves of Rome where lost to history forever.

'Oh I wish you could talk,' said Lana to Mumi without turning to face her. 'You and I would be friends back in Malibu. I would pamper you, feed you and cloth you and you would be a stunner and my friends will be jealous of you.' Lana began to whimper as she turned and hugged Mumi close to her wishing with all her might that this was some terrible dream.

'I would love to see... Mal...ee...boo.'

It was a soft whisper in Lana's ear and she immediately stiffened and pulled back from Mumi.

'What?'

Mumi smiled and clasped Lana's hands in hers. 'I would love to see Mal...ee...boo,' she replied with a broad and beautiful grin.

'You can speak?' asked Lana loudly... Mumi's left hand immediately came up to Lana's mouth, slamming the words shut behind her lips.

'Shush!' she whispered. 'Daccus mustn't know.'

Mumi released her hand and looked towards Daccus who was too preoccupied with Carl's monologue to notice anything else.

'Oh my god,' said Lana quietly, 'why have you stayed silent all this time, my love?'

Mumi frowned and hung her head then spoke softly from memory.

'I lived in a village in Ethiopia with my mother who was sold as a slave by her father and so I became a slave too. I will never know who my father was but when I became a slave at the age of fourteen I decided there and then that I will not speak, for a slave to have a tongue means they can speak their mind and a slave with a mind is a dangerous thing.'

'Especially a woman,' added Lana.

Mumi stared at Lana for a long time in a secret moment of silence. 'You are the most beautiful woman I have ever seen,' she said, warmly.

'Thank you Mumi,' replied Lana, 'you are beautiful too.'

The two ladies hugged each other for comfort once more then continued to talk in hushed tones.

After Carl had said all he could about the future, the men sat in their own world of silence, pondering upon the words of Carl's lecture. It seemed to him that they were disappointed. His words were too confusing but Carl understood. Then the silence was broken when Jesaphine called Paxus and Daccus over to him. 'I am ready to open the box,' he said whilst wiping the sweat from his beaded brow.

Paxus and Daccus quickly made their way over to the blacksmith and stared down at his handy work. The metal bands had been expertly removed whilst the box seemed only slightly damaged. Daccus breathed a sigh of relief and nodded to the blacksmith to open the lid.

Jesaphine proceeded to wedge a blade in between the lid and the case and levered it slowly open. A loud crack sounded around the smithy as bits of black seal broke away from the rim. The others rose from their seated positions and gradually sauntered over to spy on the proceedings. They watched with bated breath as the lid of the box creaked and groaned in protest but eventually gave way to Jesaphine's persistence. He raised the lid cautiously as Paxus and Daccus leaned closer to peer over his shoulder. Mounted on two wooden pegs in the centre of the box sat a large bronze key. It had an elaborately carved handle depicting a human skull with ruby-red eyes and was obviously a key to a large door. Paxus and Daccus looked to each other.

'The key to the vault!' announced Daccus.

'Or a key to a tomb!' replied Paxus, ominously.
Daccus shivered with the thought as he looked at the key. Anything to do with the dead made him feel ill at ease.

'We must leave,' announced Paxus suddenly. 'Bring the key.'

Daccus reached in and unhooked the bone clips which were holding the key in place. He hefted it heavily in his right hand and thanked Jesaphine for his work but Jesaphine didn't have a chance to acknowledge Daccus' kind words. Paxus rammed a dagger into one side of the blacksmith's throat and quickly pulled it out. The big man instantly stiffened in shock. Blood gushed out from the wound in an unrestricted flow. Gurgling and spluttering, he staggered backwards as his eyes glazed over. He reached out to grab Daccus by his toga but Daccus managed to step away, fearing his toga would be drenched in the dying man's blood. The primeval scene sickened Daccus and he felt disgusted by Paxus' murderous act. Then the blacksmith fell to his knees, drowning in his own blood.

'Why did you do that?' asked Daccus, angrily.

'Secrecy is our best option,' said Paxus as he stood in the middle of the circle of shocked onlookers. 'What I have just done was necessary for we can't have anyone questioning what we're up to. From this day on you are all under my command, you will obey my orders at all times or you will end up like the blacksmith.'

Then Paxus took everyone by surprise when he turned and slammed his dagger deep into Munos's chest. Munos stiffened from the impact. The big man gasped for breath as he fell to the floor with a loud thud. He died within seconds. The others took a step back in shock. Paxus seemed obsessively determined to carry out his plan to the letter.

'Anyone else got anything to say?' he said as he brandished his blood-soaked dagger. He looked very intimidating to Carl and Lana who stood shaking in their sandals, totally stunned by what they had just witnessed whilst Daccus, Mumi and Bastia nodded in obedience. Paxus wiped his dagger clean upon a dirty rag then threw the rag into the burning furnace. Sheathing his weapon, he picked up the empty black box and threw it into the furnace. Then he paused and stared down at the two dead men for a second. Then reached out to a metal rack and took a sword and dagger off their hooks. He quickly moved towards the body of the blacksmith and smeared the blade of the sword in the dead man's blood. Then he stuffed the sword into the man's right hand. Next, he moved to Munos' body and carefully placed the dagger in a pool of blood upon the ground next to him, making it look like the two men had had a fight to the death. He pushed over a few stands letting the tools and craftwork spill all over the floor only pausing momentarily to admire his handiwork. Looking up at his companions with a steely glare that pierced them through just as efficiently as the dagger he had used to despatch the two men, he ordered them to follow him.

The tall politician led his band of reluctant followers up to ground level and off towards an opulent area of Rome. Here, the city was cleaner, the streets were broader and there was plenty of burning torches to light their way. Apart from a few regular soldiers guarding important buildings, the streets were virtually deserted. Paxus was leading them directly towards a low building that was surrounded by iron railings. A solitary soldier stood to attention as the group approached.

'Good evening Commander Secus,' said Paxus as both men made the usual Roman salute of the raised palm and bent elbow. Carl noted that it was not the casual Nazi salute which historians would have the public to believe but rather more rigid, military and precise.

'What took you so long, Paxus?' asked Secus.

'It's a long story Secus,' replied Paxus, sounding a bit tired. 'Are the men ready?'

'They are.'

Commander Secus raised a latch to the gates and swung it inwards allowing Paxus and his band to enter. Secus followed them in and locked the gates behind him. 'The men are sleeping, the horses are rested and the cart is prepared,' he said as he scanned the faces of the strangers straggling behind. 'You look like you could all get some sleep. Follow me.'

Paxus said nothing but allowed Secus to take them through the doorway of the building where he guided them down a short flight of steps and into a large room filled with beds. It was an army dormitory with some twenty-five or so sleeping and snoring men laid out in left-hand and right-hand rows just like a modern day barracks.

'There are more beds in the next room ahead,' said Secus.

A small oil lamp set in a recess in a wall provided just enough light for the group to tip-toe their way down the centre line past the sleeping men. They entered through another doorway into a smaller room which was full of empty beds.

'Try and get some sleep,' said Secus as he lit up an oil lamp. 'I will wake you up in four hours.'

'Thanks,' said Paxus as the officer left the room silently. Paxus unhitched his weapons then promptly laid himself down upon the nearest bed and closed his eyes. The others stood for a while, uncertain what to do next, then Bastia and Daccus chose their own beds and tucked themselves in silently. Carl and Lana stood staring at each other, the longing for home growing more intense now more than ever. They had just witnessed two brutal murders, first-hand, and were straining from the effort to put the terrible visions out of their minds.

'What the fuck is going to happen now?' whispered Lana to no one in particular. Mumi placed a calming hand on Lana's shoulder but never said a word.

Carl looked into Lana's eyes and could see the mental strain tearing her to shreds. She was visibly shaking. His heart was breaking in two but, bizarrely, he found the intrigue and mystery of the situation exciting him. His archaeological and historical instincts were kicking in all the time. Ashamed of his thoughts, he took Lana's hands in his to try and comfort her but she snapped her hands away. Carl looked on in shock as she gave him a monstrous glare then she turned and walked Mumi to the far side of the room where there was a dividing panel made of wooden slats. On the other side there was only one bed so Lana and Mumi both lay upon it together and cuddled up for comfort.

Staring blankly at the wooden panel, Carl suddenly felt terribly alone, drained of emotion and bereft of feelings. He knew Lana was disgusted with him for not facing up to Paxus when he threatened her and he felt ashamed but he also knew he would be dead now and Lana would be all alone.

His mind drifted for a long time until, for some strange reason, he thought of his cell phone. He sat upon his chosen bed and rummaged through his sack until he found it. Quickly flipping open the lid he checked the battery level – one bar only and no signal. To hell with it, he thought, I'll try anyway. Bringing up the contact list, he selected his brother's name, pressed the call button and waited thinking what a foolish gesture it was. As expected, there was nothing but silence coming from the speaker. He despaired.

'Sam, Sam, answer me,' he whispered. 'Sam, please.'

Tears began to form in his eyes as his emotions got the better of him. He felt himself gripping the phone so tightly that it began to hurt his fingers. Floods of memories seared through his mind of sunny days which flashed by like snapshots. He saw himself fishing in the rivers around Red Mountain with Sam and their friend Jed Ryan; camping in Little Sage Creek under the stars where Jed would bring out his guitar and they would sing Ozark Mountain Daredevils songs by the log fire aided with a plentiful supply of Bourbon and Budweiser. The fear that those halcyon days will never be again made him nauseas. He wanted to puke but there was no food inside him to puke up. He looked despondently at the phone and sighed. The blue glow from the tiny screen was his only link to his world some two thousand years into the future.

As he prepared to flip-close the phone, the familiar sound of the message tone suddenly rang out followed by the usual vibrations. Carl almost dropped the phone to the floor in response. Quickly wiping the tears from his eyes, he stared in astonishment as the lettering read:

Missed call
Sam Mobile. Today - 15:11.

Out of habit, Carl pressed to reply and waited, thinking straight away what a stupid thing to do. But then the screen's call signal indicator showed one bar, then two, three and four. Slowly, tentatively, he raised the phone to his ear. 'My god it's ringing!' he said aloud. 'Lana... Lana.' But Lana did not respond. Carl quickly rose from his bed and made his way to the window hoping that this move would keep the signal flowing. The phone crackled...
'Hello Carl.'
It was Sam.
'S... Sam?'
'Hello Carl, where are you?'
'Sam!' yelled Carl.
'What's wrong man? National Geographic have been ringing me wanting to know where you are.'
Carl was speechless. He didn't know what to say.
'Tell me where you are man?' said Sam, sounding annoyed.
'R... Rome,' stuttered Carl, barely able to get the word out.
'You're still in Rome?' asked Sam. 'They've been searching everywhere for you. You left your car; you're credit cards and all your clothes bro'. That's not like you. Now come on. Tell me the truth?'
'We're going on a treasure hunt to Britain to find some lost Celtic gold...' Carl immediately admonished himself with such a stupid reply.
At that point the line crackled and Sam's heavy breathing began to sound intermittent. 'Sam' he screamed. There was no answer. He looked at the fascia which flashed *'battery level low'* then, in shock horror he watched as the blue light faded. The phone went dead!

9

A fine ash rained down from the darkness above, just like snow on a winter's day, but the flakes were darker and didn't melt on contact with the skin. In the short time it had taken him to ride to the top of the ridge, day had almost turned to night. As he scanned the bleak, colourless landscape before of him, all he could see was a scene of utter devastation everywhere he cared to look. Tendrils of smoke rose from numerous thermals that dotted the cracked and dried earth and a strong smell of rotten eggs was in the air. To his right, the sea had been transformed into a muddy sludge which lapped up lazily onto the coastline, disgorging the white carcasses of boiled fish all along the entire length of the bay. Inland, trees that were left standing were burnt to a crisp whilst two miles ahead of him lay the area where Pompeii once stood - now just a smudge upon the landscape.

From his hilltop vantage point, the Emperor Titus gripped the reins of his mount and grimaced. The search for survivors beyond this point would be an impossible task, he thought. Pompeii had now become a subterranean city; interred by the monster four miles to his left which was spewing out rivulets of red-hot mud that ran down her slopes like water off a duck's back. In that moment he decided that abandonment was the only solution. An exclusion zone around the entire region of Campania would have to be enforced, leaving anyone who had managed to survive to their own devices. No matter how unpopular his decision will be received back in Rome, the entire coastline must be declared uninhabitable. He knew that many influential and important people had financial interests in this region and he would have to brace himself for a backlash but dissenters will be brought here, by force if necessary, to show them the true nature of the disaster.

The ground suddenly rumbled beneath his mount's feet and the beast reared up nervously, eager to make a bolt for it but Titus' expert horse skills, honed to perfection during many years as a soldier, quickly calmed the animal down.

He turned to his escort and spoke:

'Decius, we have done all we can. I have seen enough.'

'But my emperor, there is still at least half the population of Pompeii that have not been accounted for. There must be some survivors down there that we can rescue,' replied Decius, the emperor's general of the Praetorian Guard and a close, lifelong friend.

Titus wiped the sweat from his brow and glared up at the noonday sky which had turned to a brown smudge. The previous day's rescue effort had been bad enough but today was worse. The futility of man's efforts against such overwhelming forces of nature hit home hard. Titus stared Decius hard in the eye.

'Why would the gods of the underworld want to destroy such a lovely place?' he asked bitterly.

'The gods are angry, of course,' replied Decius. 'The people of Pompeii and Herculaneum have gone soft and allowed the deities of the underworld to roam free. If we in Rome do the same we shall be the next to feel their wrath.'

Titus shifted uncomfortably upon his mount, caring little for what Decius had to say but he noted the word 'soft' and wondered if he may also have become a little lax of late.

'Fear not my friend, the gods of the underworld shall be heeded and this emperor has no intentions of becoming... soft.'

Titus geed up his horse and turned away.

'Are we leaving?' asked an incredulous Decius.

'I declare this land forsaken,' announced Titus with a heavy heart. 'We must care for the survivors and leave the dead to their own. Now let's go.'

*

Titus; a rough and ready character, in his early forties and ruler of the known world had much on his mind as he led his entourage back to Rome. His main army had welcomed twenty-thousand survivors from the surrounding area but the relief had little effect. Titus knew no emperor could have done more. The unprecedented disaster was beyond human understanding. 'The gods ways were not man's ways', his spiritual advisors had often told him but Titus was in no mood to ponder upon the vanities of the gods. All was not well back in Rome. His brother, Domitian was spending the family fortune on frivolous pursuits and claiming birth rights that he could not uphold. Titus had promised his advisors that he would rein in his brother but the eruption of Vesuvius had overshadowed everything. He also knew Domitian was jealous of him for Titus was his father's favourite son. Suetonius had written that 'Titus was the darling of the human race', a flattering statement but useful for an emperor nonetheless. Then there was the small matter of the completion of the Flavian Ampitheatre – his father's brainchild. It was already behind schedule due to the continuously revolting Jewish slaves. They were a most difficult race to subdue but Titus had promised to uphold his dying father's wish that the Jews must be seen to pay for their transgressions against the empire buy building the giant arena.

As the day wore on into late afternoon, he put thoughts of empire to the back of his mind and looked up. The sky had finally cleared and he felt relieved to be leaving the devastation behind. Then, as the late afternoon turned to dusk, Titus ordered his men to make camp. A small valley with a freshwater river running through it provided enough relief from the horrors of Campania and he needed time to clear his head.

Soon, the one hundred and twenty newly recruited guards, who were hand-picked personally by Decius, had made camp in the well-ordered and proficient way that they had been trained to do. The main body of the army, led by General Camus, were camped a few miles further on in order to set up sentries to keep the area safe for the emperor.

Removing his leather armour and undergarments, Titus washed his naked body in the river to get rid of the annoying ash that was beginning to irritate his skin and scalp. The ash even got into his mouth and he could feel it grinding away like bits of grit between his molars. After satisfying himself with his wash and dressing in a heavy field toga he decided to make his way to the campfire to go and sit with the men. It had been a long time since he had camped out and he'd always make it a point to be seated around the fire with the ordinary soldiery. This evening would be no exception. He missed being a professional soldier and all the kudos that came with it. He would eat what the soldiers ate, which, on this night, was bread, cheese, salted pork and the regulation goat's milk - something he could never get used to.

When he entered the camp the men automatically stood to attention but he quickly requested them to be seated and got stuck into the hearty rations. After several long moments of awkward silence, he deliberately brought up a loud burp to break the tension. A couple of the soldiers laughed nervously to which Titus replied back by laughing aloud. Then they all laughed as one. There was no doubt the new recruits were honoured with his presence but also a little apprehensive with the fact that the most powerful man in the world would choose to sit with them.

'Don't worry men. I was a raw recruit just like your selves once. Speak up. Don't be afraid. I won't crucify you for farting in front of your emperor.'

The men laughed a genuine laugh this time and immediately the tension melted away but he could see that their thoughts were with the tragic people of Campania.

'Now tell me men, do you think your emperor has done his duty well?'

Just as the words left his lips a rider came galloping into the camp and jumped down from his horse. He made his way directly to Titus. Decius stood and poked a warning finger into chest, stopping him in his tracks.

'General, an urgent message for the emperor from Drexa Vitanian,' said the rider to Decius as he bowed down upon one knee. Titus stood and called the messenger over, walking him some distance away from the camp.

'What is it?'

'Senator Vitanian has arrested Fario Ardenia and claimed his property for the empire, my lord.'

'Good. Has he gleaned any information from him?'

'Fario is dead!'

'What?'

'I am afraid to inform you that he took his own life whilst incarcerated in Vitanian's prison.'

Titus was stunned into silence. He instinctively felt that the message was a lie. After a long moment of contemplation he asked the rider if there was any further news. The man had nothing else to say.

'Tell Drexa to report to me as soon as I arrive,' snapped an angry Titus. 'Take a fresh horse and return immediately.'

The messenger bowed and made his way to where the horses were corralled.

Titus scowled as he watched the man go. Grinding his teeth in anger, a habit he could never shake, he cursed Drexa for allowing Fario to die. Titus wanted to interrogate the trader himself. The whereabouts of the black box was paramount, unless..., he paused and thought another thought entirely, Drexa must have found the box, but what possible use would it be to him? Then an impossible thought struck him like lightning. Has Drexa betrayed his emperor? He quickly shook such a thought from his mind and breathed a heavy sigh.

After a long pause, he requested to be left alone then walked further away from the camp to sit down upon the riverbank to listen to the water flowing by. It soothed him, calmed him and made his mind drift. His thoughts quickly turned to the emperor Claudius and the revelation that the Arverni had hidden a massive hoard of Celtic treasure somewhere in Britannia. Claudius' obsessive task with finding the treasure of the Celts had been passed on in secret to all succeeding emperors. Furthermore, Claudius had spoken of a black box that held the key to impregnable gates that guarded a large vault in which the treasure was laid. But alas, Claudius and all succeeding emperors had failed to find the key and the location of the treasure so now the charge had been passed down to Titus. Fortunately for Titus news of a black box purchased from Gaul by Fario Ardenia had reached his ear. Acting on a hunch, he had ordered that the box be seized and examined in the hope that it contained the key. He had ordered Drexa to use any means he saw fit to bring him the box but he may have underestimated his henchman. Titus castigated himself for trusting Drexa too much and cursed the bad luck that the eruption of Vesuvius had brought him. After a long pause, he rose and strode purposefully back to camp. The box must be found. He was convinced it was the secret to finding the treasure. He immediately gave the order to break camp and head back to Rome under the cover of darkness much to the chagrin of his men.

In the cool of the night Drexa Vitanian screamed at his men to search the villa again. His temper was boiling over, causing the veins in his neck and bald head to bulge dangerously. He had been waiting for six long hours and, in a rage, he kicked another alabaster vase over allowing it smash upon the marble flooring that surrounded the ornate garden.

Throughout the day his men had brought out hundreds of artefacts for him to check over but there was no black box, only crates which were full to the brim with trinkets from around the empire. There were small boxes containing herbs and spices, medicines and jewellery - but no black box. He remembered how Titus had been very specific in his demand that the box be found. He had explained carefully to Drexa that the box would be strong and sealed and would also have markings upon it in the way that the Arverni had always decorated their handiwork.

Soon, the cellar was breached and his men led him down a flight of steps to show him vases of gold and silver but no box.

Upon seeing the find his eyes widened with pleasure but this catch was insignificant to the Celtic treasure that lay buried somewhere in Britannia. Then suddenly, his attention was drawn to the fresco upon the wall. Eleven grim-faced men and one black girl stared out coldly from the stonework. His curiosity tingled for a moment as he stared at the face of Fario Ardenia. He was holding up a plaque of the Greek god, Apollo but the significance of it was lost on him. He ordered the cellar to be locked.

In resignation Drexa made his way outside and once more examined the remains of a fire that sat in the middle of the garden. The fire had long since burned out but there were no charred remains left of note except for some strangely shaped metal objects that looked like clamps or clips of some kind. Whoever made the fire had carefully removed what was left behind and probably buried them. If the black box was in amongst the pile of ash then his little quest would be a failure from the start. His heart sunk low; his hopes even deeper. He knew that his messenger would have gotten word to Titus by now of the death of Fario and that the emperor will be angered by the news but Drexa had no intentions of leaving Fario alive. His riches and property was worth taking and he also had no intentions of being in Rome when Titus returned.

The time it was taking to find the box had been unexpected but despite the fire he was sure it was here, hidden somewhere. He comforted himself with the thought that soon the box will be in his possession and then his personal quest can begin. And once the treasure of the Celts was in his hands then can he raise an army and take over the empire on his terms; terms that would make him the richest emperor to ever rule the known world.

One of his men came running from within the villa. 'We have found two slaves hiding in the loft,' he said, excitedly.

The soldiers quickly brought forth an old man and a young boy; both looked frightened out of their wits.

'Ah, perhaps you can help,' said Drexa as he turned from the fire and rubbed the palms of his hands together with glee.

*

Lana snapped open her eyes as yet another nightmare startled her awake. Mumi was already up, sitting upon the floor busily platting her hair. It was still dark outside but she could make out Mumi in the dim light from a small oil lamp upon a shelf.

'Mumi,' Lana whispered in a raspy voice - she was desperate for a cigarette. 'Are you all right?'

Mumi turned her big brown eyes towards Lana and forced a thin whisper of a smile back at her. Lana smiled back and sat up:

'I dreamt we were on a motorbike heading down the Pacific coast highway,' she said, 'when all of a sudden a giant eagle picked both of us up in its claws and took us to a wooden fort full of armed men. It dropped us before a soldier dressed in an officers' uniform. He turned to his men and ordered them to enjoy themselves at their leisure. Then many hands were all over us, ripping off our clothes and we were raped time and time again...' Lana began to sob uncontrollably.

'Don't worry, dreams are not messages,' whispered Mumi as she rose from the floor and sat upon the bed. Then, to Lana's utmost surprise, Mumi leaned forward and kissed her full on the lips. Lana stiffened but did not pull away. Then she felt a hand come up from under her bed sheet and touch her breasts, caressing them sensually and smoothly. Lana pulled away and looked into Mumi's eyes but was surprised to feel a pleasure-filled bliss wash over her. Mumi kissed her again and she found her lips were full and tasteful then both tongues met in a twisting, writhing dance of lustful wantonness. Lana needed it. She craved for it. She found it relaxing her; taking her away from the living nightmare that was Rome.

Then Mumi pushed Lana onto her back and spread her legs wide apart. Soon her warm, wet tongue was gently massaging her clitoris and she flushed with pleasure, giving in to Mumi's expertise with all her heart. Memories of her wedding night with Dennis came flooding back, memories of her first time in England with Charles Eastman on the cricket pavilion all those years ago and the memory of her first night in America, on Christmas Eve, with two hunky bodybuilders from New Mexico where they gave her the best sex she'd ever had.

Lana's pussy was dripping wet as Mumi began to slide her fingers in and out of her vagina in perfect rhythm. An orgasm will follow shortly but Lana wasn't sure if she could stay silent. She wanted to scream out her pleasure and she tried to pull away but Mumi wouldn't let her as she continued to finger her sodden pussy and lick at her clitoris at the same time. Lana pulled at the mattress and then at Mumi's platted hair, losing track of time as she writhed in ecstasy. Then she came; wave after wave, but luckily, Mumi had placed her free hand over Lana's mouth allowing her to let rip and she didn't hold back. It was perhaps the best orgasm she'd ever had, more out of relief than pleasure.

A few moments later, Mumi fetched a bowl of water and some clean linen from the far side of the barracks and helped Lana wash herself down then she combed Lana's roughened hair as best she could. The two of them dressed but stayed silent throughout. There were no words needed. What was done was done and the passionate moment will remain forever their secret. Lana wondered if she would ever get the time or the seclusion to return the favour.

A cockerel sounded somewhere in the distance and both ladies looked to each other.

'It will soon be dawn,' announced Mumi, 'but I don't want to go with Paxus and those soldiers.'

'I don't think we have a choice,' said Lana. 'We must obey, remember? And we have no one to help us.'

A loud bell rang in the other barracks and they could hear a rough voice calling out orders which was quickly followed by scuffling feet and loud groans. Then the door to their room was flung open and the bell rang louder this time.

'Up, up, up breakfast is served?'

Lana could hear the men rousing and she stood and walked with Mumi around the wooden panel to where Carl was sat up rubbing the back of his neck. She could see that he had not slept well. His eyes bore dark rings and he looked pale.

The smell of cooked food wafted through from somewhere beyond and Lana's stomach grumbled in response. As they both approached Carl's bed, he suddenly stood up. A wide grin formed on his face as he turned with both hands reaching out to Lana.

'I spoke to Sam... I spoke to Sam,' he said in English.

'What?'

'I tried the cell phone last night and Sam answered.'

Silence followed.

'Come on Carl you must have been dreaming,' replied Lana, sympathetically.

'No, it was real I tell you,' said Carl, sounding sincere enough. He reached under his blanket and pulled out the cell phone. 'I'll show you that Sam was the last caller...'

'Oh Carl don't be silly.'

'Oh shit,' said Carl alarmingly, 'the battery's dead!'

He slumped to the bed and hung his head.

Lana sat down next to him and placed a hand upon his lap. 'Let's have breakfast, I'm starving!'

'I wasn't dreaming Lana. I spoke to Sam. He said they were looking for us and that I'd left my car, my clothes and my bank cards... Jesus woman don't you believe me?'

A kick to the foot of the bed startled Carl and Lana to attention. It was Paxus. 'Let's eat,' he said as he looked down apathetically at Carl. 'We must leave by Solis Ortus.' Then he turned and walked towards the doorway followed quickly by Daccus and Bastia.

Carl knew that Solis Ortus meant sunrise so they didn't have much time.

Lana suddenly felt sorry for Carl but also a little guilty. She had fallen out with him for not defending her honour against Paxus during the incident in the blacksmith's cave. But she also knew it could have cost them their lives had Carl not appeased the politician.

'I suppose you're right Lana,' said Carl after a long pause. 'It must have been a dream.'

'Let's get breakfast then.'

Two of Drexa's men set about Tucus' torso with razor sharp knives, expertly cutting away at his little chest, peeling back the skin to expose his ribcage. The little boy's screams of agony were so highly pitched that at one point Drexa had to put his hands over his ears. Being forced to watch the torture against his will was Lucius but all he could do was weep for the slave boy.

'Tell me where the box is and I will give the boy a quick death,' said Drexa to Lucius.

'I do not know, master,' he cried as he shook visibly with fear. His hands were tied securely to one of the wooden support posts that held up the garden sun shade.

'No?' asked Drexa. 'What was burned on that fire then?'

'I don't know master. I'm telling you the truth.' Lucius slid down the post to his knees and hung forward from his restraint with his head bowed. Tears streamed down from his eyes with the thought of Tucus suffering such agony at the hands of Drexa's thugs.

'Very well then,' said Drexa as he nodded for his men to continue the torture.

The two soldiers lifted Tucus off the garden table and placed him on the ground as another soldier brought forth a large iron hammer – the type that was used for driving wooden stakes into the ground. Then one of the soldiers held down the boy's legs with both hands as the man with the hammer raised it high above his head and brought it down with such brute force upon the boy's left foot that it smashed it to pieces. Blood, bone and sinew stained the cracked marble in a messy puddle leaving Tucus screaming and writhing in agony. Lucius looked into the slave boy's brown eyes, which were streaming with tears and fear all at once, and felt nothing but pity for him. Then the soldier raised his hammer once more and smashed Tucus' right foot to a pulp. The rest of the watching soldiers laughed at their colleague's handy work.

Tucus cried out through his terrible screams, 'Tell him Lucius... tell him.'

Drexa immediately crouched down and grabbed the boy's hair. 'Tell me what?' His eyes bulged with rage and annoyance at being kept so late.

Lucius responded quickly to save the boy from further torment. 'My master's friend took the box with him to another place down by the Tiber.'

'What place?'

'The home of his politician friend, I think his name is Paxus.'

'Paxus?' said Drexa. 'So my suspicions about that scoundrel have been proven right. He is what I knew all along, an enemy of Rome!'

In one swift movement, Drexa withdrew a dagger from within his tunic and rammed it unceremoniously into the boy's heart, twisting it as it went in. Tucus died instantly - a blessed relief from his torment. Drexa removed the dagger and rose painfully from his crouched position wiping the bloodied blade on the leaf of a plant hanging from a basket.

'Mathias, let's pay Paxus Strupalo a surprise visit shall we!'

The officer stepped forward and saluted. 'I will have the men assembled at once sire,' replied the baby-faced savage who had wielded the hammer upon the unfortunate Tucus. 'What shall we do with this old man?'

Drexa asked Mathias for the hammer who duly handed it to him. Drexa thanked Lucius for the information he provided then he raised the hammer high and smashed Lucius' head wide open leaving his mushed brain to flop out onto the cold marble.

'Let's go,' said Drexa to his men as he stared wide-eyed with pleasure at his handiwork.

At a long, wooden dining table sat two-dozen burly looking soldiers seated upon benches running down either side. They were chattering and laughing amongst themselves as Carl, Lana and Mumi followed Paxus, Daccus and Bastia down the short flight of steps passing the men as they went. Carl could see that they were much older than the rank-and-file soldiery. They were veterans that had their best days behind them and were probably weeks away from retirement. Within seconds a silence fell like a veil as the eyes of the soldiers scanned the visitors suspiciously. Then Commander Secus, who had met them at the gates the previous night, stood up and addressed his men:

'Please welcome our distinguished guest, the politician, Paxus Strupalo.'

The silence continued as one-by-one the men returned to their breakfast.

'Thank you Secus,' replied Paxus as he sat upon a bench at one end of the table. The others squeezed in next to him looking somewhat nonplussed by the whole arrangement but they tucked in to the breakfast that was on offer. Secus seated himself down at the other end of the table and proceeded to eat his breakfast, heartily.

'Hey, politician,' said one of the soldiers from across the table, 'don't you know the rule, no women at a soldiers table. It's bad luck.' His comrades nodded in agreement.

Paxus turned to Lana and Mumi and simply waved them away but the two ladies stayed put.

'You heard the man,' said Paxus, angrily. 'Take your food and leave – now!'

Carl squirmed upon his seat but decided to say nothing. Death was but a breath away at all times. Then he watched anxiously as Lana slowly rose from her seat and stared Paxus down.

Please say nothing – hold your tongue girl.

He let out a sigh of relief when Lana and Mumi filled their plates with various items, exited the room and made their way back to the barracks. The soldiers resumed their breakfast but the cheery banter had ceased.

After a short while, Commander Secus rapped his knuckles upon the table for attention and spoke to the soldiers:

'Men, we have been chosen to go on a secret mission to Britannia.'

After a few awkward seconds of silence one of the soldiers bearing a scar under his right eye spoke up:

'Britannia, I have been there. It's nothing but a shithole infested with rats,' he said in a gruff voice. The men laughed as one and raised their beakers in salute. 'To Britannia!' they said collectively.

'Gentlemen,' said Secus, 'Our noble guest will explain more.'

Paxus took his time to drink his beaker of water then placed it down purposefully upon the table. When he eventually looked up all eyes were on him. The simple tactic had worked. He carefully scanned the soldier's battle-worn features one-by-one. Military action had been harsh on these men but it had made them a very tough and experienced outfit which was just what he need for this task. He shifted his weight on the hard bench and coughed to clear his throat.

'I am requesting you all to take up a secret quest that could make you some of the richest men in the empire. You will be paid handsomely on our return so you can happily retire and grow fat.'

'Oh yeah,' questioned a thin and wiry looking soldier. 'What's with the secrecy?'

'I don't want any imperial trouble in this matter,' replied Paxus. 'All I need from you men is protection for me and my comrades.' He waved a casual palm towards Carl, Daccus and Bastia. The soldiers ran a professional eye over the civilians, collectively, leaving their guests feeling decidedly uncomfortable.

'So what are you willing to pay us for protecting these shitbags?' said the same soldier. His comrades laughed aloud and raised their beakers once more.

Bastia spat a morsel of gristle onto his plate and stared the man down. The soldier stared back with menace.

'I need you to protect your interests in this opportunity of a lifetime,' replied Paxus, diplomatically. 'Wouldn't you all like to retire with a million sesterces each to your names?' The men instantly raised their eyebrows and the motion was not lost on Paxus. 'Follow me to Britannia and you will have that chance.'

Silence followed as the men pondered upon the offer.

Roman soldiers were looked after well by the army but it was tough and demanding with most soldiers expecting to do service for up to twenty years - if they lived long enough - and all for a good pension and a plot of land. But Paxus was familiar also with the practise of bribing the soldiery for political and personal reasons. He looked to Commander Secus who was himself in deep thought. Then a grim-faced soldier spoke up:

'You know the price for deceiving us, politician. These men, who are my friends, will hunt you down if you dare try any funny business.'

'I will explain all when we get out of Rome,' replied Paxus. Then he paused for a long moment to look into each man's eyes purposefully. After that he leaned forward and spoke in his statesman's voice once again. 'In the name of the mighty Jupiter, the senate and people of Rome and as an elected member of the Curia Julia, I promise to honour my word!'

Commander Secus slowly rose from his seat and stared at the faces of his soldiers to gage their mood. Then he looked to Paxus. 'Very well then, when do we leave?'

An hour later Carl, Lana, Mumi and Daccus found themselves seated inside a small horse-drawn cart heading off through the broad streets of the posher area of Rome. They had been ordered to wear rather drab looking shawls similar to slaves but of a finer cut with a simple edging pattern sewn in. A thin cord tied at the waist kept the rather flimsy garb held together neatly but Mumi was left wearing her slave clothes. Carl couldn't help but notice how Lana's amazing breasts stood out prominently through her thin covering. They bounced up and down to the rhythm of the cart as it trundled along the cobbled path. Some of the soldiers had also noticed and he cringed with what thoughts would be running through their minds. But most disturbingly, was the look in Lana's eyes. They reflected a troubled mind, withdrawn in fear and loathing. Carl closed his mind and stared ahead with fear and loathing of his own to think about.

The sun was beginning to lighten up the cloudless sky. The air was cool and the city was quiet. Few people were about, apart from a group of four women who were sweeping the steps of a rather grandiose building. It took a while for Carl to get his bearings but eventually he began to recognise certain landmarks. They were passing the Forum in all its magnificent glory. The building the women were sweeping was the temple of Jupiter which stood at one end of the Forum. This was the place where the empire's treasury was housed and in front of that stood the beautifully decorated tomb of Julius Caesar. He was stunned by the intricacy of the work adorning it. It looked tiny in comparison to the temple but just as impressive nevertheless. To the right of the temple of Jupiter stood a rather bland looking building but nonetheless more important, it was the Curia Julia – the seat of Rome, where the senate debated away the hours. How many grand speeches and political decisions have been made within the walls of this building that have echoed down through time and still resonate in modern-day Europe, he thought?

Carl indulged himself for a while as he scanned the rest of the Forum; pristine, painted and decorated unlike the ruins that he had visited so many times in the past, or the future as the case may be. The impressive site was overlooked from the Palatine hill by the emperor's palace; grand, white and gleaming in the new rays of the dawn sun. He felt the urge to reach inside his sack for the Nikon but he didn't want the soldiers to notice him.

As the entourage drew near the opposite end of the Forum he could see the foundation blocks of the newly commissioned Arch of Titus, to honour the emperor's victory over the Jews. Beyond that, the Coliseum stood gleaming in the sunlight. Already, the slaves were hard at work adding the finishing touches to the magnificent structure which will soon become a theatre of death.

Carl's overwhelming archaeological instincts were kicking in and it took some effort for him to subdue his professional emotions. He looked to Lana and spoke to her in a light tone whilst trying his best to cheer her up. 'This is incredible,' he whispered. 'What a beautiful place!' But she just stared ahead in deathly in silence.

A tap on the side of the wagon distracted Carl's attention. It was one of the soldiers riding alongside. He raised a warning finger; 'no talking!' he ordered.

Two hours later, the city of Rome was but a grey and white blotch upon the horizon. The sun had quickly warmed up the air and many birds rode upon the rising thermals on their never-ending search for food. The miniature army rode onwards through the countryside along a well-used road. Paxus, dressed in an army uniform, led the way alongside Commander Secus. Bastia had been given a horse and a sword but no uniform. He followed behind Paxus, obviously feeling the sense of his new-found freedom to his liking. Behind Bastia rode twelve regular soldiers in two-by-two formation. Following on was the supply wagon carrying Carl, Lana, Mumi and the disconcerting figure of Daccus who seemed to have retreated into a world of his own. He kept taking out the key from his pouch periodically and examining it as if he was making sure it hadn't vanished but Carl had neither the gumption nor the will power to ask what was troubling him.

The driver geed up the two horses as they increased their speed along the road which went dead straight before heading north at right angles over a series of low lying hills and off into the country. Trailing behind the wagon were twelve more soldiers riding two abreast. Carl was impressed at how 'at ease' the soldiers looked upon their horses. They rode with no saddles, of course, just thick blankets thrown over the horse's backs. The saddle would not be invented for another four-hundred years.

The quest was underway but Carl found himself suddenly pondering upon their fate. Keeping himself and Lana alive was good thinking by Paxus, he thought. Although the politician seemed driven enough to commit murder at a whim, he was no fool, that much Carl knew, but for how long would he and Lana be 'useful' to him? He knew they would have to keep their wits about them at all times and obey every order, but most of all they would have to think like Romans, act like Romans and be like Romans.

Once again he glanced Lana's way and was hit by how bedraggled and drawn she looked. For the first time ever he saw worry lines creasing her forehead and her once shiny hair looked decidedly dull and brittle. The magnificence of her California looks was fast becoming a memory. It was going to be tougher on her than him, he knew. The soldiers had already made sexual remarks to both women and in this male-dominated society he feared the worst for them but there would be nothing he could do about it. Where would he find the strength to protect Lana? He envisioned in his mind's eye a stand-off with one of the soldiers wishing to have his way with her. It would be no contest. Any one of the soldiers he cared to pick out would kill him without a second's thought. Once again he felt a sense of despair come over him. As much as it pained him to admit it, he found he was beginning to despise all that was Roman.

10

Calling everyone in the camp together, Paxus stood beneath a pine tree with his hand resting upon the hilt of his sword and one foot in front of the other ready to deliver his message. The camp had assembled by the side of a brook banked by small, sandy ridges. It was a moonless night back-dropped by the brightest celestial view Carl had ever seen in his life. The Milky Way stretched in a mighty arc from horizon to horizon in perfect clarity dotted on either side by thousands of glittering stars. Carl knew, of course, that he was in the times of the pre-industrial revolution where the atmosphere had not been polluted by millions of tons of fossil fuels; where the air in the countryside was pure and fresh. There was also no light pollution from a nearby sprawling metropolis, so it was little surprise that the view of the heavens in these times was something to behold. His concentration was distracted when Paxus spoke up.

'By being here you have made yourselves renegade soldiers,' announced Paxus in a grim but determined voice. 'Titus and his loyal army are too busy dealing with the tragedy at Pompeii to even notice that you are missing. So I ask you all on this night to make a pledge that you will take up the challenge that I am putting to you. I wish to seek and find a hoard of treasure that is said to be double the entire wealth of the empire. Somewhere buried in Britannia is the treasure of the Celtic tribes of Gaul. If you follow me I will use these riches to overthrow Titus and declare a new age for Rome and for the world.'

Silence followed for a long time. The crackling of dry wood upon the open campfire was the only sound that could be heard in the still, night air. Carl carefully scanned the faces of the soldiers to try to glean from their expressions what side of the political fence they were on. All of them looked shocked. Commander Secus eventually stepped forward and spoke:

'What assurances can you give us, Pax?'

Paxus turned to Daccus and asked him to bring forth the key. Daccus obliged by pulling out the key from his pouch and holding it up high for all to see.

'This is the key to our fortune,' said Paxus, theatrically.

The soldiers' eyes widened with surprise and they began to murmur between themselves.

Then a rather hefty looking soldier stepped forward and raised his hand for attention. 'As you are well aware, Britannia is a place where no soldier goes willingly. It is said there are witches there that can burn out your eyes at a glance. There are soothsayers that can curse you and your family with bad luck forever. And then there are the druids to contend with. It is said that they make human sacrifices to their gods and they can foretell the future.'

As one, the men began to raise their voices with concern. The soldier had reminded them of the rumours that were rife amongst the ranks. Carl knew that the Romans had abandoned the ancient rituals of human sacrifice which was now seen as a barbaric practice but the mythological tales of witches and soothsayers were very real to the ancients.

To quell the soldiers' concerns, Paxus quickly stepped away from the pine tree with raised palms for silence. 'Fear not fellow Romans,' he said in his statesman-like way. 'Put these false tales behind you. Abandon your superstitions and your gods and follow me on a path to reason, wealth and enlightenment.'

Silence shrouded the camp like a sonic vacuum.

'Why should we abandon our gods to follow you on a course that will surely fail?' called out one of the soldiers from the rear of the gathering.

'You cannot challenge the emperor,' said another soldier.

'My allegiance is to Rome and not to you,' said another.

Paxus stepped boldly into the crowd of soldiers and stared them all in the eye once again. 'I see many scarred faces in this gathering,' he said softly, 'scars that bear the marks of war, conflict and aggression. Was your salary worth the effort? Is your pension worth the time? Go and scan the face of your emperor and you will see similar scars born out of empire building. It is true that he was a brave soldier fighting from the front just like you men but Titus is far richer than any of you. He is treated like a god! He is master of all that he surveys and all because of an accident of birth; born into a family that owns the empire and its people. I tell you now if you follow me you can be masters of your own destiny.'

'How do we know that we are not trading one dictatorship for another?' asked a burly soldier in a gruff voice. His comrades nodded in agreement.

Carl was impressed at how politically aware the soldiers seemed. They were not just brutish thugs who followed orders like mindless robots which the history books would have the reader believe. These men were clued-in to the finer details of Roman politics. They had an air of awareness about them which stemmed from an innate intelligence that Carl found to be very admirable indeed.

'I represent a movement which is the very opposite of a dictatorship,' announced Paxus. 'My people wish only for a Rome that is free from the oppression of an emperor. We want to break the line of the Caesars and form a government that answers to the will of the people and not to a despot.'

'Titus will be a good emperor. We cannot go back to the days of the republic.' said a voice from the rear.

'He's a murdering bastard just like all the others,' countered another.

Quickly, all manner of insults and cries rang out amongst the men. A heated fracas ensued. Paxus stood aside to allow the men to let off steam. Ever the politician, he seemed tactically in control of the situation. Carl was encapsulated by the proceedings but then a tug on his arm distracted his thoughts. It was Lana. She looked terrible. It seemed she had grown older during the night.

'I want to escape,' she whispered in a frail tone.

Carl thought she was mad. They had no chance. Roman soldiers were experts at hunting down runaways. Lana would be found in minutes and then what would Paxus do with her?

'We can't Lana,' replied Carl in as gentler a voice as he could muster but Lana seemed on the verge of madness. She was trembling with fear and as much as Mumi could do to comfort her, it was not enough.

'But can't you see?' mumbled Lana as she forced her words out with great difficulty. 'The history books are proof enough that this quest failed because the line of emperors carried on long after all these men had died.'

Just then a fist fight broke out between two soldiers and immediately the others encircled the combatants shouting encouragement for one or the other. Lana did not wait a second. She turned and sprinted down the embankment towards the horses. Within the blink of an eye she was mounted and already manoeuvring the surprised beast away from the camp with an expertise that Carl did not know she possessed. With a quick glance back towards Carl and Mumi, Lana kicked hard into the horse's flanks and was off into the night.

None of the Romans noticed her leaving. The men were too engrossed in the fight. Carl strained to hold back his voice as he almost cried out after her. He quickly stared back at the broad shoulders of Paxus. The politician was standing with his arms behind his back waiting patiently for the fight to end.

'What are you going to do now?'

Carl stiffened when heard the words coming from Mumi's lips.

'What?'

'What are you going to do?'

Titus gripped his horse's reins and ground his teeth impatiently whilst doggedly searching for answers that would not come. He knew that the political and public fallout over the disaster at Pompeii will test his resolve to the limit. He recalled the words his father had spoken to him when he was given charge of his first legion; "There are rats in your ranks, weed them out if you wish to command". The same words applied to his reign. Humans are so much like rats, he thought; gnawing, biting and digging their way in to undermine you at all times. He could see the faces of his political enemies lining up to take bites out of him. Such was the way in Rome; a monster at times, a lamb at others. How long this uneasy affair with Rome will last he did not know but one thing was for sure, Titus will not last. What will the scribes, prophets, historians, critics and poets make of him? What will future civilisations remember of Titus – the darling of the human race!

He had been emperor for only a month and already his succession to the throne was unpopular with the public because he chose to continue his father's tough economic policies and heavy taxation. His relationship with his Jewish lover, Berenice, didn't go down well with the rife anti-sematic feelings of the day either. There was even a rumour that many feared him to be Nero, come back from the dead.

'You worried?' asked Decius as he rode alongside his emperor.

'Of course I am,' replied Titus. 'It's an emperor's duty to worry.'

He and Decius rode alone ahead of the weary soldiers. Titus stared in optimism at the horizon hoping to glimpse the outline of the city but there was nothing ahead but darkness. He thought of his enemies in Rome who were either tucked up in bed with their whores or off to some orgy organised by an ambitious socialite.

'I've already heard whispers from Rome blaming the eruption of Vesuvius on you for ordering the destruction of the Great Temple of Jerusalem,' said Decius. 'You know the people find you most unpopular don't you?'

'After one month's reign what do you expect? My late father's taxes are hurting. My relationship with Berenice is unpopular because she is a Jew and now Vesuvius has done me no favours at all. And you know that I didn't order the destruction of the Temple, it was an accident – you were there.'

'It's not a good start is it?' said Decius, 'but it's nothing that can't be fixed.'

Titus turned to his good friend. His bearded face and hardy complexion belied his true nature. Ever the optimist, Decius had kept Titus on a steady keel since they were young men. He had been a loyal and trusting friend for so long that he was almost like a family member. The first act that Titus performed after becoming emperor was to promote him to general of the Praetorian Guards. In fact, Titus favoured Decius over his brother, Domitian, which did not go unnoticed by his younger sibling.

'You worry most about Domitian, don't you?' asked Decius.

Domitian had been making big noises in Rome of late, claiming his rightful position amongst Rome's elite but just like his father, Titus ignored his younger sibling deeming him unfit to hold office.

'He's a pain in the arse,' replied Titus. 'You can choose your friends but not your family - right!'

'That's true my old friend,' replied Decius. 'But your plan to bring forward the inauguration date of the Flavian Ampitheatre is a good first step. That will keep the people's minds off the tragedy at Pompeii and take the attention away from your brother's claims.'

'A small step, but a necessary one,' replied Titus. 'I will deal with Domitian in my own time. Meanwhile, the Coliseum, as the people are calling it, won't be fully completed for a few years yet, but enough of the interior is ready. I can't see any problems there. I am also going to set up a fund for the compensation and re-housing of the victims of Pompeii and Herculaneum and the surrounding areas. These acts should endear me to my people for the time being.'

'An emperor needs the public on his side,' replied Decius, mechanically but then he turned and looked Titus straight in the eye. 'There's something else bothering you, isn't there?' he asked, rather pointedly.

Titus stared up at the night sky, breathed in deeply and sighed. He felt resigned to tell his friend a closely guarded secret that has been kept for many years.

'You trust me don't you, Decius?'

'Of course I do. You are my emperor, my friend – my... brother!'

After a short pause in which Titus wrestled with the thought of whether it was wise to confide in his good friend he eventually found the courage to speak:

'Have you ever wondered why Claudius made it his personal ambition to conquer Britannia?'

'To expand the empire, of course!' said Decius.

'Yes, that may well be true,' replied Titus, 'but his prime motivation was... treasure.'

Decius' eyes instantly narrowed with curiosity. 'Treasure, what treasure?'

'During Claudius' reign he discovered that the Arverni tribe from Gaul had hidden a vast horde of Celtic treasure from the prying eyes of Rome. During Julius Caesar's conflict with Vercingetorix, the Celtic tribes feared that their wealth could end up in Roman coffers so they took the decision to bury the entire hoard in Britannia, which at that time, as you well know, was unconquered.'

'Where in Britannia is this treasure?'

'That's the problem – nobody knows for sure,' replied Titus as he swatted away a moth that was attempting to land on his face. 'Though Claudius' conquest of Britannia was a triumph his ultimate failure in finding the treasure haunted him to his deathbed. But before he died he gave a secret order to pass on the task of finding the treasure to each succeeding emperor; all have failed. Now the task has come down to me.'

'That's a huge responsibility what with everything else going on around you.'

'I know,' said Titus with a heavy sigh, 'but alas I hear there may be good news.'

Titus explained all to Decius who listened impassively throughout. After a long pause in which he seemed to be in deep thought, Decius raised a cursory eyebrow and spoke:

'Are you sure the secret has stayed clandestine after all this time?'

'What do you mean?' asked Titus.

'Well, it's been twenty-five years since the death of Claudius and a secret as big as this can't stay a secret for long.'

Titus cringed with the perishing thought of what the implications may be if Drexa had found out about the Celtic treasure. It was the same thought he had after he dismissed the messenger from the camp. But once again, he put it to the back of his mind.

'Decius, you always state the obvious even when all around you are taken in but I am sure the secret of the Celtic treasure is safe for now.' But Titus knew he could be running out of time.

Drexa Vitanian sat in resignation of his deepest fear. Oh, the irony of it all, he thought. The secret was out and the race was on. The evidence lay all around him that Paxus Strupalo had somehow gotten wind of the Celtic treasure. The politician's study was strewn with maps of Gaul and Britannia. Celtic inscriptions, symbols and artefacts lay everywhere.

His soldiers had broken into Paxus' empty house finding no slaves, no signs of occupancy, not even the familiar smells of burning oils or incense. The building had been empty for a long time.

'Paxus Strupalo is a traitor!' announced Vitanian to no one in particular. Mathias, his captain of the guard, quickly stepped forward to examine the maps and artefacts.

'If you are correct, my lord, then he has a head-start on us.'

Drexa's heart sank immeasurably with the thought of chasing the politician all over Europe. He was heavy will excess living; unfit to ride a horse or to sleep out under the stars. His mind raced in time with his pulse because he needed to get out of the city before Titus returned. The choice was simple but daunting, nonetheless.

'Make preparations Mathias; we're going to Gaul.'

Her horse sped along the rugged, dirt road for about three miles before stumbling over a log and coming to a halt. Lana tried her best to gee up the beast but it was going nowhere. She quickly dismounted and led the horse a few feet forward. It was then that she noticed the grey mare was lame. The log had sprained her right fetlock. She knew that it was madness to sprint a horse along a rutted dirt track in the night but she was too frightened to think of anything other than her own safety.

Now her troubles began anew. She was alone in the dark with nowhere to go. Tired, bemused and utterly petrified, she stood trembling with fear then it began to rain.

Once again, she felt the gulf in time hitting home. It felt harder now than at any other moment. She wondered if she and Carl were the first human beings ever to experience such a paradox. It was a mind-numbingly absurd situation but here she was, lost on a dirt road in the dark at the height of the Roman Empire.

With an insane madness that was shredding her thoughts to pieces all she could do was laugh. She raised her head up skywards and laughed heartily as the raindrops spattered her face. But soon the laugher turned to tears, the tears turned to despair then she felt a sudden urge to run.

So she ran.

For all intents and purposes she wanted to run into the arms of her beloved Dennis or better still, run to the county sheriff's office for protection but no such things were going to happen.

After running for only a few hundred yards, she stopped; drenched to the bone. Then the heavens really opened up and the rain came down harder. Lightning flashed above her head giving her a brief snapshot of the surrounding countryside quickly followed by the deep rumble of thunder which rolled about the

black sky in perfect surround sound. Gasping for breath she tried to clear her head.
'*Don't stand under a tree for shelter in a thunderstorm*'.
She had heard that advice from her father many times as a child so she waited for the next lightning flash to see if it would show up any potential shelter. The flash duly arrived but the image it highlighted made her stomach churn; the silhouettes of several mounted soldiers stood out in stark contrast upon the horizon and they had spotted the lame horse.

Lana slinked back off the dirt road and laid herself flat upon the wet ground. There were no bushes or tall grasses to hide amongst. Soon, she could hear the sound of horse's hooves all around her and angered voices, cursing her for making them lose sleep. Then a hoof landed right next to her face. She shut her eyes out of fear, hoping the nightmare would end but then many hands were all over her, grasping and clawing at her wet tunic. A sharp pain to the back of her head made her brain ring like a bell followed by darkness.

Through blurred vision, dull sounds and dizziness, Lana stirred, feeling a sickness rising up in her stomach. She found that she was lying on her back so she quickly rolled onto her side and vomited up what little she had inside her. She didn't feel any better after that though, in fact, she felt worse. A dull pain in the back of her head quickly reminded her of her predicament. Then a kick to her legs made her jump and she turned to see a soldier standing over her. He was brandishing a whip in his hands. The look in his eye left her in no uncertain terms about what his state of mind was.

'If I could have my way with you bitch I'd make you bleed between your legs for weeks for what you did to my Sila,' said the soldier who seemed most upset about his horse. 'Thanks to you, I had to slit her throat to take her out of her misery.'

Then she felt hands lifting her and carrying her downhill towards a tall pine tree. Around the tree stood the familiar figures of Paxus, Daccus, Bastia, Mumi and Carl, illuminated in the gloom by torchlight. It was only in this moment that she noticed the storm had passed and she wondered how long she had been unconscious. Upon reaching the tree a rope was tied to one of her wrists whilst the loose end was swung around the trunk then tied to her other wrist tightly. Her tunic was then torn from her torso leaving her naked body exposed for all to see. She turned to Carl.

'Carl, what are they doing?' she cried as the men lashed her tightly up against the tree. But Carl did not answer. His eyes were filled with pity as tears streamed down his cheeks. 'Carl, stop this!' she pleaded but all he did was drop his head and look away.

The first lash of the whip shocked her more than anything but then the pain took hold. The following lashes increased the pain dramatically. The burning, cutting and slashing tore strips of flesh from her back as her tormentor got to work with relish. She screamed in agony for what seemed like ages. Then her trembling legs buckled from under her as she sagged against the tree. She could feel her bare breasts scraping down the roughness of the bark. The screams and the pain were terrifying her. She never knew she could make such otherworldly sounds and her body had certainly never experienced such brute force before. The hell of her existence had come full circle; an ever-worsening nightmare in multi-fold. Where was Carl, she thought? Where was salvation?

Then the lashes stopped and her binds were untied. She was left to flop, unceremoniously, to the ground. The pain seared through her back like bits of broken glass but she forced herself to peer through misty eyes at the silhouettes of the many feet walking away from her. Then Carl's face suddenly appeared up close. His tear-filled eyes scanned hers as he gently stroked her forehead.

'Why did you run away, Lana, why?' he said in a voice filled with emotion. Then Lana felt herself passing into darkness once more.

11

MONDAY, AUGUST 31ST PRESENT DAY:

Sam Allen sat waiting nervously in the lobby of the National Geographic's headquarters in Washington, D.C. He had received an e-mail from Ted Brooks requesting an urgent meeting and in haste he had caught the next available flight to the capital hoping for good news.

Upon his arrival he had decided to climb the main staircase up through the museum floors which were filled with many families enjoying the school, summer vacation. Boggle-eyed kids were busy playing with the hands-on exhibits, whilst partly bored parents looked on casually, obviously preoccupied with the more important responsibilities of domestic life.

Now seated in the plush, air conditioned surroundings of Ted Brook's reception and puffing from the exertions of climbing ten flights of stairs because he had a dreaded fear of elevators, he stared at a large painting of an ape-like creature standing in an upright position: the legend below read: *Lucy; Australopithecus afarensis, earliest known ancestor of Homo sapiens.* But he couldn't fully appreciate the excellent artwork for his patience was torn to shreds since the phone call from his brother, Carl two days earlier.

Sam Allen had followed in his father's footsteps and become a successful industrialist himself. He took over the running of his dad's steel business and made it profitable for the first time in a decade. Now, in his late forties, an early retirement was just around the corner and a new CEO would have to be found - but it wasn't going to be Carl.

Sam stared vacantly about the plush reception, his eyes eventually falling back again on the mature office clerk who was busily tapping away at her computer keypad making that repetitive hollow sound which bordered on the annoying. Then the buzzer on her desk sounded. She depressed the switch and spoke into the little black box.

'Yes, Mr Brooks,' she said in a sultry tone. 'Yes, ok.'

She released her finger from the switch and nodded towards the oak door of Brooks' office.

Sam rose and strode purposefully across the polished laminate flooring. After giving a light tap on the door he didn't bother to wait for a response and entered the office. Behind a surprisingly small desk in a rather grand looking room sat a burly looking black man dressed in a slate-grey suit. His bald, polished head shone like a beacon in the sunlight which streamed through the ceiling-to-floor window.

'Ah... Sam Allen,' said Ted Brooks in a softly spoken but somewhat distant voice as he stood and offered his hand. Sam recognised the southern accent which had a strong Hoosier twang to it.

He shook Ted Brooks' hand and sat down upon the chair opposite him without being invited to sit.

'You have news of Carl?' he asked anxiously.

Fifty-nine year old Ted Brooks leaned back in his leather seat and folded his arms. His brown eyes rolled about in his rotund head and he pursed his lips to let out a controlled hiss. Ted Brooks had made his way to the top despite many barriers of prejudice placed in his way due to his black African-American background. His expertise was geology and he was once an active member of Greenpeace in his younger days. He had escaped the sinking of the Rainbow Warrior, the flagship of Greenpeace, due to a toothache. His father, Charles Brooks was an associate of Martin Luther King. He was present at the assassination of the great man. Later, Charles was murdered by the Ku Klux Klan after publicly accusing them of Dr King's murder.

'The Italian police have officially declared Carl and Lana missing,' said Ted.

'What do they propose to do about it?' asked Sam, bluntly.

'It's been two days and still no sign of them,' replied Ted. 'The police have said they have done all they can and are winding down the search to second level priority.'

'But Carl phoned me only two days ago. He said he is still in Rome.'

A momentary pause passed between the two men. Sam could see that Ted was trying hard to hold back information then he spoke:

'Would you like a drink?'

'No thanks,' replied Sam.

'Did Carl say anything else during the phone call?' asked Ted, tentatively.

'Only that he was going on a treasure hunt for some lost Celtic gold,' replied Sam out of hand. 'I don't know what he could have meant by that.'

Ted didn't reply but he still seemed to be mulling something over in his head.

'What's wrong?'

'Do you have your passport with you?' asked Ted.

'Yes, of course.' Sam was the chief executive of a major company. His passport was always on his person.

'I'm flying out to Rome tomorrow morning with one of our historical investigators,' said Ted after a short pause. 'You're welcome to come with me if you want, courtesy of Nat Geo.'

Sam knew his wife, Linda, would okay it. She knew he was aching to get to the bottom of this and it would be no problem.

'Sure, I'll come,' he replied. 'I will need to make few phone calls... look, what the fuck is going on Ted – can I call you Ted?'

Ted Brooks nodded and then slid open the top drawer of his desk. He pulled out an unsealed envelope and handed it to Sam. It read, *FAO Ted Brooks*. Sam glared up at him with a puzzled look.

He quickly flipped the envelope open and pulled out a torn piece of dull, white cloth about the size of a sheet of A4 paper. Upon the cloth was faded handwriting written in red dye. The words in print simply said: HELP – CARL 79AD, followed by Carl's signature.

'This cloth was sent to me by express mail from the dig site that Carl had been working at,' explained Ted. 'It was found inside a sealed glass vial by one of his assistants only hours after his disappearance.'

'Yes,' replied Sam, 'What does it mean?'

Ted grinned back and stood up from his seat, went over to a rather grand looking cabinet and poured himself a large glass of Bourbon. He drank it down in one gulp then turned to face Sam.

'Is that Carl's signature?'

'Yes, of course.'

Ted's face went as blank as the wall behind him. He stepped forward, placed the empty glass down upon the desk, put his hands in his pockets and stared Sam down.

'That piece of cloth is two-thousand years old!'

For the first time in weeks rain clouds rolled in over the city which was good news for Rome. Water was a valuable commodity in a city of thousands and many relieved citizens were busying themselves with erecting rain catchers which were large tarpaulin sheets with a single hole in the centre that funnelled the precious water into giant vases. Although the aqueducts supplied plenty of water to Rome, they too were subject to the weather and this year had been one of the driest for many years. Soon, thunder in the hills sounded loudly across the morning sky then the deluge began.

Titus sat naked upon his bed listening to the rain hammering away at the marble floor of the palace balcony. The temperature immediately took a sudden drop but he didn't react. He was a soldier; a tough, hardened individual who didn't flinch at physical discomfort but it was the psychological discomfort that was concerning him right now. He knew that the next few days will be critical to his reign and tough decisions will have to be made. His first decision was the toughest. He will be sending Berenice back to her people to appease the growing anti-Semitism in the city but not after he had made love to her this one last time. He had already ordered her to his chamber and he waited patiently for his lover to arrive. While he waited, he deliberated over his plan to force his brother, Domitian, to take a more active role in public affairs. His younger sibling had loyal followers of a questionable character who could become dangerous adversaries in the months to come and he didn't like the way Domitian wasted his time with his friends on trivial pursuits such as chariot racing which Titus abhorred. Then there was the problem with Drexa Vitanian to sort out. Immediately upon his arrival back in Rome Titus had sent out orders for Drexa to report to him at once but he could not be found. Titus' problems were mounting and to add to them, his duty to carry on the search for the Celtic treasure was tugging at his mind all the time. Which item took priority over which, he could not decide? He wondered what his father would have done in such circumstances.

His concentration was distracted when a bell rang to announce the entrance of his beloved Berenice. In she strode like a swan gliding gracefully upon a lake, a vision of nature at its purest! As always, Titus melted before her beauty. His groin immediately flushed with blood and his penis began to twinge. She stood before him in a flimsy gown which was opened down to her navel. The inner lines of her magnificent breasts were showing from within the gown and he could see her nipples erect with expectation from underneath the purple cloth. Her dark brown eyes were filled with lust as she stared at his rousing penis.

'Fuck me!' Titus demanded and Berenice duly obliged.

After the best part of an hour of ravenous love making upon the exquisite Emperor's bed which had seen many frolicking from the emperor Tiberius to his father Vespasian, the naked and sweating couple finally rolled onto their backs exhausted but exhilarated.

'You put everything into that tonight my love,' said Berenice as she stared up at the ornate ceiling depicting Jupiter as the 'shining father', the Roman god of light and king of the gods. 'I've never known you to be so horny.'

Titus stayed silent for a moment dreading his next act but his rule as emperor was not to be trifled with. He tensed his muscles and took a deep breath then he rolled over on his side to face her.

'That will be the last time we make love!' he announced with as little emotion as he could muster for he was trying his best to stay aloof.

'What?' asked Berenice, 'what do you mean?'

'I'm sending you home to your people. You leave tomorrow. We can no longer be together. The political constraints of my office will not allow such a joining. Our creed and differences are too polarised to ever work successfully.'

Berenice sat bolt upright and stared Titus down. Her face grew dark with worry but then a slow realisation dawned upon her and she smiled a wry smile.

'I know,' she said in whisper as a small teardrop formed at the corner of her left eye. 'Somehow, I have always known that this day would come. I am a Jew and you are a Roman!'

It was customary for an emperor to turn his back on the person he had ordered from his palace and Titus duly obliged but not after kissing Berenice goodbye on her cheek first. He then turned and stepped out onto the balcony into the rain as naked as the day he was born. He could hear Berenice sobbing with emotion as she gathered up her gown and exited the bedchamber. He had made sure she would get a safe passage back to Judea and a pot of gold to boot. He thought it was good that the rains had come on this night for they disguised the tears he was shedding at this moment. He had acted like an emperor should but it didn't temper his soul. He loved Berenice with all his heart but duty calls and love will have to take second place.

Fiumicino airport was thronging with hundreds of holidaymakers. It was the height of the holiday season and Rome took its fair few at this time of year. For Sam the business class flight from Washington had gone by in a flash but the queuing was taking forever. He had not spoken much to his travelling companions whilst on route; his thoughts were elsewhere. Ted Brooks had duly brought along his historical investigator, her name was Winifred Bainbridge, a name that would suit a main character of a Jane Austen novel, he thought. She was a five-foot six inches tall, dark haired lady from Brooklyn with the typical regular office looks. She was attractive but in a strictly business-like sense and efficient looking.

Later on that day, the travellers eventually arrived at the Hilton hotel, each had their own rooms but Sam was restless. No sooner had he thrown his holdall onto the double bed and brushed his teeth he was knocking on Ted Brook's door.

'Come in, Sam!'

Sam hurried in, anxious to know what was next on the agenda. Ted was filling up a tumbler of whiskey from a bottle he had purchased at the airport and slowly turned towards Sam.

'We'll wait here for Win, she'll be along soon. Have a drink.'

Sam took the request as an order and nodded. 'I'll have a beer.'

A bottle of cold Peroni lager from the complimentary fridge went down a treat as both men sat out on the seventh floor veranda which overlooked the ancient city. The dome of Saint Peter's in the Vatican dominated the skyline and was but a five minute walk away. It was early evening and the heat of the day was dissipating rapidly. The sounds and smells of the modern metropolis wafted up to the two men as they eased back in their chairs to take in the splendour of this most famous of cities. Ted was the first to break the silence.

'Win is busy on the phone making contact with her Italian acquaintances. She has many associates around the world.'

'What does she suspect of the disappearance of Carl and Lana?'

'I never asked. I gave her all the info she needed plus the piece of cloth. She told me to leave it with her. This is probably a routine situation that will be resolved in no time Sam.'

'Routine? What's routine about a two-thousand year old cloth with my brother's handwriting on it?'

Ted stayed silent for a long while and idly scanned the rooftops of the city, seemingly thinking of something else entirely. Then a light tapping sound upon his door made him sigh with relief and he called out for the tapper to enter. In seconds the two men were joined by Winifred. She had changed from her functional office attire into a more casual white cotton pair of slacks and a loose fitting blue and white patterned blouse that billowed about her impressive figure in the warm breeze. She was bare footed and she had let her dark hair down which hung past her shoulders. Big blue eyes stared out across the balcony view but she said nothing.

'A drink, Win?' asked Ted as he stood. Sam did likewise, forgetting his manners.

'Yes please,' replied Winifred in her New York accent as she sat down and placed her mobile phone and a leather folder upon the table, 'I'm going to need one.' Win's voice cut through the air clear as a bell. To Sam, she seemed to be a smart, level headed individual but also a little sad with troubles of her own that she probably didn't share. She eventually turned and sat at the table with her back to the view. She stared Sam up and down as if seeing him for the first time. 'You are older than Carl I assume?' she asked but not in a disrespectful way.

'I am,' said Sam as he proceeded to sit down. Ted returned with another Peroni for Sam and a glass of white wine for Win.

'What's the next step?' Sam asked, leaving the question open to anyone.

'I have made enquiries,' said Win after a sip of wine. 'There is absolutely no trace of Carl and Lana. They left no trail, there was no sign of a struggle in and around the dig site – there's nothing to go on except.' She paused and quickly opened the leather folder. She pulled out the ancient cloth, holding it diligently in her hand. 'This.' She stared at Sam over the rim of her wine glass then placed the cloth down upon the table. 'Are you sure this is Carl's signature?'

'Definitely sure,' replied Sam, 'but how do you know the cloth is two-thousand years old?'

'Carbon 14 dating,' said Ted. Sam frowned. 'When I first laid eyes upon the cloth,' continued Ted, 'I could tell it was old so I sent it down to the lab and it came back - two-thousand years.'

'But how can that be?' asked Sam. 'How could Carl write on something that old?'

'Archaeologists find bits of ancient cloth all the time,' explained Ted matter-of-factly. 'It's quite easy to make a dye and use it to write a message to make it look authentic.'

'But why would Carl bother to do such a thing?'

'I don't know,' said Ted, disappointingly. 'That's why it all seems so fuckin' weird.' He took another sip of whiskey and sat back in silence.

Then Winfred spoke up and the two men listened.

'I have addressed all logical possibilities,' she said. 'The reason for their disappearance could be something simple, something we may be overlooking.'

'Like what?'

'I have spoken to a few people with little luck. The trail is cold. We can eliminate kidnapping but they could have eloped...'

'Eloped?' questioned Sam in disgust.

'It's possible,' replied Winifred. 'Lana Evans is a very stunning looking woman for her age and Carl has known her for many years.'

Sam squirmed in his seat and took a long gulp of his Peroni then sat back looking thoroughly demoralised. He had met Lana a few times at galas and charity fundraisers and had been impressed by her beauty but he hadn't seen his brother for three years and wondered whether Win had a point.

'Carl mentioned a treasure hunt,' said Sam, changing the subject.

~ 137 ~

'I know,' replied Winifred as she pondered in a moment's reflection. 'It is believed that there was a great treasure of the Celts that went missing, presumed lost forever. Legend has it that the Knights Templar found it thus making them wealthy beyond their wildest dreams but, in truth, the treasure was probably found long before that.'

'Oh, by whom?' asked Sam.

Win shook her head. 'No one knows. Historians are divided. Some say the Celts kept the treasure hidden from Rome for so long that the location was eventually lost in time and remains buried.' Then Win paused for thought for a second as if stealing herself for a major announcement. 'There are whispers of a rumour that the Emperor Constantine was the first to lay his hands on the treasure, thus funding his ambitious plans around the empire ending in the building of the city of Constantinople, which is now present-day Istanbul.' Win paused again then spoke her next words like she was revealing a secret. 'Some historians believe that Constantine had some kind of mental health issue and that the early Christian priests preyed on this, thus giving rise to the legend that he converted to Christianity. But some suspect that the priests were after Constantine's treasure and that Constantine left the treasure at the churches' mercy which ultimately gave rise to the might and majesty of Roman Catholicism.'

A short period of silence fell as all three drifted into a momentary reflection of their own.

The silence was shattered when Winifred's mobile phone rang on the glass-top table and she picked it up to answer. After a few seconds her eyes scanned the faces of the two men opposite then she stood up and walked back into the apartment, still listening to whomever was calling her. Sam and Ted stared back at her in puzzlement as they watched her move around the room like a phantom, silent and stalking. Then she suddenly stopped pacing up and down and stood as still as the many statues that adorned this lovely city. Sam's heart stopped for an instant. *Was it good news or was it bad news?*

After several long, intense moments, Win spun around and walked back out onto the balcony. Her cheeks were flushed and her breath was shallow. She stared Sam down with an inquisitive look and slight cock of the head.

'We're going to the dig site - now.'

Within half an hour they had arrived at the site and were immediately swamped by an entourage of news reporters, flashing cameras, police officers and, in particular an old man, who was making a direct bee-line for them. For all intents and purposes, he looked like a school headmaster to Sam. Win quickly paid the taxi driver and waved a hand towards the approaching man in greeting. They shook hands with one another and were quickly escorted past the barrage of reporters by two policemen. Sam and Ted were left to tag along.

In the evening gloom, the dig site was lit up like a circus and Sam glanced towards Ted who shrugged his shoulders with indifference. The two of them were left baffled by all the commotion.

They followed Win and the old man further into the site where, suddenly, all the noise and confusion was left behind and a deathly silence fell around them. Sam felt the atmosphere a little eerie to say the least. Yet, here he was, in a modern city throbbing with life and all he could feel was a similar sensation he had once felt when he was lost and alone in the Yellowstone forests back home.

Soon they had entered a large tent that had a long table running down the middle where at one end sat a metal tray covered by a towel. Next to the tray sat two smashed up boxes, one bigger than the other. The old man stopped at the table and turned to face his guests. Win quickly introduced him to Sam and Ted as Professor Terence Barnes who was the principle advisor on the dig.

'We have some news for you,' said the professor in a very British accent. 'One of my team kept digging around the spot where the piece of cloth was found.' He made his way to the end of the table with the others in tow and stopped at the tray. 'An hour and a half ago she brought this into our headquarters.' He flipped back the dirtied cloth and looked up at the three curious onlookers.

Sitting in the tray was a smashed up, rusted digital camera, crushed beyond repair. Lying next to it was what was left of its leather case, as black as the soil that was scattered around it. Beside it was a watch. The watch's face was cracked and the hands were encrusted in rust. The three companions stared at one another in silent dismay.

'I'm told the camera is a Nikon P520,' said the professor. 'Both it and the leather case were found wrapped up in linen and stored inside that wooden box.' He pointed at the earth encrusted larger box which looked as though it had been buried for a long time. 'The watch was found inside this smaller box.'

'So what are you showing us?' asked Sam, bluntly.

'These items were found at the same level as the two-thousand year old cloth,' replied the professor. 'Do you recognise any of these items?' he asked Sam.

'No, I haven't seen my brother in three years... I wouldn't know...'

At this point Sam could sense that the professor was trying his dammed hardest to keep his emotions under control. Something was troubling him deeply but he seemed determined to keep it to himself.

The professor looked up at the three puzzled faces and continued:

'We've sent a sample of the camera's leather casing to our science lab at Sapienza University to have it dated. We should hear in a couple of hours.'

'What do you mean – 'dated,' asked Sam out of pure frustration? 'You're not suggesting...?' He stopped himself in his tracks unable to finish the rest of his ridiculous sentence. *No, no, it can't be.*

At that point Win stepped forward and took out a pair of thin rubber gloves from a box that was sitting upon a shelf. She quickly put them on and picked up the camera. She turned it around in her hands, giving it a quick once over. 'Have you done a fingerprint search?' she asked, not taking her eyes off the camera.

'Our team have checked it over,' said Professor Barnes. 'It's clean.'

'What about the SD card?' she asked, 'did you get it out?'

Silence followed for a moment as the professor glanced over inadvertently to a set of computers in the far corner of the tent. 'Leave these items and follow me please.'

Sam felt like throwing up as the gravity of this preposterous situation was beginning to dawn on him. He spread his hands across the table for support feeling that his legs were about to give way at any moment. After a second or two he found the strength to follow the others to a corner of the tent where the professor was seating himself down at a monitor. Sam watched as the professor peered over his half-moon glasses and tapped away at the computer keypad. He found it odd that this very old man, with his tweed jacket and messy grey hair and long bushy sideburns could look so at home on a computer. He seemed so much like the stereotypical British upper-class twit that it bordered on the comical.

'The SD card was broken on one corner and the terminals showed signs of water damage,' said the professor, 'but we managed to retrieve seven images, though I am sure there are more.'

All eyes fixed on the monitor as a grey smudgy image flickered momentarily then flashed into clearer black and white pictures. The seven images filled the screen.

'My god,' said Win as she raised her hand to her mouth in astonishment.

Sam immediately peered closer to the screen to try to discern what he was looking at. One image stood out in particular. It was of a circular building that seemed to be surrounded by some kind of scaffolding. He pointed at the image and spoke:

'What's this?'

'That's the Coliseum,' said Ted as he scratched his bald head looking somewhat put out. The pictures were showing the construction of the Coliseum. There were many semi-naked people on the scaffolding working at it. 'I need to get the SD card to my people,' he said. 'They have the expertise to reveal more.'

Win pulled up a seat and sat down. She looked in shock. Her jaw dropped open and her hands were visibly shaking.

'What's going on here?' said Sam trying to make some sense of it all. 'What the hell have these pictures got to do with Carl?'

Silence followed once again as Sam felt his patience growing thinner by the second. 'Will someone please tell me what the fuck...?'

'... These pictures are two-thousand years old,' said Professor Barnes, more out of frustration with the whole situation than Sam's persistent questioning. His face was turning darker and his eyes were welling up with tears.

'I can't believe it,' said Win in short gasps. 'It can't be true.'

Professor Barnes wheeled back his chair and stood up. 'We tell no one,' he announced with an air of authority. 'We are the only people in the entire world who know of this. If this gets out who knows what the reaction would be?'

Sam was already shaking his head. 'No, no this is preposterous. You're pulling my leg – right?'

Professor Barnes returned to his seat and tapped away at a few more keys. Then, once again, he looked up and spoke in his soft English accent directly to Sam:

'I deliberately kept one more picture from you in the hope that it wouldn't be too much of a shock but show it to you I must. It's amazing that the SD card has survived for so long, but seeing as its made of silicon and plastic...' he trailed off and tapped the enter key on the keypad.

The screen went blank. Then, suddenly, a clear colour image appeared. It was of a man and a woman in perfect clarity. They looked thin and dishevelled and were standing by a tree holding a wooden placard between them that read in English – 'Help, we are lost in time, can't get home'.

Then, all of a sudden, Win cried out in dismay. 'Oh Jesus Christ, it's Carl and Lana, oh my god!' She immediately burst into tears as she held her hand to her mouth in utter dismay.

Sam had to squint as he peered closer at the picture, then, sure enough, it dawned on him. He was looking at an image of his brother dressed in a loose fitting garment tied at the waist by a thin cord. He had lost a lot of weight and seemed withdrawn. Even worse was the state of Lana. She looked battered and bruised. She was as thin as a rake and very ill looking. Her hair was matted with the consistency of straw and the dark rings under her eyes made her look like an old woman. Tears began to stream down Sam's face as a terrible, unthinkable truth began to sink in. Ted Brooks tried his best to detach himself from what he was seeing. He turned from the screen flatly refusing to believe it whilst trying his best to remain in charge of his emotions but he was crumbling as the seconds ticked by. Eventually he cracked. He turned back to the screen to see the sad image of the once stunningly beautiful Lana – the darling celebrity of the National Geographic - looking haggard and worn out. It broke him to pieces. All three cried for long moments until Professor Barnes found the right moment to turn off the monitor.

The professor stood once again and patted Sam on the shoulder offering precious little comfort. His heart was breaking too but he still had one more revelation for his guests to endure but he decided, in that moment, that it could wait until morning.

12

The following morning found Titus struggling with his emotions. Berenice had left for Judea, Vesuvius was still wreaking havoc in Campania but most annoyingly of all, Vitanian's mysterious disappearance was irritating him to the point of distraction. But worse than that, he felt that he was missing something; something that was obvious that he could not see. So as the morning dragged on he became irascible with everyone around him. Even poor old Tulca – the head slave – got an ear bashing for some minor indiscretion and was sent to the cellar to check on the wine store. Enraged with everything and everyone around him, the emperor decided to make a call on Decius. Decius had promised Titus that he would find Drexa Vitanian and bring him to the palace as soon as possible but there was no news. Annoyingly, the absurd thought, which had lingered in Titus' mind ever since he had returned to Rome that Vitanian was up to no good just wouldn't go away.

The rains had finally relented, turning into a fine drizzle so the walk to Decius' residence will be a sodden affair but Titus couldn't care less. Within minutes he had disguised himself as a slave and under a hooded cloak he left the palace secretively, leaving his guards none the wiser.

He slinked his way easily past two perimeter guards using the drizzle as cover and out across the courtyard towards the underground passageway that served as an escape route for emperors in times of trouble. As he entered the passageway he lit a torch and edged his way towards Decius' quarters. The trip was a short one but it was proving tricky. The rain had found its way into the tunnel where, at one point, he had to wade through knee-high, freezing cold water before he could see his intended goal. At a crossroad junction in the tunnel, where four main arteries ran off at right angles from each other, he now stood in ankle-deep water and spied his intended target. A white stone above the entrance to a set of steps on his left pointed the way up to Decius' married quarters. But as he approached, a sixth sense suddenly tugged at a nerve which forced him to stop. Something was wrong! He had come this way many times before and had never sensed this. Automatically his hand reached for the hilt of his dagger; his soldiering instincts kicked in as they raised his senses up to peak level. Then slowly, he began to pan the torch around in a full circle but the tunnel looked the same as it always had. Finely crafted brickwork ran off into the darkness in all directions but there was no sign of anything that could make him feel the way he did.

Without thinking, as if his hand had a mind of its own, he lowered the torch down to floor level. To his surprise the rainwater was crimson in colour – blood red! He brought the torch up to the foot of the steps and saw a rivulet of red liquid trickling down from above.

In shock horror he dropped the torch to the floor, bounded up the steps and burst in through the entranceway, via the open gate. The naked bodies of Decius' two sons aged ten and eight, respectively, were laying face-down on the floor in a pool of blood. He could tell that they had been dead for many hours. Their throats had been cut and their little torsos were battered and bruised. Pieces of splintered bones protruded outwards from underneath their skin at various places on their backs. Then, further on, lying at the foot of a bust of the emperor Claudius, he saw the dismembered body of Decius lying next to the body of his beloved wife, Someca. They had both been stripped naked and quartered and their severed heads were placed upside-down upon their torsos.

Titus knew what this meant, of course. It was the traditional warning and he knew exactly who was warning him. But worse than that, he feared that the secret was out. He made a quick survey of the rest of Decius' home and found what he had expected; the bodies of Homb and Lati, Decius' two slaves, were lying in the hallway, their heads had been caved in by a blunt weapon.

Within minutes he was back in his palace and calling for the Praetorian guards.

Drexa Vitanian and his accomplices will be hunted down like dogs for this, he thought. They will die a thousand deaths for the murder of his great friend and his beautiful family.

Within the hour, the palace was a hive of activity. Titus' voice echoed off every wall, bellowing out orders to everyone within earshot. By mid-morning he had gathered forty of his newly recruited soldiers in the grand hall which was adorned with the statues of many gods. He gave the young men a brief summary of the morning's events which was received with angry calls of revenge for the death of their beloved Decius. Now leaderless, the guards needed a new officer to command them and Titus wasted no time in recalling the veteran General Catrus Vitrus. Catrus had served under Vespasian and was known by the common soldiery as 'The Hammer'. He was a legend; admired, feared and revered by everyone who had served under him. The forty-nine year old stood next to Titus dressed in full combat gear. Six-foot four inches tall, intimidating and brimming with authority his cold, bright blue eyes seared through the air like a volley of arrows. The young soldiers staring back at him stood quivering in their armour. Catrus scanned them all meticulously, eyeball-to-eyeball, one-by-one, grinning back at them with an air of confidence that was definitely not unwarranted.

'Drexa Vitanian is a traitor to Rome!' announced Titus promptly as he paced up and down in front of the men. 'I declare him an outlaw and command that you find him and bring him back to me – alive! The cowardly murder of Decius and his family shall be revenged.'

'What of his accomplices, my lord?' asked Catrus Vitrus in a rasping voice that was deep and resonant and boomed off the marble walls of the grand hall.

'Kill them!'

Catrus nodded but stood waiting for more news. Titus knew that he wanted to know the motive behind the murders so he had to think quickly. *The secret must kept.*

He took Catrus aside and spoke to him softly.

'Vitanian has stolen something which belongs to the Caesar family. It is a small wooden box. It contains something of great value. Return it to me and I will reward you handsomely.'

Catrus stood to attention and saluted.

'Vitanian will be grovelling at your feet in no time, your grace,' he promised.

Titus saluted him back and spoke to the rest of the soldiers:

'Vitanian is heading north on his way to Gaul and I suspect he aims to cross into Britannia. Make haste, travel light and you may catch him before he leaves Italy.'

Within no time General Vitrus had led his miniature army down the Palatine hill, through the Forum and off to the nearest barracks to prepare for the chase. Titus watched them go from the balcony of his palace, frustrated that he could not go with them – such was his duty as emperor. The soldier in him raged with impatience as he reluctantly returned to his imperial duties.

Lana ached with every move of her body. Wracked with pain, she felt as if her back was on fire and no amount of attention from Mumi was helping. Mumi had been busily treating her wounds since dawn with a variety of leaves soaked in water. Angered and enraged by her flogging, she wished for death but Mumi quickly informed her that she had gotten off lightly thanks to the insistent begging by Carl on her behalf. Her most probable outcome would have been that she be raped by the soldiers and ritually strangled for her transgression. This fact was the last straw for Lana. She begged Mumi to kill her but Mumi shook her head vigorously, saying that she would never take the life of her lover. Lana's reply stuck in her throat and she stayed silent allowing Mumi to continue treating her.

Reluctantly, Lana stared out across the camp from her seated position by the side of the cart. She watched on as the members of the camp were getting ready to leave. The rains had gone, the ground was still sodden but the sun's early rays were warming up the air quickly. Birds chirped busily in the trees and the smell of the fresh, unpolluted air helped clear out her nicotine-riddled lungs.

She looked for Carl but he was nowhere to be seen but she soon spied Daccus who was looking strained and tired. He was standing next to Paxus who was busy sharpening his weapons. Her stomach churned at the sight of the politician. He had allowed the soldier, whose horse she had made lame, to flog her. She felt like throwing up from sheer disgust and frustration. Then the runaway slave, Bastia, appeared from behind a tree. He was stripped completely naked and was soaking wet from bathing himself in the small brook that ran parallel to the camp. He walked straight over to where Lana and Mumi were seated and reached inside the cart for a large cloth. He quickly began to dry himself not caring that the eyes of both women were watching him in all his glory. Then a call from Paxus made Bastia turn around and Lana immediately gasped at the images she saw tattooed upon his back.

While Paxus was approaching Bastia, she quickly ran over the tattoos with an expert eye. The largest image was of a wheel with four spokes and inside the gaps of each spoke were Celtic symbols for the passage of time; the phases of the moon and one of the sun, respectively. She had seen the images before during her training as a symbolist at Harvard University but the most intriguing of all was the writings beneath the tattoo. She knew exactly what they were. Then a spark of an opportunity quickly formed in her mind. So gathering what was left of her strength, she indicated to Mumi for help in standing and Mumi duly obliged by straightening out her tunic and helping her to her feet. As soon as she stood up her back felt like someone had fired a thousand pins into it. She gasped for breath as each agonising step almost caused her to pass out but she persevered, eager, as she was, to grasp this chance.

The two men were soon in deep conversation when Lana slowly approached them.

'Let me examine your back, please?' she asked Bastia who straightened in shock and turned to face her.

'I will not let you come near me, witch,' he snapped as he took a step back.

It was clear to Lana now that she was viewed as a witch. She guessed that she must have looked like one after all she'd been through. She felt old, beaten and stripped of her dignity but her burning curiosity was shining through.

'I must see your tattoos,' she said faintly as the strain from the effort of standing began to tire her out. 'I can read the letterings.'

She stumbled upon her feet which prompted Mumi to force her to sit.

'What do you mean, you can read them?' asked a curious Paxus.

'Let me see them and I will read out the meaning,' implored Lana as she sat down next to the wheel of the cart feeling disgusted at being in the presence of Paxus. She wished, for all intents and purposes, that she had Dennis's revolver at hand so she could blow his brains out.

'Bastia, let her see!' ordered Paxus sounding more annoyed than interested.

Bastia wrapped the cloth he was drying himself with around his waist and reluctantly turned to show his back.

'Sit please,' asked Lana.

The former slave sighed heavily and did what was asked. 'I don't know what you're looking for… no one can understand the writing,' he said as he sat down in front of her.

Immediately, she could see that the lettering was a form of Pro-Celtic language which was the precursor of a Welsh dialect that evolved into the modern day tongue. The ten words vaguely read; *seek Mona where under her waters there whither thine want.*

She stayed silent for a long period to make sure she was deciphering the words correctly. She knew Mona was the old Celtic word for the isle of Anglesey off the northwest coast of Wales. Then she had an idea. If she used the modern day word, Anglesey, to replace Mona then she would be in a strong position to bargain.

'Well?' asked Paxus impatiently.

'The words say; seek Anglesey where under her waters there whither thine want.'

'What?' asked Bastia 'say that again?'

Lana repeated her words but it seemed only to confuse the men even further.

Paxus stirred and grimaced. 'Under her waters!' he uttered to himself in deep thought.

'Seek angul…see?' asked Bastia, sounding irritated. 'Who is angul… see?'

Lana pondered in silence for a short while, remembering that the lettering was used by the druids as early as 300 BC.

'Well?' asked an increasingly impatient Paxus who seemed ready to walk away at any moment.

'Anglesey is not a person,' replied Lana as she shifted her weight to try and relieve the pain. 'Anglesey is the name of an island which lies off the coast of Britannia.'

'And what part of Britannia is this island situated?' demanded Paxus.

'Fuck you!' snapped Lana as she smiled back at Paxus sarcastically.

In shock, Mumi immediately gasped under her breath and Bastia jumped to his feet in surprise.

'Are you going to let the witch speak to you like that, Paxus?' he said in disgust. But Paxus got the picture straight away. He folded his arms and grinned back at Lana, giving her a cold stare.

'You are a smart lady,' he said, 'but don't be foolish in this instance. Tell me where the island is?'

~ 150 ~

Lana glared up at him in defiance, giving him a look that only a woman can give a man.

'You are a smart man,' she replied, 'but you will be a fool if you fuck with me.'

For the first time since they met, Lana had the upper hand on Paxus and she knew that he knew it. The politician smiled ironically and seemed to soften his stance a little but Lana immediately stole his thunder.

'I swear upon my father's grave that if you don't start treating Mumi and I like decent human beings; with respect and good will, you will never find the treasure you seek.'

Paxus' face suddenly turned dark and he took a step closer to Lana, staring her down with all the authority he could muster.

'We have ways and means of getting what we want,' he said as he smiled mechanically back at her. 'But I guess that would not be necessary.' He stood for a long period, contemplating his next move then he pointed a warning finger at her. 'If it is true what you say about the writings then I will do what you request but if you cross me, you and your black slut will be skinned alive and crucified. Is that understood?'

Lana forced herself to her feet despite the immense pain she was enduring and faced Paxus defiantly.

'It's a deal then, but only if you start calling us by our names and feed us properly like you do your men and horses and you had better make sure Mumi and I stay alive.' She fell to her knees, unable to stand the pain any longer.

Paxus stared down at her unsympathetically.

'There is another who can read the letterings,' he said in warning, 'and if I find him, what then for you?'

After a long pause, he walked away looking psychologically bruised and battered. Lana watched him go, knowing that he will be fuming that a woman had gotten the upper-hand on him but she was sure he would keep his word for he was driven towards one goal, and yet she wondered just how far the politician would go to achieve it.

She eventually fainted from the pain and all went dark.

*

The odour of cooked meat stirred Lana awake from a deep slumber. It smelt fresh and wholesome, reminding her of Sunday roasts at her father's cottage in the Oxfordshire countryside. Then she jumped when a loud, raucous laugh brought her fully awake. She found that she was lying on her stomach upon a lumpy but comfortable mattress. She turned a little to test her wounds. To her surprise, there was no pain, only discomfort. Raising herself up by her arms, she turned her head to gage where she was. She was at one end of a large room that looked opulent and well appointed. Sunlight shone through two large patio doors that were left wide open. The bright light forced her to squint and it took a short while for her eyes to adjust to the glare and then came the laugh once more, hearty and friendly. She sat up and swung her legs over the side of the bed. Almost immediately her head began to throb, probably because she had been sleeping on her stomach for too long, a position she hated anyway. Then she noticed that she was completely naked. Immediately, she looked about the room for her clothes but there was none. A loud thud somewhere beyond the open doors made her jump again.

Rising gingerly to her feet, she began to search the room. It could have been the emperor's palace for all she knew for it reeked of decadence. The marble floor, with inlaid mosaics depicting the many gods that the Romans worshipped, was especially exquisite and she could only but admire the workmanship that went into it. The high ceiling was also replete in splendour with intricate carvings and paintings of deities, people and animals. This truly was a wealthy establishment, she thought, but it seemed totally out of place with her recent adventures. Feeling acutely aware of her nakedness she looked about for anything that could cover her up. She eventually found a large cloth adorning a marble slab that had a small bust of an old man upon it. She did not recognise the face but judging by his appearance he seemed regal enough to warrant the effigy. She quickly lifted the bust up and pulled out the cloth from underneath. Replacing the bust she wrapped the cloth around her body and secured it tightly over her breasts. It was then that she noticed that her breasts had become smaller, a sure sign of weight loss. She frowned but wasn't overly surprised. The events of the last few days most certainly would have had some physical side-effects. She reached her hands up and tested her hair. It was matted with dried-out sweat, brittle and coarse. Her mouth felt worse but she wasn't thirsty.

Then slowly, but cautiously, she made her way to the open patio doors which were grand in design and enormous in size. Outside, she could hear talking. It sounded jovial and relaxed. She peered around the edge of one of the doors and saw several men seated at a large, round marble table eating away at a roasted pig which was on a platter in the centre of the table. The first face she recognised was Paxus'. Then she spotted Daccus who seemed at home with his beaker of wine and by the sight of him he looked to have consumed his fair share. Bastia sat impassively next to Daccus in a brooding silence. There was no sign of Carl or Mumi.

'Ah, there you are girl,' a voice sounded from behind her which made Lana almost jump. She stepped back behind the door and saw an old woman dressed in a blue toga advancing towards her. She was carrying a shawl and presented it to Lana. 'Put this on quickly and follow me.'

Lana did what was asked and followed the woman to another room where she noticed that there was a sunken bath in the middle of the floor full of steamy water. Two female slaves stood by the bath waiting to serve. With relief, she gave in and allowed herself to be bathed by the two women who washed and dried her expertly. They refused to answer questions she was firing at them so she gave up in the end. The slaves later applied scented oil and perfume to her skin. The nails on her hands and feet were manicured but she refused the offer of some rudimentary makeup knowing that some of the ingredients the ancient Romans used were actually poisonous. In no time, they had her dressed in a bright green toga, soft leather sandals and her hair was made into a bun similar to the way Mumi had done in Fario's home. Then she was presented in front of a ceiling-to-floor polished metal sheet which served as a mirror to see the results of the servant girls' labour.

'The wounds on your back have healed but the scars will remain,' said the old lady as she appeared from behind her. Lana was impressed with the work done on her but she could see in her reflection why the slaves had offered her some makeup. Her eyes bore dark rings and they were sunken into her head. Her face was dangerously thin and she could see her cheek bones protruding from under slightly wrinkled skin. She stared for long moments at the vision before her.

'Are you all right, child?' asked the old lady with genuine concern in her voice.

At that point, Lana burst into tears. The celebrity wife of a famous surfer, who was every bachelor's dream, was no more. The glamour and the glitz had gone, replaced by a shell of her former self. She felt that her world was in ruins.

'Come, let's eat, you must be famished,' said the lady as she coerced her away from her reflection.

Wiping the tears from her eyes she allowed the lady to lead her towards the patio doors. Her stomach was running on empty and her energy was spent. Food was the next best option to help rid her mind of the shocking image of herself.

'She's here!' announced the old lady to the gathering outside in the sunshine.

'Bring her out, Lydia,' a man's voice called from beyond the doors.

Moments later Lana was seated at the table with Paxus, Daccus, Bastia and three other men. The old lady, named Lydia, disappeared back into the house. The day was hot and steamy but the veranda was covered in a welcoming shade provided by a huge, white tarpaulin sheet which extended from the side of the building and was supported by two large poles at each end. Lana's eyes were quickly drawn to the food on offer.

'Eat,' said an elderly man who was sitting directly opposite her. Lana didn't wait to be asked twice and quickly tucked in to a slab of pork, freshly cut from the bone. She picked up the meat with her fingers in the customary Roman way. The smell and taste was like heaven. For the first time in her life she was famished and she found it to be a very humbling ordeal. The others watched on patiently as she stuffed her face with another helping washed down with a very fine wine. Finally, she looked up at the gawking faces staring back at her.

'What the hell are you looking at, haven't you seen someone eat before?'

Her question was followed by polite but constrained laughter and, as one the men raised their drinks in salute. When they finished their drinking the old man opposite stood and introduced himself as Ducia Strupalo, uncle of Paxus Strupalo. Lana glanced at Paxus who was seated to her right. The politician merely nodded back at her.

'Allow me to welcome you to my home in Augusta near the beautiful foothills of the Alps,' said Ducia, politely. 'I have been informed of my nephew's intentions. It is a noble but dangerous quest that Paxus has undertaken. The treasure of the Celts is legendary for they have gathered much gold and valuables throughout their vast trading routes across the known world. Long before our glorious empire was even a republic the Celts were amassing their wealth in Gaul. Now the treasure has gone missing in the wilds of Britannia; a forsaken place where no one but the brave will go.'

Lana said nothing but simply stared back at the man who must have been in his late fifties or early sixties. By the look of him she guessed he hadn't done a day's work in his life. She hated men like him. He was obviously fabulously wealthy and, most likely, a cunt to boot. Reflecting the standards of ancient Rome, he was probably a wife beater, slave beater and a paedophile all in one. She loaded up her defence mechanisms and got ready for what was to follow.

'I gather your wounds have healed?' asked Ducia as he sat himself back down, 'no small thanks to the expertise of my wife, Lydia may I add. She's so good with herbal medicines...'

'... How long have I been here?'

Ducia cringed in his seat. He was obviously not used to being interrupted. Paxus decided to answer for him.

'You have been here for four days. The first two days, you were delirious with fever. You have been asleep for the last two.'

'Where are Carl and Mumi?'

'They are with my soldiers. Don't worry, they are safe and well,' answered Paxus, tritely. Lana could see he was trying his utmost to stay patient but she was enjoying the moment. She knew they were treating her kindly for one purpose only but she was growing bored.

'Let's cut the crap,' she said as she dipped her greasy fingers in a bowl of scented water. 'I know why I'm being treated to a banquet.' She looked to Ducia who was squirming in his seat. 'Thank your wife for healing my wounds and thank you for the food but I know it's not from the goodness of your heart that you do this. You do it for what's inside my head which will remain there until I have a say in this quest.'

'What do you mean?' asked Paxus.

'Don't forget, I know the location of the treasure. I have been to the isle of Anglesey before.' She recalled her trip with her father as a girl. They were catching the ferry from Holyhead to Dublin. Her father was collecting an honorary degree from the King's College.

'When did you go there?' asked Ducia.

'Two thousand years from now,' replied Lana.

'Ha, ha... what are you saying child?' asked an incredulous Ducia who began to laugh heartily. The two men sitting either side of Ducia laughed along with him in mockery of her words. Daccus and Bastia did not. Lana glanced at Paxus questioningly.

'You haven't told him?'

'Of course not,' snapped an angry Paxus, whose mood suddenly changed like a bolt out of the blue. He stood up and planted his clenched fists down hard upon the table. 'When are you going to stop this charade about the future? Tell us where the island is?'

The three men immediately ceased their scornful laughter and looked to Paxus whose face was glowing red with rage.

'I have been held up here for four days and I haven't even left Italy,' continued Paxus. 'I may have enemies on my trail or worse, news of this quest may have reached Britannia and the treasure could have been moved to another location. Either way, we're wasting precious time.'

'That's true Paxus,' seconded Ducia.

The old man stared hard at Lana and formed his fingers into a steeple. He was pondering for a moment then he spoke like he was master of all he surveyed.

'Now tell my nephew the location of the island and I will grant you and your friends a life of leisure and peace in my villa for the rest of your natural lives.'

'Oh no, I go all the way,' replied Lana. She pointed to Paxus. 'The moment I tell you the location of the island this butcher will slit my throat.'

Ducia laughed in an attempt to appease Lana but she stayed resolute, staring the old man out; eye-to-eye.

'I see you're a woman of principle,' said Ducia, 'but how do we know that you're telling us the truth? For all we know you could be lying to us just for the favours you will receive.'

'I am an archaeologist, someone who is trained in the study of ancient civilisations such as yours. I am also trained in reading ancient writings and symbols, such as the letterings on Bastia's back.' Lana waited for a response but her words were met by silence. A gust of wind blew the tarpaulin sunshade upwards, snapping loudly above the gathering.

'It's no secret that I find you and your friend, Carl, a distraction,' said Paxus in an angry tone, 'but your words are difficult to understand. You spoke of our Roman civilisation in past-tense. Surely you don't expect us to believe that you are actually from the future, do you?'

'You saw the photographs Carl showed you in the blacksmith's cave didn't you?' replied Lana. 'They were taken by a Nikon digital camera, a tool that will not be invented for another two thousand years. Isn't that proof enough?'

Paxus sat back in his seat and threw his hands up in the air, dismissing Lana's reply with disdain. Then the old man clapped his hands together and a young slave boy appeared, carrying a tray. He placed it down upon the table and excited quietly. On the tray was the camera and watch. She stared at Ducia who slowly rose and placed both palms down upon the table.

'My colleagues and I have examined these artefacts and we find them very odd indeed. There is no beauty in them and no craftsmanship. They are made of strange materials that have strange inscriptions on them. Where did you find them?'

'I told you, they came with us when we... when we travelled back to this time.'

'Oh and how did you... travel?' asked Ducia, sarcastically.

'I don't know,' replied Lana, suddenly feeling like she was being grilled by the local sheriff. 'We went to sleep and woke up back in these times.' She was missing home now more than ever. Thoughts of her husband Dennis, her father and her community of loving friends came flooding back.

Ducia stood upright and looked to the other two old men who nodded back at him.

'These men are learned scholars who know all that there is to know. Tell them what you have told Daccus about the future?'

Lana looked to Daccus in surprise. He merely glanced at his wine but stayed silent. Feeling resolute and fearless, she nevertheless decided to lay it all on the line. She was not going to hold back anything. She was going to blind them with science and technology, chemistry and medicine, discovery and exploration. She decided to begin with Christopher Columbus.

Carl looked Mumi's naked body up and down once again, trying to decide if she was sexually desirable or not. She was sitting upon a bale of straw in a barn where they were both ordered to stay. After four days of incarceration along with the horses, Carl was glad Mumi could speak, which was a most welcome addition, but he began to imagine things. Mumi was beautiful, there was no doubting that, but her skin and hair were course and dry. Her feet and hands were calloused, cut and worn out and her breasts, though rounded and perfect were very small. She was no match for the curvaceous, full bodied Lana and yet she had a way about her that Carl found most attractive. Mumi was busily repairing her tunic with a needle and thread that the soldiers had returned. It had been torn off her body the night before by a drunken soldier intent on raping her but he was stopped by a blow to the head from Commander Secus, which rendered him unconscious.

'You like what you see, hmm...?' asked Mumi without looking up from her chore.

Carl immediately glanced away. 'I'm sorry I didn't mean to stare.'

'It's all right. Many men have stared at me with the same look that you have in your eyes. It's the way of a slave girl. We get used to it.'

'Where I come from there are no slaves and women are treated with respect - most of the time.'

Mumi stopped what she was doing and looked up at Carl with big brown eyes that looked so inviting.

'Are you in need of relief?' she asked, as she made the gesture of masturbation with her left hand.

'No, I'm fine,' replied Carl, suddenly feeling flushed with embarrassment. 'It's just that I'm not used to seeing a naked woman acting so casually in front of me.'

'That sounds very sad,' replied Mumi as she put down her work. She tucked her legs up under herself and rested her elbows on her knees. 'Go ahead and relieve yourself in front of me. I know men like to do that.'

Carl was shocked. 'I can't do that Mumi... the, the solders might come in.'

'It's not feeding time for another couple of hours. Go on, stop making excuses.'

Then, inadvertently, without thinking, Carl's right hand went down to his groin. His face was flushed with excitement and his cock began to stir.

'Oh, let me help you,' said Mumi as she jumped down from the bale.

He was surprised in himself for not reacting as Mumi's hand reached up under his tunic and grabbed his balls.

'Ooh, hot and full! I bet you haven't come for a long time?' she asked as she slowly caressed his manhood.

Her eyes looked even more beautiful this close up and the whites of her teeth were a temptation he could not refuse. In no time, he began to masturbate. Mumi tightened her grip on his balls and stared harder into his eyes.

'Go on, think of fucking Lana,' whispered Mumi down his left ear. 'I know you love her. Think of fucking me too. Think of fucking both us together.'

Carl began to race. His cock was rock hard and he wanted to bend Mumi over the bale of hay and fuck her brains out. Mumi fondled his balls expertly, soft grip and hard grip then soft again. Her breath was warm upon his face then she licked his lips, and soon, both were kissing. It was too much. Carl raised her up and threw her over the bale, face down. She didn't resist. She immediately spread her legs and he rammed his cock deep inside her. He pounded away until sweat was flowing freely from every pore on his body. Mumi was hot, wet and incredibly nubile. She made all the right moves, reacting to Carl's thrusts in perfect synchronisation with his. It felt like it was the best fuck he ever had and he didn't want it to end but, before long, he had exploded inside her with so much sperm that the relief was overwhelming. He collapsed on top of her then rolled onto his back.

He lay there to saviour the moment for a while but to his surprise, Mumi got up and returned to her chore. It was as if the special act of intercourse between a man and woman had not occurred. His come-down from ecstasy was ruined. He wanted to hold her and caress her body but she had moved on. He wondered just who was using who here? His disappointment was overshadowed by the realisation that Mumi treated sex just like going to the toilet or boiling a pan of water - functional and practical. In that moment, the gulf in time seemed to have widened a little more.

13

The sun was already up when Sam strolled out onto the balcony dressed in his standard issue hotel gown. He had not slept well. His eyes were raw from the tears he had cried throughout the night. The preposterous thought that his brother was 'lost in time' had drained his emotions to the point where he was running on empty. On their return to the hotel, Ted Brooks had sat with him when he made the call home to his wife from the hotel phone. He had to tell her the lie that the police were doing everything in their power to find Carl. The call to Linda was the most difficult one he had ever made and he could tell that she knew something was wrong. Luckily for Sam, she was the kind of woman who was patient and understanding but she would always find out in the end.

Seated at the balcony table, he stared vacantly at the Roman skyline. The hum of the modern day city from up here was just the same as any other city the world over. He could be in Paris or London, Beijing or Sydney. He wondered what kind of sound Carl would be waking up to in ancient Rome…

'… Bah,' he cried in frustration as he kicked the chair opposite him, annoyed that he was even contemplating such a thing.

It just cannot be true. I can't believe it, I won't believe it.

A knock at his door made him jump. It was six thirty in the morning and out of a natural habit he expected to be the only one awake. He was always the first up at home. He enjoyed the momentary solitude of the early morning whilst the rest of the household slept. It helped him focus his thoughts before beginning another hectic day at his company.

'Come in,' he called.

The door swung inwards and Winifred entered, dressed in loose-fitting cotton slacks and a matching white blouse. She looked prepared for anything which was, oddly, reassuring. Behind her came Ted who hadn't bothered shaving but, otherwise, looked ready in his T-shirt and jeans. Sam couldn't help but notice a print of the iconic photo of The Beatles walking along a zebra crossing emblazoned upon his white shirt. Strangely, Sam found himself trying to remember what album cover it was taken off but it wouldn't come.

'I suppose it's inappropriate for me to say good morning,' said Ted as he stepped out onto the balcony, 'but for all it's worth...' he trailed off and sat down at the table in as just a glummer mood as Sam. The two men stared vacantly out over the city in silent contemplation, neither daring to kick-start a conversation. The sound of Winifred setting out cups upon the dresser and a kettle boiling disturbed the peace for the moment but the promise of a hot coffee was always a welcome inclusion to the morning's proceedings.

'I can't accept it,' said Sam, just for something to say.

'You have to,' replied Ted, mundanely. 'The photos are not lying.'

'But they are not proof alone!' stated Sam. 'Photographs can be manipulated, especially digital ones, you know that?'

'Win got a phone call from Professor Barnes last night,' said Ted as he stirred uncomfortably in his seat. Then he fell silent, sitting motionless and in deep thought.

'And?' prompted Sam.

'The results from the lab confirm that the leather covering from the camera is indeed two-thousand years old,' said Ted said rather depressingly. He glanced at Sam with a rueful look. 'There's your proof for you.'

'And I suppose the watch strap is too?'

'I'm not a betting man but I wouldn't wager against it.'

~ 163 ~

Sam tensed up and looked away, not wanting to hear such news. Then Win appeared with a tray of mugs filled with steaming coffee. She placed the tray down upon the table and sat in the vacant chair.

'Sugar anyone?'

Neither took sugar but they were grateful for the beverage. All three sat in silence for an awkward length of time until Win eventually piped up.

'After we got back to the hotel, I rang a colleague of mine, Professor Malcolm McVie, he's a theoretical physicist, and I asked him about the possibilities of returning to the past.'

Sam choked on his coffee whilst Ted stopped midway from taking his next sip.

'Don't be surprised gentlemen. He told me that a theory exists which explains a phenomenon which they call a time fold. Apparently, they happen regularly.'

'A time fold, eh?' questioned Ted. 'I've heard of them.'

'I hadn't until last night,' said Win. 'Apparently, no scientist worth his salt would touch such a theory but, nonetheless, the theory exists.'

Sam plonked his coffee down hard upon the table with a loud clatter. 'Listen to yourselves will you? If it wasn't for the fact that you're both sitting down I'd say that you were talking out of your arseholes.'

Win glared at Sam threateningly. 'Now listen hear Sam Evans, stop living in denial of the truth and get with it or you're going to be on the next flight home.'

Sam looked to Ted for support but Ted merely replied by saying that Win was in charge.

'Your brother and Lana are gone,' continued Win angrily, 'it's possible that they have disappeared into one of these theoretical time folds back to ancient Rome and we have to try and figure out how we can get them back.'

Sam felt browbeaten. Win had spoken with such authority that he was glad that she was on his side.

'Now, Malcolm McVie has booked a flight to Rome from Scotland and will arrive at nine a.m., Rome time,' continued Win. 'He will explain more eloquently than I just what kind of situation we have here. Also, Professor Barnes has requested that we meet with him in about an hour at his apartment in Prati, which is one of the more desirable residences of Rome.' She looked Sam hard in the eye. 'He has asked that you make sure you bring along your mobile phone.'

Within the hour Sam and his two colleagues found themselves seated in a luxurious apartment, furnished with exquisite taste as only Italians can do. They sat opposite Professor Barnes in plush, leather chairs surrounded by countless shelves full of books. Two ornate window frames carved in the classic Venetian renaissance style were the most striking features of the room and Sam pondered whether he should refurbish his office in a similar style in order to get better business deals.

The look on Professor Barnes' face did nothing to lift the already gloomy mood in the room.

'I have asked you here to tell you something else about the disappearance of Carl and Lana,' he announced. He seemed a trite ruffled by whatever it was he was about to say. 'My learned friends in the museum thought it best to wait a little after the emotions of yesterday. But I must tell you now that we had a report from the meteorological department of a strange pulse of energy that struck Rome on the night of their disappearance.'

Sam's jaw dropped an inch and his heartbeats increased, tenfold.

'What are you saying?' he asked inquisitively, 'that the weather had something to do with it?'

'In a way, yes,' replied the Professor. 'The meteorological department's equipment registered a burst of energy hundreds of thousands of times more powerful than that of a lightning strike right at the point of the dig site though they are puzzled as to why the area where Carl and Lana disappeared is not scorched or damaged in any way. There were no thunderstorms forecast for that night and the sky was almost cloudless. The experts are completely baffled as to what it could be.'

'A time fold!' said Win.

Professor Barnes looked perplexed. 'A time fold you say, Winifred? What is that, pray tell?'

'It's a theory that a friend of mine agrees with,' replied Win. 'He'll be in Rome shortly. He will be able to expand more on the subject when he arrives.'

'Never heard of such a thing,' said the professor, sounding put out by Win's statement.

'I have,' said Ted as he stood up and strolled over to the windows. With his hands behind his back and facing the view of the river Tiber he spoke like he was quoting from text:

'According to the theory, a time fold is the temporary reversal of the arrow of time. This strange anomaly occurs randomly everywhere in the universe and at all times. When the universe began with the big bang, all the visible energy that we see today was created in that instant along with a lot more invisible energy that we cannot see. Scientists call this stuff, dark energy, where the laws of physics, as we know it, do not apply. There is a theory that dark energy is a link to other universes outside of our own. Within the boundaries of dark energy, time is suspended; gravity does not exist and only pure energy exists. It is a chaotic, turbulent, violent maelstrom of confused quarks and electrons. But this stuff is interwoven into the fabric of our visible universe, intertwining with gravity at random points in the vast cosmos. When a time fold strikes it lasts for much less than a trillionth of a Nano second; barely noticed and hardly felt. But where it does strike, the space time continuum is altered and depending on the amount of energy expelled decides how far back the space time is taken.'

The room went deathly silent as Ted's three pupils hung on to his every word.

'Unfortunately for us,' continued Ted as he turned to face them, 'the amount of energy that Carl and Lana were subjected to has zapped them back two-thousand years to the past, though it could have been worse: they could have ended up at the time of the dinosaurs or even on the primitive earth before life took hold... or worse than that.'

No one spoke for a while as all contemplated the situation in their own minds. Then Sam broke the silence.

'What about my phone call?' he asked, taking his mobile out of his pocket, 'how did that happen?'

'It could be that the electronics in Carl's phone had, somehow, been energised by the time fold... and... and.' Ted stopped himself in mid-sentence, looking as though he was fishing for answers in a very deep lake. 'Were you on the phone to Carl the night he disappeared?'

'Yes,' replied Sam.

Ted turned back towards the windows and fell silent.

Sam felt himself sinking further into his leather seat. The conversations were beginning to sound more like science fiction than fact. He saw himself as an earthy character. Hunting, fishing and camping out under the stars were his domain. The world of electrons and sub-atomic particles was a mystery to him. He liked the simple, homely lifestyle that helped keep a healthy balance between business and pleasure. He even found Carl's fascination with archaeology a ball ache. He never took time to listen to his brother's dining table lectures on buried artefacts and ancient monuments. He found them boring. Now he wished he had listened.

'So there you have it,' announced Lana to her dumbfounded audience, 'the future in a nutshell.' She sat down in her chair and watched the three men's faces go through cringe-worthy expressions that bordered on the comical. She had crammed their heads full with mankind's future history of discovery; from Christopher Columbus to Neil Armstrong; from Leonardo Da Vinci to Albert Einstein; from Isaac Newton to Charles Darwin. Her explanation of aeroplanes left them utterly bewildered. Her detailed tour of human anatomy held them spellbound whilst a lecture on the earth, the stars and the planets caused them to drift a little, but, nevertheless, she hoped that she had left them in no uncertain terms that she was from the future.

Ducia was the first to speak, though he looked as if he had aged by ten years after listening to Lana's tirade.

'Flying machines, a man on the moon, ships with no sails and mankind descended from pond slime, you say?'

'You better believe it.'

'You are possessed by a demon,' he replied, sounding exasperated.

Gasping for breath, he rose to his feet gingerly and ordered her from his premises, telling her to take the devilish artefacts from his premises and warning Paxus to watch his back at all times. Lana laughed mockingly into Ducia's face but Paxus was already up and shepherding her off the veranda. She didn't struggle for she was glad to get away from the odious old man.

'You're lucky he didn't order you to be flogged,' said Paxus in annoyance as he made his way through the villa.

'It would be preferable to living in these despicable times,' cried Lana, making sure the three men at the table could hear her.

After consuming his fair share of wine, Daccus took the camera and the watch and followed behind as best he could upon unsure feet. Bastia trailed in their wake feeling utterly bemused.

Within the hour Lana was brought to the barn and reunited with Carl and Mumi. The camera and watch were handed back to Carl by a soldier. He took them and placed them in his sack along with his phone which he had kept hidden.

'Are you well, Lana?' Carl asked in English.

'They fixed me up and fed me but it was all a ruse to get me to talk,' replied Lana, shaking her head angrily.

'What now?'

'We're going to Britain; Wales to be exact. I will explain all later,' she said as she walked away and sat upon a bale of hay.

'So what happened to you two?'

Carl glanced at Mumi for a moment and then back at Lana. He kept the conversation in English, finding it comforting to be speaking in his own tongue.

'We've been kept in this barn for the past four days but looked after well,' he said, without much conviction. Lana sensed something was not quite right between Carl and Mumi, but she chose to ignore it. 'Apparently you have been the guest of a merchant ship owner, one of the wealthiest men in the empire I believe?'

'How do you know?' asked Lana.

'One of the soldiers told me. And he also said that he had a famous guest at his home – someone we know of.'

'Oh, who?' she asked in surprise.

'The writer, Suetonius,' said Carl.

'Shit,' cursed Lana, realising that one of the two men sitting next to Decius must have been him.

'What's wrong?'

'I've just recounted to him the future history of the world from the renaissance to the digital age.'

A long moment of silence followed then Carl smiled, ruefully. 'Well, he must have thought you were nuts because there's no mention of you in his writings.'

For the first time in ages Lana smiled but it was then that Carl realised just how old she was looking. He tried his best to disguise his reaction but Lana had spotted the concern upon his face. She said nothing as she turned to Mumi for comfort.

After a short while, Carl reached down to a bale of hay and picked up a square piece of wood that he had been working on. He had scratched a message into its surface with an old nail that he had found in the barn.

'Lana, I want to take a photograph of us holding this message.'

Lana turned and saw that Carl had made a placard with letters scratched on it. 'Help, we are lost in time, can't get home,' she read aloud. 'What are you proposing Carl?'

'I don't know, a time capsule, just like the bottle I had Daccus bury at Fario's villa,' said Carl. 'If Sam fails to get us home then at least we can prove that we have been here. Hopefully, the camera will be found and a future generation will learn the truth.'

'You're nuts!' she pronounced. 'The camera won't survive such a long time in the ground.'

'Not if we wrap it tightly linen and put it in a sealed box. It's a long shot but what have we got to lose?'

After a long time in deep thought, Lana reluctantly agreed but still insisted that Carl was nuts.

Carl gave Mumi a quick lesson on how to take a photograph and was surprised at how fast she learned.

Within no time, they were whisked outside and ordered to wait by a large four-wheeled cart. Carl and Lana moved away to stand beside a young spruce tree and held the placard up between them. Mumi took the shot like a pro and no suspicions were raised. Carl immediately stuffed the camera back into his sack then looked about noticing that there was plenty of activity all around them as the soldiers followed orders to break camp.

Soon, the three companions were ordered inside the cart which was full to the brim with provisions. They were seated behind the driver who was joined on the front bench by Daccus, still looking the worse for wear from his drinking session the other day. Bastia was mounted alongside Paxus at the head of a line of horses. Lana could see Paxus speaking to his uncle whilst behind them stood the two other men that she had met. One of those men must be Suetonius! Lana laughed to herself knowing now that the history books were way out with his birth date. The estimates were that he was born in 69AD but that would have made him ten years old today – Suetonius looked to be at least in his mid-sixties. Paxus soon waved his uncle farewell and they were on their way.

For the remainder of the day, Lana, Carl and Mumi were taken by Paxus' mini army through the rugged terrain of the foothills of the Alps, leaving the town of Augusta far behind. The day was hot and humid but the Roman road they travelled along was smooth and even. After a while Lana told Carl and Mumi the good news that they will be treated fairly from now on if only for a selfish reason. Carl laughed aloud at the irony but he understood and thanked her.

As the day wore on she tried her best to engage Carl in conversation but he seemed reluctant for some reason; he had allowed his mind to drift as he stared for long moments at the beautiful scenery passing by. Sometimes he would open the sack that contained the camera, phone and watch and look at them briefly before closing it again. She guessed it was a source of comfort to him, reminding him of home. But, in complete contrast, Mumi was full of curiosity wanting to know more about the wondrous world of the future. So Lana passed the time with her, telling her all about the lovely things that women could do; the pampering, the jewellery, the clothes and the shoes. Mumi was delighted to hear such magical things and it helped pass the day.

As the sun began to dip below the high ridges that surrounded the entourage on all sides, a turn in a bend brought them to a sudden stop as a flock of crows scattered in fright. The birds' wings echoed off the high walls as they flew to a safe distance from the intruders. It soon became apparent what the crows were up to. Stretched out across the road were four naked bodies, each attached to wooden frames. Then, to their surprise, it suddenly dawned upon Carl and Lana that these people had been crucified. The crosses were not the classical crosses in the manner that the Christian Church depicted, but instead, they were nailed to rough-hewn vertical poles with a cross beam but no extended part that protruded above the head. They were also stuck into the earth at ground level. The grisly sight disgusted both Carl and Lana and was not helped at all by the feasting of the crows, but they were finding that they were quickly becoming accustomed to the brutality of these times and their eyes were soon drawn to the details. A large nail was driven through the palm of the victims hands all the way into the wooden crossbeam and out through the other side. A simple wooden washer stopped the nail from tearing through the palms and each of the nails was bent at the tips to hold the victim in place. Shockingly, their feet were nailed to either side of the upright through the sides of the ankles with washers to hold them in place, which must have been excruciatingly painful.

Lana felt like throwing up as she noticed that the crows had eaten out all their eyes. One was an old man; his features contorted in frozen agony. Another was a woman in her mid-thirties. Her face was twisted beyond reason. Heaven knows what her last thoughts were before she died, she thought? The other two unfortunates were black men, probably slaves. Their bodies showed signs of a beating. One had a broken leg whilst the other had hundreds of cuts to his face and arms. Lana looked to Carl who stared in disbelief at the gruesome sight.

'So that's how it was done,' he whispered in fascination.

'Is this how all crucifixions were carried out?' asked Lana to Daccus, inquisitively.

'Yes of course,' he answered ponderously, still feeling the effects of his drinking session. 'But for other reasons some are crucified upside down. It all depends on what crime they had committed. This man and woman have been executed for bankruptcy, along with their slaves.'

'How do you know that?'

'Because the mark of a sesterce has been branded into their chests,' he said, matter-of-factly.

Lana looked closer and could see a mark in the shape of a circle burnt into their torsos. She looked to Carl who seemed morbidly fascinated by it all.

My god, what's becoming of us?

'Crucified people have their crimes branded into their chest for all to see,' continued Daccus.

'I thought Roman citizens were exempt from crucifixion?' asked Carl, remembering his history lessons.

'Oh no,' replied Daccus. 'They are not exempt if the punishment is decided upon by the victims of the crime - or where murder is concerned - the victim's relatives. I dare say, in this case, the victims would have carried out the crucifixion themselves with the blessing of the magistrate.'

Lana and Carl were nonplussed by Daccus' statement. The history books were way off the mark on this point.

Then, in shock horror Lana watched on as the soldiers got to work removing the obstacles. They wasted no time as they tied ropes around all four frameworks and then simply used the strength of their horses to pull them to the side of the road. Bodies, wood and nails were sent tumbling down into a shallow ditch. She was disgusted at the way the soldiers went about their work. There was no respect shown to the victims. To them they were simply an obstacle to be removed. She looked to Paxus who had been staring back at her to gauge her reaction. She shook her head disapprovingly but Paxus returned it with a cold smile then ordered his men to move on.

The trap had been set for two days now but the men were growing restless. The mountain pass was an ideal place for it and they had set up accordingly. Drexa Vitanian's guess that Paxus had holed up in his uncle's villa was proven correct. A scout had confirmed the news and, taking advice from his general, Drexa agreed to set an ambush.

'It is good news that Paxus is on the move once again,' said Mathias as he sat next to Drexa sharpening his sword.

'Are you sure your scout is trustworthy enough?' asked Drexa, sounding mightily disgruntled to be sitting at a campfire for the fifth night in a row. He kept shifting his considerable bulk upon the tree stump that he was seated upon but never finding that perfect spot. He had left his tearful lover back in Rome and promised that he will return. That return couldn't come a day too soon.

'Tremo is a good scout,' replied Mathias. 'His word is as good as any loyal soldier.'

The scout had reported that Paxus had set out from his uncle's villa late in the afternoon with twenty-four lightly armed soldiers and a cart full of provisions including a group of civilians, two of whom were women.

'That's what I worry about - loyalty,' continued Drexa as he shifted his weight once more. 'All of your men are conscripts from around the empire; 'the dregs of humanity' as Julius Caesar once put it.'

'But my lord, the empire was built on the back of conscripts,' replied Mathias, sounding most annoyed at Drexa's statement. 'Look at me, I am not a Roman, I am a Jew and I've been loyal to the empire all my working life.'

'And so you have, but have your men? Look at them?' Drexa waved his arm in a swathe around the camp. 'There are Africans, Germanics, Celts and Spaniards in your ranks but when it comes to a fight, what will they do if the tide turns against them – run and leave me at the mercy of the traitor, Paxus?'

'I assure you, in the morning Paxus will ride straight into the ambush. He won't know what hit him. Before he can react, half of his men will be dead and you will have him begging for mercy at your feet.'

Drexa rubbed his beefy hands at the prospect. He knew General Mathias was a good soldier and his men were very professional but the worry that if it all went wrong troubled him. Bravery in the face of violence was not one of Drexa's strongest points. His father, a political commentator, had been ashamed of Drexa's cowardice as a young man and publicly insulted his only son on many occasions so Drexa poisoned him. Luckily for him, his father's inheritance enabled the young Drexa to indulge in a lifestyle of debauchery. Sex, food and wine were the order of the day in the nineteen year old's world. He came to politics quite late. At twenty nine years of age, bloated by years of neglect, he bribed his way into the senate and found that he was a good orator, often holding politicians spellbound with his late father's words. He quickly progressed through the ranks by being ruthless and efficient. Within a year he was promoted to magistrate, a respectable office for any politician. Soon, Titus got wind of his reputation and asked him to be his informer. Drexa did not disappoint the new emperor.

The following morning the early sunlight had chased away the mountain mist, leaving the pass clear for the men to see. A chill, this high up in the mountains, made them shiver but they knew that at this time of year the strong rays of the sun will be warming their backs within the hour. Drexa was still asleep but Mathias was happy to leave him be. He guessed that the slimy bastard had probably never seen dawn in his life but he had promised to wake him as soon as their quarry arrived. He approached the on-duty guard who nodded to him who then promptly spoke in broken Latin.

'Sir, the men are tired and pissed off,' said the soldier, whose name was Boruc, a Germanic conscript. 'They have decided that they will return to Rome if nothing further happens today.'

Mathias nodded but said nothing as he watched Boruc walk back to the camp to get some breakfast. He decided, in this moment, that if he didn't get the chance to spill some blood today he will return with his men.

After an hour had passed the sun was beginning to warm up his back, casting out the chill in his ageing bones. Then the unmistakable sound of hooves and the steady trundle of cartwheels disturbed the peace. He looked to his scout, Tremo who nodded back. Mathias signalled for his men to get ready then he made his way to the snoring Drexa. Placing his hand over Drexa's mouth he shook him awake. The magistrate stirred and uttered something inaudible under his breath then gasped when he saw Mathias' face up close.

'They're coming,' whispered Mathias. He let the fat magistrate struggle to his feet, unaided, as he walked back to take his place behind the mountain ridge. The sound of the horse's hooves pounding the dirt track was growing louder. It was good news. Paxus and his men would obviously be thinking that they were alone amongst the rocks of the Alps and they would be right to think so. For many years now, there had been no bandits or outlaws patrolling these mountains. Traditional trade routes through the Alps had been stopped under the reign of Claudius because of constant raids by lawbreakers. Now most of the trade from the north to Rome was transported by sea from the southern shores of Gaul.

'Are they here?' asked an out of breath Drexa, as he approached Mathias from behind.

'Silence,' he whispered as he pushed Drexa down behind the ridge. 'You don't want to give us away do you?'

Drexa said nothing and wished he was back in Rome.

Mathias cocked his head to listen to the approaching sound of hooves and a four wheeled cart. 'It's them!'

'Leave Paxus alive,' whispered Drexa, 'I want to peel the skin off his flesh and crucify him up-side-down.'

The early morning ride was proving difficult as the mountain pass seemed to grow narrower with every mile. The troop was forced to ride single file whilst the cart was left to take up the rear. In the back sat a gloomy Lana Evans who was dreading the tedium of first century travel. At this pace, she knew it will take several months to reach Britain and a further month to get to Anglesey. She was glad it was the height of summer now but what will the weather be like when they reach their destination? She dreaded the thought. Carl yawned and gave Lana a whimsical smile but then he looked to Mumi and then straight back at Lana as if it was forbidden to look at a slave girl. She could tell that he was embarrassed about something, but what?

The entourage slowly made its way through a narrow pass that was just wide enough to allow the cart through. Mountainous walls of granite on either side blocked out the sun causing the temperature to drop dramatically. Lana stared ahead at the line of mounted soldiers riding ahead. In such a confined space they had deliberately slowed down their horses to keep them calm.

After several hundred yards had passed she could see the opening up ahead where, beyond, stood a great pine forest stretching out as far as the eye could see. She was pondering whether to ask Carl as to why he was being so coy about Mumi when, from behind her, came a whistling noise that fizzed past her left ear which ended in a dull thud. She jumped back in shock when she saw that an arrow had penetrated the neck of the driver. It had buried itself right down to its quill. The driver stood up in shock, gargling in his own blood. Then he tumbled forwards between the horses and the cart and was gone. The horrific moment was frozen for an instant in her mind and then pandemonium broke out all around her. The panic-stricken horses reared and fled along the pass as arrows whizzed all around. The cart careered on through the pass, pulled along by the two terrified horses. She watched as Daccus grabbed hold of the reins and tried his best to bring the horses to a stop but the beasts were too strong for him. The cart was slammed from side-to-side against the high walls and with each slam bits of the framework broke away. She screamed to Daccus to stand up and pull back hard upon the reins but the noise of the cart's wheels and the pounding of the hooves drowned out her calls. Then an arrow hit Daccus in his left shoulder. He immediately released the reins and fell backwards into the cart, right on top of Carl. Then, to Lana's surprise, Mumi suddenly leapt up into the driver's seat and grabbed the reins, but instead of trying to stop the horses she encouraged them to go faster, screaming at them in a loud voice that belied her small frame. Arrows continued to fly all around her as she bobbed and weaved as best she could to avoid them.

Soon they were clear of the pass but the horses were hit in their heads and necks by a great volley of arrows from the opposite direction and they collapsed in a heap on the ground. The cart went careering over the dying bodies of the horses and broke apart, scattering its contents all over the pass. Lana, Carl, Daccus and Mumi were sent hurtling along with the wreckage, landing at the feet of a line of soldiers. Two of the soldiers quickly reached down and manhandled Lana to the side of the road where she was forced to sit upon the ground. Then she saw Carl, Mumi and Daccus receiving the same treatment. They too were shoved alongside her. Daccus was writhing in agony from his wound but no treatment was offered him. The shaft of the arrow had snapped off during the crash but the arrow head was buried deep into his shoulder. Carl was resisting his treatment by the soldiers as best he could whilst still holding on doggedly to his sack of contents. Then one of the soldiers punched him with a rain of blows to the head which left him unconscious in a heap next to Lana but, oddly, Mumi stayed calm throughout, accepting the situation without much fuss.

Then Lana's attention was disturbed when the clang of metal upon metal distracted her for a moment. She turned to see many men embroiled in a sword fight at the exit to the pass. In the middle of the melee was Paxus, standing tall and threatening. He was cutting and thrusting away with his sword alongside his men including Bastia who was fighting for his life. Lana was shocked by the ferocity of the fight. She guessed that there were at least ten men on each side, all going for the kill. Then the fighting men moved, on masse, towards where she was sitting; toing and froing across the mountain road. Some were taking on wounds but the fight seemed equal. Then, to her surprise, Paxus and his men rallied in an almighty savage assault that left their opponents falling backwards over one another. Swords and shields went flying out of their hands, some skidding across the road and off the edge, down into a deep ravine, clattering and clanging as they went.

In no time the fight was over. Seven of Paxus' men were left standing over their opponents who had eventually surrendered. Six of the defeated were bleeding profusely from gaping wounds. Paxus immediately ordered them to be pitched over the side of the road and into the deep ravine. His soldiers went about their orders quietly by slitting their throats and throwing them bodily over the edge. It was yet another shocking sight that Carl and Lana had to endure. One soldier came up to Paxus and announced that the rest of the attackers had fled.

Paxus quickly checked on Lana to see if she was all right but after checking Daccus over he shook his head in disappointment. Ignoring Carl and Mumi, he then checked the prisoners his men had captured. Scanning their faces individually, he quickly singled out one survivor in particular by pointing his bloodied sword down at him. 'General Mathias Bossca!' he announced, 'Drexa Vitanian's dog soldier! What on earth brings you out here with your mercenary scum to attack us in broad daylight?'

Mathias said nothing but stared glaringly back at Paxus.

Just then, a howl went up and a scuffling of feet could be heard in the pass. Soon, a fat man dressed in a robe appeared, quickly followed by two of Paxus' soldiers, one of whom kept prodding him with the shaft of a broken lance. The veteran soldiers began to laugh when they recognised who the frightened man was. Lana looked to Daccus whose face was grim.

'It's Drexa Vitanian; the man who murdered Fario!' he said.

14

After minimal effort in extracting information from Drexa about how he had gained knowledge of the quest, Paxus allowed him to grovel and whine away in the dirt. The magistrate had pleaded incessantly for his life in the most cowardly manner Paxus had ever seen a man do. The snivelling politician had promised money, favours, women, land and slaves if he would spare him. But Paxus was in no mood for mercy. After four days holed up in his uncle's villa his patience was threadbare, to say the least, and now this little skirmish was the final straw.

A blood-soaked Secus approached Paxus and looked down at Drexa with utter contempt. He had and his men had just completed the grisly task of executing the remaining soldiers by slitting their throats and throwing their bodies into the ravine. His hands were covered in blood and Drexa cowered from the sight of him.

'What do you want me to do with this bastard?' Secus asked.

Paxus could see that Secus was brimming over with anger for the death of three of his soldiers. An ambush was the last thing he expected but the bravery and professionalism of his men had saved the day.

Paxus knew his commander wanted blood and he would give it him soon. 'I have no doubt that this man deserves to die,' he said to Secus as he looked down at the pathetic sight of Drexa grovelling at his feet. 'But first I must speak with him some more.'

An angry Secus reached down and grabbed Drexa by the scruff of the neck and stared him hard in the eye. 'It's going to be a pleasure watching you die, now stand up and face Paxus like a man.' He dragged Drexa, bodily, to his feet and slapped him across the face. 'And stop snivelling like a girl you fucking pussy.'

Paxus laid a palm on Secus' arm to calm him down. 'Why don't you help your men to bury the dead? They deserve a soldier's grave.'

Secus grimaced then turned, shaking his head in disappointment as he walked away.

After he left, Paxus turned and faced Drexa alone. 'I know you and your ways, Drexa Vitanian,' he said, cynically. 'You said the emperor told you about our quest but if Titus had gotten wind of our intentions we would not have made it out of Rome alive. No. You found out by another way, didn't you?'

'I have ways and means,' was all he said as he wiped his snivelling nose on the sleeve of his toga.

Paxus recoiled from the look Drexa gave him. He was staring him straight in the eye and he could see that the wily magistrate's brain was ticking over.

'You want the same as me, don't you?' asked Drexa slyly as his eyes widened with wonder. 'The Celtic treasure would give you enough power to buy an army that could put you on Titus' throne.'

'Spare your breath,' snapped Paxus. 'I mean to use the treasure to return Rome to a democracy and destroy the house of the Caesars for good.'

Drexa recoiled from Paxus' words but then he seemed to be brewing something up in his mind.

'You will have a civil war on your hands,' said Drexa.

'Men can be bought,' replied Paxus. 'The Celtic treasure will silence many tongues.' He suddenly felt strangely uneasy in the presence of the crafty politician. Paxus knew that he wasn't as at home with words as Drexa who could hold an audience captive for hours with his narrative skills. Allowing him to live any longer would only encourage him to conjure up more words of distraction. 'Do you have any last words before I hand you over to my commander?'

Drexa cowered, knowing that Commander Secus would show him no mercy. 'Let me live Paxus,' he pleaded. 'I could help you oversee a new Rome, a new empire. With my help, you could be the mightiest emperor the world has ever seen...'

Suddenly, a shout of 'murderer' came from out of the blue shattering the conversation between he and Drexa and he turned to see Daccus approaching. He was holding his left arm tenderly and was sweating profusely. Paxus could tell now that the arrowhead imbedded in Daccus' shoulder was no ordinary arrow. Daccus came right up to the cowering Drexa and spat in his face.

'You murdered my friend, Fario, now I'm going to watch you die like the rat that you are. I hope the soldiers take their time with you, you bastard!'

Upon hearing Daccus' words, Drexa turned away and sobbed bitterly. Then Daccus, severely weakened by his wound, collapsed to the ground. Immediately, Lana and Mumi were at his side but Carl had stayed seated at the side of the road, still feeling groggy from the punches he had received.

'There's nothing you can do for him,' said Paxus to Lana. 'The arrowhead has been dipped in poison.' He withdrew his dagger from his belt and presented it to her. 'You can do him a favour.'

Lana looked up in disgust.

Just then Daccus began to cough. He writhed upon the ground for several moments, kicking violently. Then he rolled over onto his back, coughed up copious amounts of blood and lay still.

Paxus sheathed his dagger, reached down and took out the key from Daccus' pouch. Without a word, he turned away then stopped in his tracks. 'I told you so,' he said without looking back.

Lana watched as Paxus dragged the screaming Drexa towards the soldiers. Then she looked down at the body of Daccus. His face had turned blue.

'Bella,' said Mumi. 'He was poisoned by Bella. It is extracted from many plants and is very potent indeed.'

'He seemed a good man,' said Lana, trying her best to will some emotional attachment to him but failing miserably.

'He raped me many times!' said Mumi.

'What?'

'Always at parties and social events,' she said as she stood up and walked away but then she stopped in mid-stride. 'Don't ask me to help you bury him,' she said without turning.

'Crucify him! Burn him! Cut his balls off!' The calls went up from the soldiers in turn. 'Skin him alive!' With each call Drexa whined and writhed upon the ground, begging with pleading hands for mercy.

'Oh mighty Jupiter take me from this agony, I beg you, I beg you,' he cried.

'Strip him and tie him to that cartwheel,' ordered Secus. 'Let's get this over with, men. We need to get moving.'

The soldiers stripped him in seconds and he was left standing in shame.

Lana was disgusted by the sight of Vitanian's repulsive body but, strangely, felt no pity for the grossly obese magistrate. She resigned herself to the fact that this was going to be yet another example of the brutality that the Romans were so adept at.

The screaming magistrate begged incessantly for mercy as he was lashed to the wheel in a kneeling position but his calls fell on deaf ears as one of the soldiers proceeded to gouge out his eyes. Then his tongue was cut out followed by a crown of woven twigs and dry leaves, which was dipped in olive oil and was placed upon his bald head then set alight. Finally, the soldiers cut open his stomach and pulled out his intestines which were left to hang out on the ground.

Lana forced herself to watch the spectacle despite of it. For some unknown reason she felt that she must, even though her stomach was churning inside. She cared little for the magistrate and wondered how long it would take for him to die. Shocked at how she was feeling, she felt resolute, nevertheless, in her determination to stay true to her belief that she will survive this living nightmare.

Within no time, she found herself sharing a horse with Mumi as she sat astride it with no saddle for comfort. Then Paxus ordered the beleaguered entourage to follow him down the mountain pass and into the dark forest. Carl was given a horse of his own but looked ungainly upon it with no saddle or spurs to aid him. His head had cleared but his face looked puffed up like a boxers after a twelve-round bout though he was still clinging doggedly to his sack containing the camera, phone and watch. She feared for him. He would have to get stronger or die. The journey to Britannia will be long and difficult and she worried that Carl wasn't going to make it. As an afterthought, she glanced back at the dying Drexa. His flaming head exploded from the build-up of gases inside his skull. Bits of cooked brain and sinew burst out like popcorn from an open fire. She cringed from the sight and turned around. Thoughts of home, thoughts of anything that reminded her of her past life flooded her mind as she shut herself away and stared ahead at the looming forest. She decided in that moment to make it her mission to kill Paxus for all it was worth.

A grim-faced Professor Malcolm McVie stared vacantly at Winifred as she explained to him all that had transpired over the past few days. Sam scoured the professor's face with interest, hoping against hope that this man would have a solution to the problem. The young Scottish professor took the news quite well. Not once did he flinch or detract from his concentration. He seemed fascinated by Win's description. After she had finished, he picked up his cup of coffee and took a sip then ground his teeth upon the rim whilst in deep thought. The thin and wiry theoretical physicist had more of the look of an office clerk or an errand boy from a large accountancy firm than a cutting-edge scientist. His wispy ginger hair and boyish complexion seemed at odds with the stature of his profession but his bright green eyes burned with an intellect that Sam found discomforting. He guessed that the professor would win any argument that he'd care to put forward.

Malcolm McVie had duly arrived in Rome at nine in the morning and was picked up by a taxi which was provided by Winifred. It was now just after midday and it was fine and hot outside.

The five colleagues were seated in an adjacent classroom to the main lab at Sapienza University. They were brought to the university by Professor Barnes to meet Francesco Vinci, the head lecturer on physics and astronomy. Whilst Malcolm McVie continued his silent contemplations, Professor Barnes felt the need to wipe the blackboard clean should anyone want to use it. Sam casually glanced at Win in the hope that she could prompt Malcolm into a response but she sat still in her own world of thoughts. Ted passed the time by casting his eyes over the posters and wallcharts of the classroom, examining the representations of the planets, stars and galaxies but not gleaning much from them.

The time ticked by ponderously and just at the point where someone was bound to say something, the door to the room was flung open and in walked a small, diminutive figure of a man. He was dressed in a white lab coat and had a pen tucked behind his right ear. Sam noticed that more pens were protruding from the breast pocket of his coat as he stood in front of the blackboard much like a lecturer would to address his class. He looked to Sam to be in his mid-thirties, with a shock of messy black hair and a brooding disposition that was probably tempered by his devotion to his work. His blue eyes advertised immense intelligence and it seemed to Sam that a conversation with him would leave you feeling intellectually inferior. Professor Barnes shook Francesco's hand and made the customary introductions then sat at a desk ready to hear what he had to say.

'Good afternoon,' said Francesco in a very good Italian-English accent. 'I can confirm that the archaeologists, Carl Allen and Lana Evans, have been physically transported back to ancient Rome in the time of the emperor, Titus. On Saturday evening of

August the twenty-sixth at around eleven-thirty, the dig site that Carl and Lana were working at was indeed hit by what we call a time fold. A time fold is the by-product of a massive jolt of concentrated dark energy that lasts for less than a Nano-second and was the primary cause for Carl and Lana's unfortunate reversal in time. It's obvious from the evidence provided by Professor Barnes and his team that they have survived the incident; the camera and the watch are proof enough. Now, my team and I have the problem of trying to figure out a way of getting them back.'

Francesco seated himself upon the corner of the teacher's desk and waited for a response. It was Malcolm who spoke first.

'May I offer a suggestion,' he said in a broad Scottish accent as he rose from his seat and put his hands in his pockets. He paced up and down for a short while then cast a glance at Sam. Sam had the feeling that Malcolm was going ask him a question that he could not answer but then the young Professor turned away and strolled over to Francesco.

'It is fortunate for us that Sam and Carl happened to be speaking on their phones at the exact moment the... time fold occurred. It's a wild thought, but the two phones may be connected somehow which may have given us an opportunity to open up a window.'

'A window?' asked Sam.

'Yes, connecting the phones may be an option,' said Francesco, excitedly. 'If it can be possible to recreate that moment, then a portal could be opened between then and now.'

'But we have a problem,' replied Malcolm. 'The energy required to keep open such a portal for just a millisecond would be more than the entire power consumption of a large city for a whole year.'

Francesco frowned and crossed his arms in deep thought. An awkward silence pervaded the room for a short while.

'So they're stuck?' said Sam, breaking the silence. 'They are like shadows in time.'

'An apt statement,' replied Francesco, disappointingly.

Sam was crestfallen. It seemed to him that no one had a clue.
'Is that it?' he asked in frustration.
'No, Mr. Allen,' said Francesco. 'The key to getting them back is your phone, but the problem, like Professor McVie has suggested, is power. We need a source of power to generate the energy levels that are required to bring them back. May I have your phone please?'

Sam felt reluctant at first but then he looked to Win, who nodded reassuringly. He reached inside his pocket and pulled out his Nokia touchscreen phone. He handed it to Francesco who then proceeded to open up the back. When Francesco looked inside his eyes widened.

'My god!' he gasped. 'It's true!'

As one, all in the classroom gravitated towards the phone and were shocked when they saw that the phone's battery bore a scorch mark across its surface which was glowing white.

Day after day, village after village, town after town, Paxus' troop were greeted warmly by the locals. The seal of approval, given to him by his uncle was enough to guarantee their safe passage. The gold banded ivory baton depicting an image of Neptune, the god of the sea, was the recognised symbol of his uncle's merchant fleet and local businessmen were eager to do favours in return. The popularity of his uncle could not be overstated. Wherever they went, they were treated as friends, offered prostitutes for free and given food and provisions.

It had been two months since the execution of Drexa in the Alps and Lana guessed that they were now entering northern France. The weather had been glorious for the most part but now there was a distinct chill in the October air ushering in the beginning of winter's arrival.

Lana's previous fears about the boredom of first century travel had been completely misplaced. Riding a horse with no saddle was uncomfortable but every two hours or so they were ordered to walk to rest the horses and to bring back the circulation to their buttocks but all along, the journey for Lana was both beautiful and revealing. She saw countless unspoilt landscapes that showed no sign of human interference. She saw an abundance of wildlife with a plethora of birds, many she did not recognise and she wondered if they had gone extinct over time. At one point they came upon a family of bears foraging for food, a sight that would never be seen in modern day France. The rivers and lakes went by at an easy and peaceful pace and she will never forget the sight of the mountainous passes of Switzerland and Austria as they slowly rolled by in all their glory. Throughout it all, Lana felt herself becoming as one with her surroundings. She knew that if she had passed by in a car or flew over all this magnificence in an airplane, looking out on the world through a window, she would be missing something, something that most of the human population of her time would never witness, busy as they will be with their fleeting lives.

As the glow of the noon-day sun warmed their backs, they came upon a ridge surrounding a gently sloping valley which was run through by a meandering river. A mile further along the river Lana could see a large town, dotted here and there, by a few grand Roman buildings. Paxus casually introduced the village to the troop as Lutetia. Lana and Carl instantly recognised the name. Lutetia was the Roman site of Paris; the modern day city of Paris wouldn't get its name for another nine-hundred years. Lutetia, which meant 'mid-water dwelling', sat boldly upon an island in the middle of the river Seine. It was the largest settlement they had come across since leaving Rome.

An hour later they crossed a stone bridge and entered Lutetia through a triumphal arch made entirely out of wood, which was obviously a replica of one of the arches in Rome.

The town was a hive of activity and it seemed that the locals were preparing for some kind of ceremony.

'Ah, the festival of Equus October to commemorate Mars, the god of war!' announced Paxus.

'We will have a good night tonight,' said Secus. 'I hear the brothels in Lutetia have the finest prostitutes in the northern empire.'

Secus' men laughed aloud in their eagerness to get drunk and get laid.

'Come with me!' ordered Paxus as he turned to Lana, Carl and Mumi. His tone of voice left them in no uncertain terms. He ordered them to dismount and handed their horses over Secus who led his men off to the stables to prepare for a well-earned break. Turning back to the others, Paxus, accompanied by the ever-present Bastia, pointed the way to a large brick-built villa that was set back from the wooden buildings. It stood on a small rise overlooking the town and was obviously an important place. Soldiers patrolled the top of the perimeter wall who stared down apathetically at Paxus' approaching troop. Tiredness was quickly taking hold of Lana's aching limbs and the hope of a hot bath came to mind. She turned and looked to Carl who seemed ready to drop but his eyes were on stalks as he took in the surroundings.

As they walked the short distance to the building, Lana was surprised at how clean and well-ordered Lutetia looked. The people seemed well fed and healthy, unlike most of the residents of the villages they had seen along the way. Children were playing happily in the bright, noon-day sun and there was plenty of food and wares on offer at the market stalls which lined the main road down one side. The opposite side of the main road was lined with several warehouses, a blacksmiths, a tavern and a brothel.

'We are going to meet a certain Drusus Verus,' announced Paxus, suddenly. 'He is the governor of this province and a good friend of my uncle. I will do the talking and don't touch anything.'

Soon they were in the grounds of the building and were presented to Drusus Verus in a rather grand looking courtyard. The man looked to be in his mid-forties with a well-grown beard and a carefully trimmed haircut. His dark eyes looked friendly and welcoming and his demeanour was respectful and courteous but to Lana's surprise she suddenly felt an overwhelming sense of suspicion wash over her. The atmosphere within the courtyard felt laden with threat but she couldn't put her finger on the strange vibe that was causing her to feel at odds with herself.

'Greetings Paxus Strupalo, nephew of Ducia Strupalo, my slaves are yours to command.'

'Thank you for your kind words, Drusus,' replied Paxus, mechanically. 'Your great work in this province has been noted back in Rome. They speak of you in glowing terms in the Curia Julia and in the hallowed halls of the emperor's palace.'

'I try to do my best,' said Drusus as he bowed low in acknowledgement of Paxus' kind words. 'My men are loyal and the locals pay their taxes – simple eh? Now what brings you to this part of the empire?

'We've come to see the festival,' Paxus lied as he moved the conversation on quickly. 'Now let me introduce my travelling companions. This is Lana from Sicilia, Carl from Campania, Bastia from Rome and Mumi, who is a freed slave.'

Drusus eyed them all with an unconvinced look but then bowed to his guests and turned to lead them through a grand doorway resplendent in ornate carvings of victorious battles that had been won throughout Gaul. But no sooner had they entered they were immediately set upon by many rough hands and quickly subdued. Paxus didn't have a chance to unsheathe his sword nor did Bastia who struggled valiantly against the unseen assailants.

Their weapons were removed and in no time at all they found themselves being frogmarched into a cell where they were pushed to the floor, quickly followed by the sound of a heavy door slamming shut behind them. Lana looked around the empty cell noting that the only source of light available was coming from a small grid high in the ceiling. She guessed that the room was about fifteen-feet by fifteen-feet square. The floor of the dank and musky cell was covered with straw and she could make out the remains of dried-out dead things scattered here and there. She suddenly shivered from a cold chill that crept slowly down her spine as she realised that her earlier suspicions had been correct.

Paxus was the first to his feet and immediately tested the door. The others got up from the floor and waited for his response.

He turned to them and shook his head then he slowly walked over and sat down, cross-legged, upon the dank floor to await his fate. The others reluctantly followed suit.

General Catrus Vitrus unbuckled his sword and threw it down upon the table. Drusus Verus' eyes strayed towards the weapon. He felt unsure as to whether it was the right moment to correct the veteran soldier in dining room etiquette. The big man was intimidating enough and a quiet word in his ear could result in an unfortunate incident. But Drusus was not too concerned. Since the general's arrival the opportunity of a political promotion had been forming in his mind. Catrus and his small army had arrived in Lutetia several days before Paxus and the old soldier had informed him that he was under orders from Titus to apprehend the traitor, Drexa Vitanian. Drusus immediately saw this as a chance to further his political ambitions, driven by the desire to return to Rome and to rid himself of the terrible burden of governing this awful outpost.

'Would you like some wine before we eat, general?' asked Drusus in his most courteous tone.

'I never drink whilst I'm under orders.'

'I see,' replied Drusus, feeling terribly annoyed by the big man's demeanour.

'What brings Paxus Strupalo to Lutetia?' asked Catrus.

'I think he is looking for something,' replied Drusus.

'Looking for what?'

'That, I don't know but he has been seen at his uncle's villa and my spies have heard whispers that he is on a secret mission to Britannia.'

'You have spies?'

Drusus paused, still feeling intimidated. 'I am the governor of this province and I need more than one pair of eyes and ears to stay aloof. Let's keep it at that shall we.'

Catrus grinned and then stared at the food on the table. 'I can do with some water to wash it down with?' he asked as he proceeded to tuck into a plate of boiled pigs feet.

Drusus ordered one of his slaves to fetch some water then stared the general down.

'It must have been something of great importance to force Paxus to leave the luxuries of Rome to come to this forsaken place don't you think, general?'

'I do.'

'Do you think Paxus knows anything of Drexa's whereabouts?'

'I think so.'

'How would you know that, general?' asked Drusus, after a long sip of wine.

Catrus pushed his plate of food away and drank a gulp of water provided by the slave then leaned back in his chair. 'After several days of searching the northern territories of Italy, we decided to head through the Alpine pass at Augusta. As you know there is only one mountain pass through the Alps at that point, and on the pass we found the executed remains of a fat man tied to a cartwheel. There was also evidence of a fight; some freshly dug graves of soldiers, dead horses, a smashed up cart, bits of armour and broken lances.'

'Drexa?' asked Drusus.

'Not sure,' replied Catrus, offhandedly. 'I could not make out who it was from what was left of him. There was no ring of office on his finger and there were no distinguishing marks to identify him but if the body was Drexa's, then whoever killed him has what belongs to the emperor. That is why we raced here in the hope that they would pass through.'

'And you think Paxus has what belongs to the emperor?'

'He could,' replied Catrus, sharply.

'Then we must ask him.'

'My immediate concern is his soldiers,' replied Catrus. 'They will soon be growing suspicious. Are you sure your men can handle them?'

'I have seven-hundred conscripts at my command. A hand-full of veterans should be no problem, general.'
'Then let's find out what Paxus knows.'

15

Titus woke early from his sleep, just as he had done every morning since the departure of Berenice. He sat up in his sweat-soaked bed feeling totally bereft of his former lover and no amount of eager women could replace his loss. He looked to the empty side of the bed and sighed heavily. Her absence had triggered a new race for him to father an heir. His daughter, Julia Flavia, from a previous relationship, could never be emperor so it was with earnest that his advisors pushed for him to seek a new woman. But the problem of finding a partner to provide him with a son was proving quite difficult. Many offers from foreign dignitaries, wishing their daughters to be the emperor's chosen one, went by unaccepted. He ignored approaches from high-born Romans too. There were many beauties on offer but none as attractive as his beloved Berenice.

But, of course, the choice of a partner was not his most pressing problem right now. News that the imperial financial status had taken a turn for the worse had floored him. The royal coffers were taking a hammering and no amount of taxes could top-up the dwindling fortune.

The temple money from the raiding of Solomon's palace in Jerusalem, which Titus and his army had triumphantly brought to Rome ten years earlier, was now almost spent. His father had used most of the Jewish hoard to finance the building of the Flavian Ampitheatre and now, with the displacement of thousands of people in Campania, due to the devastation caused by Vesuvius, Titus had used a big chunk of the funds for the relief aid. Now his accountants were knocking at his door on a daily basis asking for more taxes.

He was displeased that the people of Rome were not wholly satisfied by his efforts to aid the unfortunates in Pompeii and the surrounding area of Campania and it was disappointing to hear that the people were growing impatient with progress at the building work on the Flavian Ampitheatre. The Ampitheatre had become a white elephant; a marvel of architectural splendour, with no equal, but nevertheless, a serious drain on the economy. The sooner the games got under way, the better, he thought. But most pressing of all was that there was still no news from Catrus Vitrus in his search to find Drexa Vitanian. Winter was fast approaching and he knew what that meant in the northern territories of the empire. Military activities were routinely put on hold by the Roman army where the soldiers would return to their barracks to sit out the winter, repair their weapons, heal their wounds and have time to reflect and write notes home. Catrus Vitrus will be lucky to convince any northern general to call for extra men, should he need to, and Titus guessed that he will have to wait until springtime for news from the north. In the meantime, all he could do was ponder upon his future.

First of all, he envisioned what a blessing it would be if he could find the Celtic treasure. It would enable him to commission grander monuments and buildings, strengthen the army, build more roads and aqueducts and bribe more foreign kings and queens into the family of the empire. He will ease the burden of taxation upon the public by decree and fund the most magnificent games that have ever been witnessed.

But lately, Titus was beginning to have serious doubts about his reign. He was overcome with terrible feelings of insecurity, suspiciousness and, for the first time in his life, he felt afraid. The brave new world which his father had promised him now seemed a lifetime ago. With all the millions of people that he had dominion over he felt desperately alone; cut off from reality and cut off from humanity. The gods had it in for him. The people had it in for him. His brother had it in for him. The rats were beginning to bite and he had no way of controlling them. So he did what was expected of an emperor. His latest decree was to order the sacrifice of a thousand bullocks near the site of Pompeii to Pluto, the god of the underworld and the judge of the dead. That simple act went down well with the public but he knew he was running out of options to placate his subjects. 'An emperor's path is a crooked one,' his father had once told him, 'but don't ever stray from that path for the wolves of betrayal will have you.'

He sighed and rose from the bed then made his way to the wash room alone. No slaves were allowed to attend his personal needs within the bedchamber. He had ordered that tradition to be suspended whilst he was emperor, feeling embarrassed, as he did, by the attention of body servants. In his own mind he was a soldier first and an emperor second and there was no vanity in him. He poured out some cold water into a trough from a beaker and washed his hands and face then he gargled with a light mixture of vinegar and honey mixed with water to take away the taste of night.

A loud knock to the door of his bedroom made him turn and he stepped back into the room.

'Who is it?'

'It's me, Domitian,' said his brother through the closed doors.

For no reason other than pure instinct, he glanced towards his sword, which was lying upon a table next to his bed, but then he glanced back at the bronze doors.

'Come in,' he announced, reluctantly.

Immediately the doors swung inwards and in walked Domitian, resplendent in his gleaming white toga interwoven with gold beading. His golden sandals skittered loudly across the marble floor as he approached his elder brother. His smile was broad and genuine and Titus warmed to his younger sibling's charms, remembering better days when they were growing up as children.

'What brings you to my chamber so early?' asked Titus.

Domitian said nothing but simply grasped his brother's hand and kissed the jewelled ring of power upon Titus' finger.

'My brother!' announced Domitian. 'The Pontifex Maximus, chief bridge builder, ruler of the world, but still... my brother.'

Titus cringed and let go of Domitian's hand. He grabbed a towel and dried himself quickly then covered up his nakedness with a purple robe. He strode over to a table in the corner of his room and invited Domitian to sit.

Domitian immediately clapped his hands and called out for food to be brought in. Scuffling feet sounded just beyond the doors as the waiting slaves rushed to obey.

The brothers sat opposite each other for a while in an awkward moment of silence. Titus stared his brother down, not knowing what to think. Domitian's looks were boyish and fresh. He seemed not to have a care in the world, as so he shouldn't, he thought.

'I have found the perfect bride for you!' announced Domitian with a broad grin.

Titus squirmed in his seat. 'I think I can manage that myself,' he replied.

'You need a son to succeed you Titus, and you're not getting any younger,' said Domitian. 'Your beloved daughter is worried for you. She knows how much you loved Berenice but she understands that it's time to move on.'

Titus gripped the arms of his seat. His daughter, Julia Flavia, lived in a palatial villa in Tivoli with her mother. The two of them were also a financial burden on the imperial coffers but he could do nothing about that. He also knew that his brother was fucking both of them and he could do nothing about that either. He had made the decision, long ago, to put himself above the incest and deception that the three 'charmers' were embroiled in. He knew that they would get their comeuppance one day and on that day he will feel vindicated.

Two slaves entered with a tray of food each and placed them down at their table, then scurried off as quickly as they had entered. Domitian immediately tucked into a piece of sliced pork dipped in honey.

Titus observed his brother intensely remembering that Domitian was terribly jealous of him. It was unfortunate that he felt that way but understandable. Their father had scorned Domitian as a child for being lazy, 'just like his mother', as he once said. He never showed much attention to him, preferring, instead, to devote all his time and attention to Titus, honing him from birth for leadership. So it was no surprise that Domitian hated his elder brother.

'The woman I speak of is Venora,' said Domitian in between bites. 'She's from Sicilia, you'll like her.'

Titus groaned and bit into a slice of pork himself. It tasted good.

'She's tall, elegant and has a great pair of tits.'

'Oh,' said Titus. 'And does she happen to be an associate of one of your many friends?'

'She is the sister of Tulus Marus, you know, he's the one who holds the record for the most wins at chariot racing in a single day.'

Titus rolled his eyes with boredom. 'Your friends are very colourful,' he replied, sarcastically.

'Would you like to meet her?'

'No, brother,' snapped Titus. 'I would not like to meet her nor any of your friends and their associates. Haven't you heeded my advice and let go of these leeches?'

'My friends serve me well, brother,' replied Domitian as he stopped eating and licked his fingers. 'How many friends have you got left since you became emperor? They've either deserted you or they're dead.'

Titus clenched his fists and slammed them down upon the table. The plates and the trays jumped up and landed with a loud clatter upon the wooden top. Domitian chuckled under his breath and scorned him:

'You may be the soldier of the family, the tough one and I could never beat you in a fight, we both know that. But I have qualities inherited from our mother that you've never had; dedication to my friends, compassion to my slaves, loyalty to the gods and experiencing the joy of life to the full. These things you do not have. You were father's pet. You were enslaved to the army, a brute; a killer of Jews; and as stubborn as an Ox.'

Titus ground his teeth in anger. He knew he could have Domitian killed for what he was saying to his emperor but brothers always talked to each other like this. Status mattered not when siblings argued. Instead, he rose from his seat and strode across the room to the window and looked out across his beloved city. The sun was rising lower in the east with every passing day, casting a diffused shadow across the forum. Winter was definitely on its way and the machinery of the empire will slowly be winding down. Travel will become more difficult and, as a consequence, commerce, trade, information and taxes will suffer. People will freeze in the north, the old and the young will die and Rome will be overwhelmed by refugees seeking shelter and warmth. It seemed that every year the annual flow was growing bigger. Long before Rome had become a small village on the banks of the Tiber the winter migration of people from the north was an annual event. They would simply up and leave their homes and head south to the warmer climates of the southern parts of Italy, but in recent times they began stopping in Rome, looking to be fed and clothed. Previous emperors had been generous and welcoming but that only served to make matters worse. And so, year-on-year the problem was getting out of hand. Now it was time for someone to come up with a solution.

'Winter is coming little brother and I need someone to take charge of the refugees from the north.'

'Why are you telling me this?' asked an incredulous Domitian who sounded distant and indifferent.

Titus turned and made his way back to the dining table. 'The city is already at breaking point with the influx of survivors from Campania,' he said, impatiently. 'The gods underneath Vesuvius did Rome no favours and I fear we will be overrun in the coming weeks.' Titus paused to gauge his brother's mood. Domitian looked bored and seemed to be thinking of other things, entirely. 'You know what that means for Rome, don't you?' pressed Titus.

'Plague,' said Domitian, with a hint of sarcasm in his reply.

'Yes, plague,' said Titus. 'For some reason, the influx of extra people into Rome causes death in the thousands.'

'It's the god's way of cleansing the city,' said Domitian. 'They have done it many times before. But you know this already?'

'It is foolhardy to rely upon the whim of the gods to protect the city that is why I am asking you to accept the honour of saving us from the threat of yet another plague.'

Domitian shook his head slowly and rose from his seat keeping his stare fixed upon his brother. 'I have appointments elsewhere,' he said, flippantly. 'If I where you I would banish all migrants from the north and send them back to where they came from.'

'Then I must order you to take this charge in the name of your emperor.'

In a move that took Titus completely by surprise, Domitian withdrew a dagger from within his toga and slashed out at his brother, cutting his upper left shoulder and leaving a six inch wound. Then he made a stab at his throat but Titus feigned to the right and punched Domitian hard in the jaw. Domitian went down on one knee but came up in a flash slashing out again with his dagger, this time nicking his groin. In a rage, Titus head-butted Domitian square in the face, breaking his nose and leaving him bloodied and dazed. The younger brother fell to the floor screaming in agony. Titus kicked the dagger from Domitian's hand, placed his right foot down on his brother's neck and pressed hard.

'You should die for this,' he said, shocked to the core that his brother tried to murder him. Domitian's eyes bulged as Titus applied increasing pressure to his neck. 'You have no allegiance to your family name and no right to be my successor. I will father a son of my own soon enough, from a woman of my choosing and he will be my rightful heir.' Then Titus released Domitian. 'I pity you, little brother. I pity your pathetic life and friends. Now get out of my sight or I will have you executed for treason.'

Disturbed by the commotion coming from the bedchamber, Tulca, the head slave, rushed in to the room followed by three burly looking companions. He looked genuinely concerned and confused at the sight of the two blood-soaked brothers and seemed at odds with himself.

'My emperor,' he asked, nervously. 'What has happened?'

Titus looked to Domitian who was choking for breath. His bloodied nose was broken and swelling up to a ridiculous size. He watched his brother as he struggled to his feet. Domitian's eyes were full of hate but he said nothing.

'I was showing Domitian a few combat moves and he slipped,' Titus lied. 'See to it that he gets treatment and send in the physician to attend my wounds.'

Tulca bowed in obedience but Titus could see that the wizened old man was not fooled by his words. But he knew that the head slave would keep his tongue and not a word would be said about the unfortunate incident.

Domitian wiped his bloodied nose and cringed with the pain of it. Titus knew his pride would hurt even more when he sees his reflection. His brother was the better looking of the two and women flaunted themselves at him on a daily basis but that will now have to wait a while.

'Take care little brother,' said Titus, mockingly, 'and mind your step on the way out.'

An angry and dazed Domitian exited the bedchamber without uttering a word, followed by Tulca and his assistants. Titus went straight to the bathroom and soaked his wounded shoulder in cold water. The cut was not as deep as he thought but stitches will be needed. The nick to his groin had stopped bleeding but was, oddly, causing him the most discomfort.

He sat for a while and contemplated his brother's state of mind. His estimation of him was seriously off the mark. Domitian clearly wanted to rule. His friends were obviously behind this, egging him on to make a challenge whilst the emperor's popularity was at low ebb. Now Titus knew what he must do. Ideally, Domitian's friends should be gotten rid of. He would only have to give the order and they will be dead within twenty-four hours but that could make his brother more dangerous. Domitian had friends in high places, friends with influence. Because of that he decided that he will order him to be watched, day and night. His every move and whoever he talks to shall be reported. It was a dangerous profession being an emperor and an emperor needed eyes and ears everywhere at all times.

The door to the cell was quickly unlocked and in walked Drusus followed by a taller man and eleven fully armed soldiers. The captives stood at once, wondering what was going to happen next. Lana's eyes strayed to the tall, brutish looking man, who was dressed in an officer's uniform. He took a short stride up to Paxus but Paxus stood his ground bravely.
'Paxus Strupalo!' announced the soldier, who looked to be past his best days. 'What brings you to this part of the world?'
Paxus stared out the soldier, eye-to-eye, then smiled a wry smile.
'General Catrus Vitrus,' replied Paxus as he turned and announced it to all in the cell, 'known to his men as the Hammer; champion of many battles and a slaughterer of women and children.'
The old soldier grimaced and placed his hand threateningly upon the hilt of his sword. The motion did not go unnoticed by Paxus who smiled back at him.
'Why are you here?' asked the general once more.
'Why, general, we have come to observe the festival of Equus October, of course.'
'I see,' said the Hammer, unconvinced by Paxus' words. 'I seek the traitor Drexa Vitanian. I am wondering whether you have seen him whilst on your travels.'
Lana took an instant dislike to the soldier. He seemed hardened by the military; an institutionalised automaton that enjoyed taking orders and following them to the letter.

'Drexa Vitanian?' asked Paxus with a disguised surprise. 'Why would that fat bastard leave the comfort of Rome to head north?' he lied.

'Because he's stolen something belonging to the emperor and I have a guess that you know of its whereabouts,' said Catrus. 'Search them!' he ordered his men.

Seven soldiers stood guard whilst four searched each captive one-by-one. They snatched Carl's sack first and handed it to Catrus whilst they carried on searching the rest. Catrus promptly tipped the contents out onto the floor and toe-poked each item in turn.

'What the fuck are these?' he asked Carl, in a gruff voice. Governor Drusus stepped out from behind Catrus and picked each item up off the floor. He stared in puzzlement at the camera, phone and watch.

'Answer the general?' he ordered Carl who stood shaking and looking lost for words.

'They... they are the tools of... my trade,' replied Carl, unconvincingly.

'Oh, and what strange trade is this you speak of?' asked Drusus.

'Never mind that,' butt-in Catrus, 'search Paxus,' he ordered.

The soldiers fleeced Paxus and quickly removed a large key from inside his pouch. It was immediately offered up to Catrus who inspected it closely. The bronze key was about eight inches long and hefty. A human skull with ruby eyes was carved into the handle giving it a sinister look.

'This looks like a key to a very large door or a gate,' he pondered loudly.

'It looks more like a key to a vault,' suggested Drusus.

Paxus stood his ground in silence, not daring to show any change in emotion.

'I recognise Celtic craftsmanship when I see it,' continued Drusus. 'What would you be doing with a Celtic key on your person, Paxus?'

Paxus stood stone-faced. His eyes pierced Drusus and Catrus in turn then he relaxed his posture and smiled wryly. 'What if I told you that this key can unlock the doors to a treasure hoard worth the entire wealth of the empire - twice over?'

A silence descended upon the cell like a veil. Everyone held their breaths for the briefest of moments and for different reasons. Then Bastia cursed under his breath and turned away. Carl and Lana's jaws dropped open in shock at what Paxus was revealing to his captors. By the surprised look upon the governor and the general's faces Paxus felt obliged to elaborate more on what he had just said.

'… A treasure so vast that every man, woman and child in the empire could live out the rest of their lives in splendid comfort.'

After a long silence, Drusus spoke in a barely audible tone:

'I have heard whispers of rumours and myths spread in these parts about a Celtic treasure hidden in Britannia, of all places!'

'Whispers and rumours,' spat Catrus, 'that's all they are.'

'You have heard them too?' asked Drusus.

'I have,' replied Catrus, looking most annoyed. 'I have heard from the lips of drunken soldiers and whores, crazy sailors and beggars alike,' he said scornfully. 'There is no treasure, none whatsoever.'

'No?' asked Paxus. 'What if I told you that the stories are true and that I know where the treasure is?'

A look of surprise crossed Catrus' face and he turned to Drusus. 'So you were right, he is looking for something.'

'Why are you so forthcoming in telling us such news?' asked Drusus, inquisitively.

'Because I need an army for protection in the wilds of Britannia and General Catrus Vitrus here is the perfect commander for just such a job.'

Bastia could hold his tongue no longer and stepped forward to speak:

'What are you doing Paxus?' he asked in a rage.

Paxus raised a hand for silence. 'It would be folly to trek across a strange land full of savages without at least a moderate sized army for protection. The Britannic tribes are dangerous and

~ 204 ~

unpredictable, are they not, general?' Catrus nodded but said nothing in reply.

'You planned this all along, didn't you?' said Bastia, sounding most annoyed at this turn of events.

'I planned to raise a small army, yes, but I hadn't foreseen that it could be led by the legendary Hammer,' Paxus admitted, 'and as a politician I seize upon opportunities whenever I can. It is most fortunate that the general is here. My original intention was to ask for the assistance of Drusus and his men but now we have an experienced commander to aid us.'

'You're forgetting one thing, Paxus,' said Catrus. 'You haven't asked me.'

'Then if Drusus will oblige maybe we could go somewhere more comfortable where I can make you an offer you can't refuse.'

Never one for passing up the promise of monetary gain, Drusus immediately dismissed his soldiers and took Paxus and his colleagues out of the cell, through the halls of his villa and into a grand dining area. He ordered his slaves to bring food and wine which was promptly placed upon the long wooden table and all tucked heartily into the fare on offer. Paxus was handed back his key and soon he began explaining his quest to the two men who both stared back open mouthed at his address. The politician held nothing back except Bastia's lineage and Lana's knowledge as to the location of the isle of Anglesey. Throughout his speech, Lana couldn't help but feel that Paxus was revealing too much to two very dangerous men. She understood that they would need a small army for protection but she couldn't shake off the feeling that the men opposite were not to be trusted and for different reasons. Governor Drusus looked sly and devious whilst the general seemed loyal to Rome and would turn them all over to the emperor on a whim.

As the meal dragged on, Lana found herself becoming more and more detached from the proceedings and a great longing for home overwhelmed her once more. On impulse, she took Mumi by the hand and walked her out into the garden. Drusus didn't bat an eyelid as they passed by such was his fascination with Paxus' promise of treasure.

The sun was beginning its descent into the west as Lana sat with Mumi upon a wooden bench and looked around the splendidly appointed garden. The typical set up, as for all Roman villas, was present here; a central fountain adorned by a god or a goddess surrounded by a low wall with a neatly laid mosaic pathway that looked exquisitely crafted. Hanging baskets and vines surrounded the rectangular building and the aroma of various flowers filled her nostrils.

'It's going to get tougher from now on, Mumi,' she said, almost without thinking. 'Once we cross the English Channel things will happen so fast that I fear we may become lost to each other.'

'What is an English Channel?' Mumi asked, innocently.

Lana laughed and cried at the same time but her heart was heavy with longing and she fell into Mumi's arms, weeping sombrely for long moments. Mumi allowed her to cry and began stroking her hair but was surprised when some of it fell out in great clumps. Lana sensed the feeling and was shocked to see Mumi with her hands full of black hair. She cried out for home and sobbed bitterly this time. After a while, Mumi forced herself away and stared Lana in the eye.

'There is something I have to tell you,' she said.

'What is it, my dear?' asked Lana as she wiped away the tears and held Mumi's hands in hers.

'I am pregnant!'

Lana stopped breathing for a while then released her grip from Mumi's hands.

'But who…?' stuttered Lana innocently. Mumi stayed silent allowing the words to sink in. She watched as Lana's expression went from dumbfounded to realisation then exasperation all in a few seconds.

'Not Carl?' asked Lana sounding terribly shocked at the thought. 'When… how… where?'

'In the barn back at the villa in Augusta,' replied Mumi sounding a little afraid. 'When the baby is born I will cast it into a river and be done with it.'

In the shadows beneath an archway, Carl stood and watched Lana go through all sorts of emotions as she tried to explain to Mumi about the sanctity of life and how the baby should not be considered an inconvenience. Tears welled in his eyes but for some unknown reason he couldn't bring himself to join the conversation. He had his own demons to deal with. Two-thousand years adrift in time was a dilemma beyond comprehension. His feelings for home were just as powerful as Lana's but his introverted way of dealing with it was keeping him sober on thoughts of getting home. Now, the revelation that Mumi was pregnant had turned his upside-down world inside-out. He cursed himself for falling for his base instincts. He had to think quickly. He was to be a father for the first time in his life. The dilemma he now found himself in would be a major distraction. He had to stay focused. The best chance for them to get home was for him to keep a clear head and think. He looked down at his sack. For some unknown reason, he had been given the camera, phone and watch back and he stared down at the sack absentmindedly. The Romans had obviously showed no interest in the modern marvels that he had in his possession. Then, without knowing why, he opened up the sack and took out the phone. He flipped it open hoping it would spark back to life but, of course, it was dead. In a last ditch effort he turned it over and opened up the back to see if he could prompt life back into it. The cover came away easily and he carefully removed the battery then, to his utter astonishment, he saw that the battery was scorched along the length of its back like a miniature streak of lightning frozen in time but the most surprising fact was that it was glowing white. Then a thought flashed through his mind and it made him jump. Without further ado, he silently slinked back into the shadows to ponder upon his thought.

16

Two days later, Lana found herself mounted upon a horse and on her travels once again. There was a distinct chill in the early morning air, reminding her that winter had definitely arrived. The two-day festival of Equus October was over and all around here lay the evidence for it. Broken barrels of wine scattered the main street; half eaten animal carcasses lay in the dirt and were being fought over by scavenging dogs. The incredible notion that she was riding across the same ground that would, one day, become the city of Paris seemed a world away. But at this moment in time her main thought was the daunting task of crossing the English Channel and entering a wild and unspoiled Britain.

She harkened back to her childhood memories of the southern coast of England. Her father had often holidayed there, taking his daughter to the lovely coastal towns and villages of Hampshire, Dorset and Sussex but soon she was about to see the area bare of its picturesque buildings and harbours; no ice-cream vans or fairground rides; no piers to walk along or speedboat rides, which she loved so very much as a child - all yet to be.

Her dread of the journey ahead was filling her with fear and trepidation. What horrors awaited them all? What path will this foolish quest lead them on? Who will live and who will die? Her heart was racing as she looked to Carl mounted upon his ride. He seemed withdrawn into deep thoughts of his own. His once handsome features had deserted him. He looked more like a hobo than a respected archaeologist. He was still clinging to the now useless items in his battered old sack, but as she had concluded before, those items were his only link to reality; they were the only things keeping him from going crazy. And now with the added complication of Mumi's pregnancy it was small wonder he hadn't topped himself. She had wanted to talk with him about how foolish he had been by getting Mumi pregnant and how it could jeopardise their chances of survival but she didn't have the heart to carry it through. There was no jealousy or ill will towards him, only pity. He looked pathetic sitting upon his horse and she feared for his sanity. On the other hand, Mumi seemed indifferent to it all, showing a calm restraint.

Behind Lana followed six-hundred foot soldiers belonging to Drusus' garrison whilst alongside them rode the forty soldiers of General Catrus Vitrus' troop; young and green behind the gills but well trained. Also on horseback were Bastia and Paxus riding alongside Secus and his veterans. The old soldiers eyed the rest with suspicion. Paxus had spent hours persuading them that they needed more men. In fact, Lana found his power of persuasion most impressive. Oddly though, Catrus Vitrus, a highly experienced and loyal officer, was easily persuaded by Paxus after a lengthy discussion to discard direct orders from his emperor and join him on his quest. And as for Governor Drusus, he jumped at the request without hesitation, demanding a sizeable percentage of the treasure in return for offering the services of his soldiers.

The following four days took the miniature army north towards the coast and in the late afternoon on the fifth day they spotted the channel. At this point many of the soldiers made signs to their gods. The fear of crossing the Britannia Sea, as the Romans called the English Channel, was very real. This was the edge of the world for some of them and Britain was seen as a mystical, mythological place. The stories of witches and druids who could conjure up dangerous magic ran wild amongst the ranks but commanding officers shunned such tales, often quoting that it was the Brits who made up the stories to frighten off superstitious foreigners.

They made camp along the beach at Morini Port which Lana guessed was probably somewhere in Normandy. She had no way of knowing if this may be one of the beaches where so many soldiers had died during the D-Day landings which, to her, seemed a very long time ago in the distant future. This odd paradox was a constant refrain in her thoughts and it bothered her like an annoying fly that wouldn't go away.

Morini Port was full of vessels of all sizes, moored and ready for loading. It was large and thronging with people. The decision to camp on the beach was made by General Vitrus to keep secrecy a priority. From experience, he knew that any mere whisper of their quest would spread like wildfire throughout the port. News from anywhere was ceased upon by the townsfolk in the northern territories of the empire for they saw themselves as being the last to know anything coming out of Rome.

Lana sat with Mumi upon a small sand dune at a spot set aside for the two women whilst the soldiers went about making camp. Paxus was going out of his way to ensure their safety and comfort and in no time at all a tent was erected for them both. As night fell, the two women retired to their tent which was comfortable enough in the circumstances. Before long, Carl showed up and was welcomed inside. He sat and ate in silence but as soon as he had finished his meal he quickly opened his sack and brought out the phone. He removed the back cover and showed the battery to Lana. He smiled broadly and spoke in English for fear of someone listening from beyond the tent:

'Look Lana, do you see that glow?'

Lana glanced down at the battery and could see a faint glowing and pulsating, thin white streak across the black surface.

'What the...?'

'Don't touch it!' he ordered, protectively. 'I think it could be our ticket home.'

'What?'

'That glow is a connection... a tenuous thread through time that will take us back to where we belong.'

Lana looked up at him, checking to see if he had finally gone mad but he seemed sincere.

'It figures,' said Carl as he replaced the cover and put the phone back in the sack.

'What figures?' asked Lana with disdain.

'I've been thinking about it. There must have been a tremendous surge of energy that sent us back through time, something so powerful that it lingers on in the battery.'

'But what's keeping the energy going when the battery is dead?'

'I reckon that the battery is still connected to our time,' replied Carl, 'and the energy is flowing through it from the future to the past and vice-versa.'

'Oh and how can that be when the battery is here?'

'Simple, the energy flowing through the battery is operating in its own time but we physically brought it here with us when we were 'zapped' here.'

'Are you saying that this... energy... also exists in the future... in two places at one time?'

'Not two places at one time... but in two places at two times. That's how Sam was able to talk to me that night in the barracks. Somehow, a kind of worm-hole exists that transcends time – back and forth.'

'And you've figured this out all by yourself?'

After a quick nod and a short pause, Carl spoke in a whisper. 'I've figured something else out too.'

'Oh, and what's that, pray-tell,' snapped Lana, her patience was wearing thin. 'Is Captain Kirk going to turn up on board the Starship Enterprise and beam us up?'

'My guess is that the battery in Sam's phone bares this same mark and the two are linked. I'm sure our people back home know this and are working on it.' Carl paused and flashed a thinly disguised smile back.

This time Lana could not contain her feelings as she grimaced at Carl. 'You've finally lost your marbles, haven't you?'

Carl straightened up in surprised as Lana continued:

'I've seen you struggling with your thoughts,' she said whilst trying her best to contain herself. 'I think you've given up the will to survive. Look at me. I've kept my wits about me whilst you mope about feeling sorry for yourself and now this. This pathetic idea that we can go back is never going to work. We're lost, Carl, lost forever.'

'But Lana I know it can work, the link is there, I'm sure that's the key.'

Lana shut her mind away and buried her face in her hands. 'Get out. Get out of my tent,' she screamed through her fingers.

Carl reluctantly made his way out of the tent without a further word.

After a long spell of silence she dropped her hands and sighed. She felt sure that she will be sorry for her outburst by the morning but his proposal seemed more preposterous than their actual situation. She wondered if she did the right thing by confronting him, but then her concentration was distracted when a warm hand touched hers. It was Mumi.

'Can you explain what you were talking about?'

Catrus Vitrus spat a morsel of pork into the campfire and burped loudly. 'That piece of meat is rotten,' he complained to Drusus who was sitting opposite him upon an upturned barrel. All contents of the three carts that they had brought with them from Lutetia had been off-loaded onto the beach. The camp resembled a small town that would attract curious locals but Catrus had ordered a perimeter of guards every ten feet.

'It was the only meat left after the festival,' replied Drusus.

'It looks like my soldiers and I will have to live off the land from now on.'

'I can do that, general. I was a soldier once, you know,' said Drusus.

'Oh yeah, what legion?' asked Catrus, mockingly.

'I was no legionnaire. I was an Agremensor - a surveyor.'

'A road builder?' laughed Catrus.

'I surveyed the land for the building of forts and out-posts.'

'You never saw active service then?'

'No, but I trained for it.'

Catrus laughed to himself and turned to Paxus who was casually sharpening his sword. 'Maybe you could order this amateur into the tent with the ladies where he will feel safer.'

'I can fend for myself, general,' replied Drusus as he stood up to stare Catrus down. Catrus didn't even care to look up at the governor. 'I would like to remind you, general,' continued Drusus, 'that I have six-hundred soldiers at my command, all of whom are loyal to me.'

Catrus shook his head and pointed towards Paxus. 'Your men are loyal to him now.'

Drusus was stunned into silence and immediately sat back down to contemplate the meaning of the general's words.

'Don't worry, Drusus,' said Paxus after a short while. 'Your men will respect you even more as long as they get their cut and can return home to their families with their arms full of gold.'

After a long pause, Drusus stood again and walked off into the night to camp with his men.

'He looks scared,' said Catrus.

'Maybe, maybe not,' replied Paxus.

'Well, he should be. A foray into Britannia is not the first item on the list of the conquests of the average soldier. Britannia is a bad place.'

Paxus stopped sharpening his sword and looked the battle-hardened general up and down for a moment then he spoke:

'What do you remember of Britannia?'

Catrus stared hard into the flames of the fire and crossed his arms whilst he recalled his memories. 'The worst thing is the weather; the wind, the rain and the cold. How people can thrive in such conditions is beyond me? I served under Vespasian on many campaigns throughout the empire and all of them were glorious but victory in Britannia was, somehow, underwhelming and tainted by doubt. There was always a lingering feeling that we, as an army, had achieved nothing. Some of my best men died a terrible death upon the battlefields of Britannia, and for what? It's true that here are resources to mine in Britannia, but all that effort for such scant reward never seemed to justify the sacrifices made by the soldiery. Morale in the ranks was low at the best of times and when morale is low rumours are rife.'

'What kind of rumours?'

'Some said that Rome wanted to conquer Britannia so the emperors could learn the magic of the druids and become more powerful whilst others speculated on finding the mythological unicorn or cures for illnesses and there was even a rumour of a valley full of beautiful six-foot tall women who would allow you to fuck them 'til your heart's content.'

Paxus frowned and sheathed his sword. 'The imagination runs wild when speculation is all we have to go on.'

'That's true,' said Catrus keeping his eyes fixed upon the flames. 'So what's a politician's opinion on the conquest of Britannia?'

'I had an opinion once,' replied Paxus, on reflection, 'but all that has changed now.'

'Changed, because of the treasure?'

Paxus smiled to himself.

'The reason why Rome chose to cross the Britannia Sea is the same reason why we are about to.'

Catrus cocked his head and stared hard at Paxus. The general's glowing face, reflected in the campfire light, was ablaze with astonishment and disbelief all at once.

'Yes general, it has all been a ruse since the time of Claudius,' said Paxus. 'It was he who discovered that the Celtic treasure was buried across the Britannia Sea. That is why his conquest to conquer Britannia succeeded where others failed. His quest became a lifelong obsession but he never found the treasure. The task has since been handed down to succeeding emperors in absolute secrecy.'

'So Titus knows about the treasure and your key?'

'Yes,' replied Paxus. 'The key was kept safe in a box; the box that Titus ordered you to bring to him.'

'Then it was fortunate for us that you stopped Drexa Vitanian from getting his grubby hands on the treasure.'

'That's true.'

'But if it was an emperor's secret, how did you come to know of the treasure's whereabouts?' asked Catrus, out of curiosity.

'That's a long story and soon I will tell it to you, but for now, I will retire for the night.' Paxus stood and made ready to leave.

'Wait one moment,' said Catrus as he stood up to his full height. 'If you need me to lead this rag-tag army of yours into a wild and dangerous country I think I deserve the right to know just how you became aware of the treasure's location and just exactly where I am about to lead them.'

For once, Paxus was lost for words. He needed to protect Lana and Carl at all costs. If he was to let anyone know that it was they alone who knew the location of the treasure it would leave them vulnerable. He paused for a brief moment and then smiled back at the general.

'If I told you of the treasure's whereabouts the quest will be compromised,' he replied in a calm voice. 'It is better that only I should know, for now.'

'Then you'd better hope that I keep you alive, for now,' snapped Catrus with a hint of a threat in his voice. 'But then, what's to stop you from slitting my throat after I get you to within a mile of the treasure, eh?'

Paxus turned and bowed courteously.

'Good night general. Tomorrow will see the beginning of a great adventure - for both of us.' He made a move to walk off but Catrus was persistent.

'Wait a moment. What's with your women friends and the two men? Who are they - really?'

Paxus turned to Catrus and smiled back. The wily old soldier was smarter than he let on. 'The shorter man is an Arverni King whilst the other man and the white woman are from a far off land they call America - the land of the free.'

Catrus chuckled to himself not believing a word of it. 'And don't tell me, the black bitch, she's the Queen of Sheba, right?'

Once again Paxus bowed and smiled broadly then made off into the night leaving the general to ponder.

Sam was handed a note halfway through his board meeting. It was Winifred. She had asked to meet him right away. He excused his managers and immediately left the room. It had been nearly three months now since Carl had vanished and not a word from Rome. He had come home from his trip none the wiser. Carl and Lana's mysterious disappearance was still unresolved. The media had rumoured that they had become recluses and assumed new identities. The National Geographic put up a reward of one-million dollars to anyone who could offer information in finding the two archaeologists. But Sam knew this was a disguise; a clever ploy by Ted Brooks to keep the media guessing. Sam also knew the scientists in Rome were working day and night to resolve the problem of bringing Carl and Lana back from the past – a thought that still sat heavily on his mind. If news got out that Carl and Lana had travelled back to the time of the emperor Titus careers will be under threat. Questions about the state of the mentality of Ted Brooks, the head of The National Geographic, and Sam, a CEO of a steel company, will be asked. Scorn and incredulity, mockery followed by suspicion will rear their ugly heads and the disclosure of the truth will be demanded by the authorities. It was a difficult situation that Sam was in. He had returned to the US and tried his best to carry on as normal but nosy investigative journalists were constantly on his tail. Local TV stations were not giving up the goat and even suspicions of murder were uttered.

Sam made sure he was alone and rang Winifred back immediately from his office phone. The phone had not been tapped, that was one of the first things he took care of upon his return.

'Sam, Ted Brooks wants you to come to Washington right away.'

'What is it, Win?'

'They've found a solution.'

*

Within three hours Sam was sitting in Ted Brook's office riddled with anticipation and expectation all at once. Winifred Bainbridge was seated next to him looking anxiously towards Ted who was on the phone to Professor Francesco Vinci in Rome. Something had happened, something new had cropped up and Sam's nerves were being torn to shreds by the second as he tried to catch snippets of Ted's conversation. He heard the mention of wormholes and the space time continuum and the cosmological constant, all of which were now familiar phrases after he had avidly read many science books since returning home from Rome. His wife Linda had, sort of, half-believed the closely guarded secret that Carl was lost in time but she had encouraged him to read up on the subject and he threw himself into it with relish. The great books of Carl Sagan, Laurence Krauss, Kip Thorne and Paul Davies were read in weeks and now, armed with a bastion of information, Sam felt he could handle himself better when confronted with the mindboggling stuff he was up against.

Ted finished his phone call and replaced the receiver. He glanced up at the two opposite him and sighed.

'What is it, Ted?' asked Sam, impatiently.

'We're off to Rome. Professor Vinci wants us there for when they try...'

'Try what?' cried Sam.

Ted stood and made his way to the drinks cabinet and quickly poured himself some Bourbon. After swallowing the contents of the glass in one gulp he turned and spoke with a tremble in his voice.

'They're going to try to make contact with Carl and Lana.'

Exactly at the same time Ted had spoken to Sam and Winifred, four-thousand miles away in Rome, Carmarello De Conte, a nineteen year old Italian archaeology student, was scratching her way through a pile of dirt near the base of the fresco at Carl and Lana's dig site and came across a large bronze key. She cleaned off the dirt, raised it up to eye level and looked at it in wonder. She could only guess what lock the key could have once opened? It was heavy, worn and a little grubby after so long in the ground. She cleared the dirt away from the handle to inspect it more closely and soon noticed the form of a human skull encrusted with ruby eyes. She quickly placed the key into her tray and headed back to the field tent. The tent was occupied by Natalie and Stephan, two French students who were busily cleaning the day's findings. It was already dark and Carmarello had promised to meet with Vito for a few drinks. She would be late for her date if she stayed to itemise the new find so she slipped the key silently into her handbag and quickly left. The key can be cleaned and categorised in the morning, she thought as she headed off into the night for her romantic rendezvous.

A shadowy figure detached itself from a doorway and followed Carmarello into the night. The narrow, quiet streets in the suburbs of Rome was perfect cover for what she was about to do. The expert killer moved like a phantom. Tall, dark haired and athletic looking, she slinked up behind her target and rammed a seven inch dagger deep into the back of Carmarello's neck. Carmarello fell forward, smashing her face into the cobblestone path with such force that her skull cracked open.

The assassin quickly removed the dagger and searched the dying student's handbag. She pulled out the skull key along with her phone and purse to make it look like a mugging. Looking around for any sign of witnesses and finding the street completely deserted she walked back the way she had come. When she turned a corner she took out her mobile phone and rang her paymaster.

'The duck is in the water.'

There was no reply from her paymaster, only a heavy breathing. Then the call was ended. The assassin looked up the hill at the dome of Saint Peter's Basilica and scurried off to her rendezvous point.

17

The shale beach couldn't be less welcoming for the miniature army as they landed their boats at Cantium, which would one day become the English county of Sussex. The grim scene before them did little to raise their spirits after a difficult five hour voyage across the rough waters of the channel. The rickety boats had been tossed about the waves like matchsticks. Some of the occupants were overcome by sea sickness whilst others began to rue their decision. It was now around midday and the sky was clouding over ominously. Lana, Carl and Mumi were shaken but not unwell. The three looked up and down the beach feeling grateful to be on terra firma once more but not overjoyed at the prospect of spending the night camped in such bleak isolation.

High upon the cliff stood a collection of huts and shacks but they had been abandoned by their owners for the winter. A wooden set of stairs meandered their way up the cliff face to the buildings but there would be no one there to greet them. Above, the ever-darkening sky was brewing up a storm so the soldiers quickly made haste in retrieving their provisions from the boats. Once they took stock, they dragged the sixteen sailing vessels up the beach, flipped them upside down and lashed them to the mooring posts.

The journey across the channel was overshadowed by the fact that only three hundred of Drusus' soldiers found the courage to sail across the Britannic Sea, the others had decided, at the last moment, to stay and return to Lutetia. Their superstitions of Britannia had gotten the better of them but Bastia was outraged with Paxus that he had allowed three-hundred men, who had knowledge of their quest, to stay home. Paxus had reminded him that the location of the treasure was a secret and that any following bandits wishing to muscle in on their prize would spend years trying to find the whereabouts of their small troop. Bastia was duly persuaded but he didn't disguise the fact that he was disappointed.

The miniature army were ordered by Catrus to ascend the stairs before the storm struck. But no sooner had the troop gathered up their provisions and began making their way up, the heavens opened. In a rush, they made it to the top and headed for the abandoned shacks that were assembled in random clusters. Lana, Carl and Mumi found themselves huddled together with a group of soldiers inside a large wooden-built structure. The building was obviously a store of some kind, built to hold bulky stock. Deep impressions of large square objects were evident in the earthen floor and Lana could only guess at what had been stored here.

The rainstorm battered the coast for almost two hours as the drenched occupiers sat it out in almost total silence. Lana's earlier fear of being in close proximity to the soldiers who might be tempted into abusing her and Mumi were waylaid. In fact, she was surprised at how preoccupied they were with the storm. Some of the soldiers incessantly prayed to their gods, whilst others were riddled with apprehension bordering on fear. She recalled that in these times storms where interpreted as the wrath of the gods and by the reaction of the soldiers it must have seemed to them that the Britannic gods did not want them here. The tension was very real and she found that she could only sympathise with them for they would not understand the explanation that the storm was actually due to temperature variations caused by fluctuations in the barometric pressures of the upper and lower atmospheres.

When the rains finally broke and the clouds cleared, Catrus assembled the troops together to plan out their journey. After a short briefing the bedraggled soldiers seemed unwilling to go a step further. Catrus' assurances could not sway their misgivings and it came to a point where a decision had to be made. Paxus decided to speak to the soldiers in an attempt to convince them. He stood upon a low wall that surrounded a large monolith; a sure sign that stone-aged people were here long before the natives of Roman Britain.

'You are all volunteers and you have the right to change your minds and return home,' he said in his statesman's voice. 'But you will not receive any gold reward should we be successful in finding the treasure. The choice is yours; go home and live as before or stay with me and be rich enough to build your own villa, have your own slaves, drink the finest wine and choose the best women to keep you warm in bed at night.'

The soldiers looked dumbfounded and terribly unsure of themselves. Paxus didn't want to lose any more men so he decided to up the offer to twice the amount of gold that they were previously guaranteed. Unsurprisingly, this had the desired effect as the men voted, unanimously, to carry on. Drusus rubbed his hands gleefully at the news and ordered his men not to change their minds. The soldiers said nothing.

With great relief, Catrus set out his plans for them to trek fourteen miles west across country to the Roman fort at Noviomagus. They needed horses and a cart for their provisions and he was adamant that the commander at Noviomagus would be generous enough to rent them out to him. Lana, Carl and Mumi were each given dry clothes, standard footwear and a heavy cloak made of animal hide to keep them warm. Within the hour, they found themselves trekking across fields of open grassland, past herds of wild sheep and cows. Lana was surprised at the apparent lack of trees. She could have been strolling through modern day Sussex for all she knew but Carl had assured her that the days of when you could go from Land's End to John O'Groats without touching the ground because Britain was covered in a blanket of trees had since long gone. Early bronze aged man had seen to that.

As the day wore on, the sun began its descent to the west. The sky was clear but a chill from the ground up was making the walk uncomfortable. Then the small army came upon a well-worn pathway which meandered through fields and brush, over hills and dales. The first thing that struck Lana was the total absence of people along the trail. There were no buildings or settlements to be seen either and it made her wonder just what the population of Britain was during the Roman occupation. The best estimation by modern-day historians was around four-million but, so far, the southern fields of England seemed bereft of human life.

After two hours of drudgery, Carl and Lana's feet began to ache incessantly. The sturdily constructed sandals that they had been provided with, which the Roman army wore for long marches, were wholly inadequate for their modern day feet which were used to trainers and slippers. Although they wore socks, which themselves were not very comfortable, blisters began to form under the ball of their big toes and every step was becoming a task as the relentless march went on. Then, after another arduous hour, Catrus finally called a halt. The sun was now touching the western horizon and soon darkness will shroud them. They were now just two miles from their destination and Catrus sent two scouts ahead to make sure that Noviomagus was still standing; a regular tactic employed by the army to make sure that the fort had not been attacked by an enemy.

The troops were ordered into a small wooded area to rest up and await the scouts' return. Paxus asked Lana, Carl and Mumi to sit aside from the soldiers and then went off to consult with Catrus and Drusus with the ever present Bastia in tow.

Lana sat beneath a tree with her back to the trunk. She slipped off her sandals and socks and began massaging her aching feet thinking how much she missed her Minnie Mouse slippers back home. Carl was following suit, but he seemed deeply withdrawn and unwilling to make conversation.

'Carl, I'm sorry for my outburst the other day. It was unfair and unjustified,' said Lana in English.

Carl simply smiled back at her and sighed.

'Did you mean what you said about us getting back?' she asked, nicely.

'Of course I did,' replied Carl without looking up from his massaging efforts. 'It's just that...'

'What?'

'It's just that I wish I had thought of it earlier, when we were in Rome. Now we're hundreds of miles away on this foolish errand and no foreseeable chance of getting back.'

'But surely Carl, the possibility of us returning back to our time is nil. You must know that.'

Carl looked up and stared blankly at Lana without a word passing his lips. He seemed disappointed in her and went back to his massaging.

A long spell of awkward silence passed between the two of them and they fell into a world of their own thoughts.

'It's dark,' said Mumi, breaking the silence. 'We must get some sleep.'

Lana could tell that Mumi was disturbed by the sound of her conversation with Carl. It was unfortunate in the circumstances but she would not understand any kind of explanation of their predicament no matter how simply Lana would choose to put it. To Mumi, life had always been simple and uncomplicated, which is something that modern day humans had lost over time. The peoples of both worlds may as well be alien beings from different planets such was the vast gulf in technology and knowledge. And yet, Lana felt that she will have a lot to learn from Mumi; things that she had forgotten, experiences that she had never had and ways of looking at things from a different perspective. She nodded to Mumi and cuddled up to her and her ever-growing bump for warmth. The two were asleep in no time.

The following hours passed slowly for Catrus as the camp fell into a lull. He watched his rag-tag army from his resting place noticing that most of the soldiers were asleep whilst a group of younger men played a game of knucklebones, which were made out of the ankle bones of sheep or goats, in which you had to throw up one of the knucklebones and scoop up as many of the others that you could then catch the first one before it hits the ground. Perhaps they were gambling away their fortune of gold, he thought, as he yawned and stretched his ageing limbs but pretty soon his thoughts turned to his decision to take up Paxus' challenge to go in search of the Celtic treasure. He knew this will be his last escapade. The onslaught of age had seen to that, but the alternative was retirement and that didn't sit well with him. He hated the idea. He had been officially retired for nine months now but that was already too long. He was a soldier through-and-through and this chance of glory offered by Paxus will be his swansong. In a strange kind of way he liked Paxus. The politician reminded him of himself as a younger man; eager, ambitious and restless. To Catrus the Celtic treasure did not matter much. His pension was decent and the land and possessions he had amassed throughout his illustrious career would see him live comfortably for another lifetime. He knew it was foolhardy to be going against his emperor's orders but in the same breath, he felt exhilarated.

Then his thoughts turned to Paxus' strange companions. The one called Bastia, whom he had jokingly referred to as an Arverni King and who seemed to be fretting all the time, edgy and nervous. How could such an individual be the heir to the lost kingdom of the great Celtic Arverni tribe? They had been disposed of by the Roman army and enslaved by the empire. Soon after their enslavement, rumours of the treasure began to spread throughout the northern territories. It was no wonder that the strange tales of giants or demons guarding the entrance to the hoard were passed around by the folk in the north. The imaginative stories as to the whereabouts of the treasure were just as fantastic. Some said the treasure was buried at sea off the coast of Lusitania whilst others said it was given to the gods for safe keeping. Catrus smiled at the absurdity of it all, but then he wondered how the mission to find the treasure had sat with Emperor Vespasian under whom he had served his entire career. Titus' father never mentioned anything about treasure. Catrus' many campaigns in Britannia were entirely taken up with pacifying the natives and not ever in search of any gold.

He allowed his thoughts to drift for a while then he focused on Titus. The emperor would not know about his 'treachery' for many months to come and by that time, Catrus would hope that the treasure will be found. He couldn't care less what plans Paxus had in stall for the empire but what he did know was that his plans will bring civil war and General Catrus Severus Vitrus, first general to the Emperor Vespasian will once again have a purpose to his life. It was an opportunity he could not refuse.

Just then, his thoughts were disturbed when his guards suddenly appeared. They had with them the two scouts that he had sent out four hours earlier. The scouts quickly reported that Noviomagus was under siege and was surrounded by up to one-thousand natives.

'Is the battle under way?' asked Catrus as he reached for his sword.

'No,' replied one of the scouts. 'It seems that there's a stand-off.'

Catrus paused in deep thought. He could do without this. He had an ulterior motive at Noviomagus that he was not keen to share. Now he had a choice to make. Should he wake up the camp and move on, away from trouble and keep the quest on track or should he do what is in every soldier's military code and come to the aid of his fellow Romans? He had been in this situation many times before and he had always answered the call but this time the call was personal. He needed to know what Paxus will have to say about it.

Within minutes, Paxus and Drusus had been woken up and brought to him. The two turned up looking ready to go back to sleep. They sat with the general, awaiting his reason for waking them at this hour.

'My scouts report that Noviomagus is under siege by a thousand hostiles,' said Catrus

'Then we must find horses from somewhere else,' snapped Drusus sounding most annoyed at being woken in the middle of the night.

'How many soldiers are posted at the fort?' asked Paxus.

'From memory, I guess around three-hundred,' replied Catrus, 'but I'm not sure if they have extended the grounds since I was last there some fifteen years ago.'

'The moat and stockade should keep the savages at bay,' stated Drusus, flippantly. 'They'll be alright.'

Catrus looked down in silence.

'You intend to go to their aid, don't you general?'

'It is my duty as a soldier,' he replied, proudly.

'I cannot allow it,' replied Paxus.

'No way, general,' seconded Drusus. 'I will not jeopardise this quest to save three-hundred professional soldiers who are more than capable of looking after themselves against a bunch of savages.'

Catrus did not answer but merely stared into the middle distance. He seemed to be thinking of something else entirely. After a long pause, Paxus took a step closer; curious as to why the general was so eager to intervene.

'What is it?' he asked in a softer tone.

Catrus sighed and looked up. 'My son is posted there. He is the new commander and I haven't seen him for a long time.'

Drusus threw up his arms in despair as he stood up and turned away in disgust. 'Now I see why you were so keen to join this quest.'

Paxus shook his head. 'General, you're putting the quest in serious danger.'

'I must do this Paxus,' demanded Catrus. He stood and stepped up close to the two men in an intimidating fashion. 'My son and his men may well be capable of withstanding an assault but as a Roman soldier I cannot take that chance and leave them to it. Besides, we have the advantage of surprise and knowing the tribes in these parts, they will scatter without a fight and no one need not lose their life.'

Paxus pondered for a while and then looked to Drusus who was shaking his head vigorously.

'Are you sure they will scatter?'

'When you undermine their numerical advantage they will scatter like sheep.'

Paxus nodded and crossed his arms. 'I will leave the decision up to Drusus,' he announced like a true politician.

Drusus looked positively annoyed. He stood in stunned silence for a long period.

'What's wrong governor?' asked Catrus, mocking him. 'This is a fine opportunity to put your military training to good use.'

'This is ridiculous,' snapped Drusus. 'We've only just landed in Britannia and you want to go to war?'

'I assure you,' said Catrus as he stepped up to face Drusus, eye-to-eye, 'the savages of these isles can put up a good fight but only when it is on their terms. And don't worry it will be over in the blink of an eye.' He slapped the governor on the back and grinned back at him then he turned and spoke to his guards. 'Wake the men. Tell them we will approach in the dark and show ourselves at dawn with our swords unsheathed. Make sure the enemy see us with our swords at the ready. It will show that we mean business.'

Drusus sighed and nodded reluctantly. 'I will go and wake up my men but I want you to promise me one thing, general. The men inside the fort are not to know of our quest, not even your son.'

Catrus nodded in agreement.

Within the hour, the camp was on the move. Silence was paramount. Buckles, belts, helmets, straps and metal weaponry were either tied down, tightened up or wrapped up to keep the noise to a minimum. Catrus had ordered that no talking was allowed and they will have to trek in single file so as not to disturb too much of the ground that they were walking on.

Dawn was at least four hours away when the trek began in earnest. Paxus had requested that ten soldiers be assigned to Lana, Carl and Mumi as bodyguards, Catrus didn't argue the point but he insisted that they stay at the rear of the column at all times.

Two hours into the hike, Catrus ordered a halt behind a hillock topped by a line of bushes. Beyond that was a forest. They were now a short distance from the fort and it was a perfect place for them to await the return of the scouts who had gone on before them. It was at this point that Catrus ordered them all to remove their footwear. This was done to ensure that everyone will be forced to tread carefully as they approached the enemy. Nothing was left to chance. The natives will have no idea that over three-hundred soldiers, led by one of the most revered generals in the Roman army will be breathing down their necks.

Lana and Carl were, once again, relieved to be free of their cumbersome sandals but dreading the next stage. What will be expected of them? They were given no weapons and ordered to stay with their bodyguards at all times.

Soon, the scouts arrived and gave the all clear for Catrus to advance. Within no time, they found themselves tip-toeing through the forest in almost total darkness whilst trying to avoid twigs and roots, fallen acorns and stinging nettles. This was clearly not the ideal way to go for a night time stroll through the English countryside. Carl and Lana both held their breath at every footfall. Any cry of pain would give their position away and they did not want to be the ones responsible for ending the quest before it got started.

After almost an hour of painstaking progress they caught the smell of burning wood upon the light breeze trailing through the trees. Catrus immediately ordered them to halt with a hand signal. Noviomagus lay just beyond. They could hear cattle mooing in the distance and the sound of someone chopping wood reverberated off the surrounding tree trunks. Then, after a further hour of waiting, the sunlight penetrated the foliage above them ushering in the early rays of dawn. In an ironic twist, the view that greeted them was stunning in its beauty. Sunlight reflected off trillions of lines of gossamer that blanketed the forest floor as far as they could see. All kinds of flying insects danced in the warming air and a cacophony of birdsong rang out all around them. Then a nudge in the small of their backs from one of the soldiers ended the moment. Within no time they were following on behind at the rear of the column as they moved like silent phantoms. Ten minutes later they had reached the edge of the forest then Catrus gave the hand signal for them to spread out. Everyone was ordered to put their sandals back on and wait for the signal to attack.

Lana and Carl's group stayed back a little and they both strained their eyes to look past the heads and shoulders of the soldiers in front of them. Then Lana spied the fort. It was larger than she was expecting, built of wood with high walls rising some thirty feet into the air. As Catrus had ordered, the men had their swords out at the ready. The atmosphere was tense and laden with an air of foreboding. Carl and Mumi followed Lana's stare and all three peered out across the clearing from just within the fringe of the forest. The silence was tangible. There was no birdsong now. It was as if the birds had flown away in anticipation of what was to follow.

The fort stood at one end of the clearing with sentinels posted all along the top wall. On the other side of the moat that surrounded the fort gathered the natives. Most were seated on the grass whilst others were standing in groups and talking amongst themselves. Campfires were burning full and there were men chopping wood to keep the fires burning. Lana and Carl were both surprised at how casual everyone seemed. It was as if there was an acceptance of the inevitability of the coming battle.

Carl moved closer to Lana and placed his sack at his feet. He looked at her with dismay. He mouthed the words *my god* and stared in fear at the scene ahead. Then, unbelievably, Carl's phone began ringing. The sound of Creedence Clearwater Revivals' song, 'Travelin' Band' split the peaceful silence like a sudden clap of thunder. Catrus glared in Carl's direction wondering what in damnation the noise was. In response, the natives turned and raced to their weapons. Battle cries went up and they quickly grouped together to face the trees. Lana cringed and hunkered down further into the foliage whilst Carl struggled at untying the string to his sack. He quickly brought out the phone and flipped it open.

'Oh shit,' he cried, 'its Sam.'

Then all hell broke loose. Arrows came hurtling through the leaves. Some buried themselves into the tree trunks above Carl's head. He immediately scurried away and ran back into the forest. Catrus was forced to order his men to attack and a roar from the mouths of angry men filled the air all around him. But Carl's only thought was the phone. He answered with a hello and almost fainted when he heard Sam's voice. Sam was asking him where he was but the noise of the battle was drowning him out. Carl screamed down the phone for Sam to help him but all he could hear were garbled words that sounded something like 'stay safe, we are trying to bring you home'... then the signal started to fade and crackle. Carl screamed down the phone once again for help but it went dead. He fell to his knees and cried out bitterly. Once again, the only link to his life was gone.

An enraged Catrus had no option but to order an attack. The natives had no option but to fight. The moment of surprise was lost to the Romans but the natives had nowhere to flee. The Roman's raced from the trees and went about their duty with stunning expertise. Within a minute, the front line of the enemy had fallen but at least twelve Roman soldiers lay dead or dying. The Brits were fighting for their lives and they rallied in one huge push wielding their clubs and axes with wild abandon. Heads were cracked and bones were broken. Cowering in fear behind a tree trunk, Lana and Mumi watched the proceedings in horror. A Roman soldier stood to their left holding in his guts which were spilling out between the gaps in his fingers. To their right a young native boy, who must have been around fifteen years of age, was on his knees bleeding profusely from a gaping wound in his neck. The gargling noises he was making as he struggled to breathe sent shivers down Lana's spine. Then the boy caught Lana's eye and he raised his hand to her in pleading for help. Lana buried her head in Mumi's shoulder. She couldn't watch anymore. Mumi grabbed Lana's hand and raced her back into the forest in a desperate search for Carl.

As the battle wore on, Catrus sensed that the natives were gaining the upper hand. Although the highly trained Roman soldiers were making their regulatory quota of kills per man he knew that without the soldiers from the fort there will be too few of them to win this battle. He looked to the fort in hope. The doors were firmly shut and the sentries on the wall had not moved. Angered at how slow their response was, Catrus slashed his way through several Brits in a fit of rage and raced to the moat screaming up at the men upon the wall.

'Open the gates and help us you bastards,' he cried. 'I am General Catrus Vitrus, father of your commander, Juna Vitrus.'

Then suddenly, bunch of fighting men stumbled into Catrus and knocked him, head-over-heels, into the dry moat. Two Brits quickly followed him down and made ready to attack him with their axes raised high above their heads. Catrus sprung to his feet and swung his sword down upon nearest assailant cutting straight through the knuckles of his right hand. The big, hairy man dropped his axe at once and screamed in agony. The second man, who was even bigger and hairier than the first, attacked him at once. Catrus feigned to his left then to his right avoiding the flailing axe by inches then he went down on one knee and with both hands he rammed his sword up into the man's genitals and then deeper into his bowels, twisting the blade as he went. Hot blood cascaded down onto Catrus' hands and forearms from out of the gaping wound. But his training had taught him not to waste a second admiring his handy work. In a flash, he let go of his sword and jumped to his feet then he wrenched the axe from the man's hands and head-butted him flat in the face. The Brit's nose exploded into a fountain of blood and he fell to his knees. Catrus brought up the axe and buried it deep into the man's skull. His head split open wide enough for his brains to spill out all over Catrus' feet. The other Brit, whose right hand was rendered useless brought out a dagger with his left hand and stabbed Catrus in his right thigh. The general reacted automatically. He grabbed the man's hand and stepped back from the dagger. It slipped out from his wound easily. But then the man rose to his feet, snapping his hand free from Catrus' grip. He brought up the wicked looking bronze dagger and made a lunge at Catrus' throat but his lunge was stopped in its tracks when an arrow went zipping through his face. It entered just above the right eye socket and out through his left ear. He staggered for a moment and then collapsed in a heap on top of Catrus. The general was relieved but he was bleeding profusely from his wound. With an almighty effort, he rolled the dead Brit off and looked up at the fort. The archers were firing volleys of arrows from atop the walls at the enemy. He painfully clambered up the rise and peered over the edge of the moat wall to see the gates opening inwards. The fort's cantilevered bridge was lowered and out rode the cavalry. He counted forty in all and it wasn't a moment too soon. The cavalry had the Brits on the run as they scurried away for their lives, back into the forest.

In no time, the short but bloody battle was over. Catrus managed to crawl out of the moat and get to his feet where he quickly surveyed the scene. He had lost many men in an encounter that should have been well in their favour. Why had the fort occupants been so slow to respond and what the hell was that infernal noise that had alerted the enemy to his soldier's presence? Paxus' strange companions will pay for this, he vowed. In frustration he called out for aid but he quickly succumbed to fatigue and blood loss. He fainted and rolled back down the side of the moat, landing unceremoniously on top of the two dead Brits.

18

Sam wiped the tears from his eyes and stared forlornly at his phone which was suspended in a bracket contained within a metal framework. Various wires led away from the contraption that connected it to a large metal box which was about the size of a microwave oven. Hundreds of multi-coloured wires led out from the back of the box and ran along the floor to a bank of computers standing tall against the far wall. The computers whirred and hummed with various degrees of regularity. Green lights, red lights and white lights flickered off and on at random. Sam pushed the microphone away from him and leaned back into his chair. He looked into the faces of his companions who were seated either side of the table. Ted Brooks seemed positively stunned. Winifred had a tear in her eye whilst the three professors looked totally flabbergasted. No one spoke for an age. The only audible sound in the lab came from the computers obediently performing their calculations at a lightning fast rate.

Sam spoke up:

'Anyone got anything to say?'

Malcolm McVie leaned forward in his seat and shook his head. 'I can't believe it. The experiment worked, it actually worked for Christ's sake!' Then he burst into a half-laugh, half-cry splutter.

Ted Brooks slammed an open palm down hard upon the table and smiled a broad smile as wide as the Mississippi. 'We just might be able pull this off, you know,' he said, excitedly. 'If we can bring them home it would be the most amazing story of all time.'

Professor Francesco Vinci raised a calming hand towards Ted. 'I know we are all a little emotional at this time but we need to listen back to the recording to verify the call.' He signalled to his assistant who was seated in a booth at the far side of the lab. The assistant nodded back and made a thumb's up signal to Francesco. The ten watt speaker on the table crackled for a moment then a hail of noise split the silence in the room. It sounded like a lot of men were shouting mixed in with a crashing noise. Then Carl's voice said hello. Sam began to fill up once again and Win reached out her hand across the table to his. Both listened intensely as Sam's voice repeatedly asked Carl where he was. Then the static increased but the last sound they heard was a barely audible cry for help from Carl. Then the speaker fell silent.

Winifred burst into tears as both she and Sam grasped both each other's hands tightly for comfort.

Professor Terence Barnes had looked the most shocked out of all of them. 'My god,' he said, 'poor Carl and Lana must be going through hell.' He brought out a handkerchief from the inside pocket of his tweed jacket and blew his nose. Tears welled in his eyes as he looked at everyone in turn. 'The recording sounds like Carl was in the midst of some kind of fracas.'

'Yes,' said Francesco, 'or it could have been a noisy market place or a sporting event of some kind.'

'Whatever it was, he sounded in trouble to me,' said Sam. 'We have to get them home as soon as possible or they're going to die.'

After another long moment of silence Francesco asked for a rerun of the recording. During the following hour they listened to the recording over and over but could conclude nothing new from it. Francesco then requested that they go back to their hotels and return the same time tomorrow for the next try at contacting Carl. After several goodbyes and handshakes Francesco and Malcolm McVie were left alone in the lab to discuss matters further.

The experiment had worked because the battery inside Sam's phone had been linked to a powerful superconductor which was stored under the grounds of the university and the superconductor was linked to several power stations throughout the southern region of Italy. The logistical nightmare of setting up the experiment, which they managed to keep a secret from the energy companies, had exhausted both men, but the endless negotiations with Dolomiti Energia and Enel to provide enough power for them, had paid off. Now they hoped the two companies would not go back on their word for a further try tomorrow.

'You were right about the battery in Carl's phone having the same time link to Sam's,' said Malcolm, acknowledging Francesco's insight. 'It seems that the microscopic thread through space time has kept the two phones connected.'

'Yes indeed,' replied Francesco. 'I have calculated that at the atomic level the bond is unbreakable but it could all unravel when we try to enlarge the window to bring Carl and Lana back through a worm hole of some kind.'

'It's risky but not impossible.'

Francesco flipped through a few sheets of graph paper and looked up at Malcolm.

'Your calculations to get them back seem plausible but as we have known all along, the problem now lies with boosting the power.'

'Italy's power companies alone cannot provide enough power to bring them back,' said Malcolm. 'Their national grid will be burned out by the end of it and then we will have a lot of awkward questions to answer.'

Francesco nodded but seemed to Malcolm to be thinking of other things.

'As much as I would prefer to keep this a secret,' continued Malcolm, 'we may have to go public to generate enough support for the project. Two people's lives are at risk here.'

'But the public will laugh at us, surely?' questioned Francesco. 'They're not going to believe that two archaeologists are lost in time.'

'The National Geographic is a respected publication,' replied Malcolm. 'I'm sure Ted Brooks will pull out all the stops on this one.'

Francesco twiddled his thumbs and sighed. 'There maybe another solution.'

The Italian professor seemed edgy and nervous all of a sudden and it disturbed Malcolm a little.

'What other solution?' he asked.

Francesco shook his head and smiled back at the young professor. 'It's nothing, just a thought, that's all.' He rose from his seat and ended the meeting promptly. Both men were tired from being awake all night. They had set up the experiment which required absolutely precise calculations that dealt with the strange world of quantum mechanics. So, after gathering up his papers and putting on his Adidas track top, a puzzled but grateful Malcolm shook Francesco's hand and they exited the lab.

Francesco waved Malcolm off at the door to the university and watched him jump into his taxi. The young Scottish professor was exhausted and needed to get a good stretch of sleep before another long day tomorrow. But for Francesco, his day was only beginning. Instead of returning to the lab he decided to take a walk. Leaving his white lab coat behind, he strolled along the Piazalle Aldo Moro in his short sleeved white shirt and grey slacks. The early morning November air was sharp but not cold. He lit up a cigarette and took a long drag as he walked. At five-thirty a.m. there were not many souls about on Sunday except for a stray dog and a young man on a bicycle. He pondered upon whether he should have told Malcolm about the 'other solution'. He knew the young professor would have been shocked by it and he wouldn't blame him but Francesco was convinced that his idea would work. A nuclear bomb would generate more than enough energy to widen the portal just long enough to allow Carl and Lana through.

Titus had heard nothing from General Vitrus. The usual communication lines had not been utilised. A general on a special assignment was required to send progress reports to the emperor at least once a month. Three months had now transpired and he began to wonder if there had been another disaster, or could

Catrus have been killed or taken prisoner? The permutations were endless, but more than likely the reason would be something mundane. He had ordered Castillius, his finest horseman, to go in search of the general but he had reported nothing of any significance. The emperor's patience was wearing thin.

All was not well in Rome either. Building work on the coliseum had been halted for two weeks due to an archway that had collapsed causing a large section of the outer wall to fall. Thirty slaves and three Romans were killed in the accident. One of the Romans killed was a promising young architect called Bastera who was also involved in the building of the gleaming new triumphal arch of Titus. There was also plenty of unrest caused by the annual influx of the winter refugees from the north. Food shortages and reports of the early signs of a plague from the eastern borders were also bothering Titus. Adding to that was the complete silence coming from Domitian's camp. Titus' observers had reported nothing out of the ordinary with his brother's behaviour. He was still living the life of indulgence that his standing allowed but not as extravagant as he had done in the past and it seemed he had taken heed of Titus's advice but still, a nagging thought simmered just below the surface of his conscience and he couldn't help but feel that his brother was up to no good.

Rome was creaking under the pressure of too many people. The steady influx of northerners plus twenty-thousand survivors from the eruption of Vesuvius who had opted to come to Rome were now a major problem. Since the reign of Augustus, Rome's population had grown enormously to a point where even the sacred areas of the city now had beggars and vagabonds of all kinds inconveniencing the citizens. It was an outrage and something had to be done. Titus decreed that an exclusion zone be set in force around the sacred sections and anyone found begging or trading in these areas will be imprisoned or flogged for their transgressions. But that was all he could do? His hands were tied. Winter was coming and that meant a change throughout the empire and, as always, change was felt more acutely in Rome.

He walked out onto the veranda and sat upon his favourite chair which overlooked the palace gardens. He took in a deep breath and allowed the crisp morning air to help chase away his troubles. The chair he was sitting upon, which was commissioned by Nero, was made of oak inlaid with gold and silver floral patterns. He called it his 'thinking' chair and was the most sumptuous piece of furniture in the entire palace. Whilst he sat and recalled his early years of conquest in an attempt to forget his troubles, a bell rang announcing a visitor. A praetorian guard brought in a message from Castillius. The clay plate was handed to him and he read it carefully:

My lord emperor, I have received news that Drexa Vitanian has been slain and that all of his soldiers were murdered during a battle that took place on the mountain pass in the Alps just north of the town of Augustus. A merchant from the northern port of Morini has also informed me that a small army belonging to Governor Drusus Varus has sailed across the sea to Britannia. It is believed that on board one of the boats were two men, one was General Vitrus and the other answered to the description of the politician, Paxus Strupalo. I will keep you informed of any more developments.

Castillius

Titus ground his teeth in anger and growled. He threw the clay plate to the marble floor where it smashed into several pieces. The guard took a step backwards wishing he was somewhere else.

'Leave me!' he ordered the guard who left at once.

Titus dared not believe what he was contemplating; a conspiracy upon the high road; a traitorous act of allegiance against him? General Vitrus, a traitor? He was once his father's most trusted soldier and now an outlaw; and the politician, Paxus Strupalo who was the nephew of Ducia Strupalo, a wealthy merchant shipman whose ships supplied goods to Rome. He remembered Drexa Vitanian often talking about Paxus, stating that the young rising star of politics was too clever for his own good and that he would be a problem in the future.

'It can't be,' he said aloud. 'They dare not take my treasure!'

Feeling helpless and utterly betrayed by General Vitrus, Titus thought long and hard for well over an hour. Then a thought occurred to him, a strategic masterstroke befitting his status as a great general. He will set up guard posts to every mountain road leading in and out of the Alps.

Within the hour he had given the order for his commanders to make plans for the new guard posts to be set. Now, all he had to do was wait out the winter.

Why go in search of the treasure when your enemy can bring it to you?

General Vitrus woke from his slumber and sighed with relief. He was glad that the fort of Noviomagus had been saved but he knew the fort soldiers would not be overly keen to see him on their doorstep. His reputation always preceded him wherever he went. Exaggerated tales of his exploits had been told by the common soldiery down through the years, but he had grown accustomed to them. He allowed the soldiers to ponder upon his legendary career which he knew would, at least, keep them on their toes.

After the battle, he had been rescued from the moat and had his wounds cleaned and dressed. He guessed that it was evening time as he forced himself upright in his bed and looked around the tiny claustrophobic room which was filled with burning incense and candles to ward off evil spirits. He cared not for such trivial remedies. Angered that he allowed himself to be wounded and choking from the fumes of the incense, he was already becoming restless. He swung his legs over the side of the bed, feeling a mild pain from the wound to his thigh. He called out to whoever was beyond the door. The door immediately swung inwards and in stepped his son, Juna, followed by an old man who was carrying a bowl of hot water and a roll of linen.

Catrus looked Juna up and down. He was dressed in a gleaming new uniform with his hair cropped close to the scalp. A deep scar ran vertically down the left side of his face and his left eye was half-closed. Catrus was aghast at the sight of his only son. He was twenty-five years old but looked more like forty-five.

'Good morning, father,' said Juna, as he nodded courteously.

'You look like shit.' said Catrus.

'Is that all you can say to me after all these years?' replied Juna as he took a step forward to the foot of the bed.

The old man busied himself with removing the bandage around Catrus' leg wound and it pained him much but he didn't show his discomfort.

'It seems that you've been in a few scrapes,' said Catrus.

'A few too many, father.'

'You said good morning but it is dark outside, how long have I been asleep?'

'Almost twelve hours,' replied Juna. 'It will be dawn soon and I have made the fort ready for your inspection.'

Catrus grimaced as the clumsy physician worked away at his stitched up wound, cleaning it with herbs soaked in warm water.

'I am proud that you are camp commander and thank you for rescuing my men.' He said it more to help forget the uncomfortable pain rather than to be polite. 'How many were killed?'

'Twenty-three,' replied Juna who then paused for a moment's thought. 'I had the situation under control. Why did you attack?'

Catrus could see that Juna was distant. He must have had a hard time being the son of a revered general. It would be tough for him to follow in his father's footsteps but he could see it also made a fine man of him. Juna's mother had died during labour and he was left to be brought up by his aunt Justa. Catrus had made sure that his sister Justa was financially taken care of but he had never been able to see his son grow up. It was only until the boy was fifteen years of age that Catrus found the time to spend with his only child.

'I will explain later but first tell me why you hesitated in coming to our aid.'

'I thought you could handle the situation. From my vantage point your men were doing fine but then the tables turned quickly. Most of them seemed to tire rapidly. Are they fit enough to fight?'

Catrus frowned. Drusus' men had grown lazy under the governor's command. They had probably not seen combat for years and were wholly unsuited for battle.

'I will explain that later too, my son,' he said feeling slightly annoyed with himself for not foreseeing the shortcomings of Drusus' men. 'Now tell me, how are you doing?'

After Juna had informed his father of everything that had happened to him since he left Rome, he insisted that Catrus ate a meal and allow his wound to be dressed properly. When all was done, he helped dress his father in his freshly cleaned uniform and led him, limping outside into the torch-lit courtyard. Catrus immediately caught sight of Paxus standing with his group of friends along with Drusus who looked like he had seen a ghost. The man they called Carl was with them and he immediately made a beeline towards him.

'You there,' called out Catrus as he limped towards the group. He could feel his anger rising. 'You could have had us all killed. What in the gods name was that terrible noise that you made with your... your strange... device?'

In an attempt to appease the general, Paxus took a step forward but Catrus raised a hand for silence. 'I want him to answer for his actions. Twenty-three men under my command are dead because of his foolishness. Now tell me, what was that noise?'

Fortunately, Carl and Lana had had time to come up with a plan. It was going to be risky but if it meant saving a life it was a risk worth taking. Carl flipped open the phone and showed it to Catrus.

'This is how I communicate with the gods of my world. They talk to me through this and I speak to them.'

Carl looked to Lana who stood wide-eyed and rigid with fear but she had managed to stay silent then he looked to Paxus who showed nothing but puzzlement but said nothing. He quickly looked back at the general whose face had grown dark with contempt.

'Your gods speak to you, ha?' raged Catrus. 'Who are you?'

'Lana and I are from a far off land you could not begin to imagine. We are as one with our gods. They can talk to me at any time and at any moment through this communicator. It was unfortunate for your men that they chose the wrong time yesterday to speak to me and for that, I apologise.'

'Your gods mean nothing to me,' said Catrus.

'Our gods are very powerful and their words are not to be taken lightly.'

'Who are you that you can speak to your gods directly?'

'I am a priest of the temple of rock,' said Carl, whilst trying not to sound too hesitant, 'and they have spoken many words of wisdom that have enriched my life and the lives of my people.'

'Who are these gods you speak of, name them?' ordered Catrus, mocking Carl's words.

Carl's mind raced. He didn't want the general to catch him out so he stuck with the rock stars of his day. 'Well, there's Fogerty, the god of music, who spoke to me the other day then there's Elvis, king of the gods then there's Lennon, the god of peace and McCartney, the god of love and then there's Springsteen, the god of the people and Wilson the god of the sea...'

Catrus stopped Carl in his tracks by raising his hand then he took a step closer. Carl tried his best not to think too much about what the general would do to him if he did not believe his lies. This was a man who, as the old cliché went, had killed more people with his own hands than he had hot dinners, but in this case it was probably true.

'At dawn my men will crucify you,' announced Catrus without a second's thought.

Paxus immediately placed a calming hand on Carl's shoulder, took a step forward and asked to speak with Catrus in private. The two men moved several steps away from the gathering and faced each other.

'Back at Morini port I didn't tell you everything about this man and his woman. They are both important to the success of our quest,' said Paxus. 'They alone know the location of the treasure, not I. If you execute him the woman will not reveal her secret.'

'There are ways of making people talk,' replied Catrus. 'The make-up of a woman's body makes it especially easy at extracting information.'

Paxus cringed at the prospect of allowing Catrus go to work on Lana's body.

'You know the penalty for causing the unnecessary deaths of fellow soldiers on the battlefield?' continued Catrus.

'I know, general,' replied Paxus, 'but you're putting the quest in jeopardy. Lana would rather die than reveal what she knows. She is unlike any woman I have met before. She is educated, strong willed and not afraid to speak her mind.'

Catrus had had enough. He raised his hand for silence in the typical Roman manner and Paxus was forced to obey.

'She will talk,' he said to Paxus with a finality heavy with authority.

Paxus knew that a Roman general was god in enemy territory and Catrus was now the senior officer of the fort and therefore commander. Catrus turned from Paxus and approached Carl.

'So, we wait until' dawn,' he said to Carl, staring him down with a menacing look that stabbed at every living fibre in his body. 'Under military law I have no option but to carry out the punishment of crucifixion. You have about an hour left before you get to meet your gods.'

Catrus turned then looked about the camp, casually nodding here and there seemingly impressed with how the place had changed. 'You have done well, my son,' he called to Juna. 'The fort looks a safer place than when I was last here.'

'Thank you, father,' replied Juna looking somewhat put out by the appraisal.

*

The wait for Carl was an agonising one. It was going to be the longest hour of his life. His palms were sweating profusely as all he could think about was the terrible death that awaited him. He threw up repeatedly and begged Paxus to talk sense into the general but Paxus regrettably informed him that the general's words were final. He stood up and walked away, leaving Carl, Lana and Mumi to ponder alone.

Lana was suddenly overcome with a sense of guilt for the way she had treated Carl since leaving Rome but she knew now why Carl had retreated into himself; he was working out a way to get them home; he was being tactical in his approach by staying out of trouble and avoiding confrontation. Lana had misinterpreted him badly and she felt terrible about it.

'Oh Carl I'm so sorry for being such a bitch to you at times,' she said in English.

'It's okay. You helped our situation by being a bitch,' he replied in English also trying valiantly to make light of the situation and failing miserably. 'If it wasn't for your headstrong approach and god-damn stubbornness we may have been killed. Thank fuck for the women's liberation movement, eh!' He burst into tears.

Lana gripped his hand tightly and thanked him. Then she planted a kiss square onto his lips and hugged him.

'I'm scared, Carl,' she said as she pulled away. Carl hugged her tight, feeling the bones of her shoulder blades and spine sticking into his arms. He gently stroked her scrawny neck and ran his fingers through her hair. He was shocked to feel her once silky smooth bonnet so brittle and lifeless.

'I want you to know that I love you as I have always loved you,' he whispered with as much conviction as he could muster.

Lana gripped him tighter and cried harder as she buried her face deeper into his shoulder.

Although she could not understand a single word they had spoken, Mumi cried along with Lana and she threw her arms around the pair of them.

An hour later, the sun peaked over the horizon and three soldiers from the barracks came for Carl. They withdrew their swords and ordered him to stand.

Then suddenly, John Fogerty's voice boomed around the courtyard...
Seven-thirty-seven comin' out of the sky,
Oh, won't you take me down to Memphis on a midnight ride.
I wanna move...

The camp was in uproar. Horns sounded and the barracks was alerted. Shouts from all around them came from all quarters. Carl immediately grasped for the phone at his side, fumbling in his anxiety to flip it open. He almost dropped it from his trembling hands then he opened it up and pressed the green button.

'Sam,' he shouted down the phone in English.

'Carl, I don't have much time to talk so listen up. Are you still in Rome?' Carl told him they are in England on the treasure hunt. 'Don't worry, we're going try and get you back home, but you must not lose your phone. It is vital to the rescue mission...' Static began to build up as Sam's voice began to fade. 'Tell Lana we love her very much... and stay strong for each other... good b...'

The line went dead and the phone's green glow fizzled out. When Carl looked up he found himself surrounded by a dozen open mouths. It was like he was a special toy in a shop window looking out at goggle-eyed kids staring in wonderment at him.

'What did your god say?' asked Catrus as he stepped forward from behind the ring of soldiers.

Carl's mind was numb. He couldn't scramble any sequence of thoughts together to answer Catrus. Luckily, Lana answered for him.

'Our great god, Elvis has spoken and he has ordered that Carl and I return home and if you do not let us go he will kill every last one of you.'

A long spell of silence followed. All eyes were on Catrus. To Lana, the other Romans looked shaken. They glanced at each other in trepidation and fear. The sound of Sam's voice coming out of the phone must have been convincing enough but Catrus looked unperturbed. His mind seemed to be racing. She knew this display of 'magic' was frightening enough for the ordinary Roman but the general was no ordinary man. After a long and awkward pause, Catrus turned to his soldiers and pointed at Carl. 'Crucify him!'

19

The unwilling soldiers immediately took a few steps back from Carl and Lana; unsure what to do. Some drew their swords for protection and uttered words of comfort to their gods.

'Crucify him,' bawled an enraged Catrus to the soldiers, but no one moved.

Within seconds a circle had formed around Carl, Lana, Mumi and Catrus. Other soldiers from the fort gravitated towards the circle, curious as to what the commotion was all about. Even Paxus' men came over and, in no time, a sizable crowd had gathered. It was good news for Lana as she felt a great sense of relief come over her. The situation had turned in their favour and to emphasise the point she took a step toward Catrus and glared up at him. He towered over her threateningly but she didn't flinch one bit.

'Now back off or I will bring forth the will of our god and have him blind you.'

'This is an outrage,' cried Catrus as he looked to his men. 'In all my years of service I have never been threatened from within my own ranks, especially by a woman.'

Lana pressed home her advantage by announcing to all that they intended to leave and if anyone should stand in their way they will feel the wrath of their gods. The circle of soldiers widened even more. Carl was astonished by Lana's fearlessness. He felt acutely aware that she was taking a big chance but she was making a fine fist of it. Then, from out of the blue, Paxus appeared carrying a large club in his hand. He stepped into the clearing and pushed Lana to the floor. Then he turned to Carl and slammed him hard in the chest with the head of the club. Carl went sprawling to the floor but before he could react, Paxus had pressed his left foot down hard upon his neck. Carl was astonished at Paxus' behaviour as he choked and struggled desperately to breath. Then suddenly, he felt the back of his head cracking and all went dark.

Paxus turned to the general and spoke:

'It would be wise not to offend their gods, don't you think general?'

Filters of light danced in and out of his half-closed, half-open eyelids annoying him to the point where he had to turn his head away. The sudden movement made Carl cringe from a jolt of pain to the back of his head and neck but it only served to jog his memory...

Paxus; his foot on his neck and the club...

After a few seconds, he got his bearings and found that he was lying on his side upon the floor of a moving vehicle. The familiar pitch and roll and the creaking of wood brought him back to full consciousness. Then he remembered his phone; the only chance they had to get back home. He looked about for it but it was gone. He gasped in fear that it could be lost. Then he spied Mumi. She was fast asleep sitting up against a metal framework with her head bowed. He realised the framework was covering the back end of a wagon. He scanned the framework up and over to the other side where his eyes eventually fell upon Lana. She was staring back at him but she seemed distant, almost lifeless. She was sitting with her knees up and arms crossed looking thoroughly pissed off.

'What the...' he mouthed to her.

Lana turned away from him then looked back again. The lifeless look was still there.

Then Carl gasped when he noticed that her face was covered in bruises.

'What happened to you?' he asked.

Lana hesitated as tears welled in her eyes. Then she slowly spread her legs apart to show Carl a multitude of bruises and gashes to the insides of her thighs. Further up, he could see that her crotch was covered with a blood-stained rag. He looked back at her with the unasked question burning in his eyes. She had been raped! Instantly, his heart felt like cracking open then anger boiled up inside him as his mind raced with unwanted thoughts. Poor Lana had been raped and he wasn't there to stop it. He made a move to comfort her but he was stopped by a shackle that was attached to his left ankle which was anchored to the bulkhead of the wagon. It was then that he realised that he, Lana and Mumi were incarcerated like criminals.

'What the fuck?' he cried to Lana but she was beyond reproach. It was like a light had gone out in her that would never again be ignited. In despair, he turned and raised his free leg to push Mumi awake. She groaned and raised her head groggily. Luckily for Mumi, it looked like she had been spared.

'Mumi,' he said in exasperation, 'what happened? 'Is the baby all right|?'

She jumped with a start after hearing Carl's voice and instantly burst into tears. She cried in high pitched wails as only Africans can do then she stopped as quickly as it started.

'Keep the fucking noise down you vermin,' ordered one of the two men riding at the front of the wagon. 'We're in enemy territory.'

Carl strained to raise his head up and looked about. They were travelling along a dirt track through a heavily wooded forest. Following behind the wagon was a line of mounted soldiers as far as his eyes could see. To either side of them were foot soldiers, three on each side.

'How long have I been unconscious?' he asked Lana, hoping she would answer him this time.

'All day yesterday and several hours this morning,' she replied but then she rolled over and lay down on her side facing away from him. He thought it best not to say anything more so he turned to Mumi instead, but she had gone back to her original position. Alone, in his own world of thoughts and chained up like a dog, Carl sat for hours wondering why he hadn't been crucified.

At the end of the day the call went up to make camp. The three prisoners were left inside the wagon whilst the soldiers busied themselves with the task. In no time at all, a fire was raging and a few tents had been erected. Carl was, once again, impressed at how efficient the Romans were at building a camp. They had surrounded this one with thorn bushes to shoulder height for protection and posted guards at every few paces. The three incarcerated friends were thirsty, tired and hungry. The day had been long and wearisome, cold but sunny. Lana had not spoken a word since but he managed to coerce Mumi into telling him that Lana had been raped by many soldiers under direct orders from Catrus. Carl's instincts were reminding him that these were brutal times for women. It was obvious that Catrus sought retribution upon Lana for failing to crucify him and that Paxus' little show of aggression with the club had something to do with it.

A loud bang on the side of the wagon startled all three and they jolted to attention. A brutish looking soldier stared back at them through the iron grills of the cage. His ugly face looked grotesque in the flickering flames of the campfire. His fat, bald head was covered in lesions and scars and his grinning mouth showed a row of crooked teeth.

'My name is Vaco,' he said in a gruff voice, 'I am your jailor. I will water you and feed you until we reach our destination and if there's any insubordination I will fuck you two ladies.' He eyed both Lana and Mumi up and down then he turned to Carl. 'And that goes for you too. I'm not fussy when it comes to fucking... ha, ha...'

Carl cringed with the thought. The man was foul and uncouth. He watched him as he unlocked the door to the cage. Then he picked up a bucket and a tub of water from the ground and placed them inside the wagon. The bucket contained what looked like pig's swill; a grey, watery mixture of a hot concoction that had things floating in it. Carl shuddered to think what those 'things' were.

'Eat,' ordered Vaco as he placed a wooden ladle beside the bucket then locked the door behind him. He gave Carl a lingering look which was loaded with threat, licked his lips in a suggestive manner then strode off back to camp, laughing as he went.

Carl watched him go then stared at the fare on offer. It had a strong odour, something akin to corned beef, but that's where the similarity ended. Then Mumi reached out from behind, grabbed the ladle and scooped up a portion from the bucket. She tasted it, nodded then swallowed a mouthful.

'Scour,' she said after wiping her lips with the back of her hand. 'It's a dish I have made many times.'

'What's it made of?' asked Carl.

'The meat is usually rats or mice but the vegetables are whatever can be found in the kitchen, hence the name scour. It's a slave food.'

Carl felt like throwing up but he knew this fare was all Vaco was ever likely to offer them so he forced himself to indulge. It tasted bland but at least it was hot and contained some form of nutrition.

'Lana, come and have a taste,' he said, trying his best to encourage her but she sat as still as a rock, gazing over at the campfire with a forlorn look in her eyes.

'Why has Paxus not shown his face?' she said to no one in particular.

'I don't know,' said Carl. 'He'll show. He needs us, remember! Now please eat.'

Lana turned from gazing at the campfire and looked at the food in the bucket.

'I'm not hungry,' she said.

'You need to eat,' said Carl. He took time to look Lana up and down and noticed that her arms and neck were covered in bites. Her eyes were bruised and sunken further into her skull making her look more like the witch that the Romans were accusing her of being. The last vestiges of her tremendous will-power seemed to have been stripped away. He knew, in that moment, that Lana will be changed forever. How could she be the same woman after what had happened to her? He wished with all his might that he had a semi-automatic so he could blow away the perpetrators of such a despicable act.

'Catrus tortured me, you know,' said Lana from out of the blue, whilst keeping her eyes fixed upon the distant campfire 'He tried to get the location of Anglesey from me but I didn't crack. I stared him out whilst his soldiers took turns at raping me. But I stayed defiant, so they turned to Mumi to get at me. But before they could lay a hand on her, the Brits returned and lay siege to the fort. Catrus ordered an all-out assault on the enemy but they were too strong. The Brits chased the Romans away from the fort and burnt it to the ground. The Romans were forced to battle out in the open for many hours but eventually had the Brits on the run. They killed many but they had no fort to return to. So now we're heading north to another fort.'

A loud bang on the side of the wagon made all of them jump once again. It was Vaco.

'Your friend is here,' was all he said as he turned away and disappeared back into the gloom. A few seconds later Paxus strode forward to show himself in the light of the flames. His eyes strayed to Lana then he dropped his head in shame.

'My lady I am so sorry for what has happened to you. It is with great sadness that I ask your forgiveness.'

'Fuck you!' said Lana in reply. Carl could see her eyes were burning with raging hatred.

Paxus raised his head and stared back at her. It was not lost on Carl that his reaction at the sight Lana disturbed him somewhat.

'Go ahead,' said Carl in disgust and anger, 'look at her. Look what your Roman friends did to my beautiful lady. How could you have stood by and watched this happen to her?'

Paxus raised his hands in pleading. 'I was restrained by the soldiers under Catrus' orders. There was nothing I could do to stop it. Catrus was in a rage… he wanted to kill the three of you but my intervention with the club had bought you time and then, an hour later, the attack on the fort came.'

'Why did you feel the need to knock me out?'

'I needed to distract his attention. I told him that your gods are unforgiving and that they will kill all of them.'

In a surprise move Mumi lunged forward and spat Paxus square in the face. 'You should have let him kill us,' she screamed. 'Look at Lana, she may as well be dead, you bastard!'

Paxus took a step back from Mumi, more out of shock from hearing her speak, guessed Carl, than the spit in the face. After wiping himself clean Paxus reached forward and grasped the bars of the cage with both hands.

'Now listen here,' he said with a serious intent. 'Catrus and his son, Juna, want to take the treasure for themselves. They will torture the three of you to get what they want and when they have done that they will kill us all but I will not allow it. A few hours before dawn we are going to make our escape. Bastia, Drusus and a few of his loyal men and I will come for you. Be ready on my return. Now I suggest you all try and get some sleep.'

'But Lana needs medical attention,' pleaded Carl.

'Don't you think I know that?' questioned Paxus, sounding angered but also painfully aware of Lana's condition. 'Fortunately for Lana, Drusus has brought along his physician.'

With that, he left them alone, disappearing silently into the night like a ghostly apparition.

All three looked to each other. The unasked question stayed unasked. Their quest was about to take another turn and they feared it would not bode well for them.

After a long spell of silence, Carl slammed his fist on the floor of the wagon in frustration. Lana groaned then rolled over painfully onto her side and was asleep within seconds. Mumi returned to eating scour like it was her last meal but Carl had lost his appetite. He sat and pondered long into the night wishing he would wake up one day and this living nightmare was but a dream.

*

The three were woken by a sudden shaking of their cage quickly followed by the familiar sound of a key in a lock. Before they had a chance to stir they were unshackled and manhandled off the wagon then frogmarched into the forest without a moment to pause for a breath. Time went by in a flash; sounds of the rustling of foliage mixed with the tramping of the undergrowth and images of light and shade and sensations of pushing and shoving all hindered their sleepy senses which took an age to dissipate. After what seemed like forever, Carl finally found himself in amongst a troop of soldiers who were leading him, along with Lana and Mumi, through a tangled mass of overgrown bramble and weeds. Lana was being helped along by two soldiers who handled her roughly but firmly. As the trudge wore on it began to grow darker with every step. Then, before they knew it, they were inside a large cave. The echo of dripping water reverberated around the walls giving the cave an eerie feel.

'It will be dawn soon,' Carl heard Paxus' whisper but could not see his features. All he could make out was the dark outlines of the soldiers guarding the entrance but then he heard Lana groaning from the pain of the walk. The soldiers had left her limp body to slump against Carl's and he reached out, automatically, to catch her from falling. Mumi came to Lana's aid at once and helped to lay her down upon the sodden ground.

'She is bleeding to death!' she announced. 'If we don't get her some help soon she will be dead.'

'When the light of the sun brightens up this cave the physician will get to work,' replied Paxus. 'In the meantime we must stay silent.'

Suddenly, the sound of shouting could be heard coming from the camp. The alarm had been raised. Carl guessed they had travelled only about a hundred feet and was sure they will be found in minutes. The atmosphere in the cave suddenly grew darker than the surroundings. Everyone held their breath for long moments. Then torchlight flickered through the bramble outside and as one, they retreated further into the cave carrying Lana along with them. She didn't make a sound and Carl feared she had passed into unconsciousness. The sunrise couldn't come quickly enough.

Minutes passed as the shouts grew louder. Then Carl heard the voice of Catrus calling out. The wily general knew they had not gone far and was making sure they heard him.

'Give up the game, Paxus,' said Catrus. 'We need the woman and her man. Hand them over and I will pardon you and your men.'

Paxus knew he was lying, of course. The moment they will be found they will be tortured. So the wait went on. The search went on. Then sunlight began to filter through the cave entrance. The gnarled features of the cave ceiling appeared high above their heads. Crystals, imbedded in the rock, reflected the light in a dazzling array of colours and within a few minutes there was enough light to make out the form of Lana lying in a pool of her own blood. Her withered and battered body looked pathetic. Her once athletic and immaculate figure was gone. Without realising it, Carl found that he was crying and it took all he had left in him to hold his sobbing in check. He looked to the others for help then one of the men, the youngest amongst them, came to Lana's aid. He had a small bag with him and he proceeded to examine her.

'Paxus,' screamed Catrus from outside. 'Reveal yourself and the treasure shall be yours, I promise.'

Paxus raised a finger for them all to stay silent, determined as he was to outwit the general.

After another eternity, Catrus began to turn his anger upon his men, calling them useless and incompetent and blaming the guards for allowing his captives to escape. Soon, the soldiers' search quickly became erratic and futile. Then the sounds of the search began to fade as they looked further afield for their quarry. It was then that Paxus ventured to speak.

'How is she, physician?'

'She is losing a lot of blood from her vagina. I need to stitch her up soon or we will lose her.'

'Can you do it here?' asked Paxus, sounding sincere for once.

'Yes, but I need more light,' replied the physician. 'Help me with her,' he pleaded.

Within seconds, Carl, Mumi and a few men had Lana raised up onto a slab of rock. They gagged her just in case she made a noise whilst the physician removed her rags. The young man got to work immediately.

Carl came away from the proceedings. He couldn't stomach seeing Lana in such a state. Maybe death would be welcome for her right now, he thought.

'She is a strong woman,' he heard Paxus say as he, Bastia and Drusus stood next to Carl. 'She did not deserve this.' Carl said nothing in reply. He was drained of emotion and will power. 'The ambitions of Rome spare no thought for sentiment or morality,' continued Paxus, 'and wherever that ambition takes Rome, men of dishonour and cruelty will follow.'

'Spare me the words of a politician, Paxus,' replied Carl, holding back his anger which suddenly spilled forth from within him. 'Lana is dying, all because of you.'

'I did not foresee this,' pleaded Paxus. 'My only mistake was trusting General Catrus Vitrus. Now the entire garrison of Noviomagus is after the treasure.'

'If Lana survives I will tell you where the isle of Anglesey is but only if you let us go,' said Carl.

Paxus pondered for a while then he turned to Drusus and Bastia who both nodded their approval.

'Why are you so keen to get home when you can live like royalty after we find the treasure?' asked Drusus.

'We want to go home to our time.'

Paxus rolled his eyes. 'You still insist on this stupid story that you are from the future?'

'It is true. Everything you have heard is true.'

Paxus reflected for a while then recalled Lana's description of the future of mankind at his uncle's villa in Augustus. 'Man has walked on the moon?' he laughed; 'flying machines and ships with no sails?'

After a short pause Carl decided to turn the tables on Paxus. 'Why are you insisting on continuing this quest when the history books tell us nothing of the Celtic treasure or your triumphal return to Rome? You are not mentioned in any of the writings passed down through the centuries. Your quest must have failed.'

Paxus said nothing in reply. It was obvious that he didn't believe a word Carl was saying. 'You will be free from me when I get my hands on the treasure. But be sure to get yourselves home before I bring the empire down to its knees.'

Carl shook his head knowing no such thing ever happened. He couldn't help but feel pity for Paxus. He will be forgotten to history like so many ambitious men of these times; the trials and tribulations that these countless individuals willingly put themselves through for the sake of financial gain or power just to become the momentary masters of a fraction of the planet is, ultimately, a selfish act.

'Very well then,' said Carl. 'We will leave as soon as Lana is able to travel.'

Paxus reached under his cloak and brought forth a small sack which was tied to the cord around his waist. 'Your things,' he said. Carl gratefully accepted the sack and sighed with relief. The camera, watch and phone were safe.

'Try not to lose them,' said Paxus with a forced smile.

Throughout the morning there was no hint nor sound of Catrus and his men. The hidden cave had done its job but Paxus was cautious about leaving just yet. Besides, Lana was gravely ill. It was a miracle that she was still alive. The young physician had done all he could but he insisted that she needed more comfortable surroundings to recover. They were all hungry, tired and a little afraid. Drusus seemed the most afraid of all. He looked positively stir-crazy and ready to bolt out of the entrance at any moment, but worst of all, he was angry at Paxus for allowing the general in on their quest.

'This quest is doomed,' said Drusus. 'We have been reduced to a handful of individuals who will be hunted down like dogs.'

'Don't be so certain, my friend,' replied Paxus. 'Men like Catrus will lose interest soon enough. The Celtic treasure will be but a memory to him when he realises he can't find us. He will end up back in Rome with his wine and his whores soon enough.'

Just then the smell of burning wood wafted in through the cave entrance. Black smoke crawled along the top of the cave and began to descend down the back wall. They had been found!

Drusus cursed under his breath. 'We're dead!' he said. 'Catrus is going to skin us alive!'

Paxus turned to Carl and then he glanced down at the forlorn figure of Lana who lay blissfully unaware of the proceedings.

Within seconds, everyone was choking, including Lana. The smoke was thick and heavy and they had no option but to exit the cave. Carl, Mumi and two other men carried Lana outside where, to their immediate left they could see the bramble had turned into a raging fire. Desperate for fresh air, the small troop pushed and shoved their way through the thick undergrowth in the opposite direction, back the way they had come. It seemed to take an eternity but eventually they spilled out into a clearing coughing and spluttering. They lay on the ground taking in deep breaths to try and clear their lungs. Lana was stirring. Her eyes blinked open and she sat up, then the pain hit home. She doubled up in agony but nobody could come to her aid.

After several minutes had passed, Carl managed to clear his streaming eyes enough to look about. He was fully expecting to see Catrus and his men gloating over them but he saw that the clearing was empty. Then, in the far distance, he heard the sound of men shouting followed by the clashing of metal upon metal. He looked to Paxus, quizzically.

'They're under attack!' he announced with surprise.

In the next instant, the burning bramble had caught up with them. Flames and smoke began to engulf the clearing. Then, from out of the blue, Vaco, the jailor appeared. Carl reeled at the sight of him but Vaco put a finger to his lips and ordered them to follow him.

Within seconds he was leading them down a gully and out across a field of tall grass. Lana was groaning in agony as she tried her best to stay on her feet. Then in a surprise move, Paxus picked her up and carried her over his shoulder. Vaco led them at a fast pace, but breathing heavily from the effects of the smoke, the troop found it a difficult task to keep up with the jailor. Luckily, Lana had stopped groaning but kept grunting from Paxus' every footfall. Every hundred yards or so, they had to stop for seconds at a time to regain their strength. Behind them, the sound of the battle raged on but Vaco's sense of urgency forced them to keep moving.

After half an hour of painfully slow progress they came upon a fast flowing river. The sound of the battle behind them had faded and Carl frantically looked up and down the river for a sign of a bridge or a way to cross but there was nothing. Then, on the opposite bank, a tall, bearded man suddenly appeared from over a rise. He stood alone, watching them intensely. He was dressed in a grey cape and was holding forth a wooden staff. He began calling out some kind of incantations in a strange language. His long, brown hair swirled about in the light breeze. The man reminded Carl of Gandalf, the wizard, from The Lord of the Rings. Then suddenly, he dropped his staff to the floor and laid down, head first, upon the ground. Vaco stepped forward and called out to him.

'Velen, Velen?'

The man did not respond and after a few seconds had passed, Paxus spoke to Vaco. 'Did you just say the name, Velen?'

'Yes, Velen the druid of the Borgoni tribe,' replied Vaco out of hand. 'He is their spiritual leader. He is determining whether you are good or evil. If he thinks you are good, he will allow you into the village. But if he decides you are evil, he will have you sacrificed to the gods.'

'Are you a Brit?' asked Paxus to Vaco who grinned back at him knowingly.

'I am a mercenary spy,' he replied without expanding upon the subject.

Stepping casually aside from Carl and Vaco, Bastia whispered to Paxus. 'We have found the druid Velen, at last!'

Paxus said nothing in reply but kept staring at the prostrate man who was continuing his incantations. Then the druid suddenly stopped talking, rose to his feet, picked up his staff, turned and waved them on as he walked back over the rise.

'You are all safe, for now,' said Vaco. 'Now, follow me and do what I say!'

20

Carl sat across from Velen who was busily scanning the faces of the Paxus' troop with an air of caution. Weapons and belongings had been removed and were stacked in one corner of the large building where all were seated. The druid's wizened and craggy features seemed at odds with his blue eyes that were both bright and piercing. A long, brown beard went all the way down to a fine point. A broad nose that had been broken in the past was the dominant feature of an, otherwise, friendly and appealing face but there was also a threat in his look that simmered just below the surface. Carl guessed he could be in his early sixties but, true to these times, he looked much older. Next to him sat the chief of the village whom Vaco had introduced as Bedor Longshadow, son of Vestin, the Greyheart and he looked very old, frail and tired of life.

The gathering was seated in a circle around a central fireplace that smouldered with dying embers. Various carved wooden pagan objects hung from the ceiling depicting deities and animals that the druids worshipped. Carl was surprised at how many there were and even more amazed with the attention to detail that went into them.

A terrible fear that he may not get his camera, phone and watch back plagued his mind. It was imperative that he had the phone back. The loss would be incalculable. In the same vein, he could see that Paxus was immensely annoyed over the removal of his key. The politician was brimming over with barely disguised anger but he managed to keep his nerve.

The silence within the building was continuing on for an age and soon Carl's patience began to waver but, as Vaco had mentioned beforehand, this kind of treatment was customary before talks began. A period of silence was a show of respect but it seemed to Carl that the druid and the chieftain were also checking out the worthiness of their guests. As the spell of intolerable silence continued Carl chanced a look across at Lana. Once again, she was at death's door. She was slumped up against Mumi, who was barely able to keep her from falling off her stool. He thought to prompt the gathering along just so Lana could get some treatment but he dispelled it a once. Then, without warning, Bedor Longshadow rose gingerly from his seated position and pointed a long, bony finger at Bastia. Carl was astonished at how tall he was; at least six-foot-seven and it was easy to see how he got his name. Bedor directed his words at Bastia in a strange language that Carl did not understand. After he had spoken he sat back down and stared vacantly at no particular point. All eyes turned to Velen.

'The great Bedor Longshadow of the Borgoni tribe says you are welcome to stay,' he announced in Latin, 'but only until the woman gets better, then you must leave and never return.' He clapped his hands and several tribes women came rushing in to Lana's aid. They carried her off to another location, quickly followed by a deeply concerned Mumi. Carl sighed with relief. At last, she's getting some care, he thought.

Another period of silence followed until Velen eventually stood up and stared down at Bastia.

'You are the son of Banax!' announced the druid out of the blue, 'the good king of the Arverni.'

Bastia's jaw dropped wide open and was unsure what to say. He glanced at Paxus and Drusus who both sat stone-faced not daring to give anything away.

'You are here to reclaim the great treasure of the Celts in your father's name, are you not?' asked Velen.

Bastia's face went crimson. Once again he glanced to Paxus and Drusus for some guidance but they both sat as still as statues.

'Your father was the last king to see the great treasure hoard of the Celts before it was moved to Britannia,' continued Velen as he scanned the eyes of his guests one-by-one. 'It took eight-hundred men with five-hundred carts sixteen months to bring the treasure to its resting place. Bedor Longshadow here oversaw the whole journey along with his father, Vestin, the Greyheart. Between them they managed to keep the task a secret, covering the carts at various points along the way with manure, rotting fish and even human excrement. At one point Vestin ordered the slaughter of an entire village when a particularly nosy bastard questioned why the carts were making such deep grooves in the ground for such light loads.'

The watching Paxus could not sink any deeper into his stool. The druid had sussed out their quest which had now taken another twist. His quick mind dithered for once and he struggled to think of a response. Drusus fared even worse. His dreams of riches were fading with every word that Velen uttered and he began to perspire and tremble with an almost uncontrollable anger. Then, to both men's surprise, Bastia rose from his seated position and stepped forward.

'How do you know of me?' he asked inquisitively.

Velen took a step forward and stared at Bastia with a hardened look. 'It had been foretold by my predecessor, Ulnur that you will show up one day,' he replied. 'Ulnur was your father's closest friend. It was he who first suggested that the treasure be moved from under the prying eyes of Rome. But alas, Ulnur betrayed your people because your father had the foresight and wisdom not to inform him and the village elders of the chosen destination of the treasure. He entrusted that only to Vestin, the Greyheart. So you see, that is why Ulnur sought an audience with the emperor Claudius to inform him that the treasure had been moved to Britannia. He wanted the treasure to be found before you had a chance claim it back. He wanted to avenge your father's betrayal of trust and he searched Rome's streets looking for you.'

'Looking for me?' asked an incredulous Bastia.

'Oh yes. Ulnur wanted you dead and he wanted to bring your head to Claudius, but his wish for favours in return from Claudius ended abruptly when Bedor Longshadow here, under orders from his father, travelled to Rome in disguise and killed him.'

Velen turned away from Bastia and sat down upon his stool. He looked a little sad and reflective. 'And so it was, because of Ulnur's treachery, Claudius began his conquest of Britannia where many of the Borgoni would be crushed under the heel of Rome.'

A strained atmosphere descended upon the meeting. Then the sound of cheering men came crashing through the village disturbing the melancholy. Cries of joy mixed with the familiar clatter of metal and wood along with the unmistakeable sound of weapons and armoury filled the air. Bedor exited the building at once to see what the commotion was, the others quickly followed behind. Within minutes a gathering had assembled as cheers of adulation for Bedor Longshadow by an army of Borgoni warriors echoed around the village. To Carl they looked jubilant and overjoyed, but then he noticed the reason why. From behind the throng General Catrus Vitrus, his son Juna and about forty other Roman soldiers were paraded in front of Bedor Longshadow. They bore the scars and wounds of battle. General Vitrus' face was covered in bruises. His eyes were puffed up black and blue and Juna had fared no better.

All the Roman captives were lined up and forced to kneel before Bedor. The great leader clasped his hands with delight and took a step forward to eye his prize. Next, a two-wheeled wagon was brought forth and tipped upwards. Out spilled the decapitated heads of the defeated Romans at the feet of Bedor. Carl estimated there to be at least two hundred. His stomach churned at the sight but, once again, he found he was getting used to such brutality.

Bedor bowed in honour of his brave warriors then gave a command. His men immediately stripped their captives naked and bound their hands together behind their backs. Then up stepped Velen who raised his staff to the sky and spoke some incantations over the soldiers. Some of the younger Romans began to shake and quiver in fright at the thought of what might happen to them. Carl turned to Vaco with a questioning look that did not require the spoken word.

'They will be sacrificed to the gods,' Vaco whispered in return. 'All captives in war share the same fate.'

Carl looked to General Vitrus who seemed resigned to his fate. The general caught Carl's stare and smiled back at him.

'I will meet you in the afterlife,' he said, 'where we can talk more about your gods.'

In a move that took both Paxus and Bastia by surprise, Carl turned to Velen and pointed a finger at Catrus.

'That man is General Catrus Vitrus,' he said forcefully. 'He is the most highly decorated general in Rome. If you execute him and his men your village will face the wrath of the Roman Empire. Your people will be annihilated and your bones scattered to the four winds. History will have forgotten you ever existed and all you have lived for will be wasted.'

Velen raised his eyebrows in surprise. 'You speak as though you want this man to live.'

'I promise you, if you let him live Rome will not avenge you. Paxus here is a politician and he will speak to his leaders.' Carl glanced at Paxus who nodded back at Carl's ridiculous assertion.

'And furthermore,' continued Carl as he raised a hand out towards Bastia. 'Bastia, the son of Banax, decrees that the treasure of his forefathers be left in Britannia under the stewardship of Bedor Longshadow and his people; never to be disturbed, never to be found.'

Bastia threw a glance in Carl's direction with a look that could kill a thousand men. It was almost too much for Drusus to bear as he made a move towards Carl but Paxus placed a restraining hand on his arm. The governor was livid but wise enough to stay put.

The moment was not lost on General Vitrus. 'So these savages have the treasure?' he asked Paxus who grimaced with rage but had the foresight to remain silent.

Velen contemplated Carl's words for a while then spoke to Bedor in hushed tones. After several long minutes, he came up to Bastia and smiled a warm smile.

'Bedor Longshadow is most pleased that you have given him this honour in your father's name. He will see to it that the treasure will remain in this land forever.'

Bastia could do nothing but force the thinnest of smiles back at the druid. He wanted to strangle Carl's scrawny neck but a slight nudge in the foot from Paxus made him realise that he had no choice but to agree so he bowed his head in response to Velen's statement.

Carl bowed to Velen and asked that he thank Bedor for sparing the lives of the soldiers.

'He gives them their lives back but he asks a small price in return.'

'What is that?' asked Carl.

Velen turned and gave an order in the strange, Brit language to one of the warriors who looked most displeased with his request. It was clear he wanted blood. Then Bedor stepped forward to face the warrior down with a threatening look. The warrior reluctantly bowed in respect. He turned and gave the order begrudgingly. Immediately, the Roman soldiers were untied from their bonds and led, in single file, over to a tree stump where an old man was untying a set of tools from a leather holder. He took out a hammer and what looked like a broad chisel. Then Carl looked on in horror as the first soldier in the line had his right hand forcibly placed down upon the tree stump with his palm downwards. Then the old man placed the wicked looking chisel on the soldier's wrist and raised the hammer. He brought it down hard with a loud thud upon the chisel. The soldier's hand came away with ease. His screams reverberated around the village and the surrounding woods. Birds flew from their branches in fright from the bloodcurdling echoes.

Carl looked to Vaco for an explanation.

'The Borgoni do not let their enemies get off lightly,' he said. 'Bedor will send them back to Rome alive all right, but they will not be able to return as soldiers.'

Carl watched on as another man, brandishing a white hot rod of iron came up to the unfortunate soldier and raised it towards him. Two men held his bleeding stump outwards and the man with the hot iron cauterized the wound. The soldier's screams were even more bloodcurdling this time around.

'Now,' said Velen to Bastia. 'Would you like to see the treasure for yourself?'

Malcolm McVie placed the phone down upon its receiver and sat back in shock. Professor Barnes had been arrested on suspicion of Carl and Lana's murder. He turned on to Sky news and saw the old man being whisked off in the back of a police car outside his London home. It was time that the world knew the truth, he thought,

He immediately rang Ted Brooks at the National Geographic office in Washington DC. The phone rang for several moments then a woman answered. He looked at his watch. It was 14:30 in his Glasgow office so it will be 9:30 in the morning, Washington time.

The woman directed Malcolm's call to Ted's office. The ringtone seemed to take an age before Ted finally answered.

'Good morning, Ted Brooks speaking.'

'Hi Ted its Malcolm McVie here. Have you seen the news?'

'I have it on as we speak, Malcolm. It's terrible. The poor man wouldn't hurt a fly.'

'I fear he will talk and they'll definitely think he's a crank unless…'

'Unless what Malcolm?' asked Ted, apprehensively.

'Unless you go public and I will back you up.'

'What about professor Vinci and his team? I hear they are close to a solution, aren't they?'

There was a long pause on the line until Ted prompted Malcolm for a reply.

'Ted, they have found a solution… they're going to use a nuclear bomb.'

There was another long pause on the line before Ted finally spoke.

'You're kidding me?'

'No, it's true. I have the plans on my computer.'

'This is unbelievable Malcolm,' said Ted sounding excited but a little apprehensive. 'How are they going to pull it off?'

'Leave it with me and Professor Vinci. The operation is already in motion. Your job is to go public so we can get Professor Barnes released. I will inform Sam. In the meantime stay positive.'

'We should have informed the world right from the start to lift the cloud of suspicion off our shoulders,' replied Ted. 'I will type up a draft and let you and Sam read it before I publish. In the mean time I will get Winifred to make a statement to the press, some kind of teaser to the keep media on their toes.'

After they said their goodbyes, Malcolm sat back in his chair feeling a sense of relief wash over him. Ted was right. The world should have known about this, months ago. A report claiming that two respected archaeologists of our day have ended up in the time of the Roman Empire would not be believed, of course; it would even be laughed at. The reputation of the National Geographic would be at stake. Ted Brooks' job would be on the line but at least it would keep the focus on Carl and Lana, but the truth will still remain; they are both lost in the mist of time, alone and afraid.

He picked up the phone once more and made the call to Sam.

Sam was at home, still off work with depression. His workload was being covered by his chairman, Peter Marshall whose daily phone calls were becoming a nuisance. This one will be the same, he thought. He got up from the porch lounger, placed Carl Sagan's book, Pale Blue Dot down upon the table and sauntered into the kitchen to answer the phone.

'Good morning Peter,' he said expecting the annoying high-pitched tone of his chairman's voice to fill his head with yet more figures and chart readings.

'Sam its Malcolm McVie here,' said a voice on the other end.

It was a welcome change to hear the softly spoken tones of Malcolm's beautiful Scottish accent rather than the sharp nasal whine of Peter Marshall's.

'Hi Malcolm,' said Sam in surprise. It had been almost two months since he had heard from any of the science team. Hope of finding Carl and Lana had diminished over time and this led to him spiralling into a deep depression. The finger of suspicion from the media and even his close friends and associates was a constant presence. The local police even had a team of officers assigned to his every move.

'Have you seen the news, Sam?' asked Malcolm, 'Professor Barnes has been arrested outside his London home on suspicion of murder.'

'What?'

'Sam, Ted is going to go public,' announced Malcolm without much ceremony.

'Are you sure?'

'Yes it's time.'

'But we'll be laughed at. We'll be on the news for all the wrong reasons.'

'Ted has the photos, the camera and the watch. Independent scientists can verify, cross examine and corroborate our claim. The evidence is there Sam.'

'I know, but what about Professor Vinci? He will say we're jeopardising his plans to get Carl and Lana back...'

'Professor Vinci has figured out how to get them back,' butt-in Malcolm, 'he's going to use a nuclear bomb.'

'What, a nuclear bomb? But that will kill them Malcolm.'

'The theory works Sam. It's all to do with energy, a lot of energy in a short space of time. Ted Brooks is going to go public. He will send you a draft copy before going to print. It's imperative that the world knows Sam.' There was a long pause on the line. 'We must do this for the sake of Professor Barnes' reputation.'

'Oh the poor man,' said Sam feeling desperately sorry for the likeable professor. 'He wouldn't hurt a fly.'

'That's just exactly what Ted Brooks said,' replied Malcolm. 'Now don't you worry Sam, everything is going to be fine.'

After his phone call, Malcolm immediately left his office and flagged down a taxi. He was going to take the next available flight to Rome. He knew Professor Vinci will be against going public but he had no choice. The silent approach had not worked. There were too many prying eyes and ears on the case which would inevitably lead to more arrests. Reputations and jobs were on the line here but even more than that, Carl and Lana's very lives were at stake.

The following morning, Carl, Paxus, Drusus and Bastia were led by Velen from the village, flanked on either side by a large troop of warriors but Vaco was left behind much to his chagrin. Carl's three Roman companions were puzzled over the revelation that the treasure was within walking distance and not on the Isle of Anglesey as Lana had said. It was yet another twist in this extraordinary quest.

They were taken along a dirt pathway that wound its way through a dense forest. The trail undulated for several miles with many twists and turns. As the day wore on the foliage above grew thicker blotting out the afternoon sky in an almost sinister way which made Carl feel a little disconcerted. Thoughts that they were being led to a place of worship and that he and the others were to be the sacrificial lambs crossed his mind. He quickly put that disturbing thought out of his head and thought of Lana. He was forbidden to see her, but Mumi had managed to inform him of her progress. Apparently, she had been treated for her wounds with herbs, crushed insect larvae and diced birds brains and was resting in a bath of warm ox milk mixed with the bile of pig's stomachs to help the healing process along. Carl was pleased for Lana but a little apprehensive about the style of first century medical care. Then he concentrated his thoughts on General Vitrus and his men. His kneejerk reaction to plead for their lives was a selfish act. He wanted Vitrus alive so Lana could get her revenge. He knew that that was the least he could do for her. Lana would want nothing more than to light the tinder at his feet and stare the general in the eye as he burnt alive. Her savage mutilation at the hands of the Roman soldiers was worthy of such a revenge ten times over.

After the soldiers were brutalised and had their wounds cauterised by the Borgoni they were washed down in horses urine, 'to purify their souls' as Velen had put it and then given their decapitated hands back and sent on their way totally naked as the day they were born with no food or water. The look that Catrus Vitrus gave Paxus, Drusus and Carl suggested that he would be back with vengeance aplenty.

Then Carl thought of his fellow companions and how they were shocked by his offer for the Britannic tribe to keep the treasure. He had acted on instinct, thinking only for the life of Lana. Surprisingly, Paxus calmed down after a while as he pointed out that Velen was foolishly about to reveal the location of the treasure to them and that they could return one day and claim it for themselves. But Drusus argued that raising a rebel army to take on the Brits could take years and in that time the treasure could be moved to another location.

As the march continued, Carl shut his thoughts away and concentrated on what plans his brother had install for getting them back home. He was anxious about his phone. It was his only link to the future. He knew without that, he and Lana will be trapped in the first century for the rest of their lives; a prospect that filled him with dread.

Then, to his surprise, the path ended and he was quickly blindfolded and his hands were bound together along with the others. They were led by their bonds for the remainder of the trek.

After another hour of trudging through the forest they suddenly came to an abrupt stop. Their bindings were removed and they found themselves standing in front of a thirty foot wall of impenetrable thorn bushes. Carl noticed that on either side of the wall hung a collection of bones. He recognised them as human but there were no skulls. A terrible sense of foreboding crushed him and he looked to Paxus for some sense of understanding but the politician was unaware of his gaze.

'We are here, Bastia, son of Banax!' announced Velen as he turned and shoved the base of his staff into the soil at his feet. 'This is the chosen place of the great treasure of the Celts. Your father and Vestin the Greyheart ordered that it should stay here, once and for all. You may be aware that the Isle of Mona was chosen but that was a clever ruse to throw off the attention of potential looters even to the point of tattooing the location on your back.'

Bastia and the men from Rome shot Carl a curious look when Velen had mentioned Mona but Carl simply shrugged back knowing that he will have to explain to them that the name Anglesey, which Lana had chosen, was the modern day word for Mona.

Without further ado, Velen turned and approached the wall of thorns. He raised his staff high and called out loudly in the Britannic language then banged the staff on the floor three times. Strangely, no echo rang out which confirmed to Carl that they were in a very densely packed forest indeed and it was no wonder that Vestin had chosen this spot. Then, all of a sudden, the bushes split apart as if someone or something was pushing from within. A loud creaking and splintering of wood and twigs split the air and within seconds the bushes were wide enough for a man to enter. A rain of loose thorns and leaves showered down upon the gathered men which forced them to cover their eyes. When Carl eventually looked up he saw a man standing in the entrance. He was dressed in a white robe and holding a flaming torch aloft. The man raised the torch up and turned away disappearing back into the gloom beyond.

'Follow me,' said Velen to Bastia.

Bastia looked nervous as he tentatively took a few steps forward. Paxus nodded to Carl and Drusus as the three of them followed on behind. The accompanying warriors turned and trudged off back to the village without a word.

As soon as Bastia and the others passed through the entrance they were hit by a chill of cold air that came from above. As one, they looked up and could see nothing but blackness above them. Then the man in the white robe touched his torch to something hanging above his head and instantly another torch lit up followed by another and yet another. The torches ran off into the distance, each one lighting another further on in a straight line until they disappeared down a steep gradient. The four men now realised that they were inside a huge cave that sloped down into the depths of the earth. Then the entrance behind them was slammed shut, cutting them off from the outside world.

'Do not fear,' said Velen in a calm tone. 'This is the place of the skull. There are no spirits here to bother you. We Borgoni believe that when a head is removed from the body the spirit dies.'

Velen turned and followed the man with the torch without once speaking to him. After several minutes of descent, the line of torches above ended abruptly. Carl found that they were standing at the top of a long set of stone steps that descended into the darkness below.

'The treasure is down there,' pointed Velen.

Bastia cursed under his breath. 'What else is down there?' he asked sounding very unsure.

'Skulls,' answered Velen.

Bastia took a step back.

'Ha, the son of Banax scared of a few skulls?' mocked Velen. 'Your father would be turning in his grave.'

Bastia cursed again then gathered his thoughts. He stood up straight and proud then turned to Velen. 'Let's go,' he said. Velen smiled a wry smile then took the torch from the man in the white robe and led the way down the steps leaving the silent man behind.

21

At the base of the steps, Velen strode across the earthen floor without waiting for the others. As soon as the following men reached the bottom they hastened after the druid, circling his torchlight like moths around a lamp, eager but a little apprehensive of the looming darkness up ahead. Within minutes the entrance to a tunnel appeared from out of the gloom. It seemed to be beckoning them towards it like a demon waiting to devour their flesh. Drusus stumbled and caught his breath at the sight of the cavernous void ahead. He looked petrified and ready to bolt back up the stairs at any moment. But soon, they were at the entrance. Velen forged ahead into the gloom, unconcerned. The men had no choice but to follow.

The atmosphere inside the tunnel instantly felt claustrophobic, cold, damp and dangerous. Carl could sense an overriding presence of danger coming from ahead but he dismissed it out of hand, of course. He knew that they were walking inside an extinct lava tube, probably millions of years old when the British Isles was once part of a much larger landmass.

Velen suddenly came to a stop and turned to face the men.

'Another league ahead is the great treasure of the Celts. It has been interred here and will remain here forever. Do not even think about changing your minds and returning to steal it for it is impossible to take even the smallest of items. Vestin the Greyheart has seen to that.'

Paxus was puzzled by Velen's words. What did he mean, 'even the smallest of items'? Surely a couple of legions could take the Borgoni tribe in a single battle and then it would just be a matter of time before they would find the treasure and haul the lot of it back to Rome? Velen was either being very foolish in revealing the treasure to his sworn enemy or he had a motive behind all of this.

'Show us?' asked Paxus, impatiently.

They followed Velen for a short while until they came upon a huge, iron gate that straddled the entire archway of the tunnel, some one-hundred and fifty foot tall by sixty foot wide, it looked impregnable and stood like a sentinel barring all who dared to pass. Hanging from the gate was a single human skull.

'This is the head of the traitor, Ulnur,' explained Velen. 'Bedor brought it here all the way from Rome.'

Velen turned and reached inside his robe with his free hand and pulled out Paxus' key. He handed it to Bastia who looked to Paxus in surprise.

'Take the skull key, Celtic king and enter,' said Velen to a dumbfounded Bastia. 'It is the only way to pass through these gates, fore they cannot be forced open by man nor beast.'

'The skull key?' asked Paxus with a hint of sarcasm.

Velen nodded in response but stayed silent for a short while. Then he spoke in a distant tone:

'The skull key was handed to King Banax by Vestin, in trust for when he returns to claim his treasure,' said the druid. 'But before the Romans murdered Banax the key had vanished; stolen by Ulnur. Ulnur's plan to lead the Romans to these gates was ambitious in the extreme as it was foolish and he paid for it with his life. Even until his death he would not reveal the whereabouts of the key such was his hatred towards Banax. The mystery of the lost skull key plagued Vestin for many years. Foolishly, before leaving for Rome, Ulnur had interred the key in a box and buried it under his temple mound. After his death it seemed someone had found the box and sold it off for monetary gain and hence therein the box led a charmed life. Legend grew that it was cursed. It was eventually sold off to a trader from Rome and the people were glad to be rid of it.'

Carl recalled that it was Fario who brought it to Rome and thus, inadvertently, started all this trouble.

Velen paused for breath and closed his eyes in deep thought. Then he opened his eyes once more and rested a hand upon Bastia's shoulder. 'I have waited a long time for this moment. I have not seen the treasure since Vestin handed the skull key to your father all those years ago. And now, as fate has deemed it so, the son of Banax shall open the gates of Dragor and take the place of his father.'

Bastia swallowed hard as his mouth dried up instantly and a cold chill ran down his spine.

'Oh Dragor, god of the Borgoni, hear me,' cried Velen as he raised his arms in praise. 'Give your blessing to this Celtic king so that he may understand.'

All the men looked to each other in puzzlement at Velen's last words – *so that he may understand,* but they chose to say nothing.

Bastia was prompted by Velen to continue. He trembled as he hefted the cumbersome key in his right hand then placed it in the lock. The gates echoed on contact reverberating in a metallic chorus that sounded threatening. Carl was amazed at the craftsmanship that went into the gates. They must have weighed at least ten-tons each hanging upon enormous hinges that were hammered deeply into the basalt rock. Then, with shaking hands, Bastia slowly turned the key. The lock creaked and groaned in protest but kept turning, nevertheless. A loud click confirmed the lock was open and the gate swung ever so slightly outwards. A nod from Velen reassured Bastia who left the key in the lock. He then reached out and grabbed a single bar with both hands. With all his might he pulled back but the gate wouldn't budge. An impatient Paxus jumped to his aid and between them they managed to open a gap wide enough for a man to enter. The grinding sound of the rusting hinges, as they gave way, reverberated around the cavernous void for a long time, signifying to Carl that they were inside a very big lava tube indeed.

'Lead the way Celtic king,' said Velen as he handed the torch to Bastia.

Bastia, followed by Velen then Paxus, Drusus and Carl entered the chamber like phantoms in the night. The feeble torchlight penetrated barely more a few feet in front of them as they passed through a void of darkness. The only familiar source of comfort for them was the reassuring presence of the earthen floor which was littered with bits of fallen crust from the roof above. After several long minutes had passed, flecks of white began to appear up ahead of them. Then the vision grew clearer until the familiar sight of human skulls stared back at them.

The men stopped in their tracks when they saw hundreds of human skulls embedded in the walls of the cave.

'These are the heads of the men who helped bring the treasure here,' said Velen. 'The secret had to be kept safe so they were sacrificed.'

Carl shuddered at the thought of the mass slaughter of the men but of course, life in these times was cheap.

Velen urged Bastia onwards. Another few minutes had passed until the druid eventually called a halt.

'Lift the torch upwards and let the light reveal the treasure.'

Bastia did what was asked and slowly raised up the torch. Over his head was another torch hanging in a bracket suspended on a long chain that ran off into the blackness above. The torch was obviously dipped in some kind of oil as it instantly caught alight and, as before, it set off a line of fire that ran to another torch further up which then lit a multitude of torches that spread out in all directions, higher and higher, upwards and outwards until there were literally hundreds of them burning brightly like stars in the night sky. The darkness was instantly chased away as the men looked up in awe at the vast arching ceiling high above their heads. To them it looked as bright as early dawn on a summer's day. Bastia dropped his now useless torch to the floor where it fizzled out in a whisper. But then the men's eyes were soon distracted from the spectacle above as a golden glow reflected off the cave walls. They followed the glow downwards until their gaze finally fell upon a mountain of gold as big as a ten-storey building. But they quickly realised that there was something wrong. Something was amiss!

Paxus took a short step forward to make sure he wasn't seeing things. Drusus gasped in shock and turned away in disappointment. Bastia stood in disbelief with his jaw agape whilst Carl struggled to discern whether to laugh or to cry.

In front of them sat a solid pyramid of gold, melted into a single, immoveable mass. Its familiar shape reminded Carl of the great pyramid of Egypt. It stood at least two-hundred foot high and was about a hundred and fifty foot wide at the base. In front of the mountainous pyramid sat a stone altar or table which was littered with bits of dried-out moss. But Carl's attention quickly returned to the gold. He scanned the surface looking for a sign of a bracelet, a ring or even a crown, but there was nothing. The entire hoard of the Celtic gold, from the intricate artworks of delicate earrings and tiaras to the great statues and shields for which the Celts were famed for, had been melted into one giant ingot. Then he noticed that a single eye had been carved into the pyramid, just below the apex. A memory suddenly flashed through his mind. It looked very much like the eye of providence that was printed on the back of every American dollar bill. This symbol, a pyramid with an ever-seeing eye at the top had been open to interpretation ever since its inclusion and was still hotly debated over. He shook his head, thinking that this could be an odd coincidence or was the conspiracy theory right about the mysterious origins of the symbol?

Carl looked to Paxus who suddenly turned in rage and bounded over to Velen to confront him, face-to-face.

'What in the world have you people done?' he screamed tensing both fists as if he was making ready to pummel the druid into the ground, but Velen stayed calm and smiled back at the Roman.

'You didn't think we savages were stupid enough to leave the treasure as it was, do you; easy to carry off by any common thief?'

Paxus was beside himself with rage. He was speechless for once and he turned away from the druid in disgust.

'We've come all this way for nothing!' announced Drusus who began to laugh at the irony of it all. 'I should have stayed at home with my whores and my juicy fat pigs instead of coming to these cursed isles.' His ironic laughter grew louder and louder, echoing off the vaulted ceiling in a chorus of rebounding voices that seemed to be laughing back at him. But pretty soon, his laughter turned to cries of anguish and he swooned to the ground cursing his luck.

Carl relished in the poetic justice that these greedy Romans were receiving. Then a thought struck him from out of the blue. What that if Paxus had been successful in returning to Rome triumphant with all this gold? Would he have read about him in the text books? Would the empire have ended there and then? Would Christianity have been lost to history like so many early cults? One glance at the giant mound of gold in front of him confirmed that if Paxus had been successful he would have most certainly rewritten the history of the western world.

'Why have you chosen to reveal the gold to us?' asked an incredulous Paxus, still angered almost to the point of violence.

'It is Bastia's birthright to see the great hoard,' replied Velen. 'I could not deny him this opportunity.'

With his back still turned, Paxus spoke out of a burning curiosity: 'Earlier on, you said, 'so he may understand'. What did you mean by that?'

Velen moved towards the treasure and laid a palm upon its gleaming surface.

'The great Celtic Kings of old, including the mighty Vercingetorix, watched the treasure hoard grow with trepidation,' he said as if reciting from a manuscript. 'Their ancestors had amassed so much gold over the centuries that they realised it would eventually become more dangerous to them than their sworn enemies. And of course, their suspicions were realised when Julius Caesar arrived in Gaul. You know the history of his conquest and subsequent triumph over the Celts but what you don't know is that Caesar played an unwitting hand in protecting the gold. Following the defeat of Vercingetorix, the Celtic Kings were forced to make a drastic decision. They knew that if the gold ended up in Caesar's hands the world would be plunged into a terrible and deadly war that would spread well beyond the borders of the empire. It would see an end to the Celts forever.'

'So it ended up here,' said Drusus mocking Velen's words, 'hidden away from people who could make use of it. People like Paxus here who had a plan to overthrow the Caesars and return Rome to a republic.'

'A noble gesture indeed,' replied Velen, 'but men are corrupted by gold. It destroys their spirit and opens the door for all their vile traits to come to the fore; treachery, betrayal, lies, corruption, violence and murder. This is the world as foreseen by the Celtic Kings of old.' Velen paused for breath and looked each and every man in the eye. 'Is this the world you would want to live in?'

Drusus raised his hands and applauded Velen in a sarcastic gesture. 'Thank you for the moral lesson,' he said as he turned and ran an envious eye over the gold. 'So what happens now?'

Velen tapped his staff to the floor three times. Almost immediately, footsteps echoed off the high walls growing louder with each step. Before they knew it, twenty or so white robed figures, similar to the man they had first seen at the entrance, appeared from out of the gloom behind them. They looked threatening and ready to do something.

Velen nodded to the men and at once then several of them seized Bastia and pulled him aside from the others.

'What the hell are you doing?' screamed Bastia to the druid.

'Your life will now fulfil its purpose, Bastia, son of Banax,' said Velen. 'Your royal blood will protect your ancestor's legacy forever.'

'No. Paxus do something,' pleaded Bastia.

The politician took a step forward but thought better of the situation. He was heavily outnumbered and had no weapons to help him. Drusus cursed Velen vehemently saying that human sacrifices had been outlawed in Rome for decades and damned him for such barbarism. Carl was left speechless. The fear upon Bastia's face struck horror in his heart and he felt for the unfortunate man.

'I have not come all this way to die,' cried Bastia, but his words fell on deaf ears as the robed men stripped him naked and held him firm by the arms. It was too much for Paxus who rushed to his aid, but Bastia's captors kicked and punched him away from them. Then they shoved him bodily towards Carl and Drusus and gave the three of them a look that simply said; 'don't you dare'.

A screaming Bastia was frogmarched towards the mountain of gold then lifted up and laid out on his back upon the stone altar. Then they grabbed his legs and arms and stretched him out to his full extent. Bastia was pleading for help but there was nothing Paxus, Drusus or Carl could do.

'I can't watch this,' said Drusus as he turned away.

One of the robed men pulled out a dagger from within his robe and held it high. He began to whisper incantations over the prostrate figure of Bastia whose struggles were useless against the combined strength of his captors. Velen took a step forward and began to circle the altar. He shook his staff at intervals over Bastia calling out in the Britannic language to his gods. When he completed his circling, he took the dagger from the other man who bowed and moved away.

'No,' cried Paxus, 'let him be. I beg you.'

Velen looked up from the altar briefly and grinned back at Paxus.

'Do not fear for him,' he said impassively. 'The line of Celtic Kings will end with this final act. Bastia will join with his ancestors and the world shall see their likes no more.'

Without hesitation, Velen plunged the dagger deep into Bastia's chest and the former slave cried out in anguish and pain. Then Velen twisted the blade at right angles and began to cut downwards, opening up a long gash all the way down to his navel. Bastia's bloodcurdling screams echoed off the vaulted ceiling high above causing Carl to vomit up what little he had in his stomach. The poor man was suffering a terrible death at the hands of these savages and there was nothing he could do about it. He had never felt so helpless in all his life. Paxus stiffened with rage but stood his ground whilst Drusus raged at Velen, calling him a devil and a barbarian animal.

The men watched on in horror as Velen cast aside the dagger and plunged both hands deep into Bastia's torso. He proceeded to pull out his innards whilst calling out loudly to his god over Bastia's hysterical screams. Then some of the robed men took it in turns to reach in and rip out vital organs; lungs, heart, liver and kidneys. Carl and his companions looked on as the men walked over to the gold mountain and rubbed Bastia's organs all over the surface, calling out in their strange language.

Bastia lay dead. Rivulets of his blood ran down from the altar. The remaining men cupped their hands beneath the altar to catch Bastia's blood. Then they took turns in splattering the blood over the gold whilst chanting prayers to their god.

'Run,' whispered Paxus into Carl's ear, 'quickly now.'

The next few minutes went by in a flash for Carl. He followed Paxus with Drusus tagging along as the politician led them back the way they had come. The light from the torches guided them safely for only five-hundred feet or so but then the darkness shrouded them. Carl knew that one wrong turn down here could see them lost forever in an endless subterranean world but soon the gates appeared, grim and foreboding. Paxus wasted no time as he passed through the opening followed by Carl and Drusus. Then the three men pushed hard against the gate slamming it shut with a loud clatter that must have reverberated all the way back down towards the druid and his savage accomplices. Shouts immediately sounded out as the druid and his men realised that their guests had left the party. Paxus locked the gate behind him and removed the key. Holding it up like a trophy, he spoke with a glint in his eye.

'Good on Bastia for leaving the key in the lock,' he said with a broad grin as he nodded for them to move on.

They wasted no time as they quickly found the flight of steps that led up to the exit. They fumbled and felt their way upwards in the near dark for what seemed like an eternity until they made it to the top step. The torches that the first robed man had lit were still ablaze but Paxus called a halt before they went any further.

'Always take stock before your next move,' he said to Drusus and Carl like a scout. The men scanned the way ahead for a sign of life but there was none. The cave seemed devoid of anything living. The cold air from above indicated that they were not far from the thorn bushes that guarded the exit.

'Let's go,' whispered Paxus cautiously.

They slowly advanced taking care not to make a noise. Carl could think only of Lana. An urgent need to get to her as quickly as possible filled his thoughts but he wondered just how were they going to find their way back to the Borgoni village? Soon the thorn bushes appeared in the distance. The doorway was still shut but they opened easily with one shove and in no time they found themselves out in the open. It took several minutes for their eyes to adjust to the diffused sunlight streaming through the canopy above and when they eventually did they quickly spotted a lone man leaning up against a tree stump with his arms folded. It was Vaco. His gnarled and grim features were unmistakeable.

'Welcome back to the world of the light,' he said as he looked past the three men quizzically. 'Where is Velen?'

'We locked him behind the gates,' said Paxus getting straight to the point. 'He sacrificed Bastia with help from his cronies.' Paxus stood tall and threatening over Vaco who shied away from the politician's stance. His eyes darted from Carl then to Drusus and back to Paxus.

'So, you'll want to be getting yourselves back to Rome then?' he asked.

'Can you help us, Vaco?' asked Paxus.

After a long pause, Vaco stood upright and took a step towards Paxus. He seemed pleased that he was asked for help. He had several swords upon his person and he quickly unbuckled one of the straps around his waist and offered up a gladius, the preferred sword of a legionnaire, to the politician.

'You know how to use this, don't you?' he asked, mockingly.

'I can look after myself,' replied Paxus who snatched the sword gratefully from Vaco's hands. He then unsheathed it and pointed the tip at Vaco's throat. 'Who are you?'

Vaco smiled broadly and slowly pushed the sword away. 'My real name is Torus Vacos. I was a ballista in Vespasian's seventh legion.'

Carl recalled what a ballista was. They were expert exponents of the catapult who flung lead balls from within their ranks at the enemy, often to devastating effect.

'I was wounded in battle many moons ago and left for dead by my men,' continued Vaco. 'I managed to survive alone for weeks in the forests around here until the Borgoni found me. Instead of killing me they took me in and treated me as one of their own but I quickly discovered why. They wanted me to spy for them in return for payment but I have yet to see any gold lacing my palms. Now you have come along and given me hope. I am done with the Borgoni and their lies; to hell with their gold. I want to return to Rome and kill the bastards that left me behind.'

'You're forgetting one thing,' said Carl abruptly. 'What about Lana and Mumi?'

Vaco smiled at Carl with a charm that failed to materialise. 'Your women are safe and waiting for you,' he said but then he frowned. 'Why are you so concerned about them anyway, they are only women?'

Carl immediately stiffened with rage but Paxus raised a hand for calm and turned to Vaco. 'They come with us or we don't go to Rome,' he said in his most threatening tone. Drusus seconded Paxus' words which made Carl feel humble and grateful all at once.

After a long pause in which Vaco eyed Carl up and down with an unsatisfied curiosity he turned back to the tree stump that he had been leaning against and reached down behind it. He picked up a small sack and presented it to Carl. Carl immediately opened it up and there was his camera, phone and watch just as he had left them.

'The Borgoni thought them to be instruments of evil,' said Vaco, 'so they ordered me to destroy them. What the fuck are they?'

Carl nodded back gratefully and tied the sack to the cord at his waist. 'They are the tools of my trade,' he lied.

Vaco shrugged with indifference. 'You can tell me what they do another time.'

Without a second's pause, Vaco ordered that they follow him quickly. The men obeyed at once and soon they were plunged into a semi-dark world of dense forest and thick undergrowth. There was no visible trail ahead only the balding scalp of their guide as a point of reference. With no sign of a chase or alarm being raised, Carl began to relax, thinking of his reunion with Lana and wondering if she would be fit enough to travel. With his phone in his possession and the chance of returning to Rome where they can hide until Sam could bring them back he began to feel a sense of hope at last. He knew Sam would not let him down.

And so, another quest was about to get under way; the quest to return home. He and Lana's only problem now was to stay alive, but in these times that was an uncertain proposition. He chanced a look to Drusus who seemed anxious and nervy. He seemed like a man who was ready to explode at any minute and Carl thought it better not to stir his pot too much. But Paxus' face told a different story. Disappointment was reflected in his eyes. Thoughts of glory and reward had been snatched from his grasp and the death of Bastia hung over him like a raincloud but he could also see a grim determination behind the mask. He had the willpower to succeed and he had the contacts in Rome to pull the strings for him. Carl knew from history that Paxus' ultimate failure to return to Rome with the treasure was probably down to his sheer pig-headedness which was a trait that was the most likely cause that led to his eventual demise.

*

After almost an hour of trudging through the dense forest, the small troop came to a clearing filled with bright sunlight. Carl had to cover his eyes from the glare for a brief moment but as his sight got used to it he noticed several horses tied to a log and beyond them stood a two-wheeled horse and cart. Sitting upright in the back of the cart was both Lana and Mumi.

'Your women,' announced Vaco, not sounding too pleased.

Carl turned to Vaco and thanked him then he immediately raced over to the cart and went straight up to Lana. He made to give her a big hug but she stiffened and brought up her legs to her chest in a protective way. Carl stood back feeling puzzled by her reaction.

'Don't touch me,' she said in English as she stared back at him with those same lifeless eyes he had seen only days before. 'Give your attention to the mother of your child.' Carl immediately felt crestfallen.

'It will be a long time before she can trust another man,' said Mumi.

Out of the eyesight of the others, Carl placed a hand on Mumi's ever-growing bump in a pathetic attempt to show compassion but she pushed it away.

'Ha, ha, ha,' laughed Vaco as he approached the cart. 'That's women for you. Your best will never be good enough.'

Carl ignored the ignorant pig behind him and looked Lana up and down to inspect her. If ever there was a case to be made for the biggest fall from grace, surely Lana was it. She looked more like a stick insect than a human being. There was nothing left of her great beauty, just a bag of skin and bones.

'Let's get moving. We have a boat to catch,' ordered Vaco as he jumped up onto the seat of the cart and took up the reins. 'Choose a horse each of you men. It's a half day's ride to the sea so let's make haste.'

A trail led through the forest that meandered uphill and downhill for a few miles. The canopy above began thinning out with every mile and soon the travellers found themselves out on a dirt path that wound its way through wide open meadows covered with endless sheets of gossamer. It felt good to be clear of the claustrophobic atmosphere of the trees and in the open once more. The air was fresher out here and it helped to clear their heads. It seemed that spring had arrived early on this day and that winter had skipped past without notice.

Carl rode alongside the cart with his eyes fixed upon Lana who had fallen asleep. He was worried for her. The wounds to her vagina and pelvis may be on the mend but the mental trauma she had suffered at the hands of the soldiers will never heal. In a funny way, if she was to die soon it would be a blessing and he didn't mind thinking like that. In these ancient times, where death was a constant companion, it was also the only way out of the desperate struggle.

'Are they your wives?' asked Vaco shaking Carl out of his grim thoughts.

'They are my companions,' he replied without thinking.

'The white one has great spirit, for a woman?'

Carl did not reply but merely shrugged. 'Why haven't the Borgoni come after us?' he asked wanting to change the subject. Paxus and Drusus listened in to Vaco's reply with interest.

'The villagers are forbidden to enter the place of the skull. It will be a long time before they figure out that Velen and his priests will not be returning.' Vaco laughed to himself.

'How come you were waiting for us back there?' asked Paxus.

'I was given the task of selling off your women to the neighbouring village to be used as slaves so I stopped by on the way in the hope of rescuing you but, thankfully, you made it out by yourselves.' Vaco's expression suddenly grew dark with threat as he stared Paxus hard in the eye. 'You're my ticket to Rome, politician, and I want to be rewarded handsomely for this.'

The troop rode on in sullen silence for several minutes until Carl spoke up out of the blue:

'Did Velen mean to sacrifice us all?'

'Of course he did. His bloodlust is insatiable and your skulls would have joined the thousands already down there. But don't worry, my friends. By the time the Borgoni discover that you have locked away their druid and his priests, I'm sure we'll be at sea and heading for Gaul.'

The men looked to each other and breathed a collective sigh of relief but said nothing. The ride went on in silence.

Carl kept his eyes fixed on the track ahead. His thoughts soon turned to home and to his phone which, thankfully, had not been tampered with. He was grateful that the people of these times were totally ignorant of the modern marvels that he had in his possession. If they only knew, he thought but then, they would never understand.

Several hours passed and the troop made good progress across open fields stopping only to rest the horses and to eat. They eventually reached the coastline in the late afternoon. Vaco let loose the horses and left the cart by the side of the trail then he took them on foot down a steep, narrow pathway that led all the way down to the beach. Lana found the walk a bit tiring but she showed great inner strength to walk unaided. Mumi's bump was becoming more prominent now but Carl was relieved that the others showed no interest in her pregnancy at all. The secret that he was the father was safe for now.

After another hour, they eventually spilled out onto a shale beach which was full of boats bobbing gently in a small, natural harbour. Many men were busy at preparing the rigging and loading provisions.

'You see that big one there?' said Vaco as he pointed at the largest in the fleet. It was brightly decorated with sea monsters and gods of all descriptions painted along her sides which Carl found fascinating indeed. 'She's called The Dawn Rose. She was a Roman merchant ship at one time, until she ran aground. Now she belongs to me and my good friend Decada – a Roman deserter who hated the army life.' Vaco turned to Paxus and Drusus and smiled. 'Don't look down on him for deserting for he has done more good for Rome as a trader than he could ever have done as a soldier.'

Paxus and Drusus said nothing in reply. The two Romans wanted to get to Gaul more than anyone on the beach and they were willing to sail at any cost.

After Vaco had introduced Decada to his traveling companions, the very tall but slim deserter ordered his crew to set sail and pretty soon The Dawn Rose was under way. Paxus had greeted Decada warmly upon boarding but Drusus was less friendly, deeming all deserters worthy of crucifixion. Decada had seen it all before but stayed aloof and unperturbed.

The boat made good progress across the English Channel. The waters were calm and a warm, stiff breeze helped them make the crossing quickly. They landed in Gaul by nightfall and were met by a group of riders who had horses ready for them. After Vaco had said his farewell to Decada they were soon on their way again but the ride was short for they found themselves in a small village atop a high ridge. Vaco was welcomed by the elders but they seemed suspicious of his company, especially a black woman whom they had never seen the likes of before. He quickly reassured them that they were traders seeking out new prospects in the south.

They stayed the night and were fed well. Sleep came quickly to Carl and it was the first decent rest he had had in ages. They were woken at dawn on the next day and sent on their way with only enough supplies for a day upon a rickety old one-horse cart that looked ready to fall apart at any moment. Carl, Paxus and Drusus were given horses to ride but the horses were diseased, dirty and weak. By the night of the third day, the horses were dead, the cart had fallen apart and Vaco slaughtered the carthorse for meat. Rome seemed further away now than when they set out from Britannia.

'To walk to Rome from here would take about six months,' said a despondent Drusus who began to gather wood to make a fire to cook the horsemeat.

'Let's make a big fire, on top of that hill,' said Lana shocking everyone into silence. It was the first time she had spoken since leaving the shores of Britannia.

'Why a big fire?' asked Drusus, sounding confused.

'How far would you say we are from your fort at Lutetia?' asked Lana.

'We are about three days ride west from it,' guessed Drusus.

'Don't you have smaller forts posted around this area?'

'Yes, but the winter…' Drusus stopped himself in his tracks. It was not winter. The soldiers will be returning to their outlying forts, ready for the spring and summer months.

'She's right,' said Paxus. 'The soldiers will come if we build a big enough fire.'

Within the hour the troop had dragged the cart up the hill, piled it up with plenty of extra wood that they found scattered around and set it alight.

22

THURSDAY, MARCH 11TH PRESENT DAY:

Ted Brooks cast an eye over the headline news of the many tabloids which he had spread out all over his office desk. One in particular cut straight to the bone: *American archaeologists stranded in ancient Rome. Extraordinary claims by respected journal, trashed by experts. Has the National Geographic gone mad?*

It was just as he expected. Ever since the hurried publication of a special edition of his journal revealing Carl and Lana's plight and the imminent rescue attempt, his phone never stopped ringing. The police requested that he remove the magazine article from circulation but his lawyers stepped in on that point. Television chat show hosts were ridiculing the article and inviting, so-called experts, to comment. It brought home to him just how stupid the human race can be.

Ted Brooks, a champion of science, was once again, on the defensive. He hated the near total absence of scientific understanding within the public domain. The failure of the education system which had always been stymied by religious beliefs, and which he knew was steeped in ignorance and creates a long line of generations that are lost to science, grated on him immensely. He despaired that the great works of contemporary science educators like Carl Sagan, Richard Dawkins and Neil DeGrasse-Tyson clearly haven't been heard. Their calls for logic and reason to be at the forethought of everyone on the planet have fallen on deaf ears. Instead, the world carries on steeped in mysticism and ideology; ideologies that, not so long ago, were the very foundations upon which every pious nation of their day was built upon, where science was suppressed and often ignored and many of the exponents of science were tortured or murdered for their thoughts and ideas. That time was called the Dark Ages but it seemed to Ted that the Dark Ages had never gone away. His long standing disgust for humanity's lazy intellect was always an unsettling thought and now he had to ready himself for the storm of ignorance that was to come his way.

A knock on his office door jerked him back to reality. June, his secretary, popped her head 'round.

'Excuse me Ted it's the mayor here to see you.'

'*Oh that Judeo/Christian idiot,*' he thought as he rolled his eyes with displeasure. '*He'll be bringing along his portable pulpit to give me a grilling with all his godly authority.*'

'Send him in June,' he said wearily as he readied himself for the dressing down by reaching for a large glass of Bourbon.

Big John Muldoon strode into Ted's office like a crusader on his way to slay the infidel. Without a handshake or even a nod the mayor of Washington DC sat down and crossed his legs looking mightily annoyed.

'I just got a call from the president,' he announced in his '*I shout the loudest so I win the argument*' voice. 'He wants you to issue a public apology and withdraw your article at once.'

'Tell the president to call my lawyers, sir,' replied Ted as he sat down opposite the huge and dominating figure before him. He made it a point not to offer the mayor a drink. He wanted him out of his office as quickly as possible.

'What the hell are you thinking, Ted?' asked the mayor as his fat balding head began perspiring even though the room was a cool sixteen degrees Celsius. 'The National Geographic has become the laughing stock of the world. This city cannot be the centre point of ridicule.'

'I have provided the evidence that Carl and Lana are lost in time due to what theoretical physicists call a time fold. It's all to do with the quantum link between Carl and Sam's phones.'

'Ha, quantum link you say?' asked the mayor in frustration. He slammed his beefy fist down hard upon the desk. 'For fuck's sake man where are Carl and Lana?'

'At this moment, they are somewhere else in time – Rome, two-thousand years ago.'

The look upon the mayor's face was a picture. Ted was brimming over with smugness. The big dummy in front of him couldn't grasp his simple statement, yet this man was an elected representative of the people of Washington DC.

'Is it true that this Italian physicist friend of yours is going to use a nuclear bomb?' asked the mayor. Ted nodded. 'Do you know that it is causing me a serious diplomatic headache?'

'It's the only way to get Carl and Lana back,' replied Ted after he took a long sip of Bourbon.

'You truly believe that these archaeologists are lost in time, two-thousand years in the past, don't you?'

'All the evidence points towards it,' said Ted who was now becoming a little irritated. 'Christ John, you've heard the recording on TV of Carl speaking to his brother. He sounded afraid for his life.'

'The public don't buy it and neither does the president. No nation wants to lend your professor a nuclear bomb to perform a half-assed experiment just so he can get himself a Nobel Prize for physics. What are you hoping to gain by this publicity stunt Ted? You don't need to drag the National Geographic through the gutter just to sell more copies.'

'You're right Mr Mayor,' replied Ted mockingly as he threw a hand up in the air in a flippant manner. 'Why on earth would a respected journalist like me risk so much on a trashy storyline like this? I must be nuts, just as the tabloids are claiming, right? I must have been involved in Carl and Lana's murder somehow and invented this wacky tale to cover my back, right?'

John Muldoon leaned back further in his chair, twiddling his thumbs and looking as though he was trying his damn hardest not to be convinced by Ted's argument. After a long pause the mayor finally spoke up.

'I have powers that I can invoke, Ted,' he said as a mild threat. 'You don't want me to exercise my authority do you?'

Ted had had enough. He slammed his tumbler down upon his desk causing the glass to crack and stood up. He paced up and down several steps then turned to the mayor.

'Two of my friends' lives are at risk here. They are lost and alone in a time when the wheelbarrow was considered to be cutting edge technology and when everybody on the planet didn't know where the sun went at night. Damn it John, just look at the picture.'

Ted leaned forward and shuffled the tabloids aside on his desktop. He pointed out the colour photograph of Carl and Lana which was used on the front cover of the National Geographic. It was the one that he had first seen at the dig site in Rome. John Muldoon stared at it as if seeing it for the first time but the picture was now on almost every publication around the world. He shied away from the image of the two archaeologists holding up a placard that said 'help, we are lost in time, can't get home' and looking a shadow of their former selves. He pushed the magazine aside and looked up at Ted.

'Cardinal Bell is concerned that your article will cause unrest within the religious community.'

'Heaven forbid!' cried Ted sarcastically. 'Why on earth would the cardinal think that?'

'Because, if what you claim is true,' replied the mayor, 'and by some unfortunate circumstance Carl and Lana should meet our lord Jesus Christ, then it could undermine the churches authority and all that it stands for.'

Ted was stunned into silence. He could not believe what he was hearing. Once again the ignorance shown by these people was staggering. He slumped back into his seat and stared in disbelief at the mayor.

'As I have explained in my article,' said Ted with a restrained anger. 'Carl and Lana have been sent back to the time of the reign of Titus, that's a good fifty years after the supposed death of that fucking first century hippy.'

The mayor raged at Ted's stinging words about his beloved Jesus and shifted his position in his chair. It looked to Ted as though the simple fact of the difference in time between Carl and Jesus was too hard for him to fathom.

'And furthermore,' continued Ted, 'the Jesus of the bible was nailed to a cross in Judea, a good one and a half thousand miles from Rome. There would be no way that they could ever meet.'

'All right, Ted,' cried the mayor, as he stood up and leaned across the desk, 'let's say Carl and Lana are lost in time. What if this… experiment with a nuclear bomb works and it brings them back. That would be a triumph on its own but the cardinal thinks that the scientists might want to take it a step further and keep the doorway open so they could drop in on the crucifixion?'

Now it all seemed clear to Ted why the mayor was paying him a call. Cardinal Bell had sent along his lapdog to grill him on the potential possibility that the Jesus story had been a myth all along. Ted shook his head in pity.

'Tell the cardinal his little secret is safe with me. His church have been selling their invisible product for two-thousand years and making a good living out of it. Why would I want to spoil their party?'

The mayor's face went crimson with rage but he did a good job of keeping his tongue in his head. He turned and made ready to leave, much to Ted's relief.

'I know that you are an atheist Ted,' he said. 'And I know that you lost your faith after what happened to your father with the Ku Klux Klan and all that, but please, show some respect for once. There's no need to be arrogant, it's so unbecoming of you.' The mayor straightened his tie then turned to make his way out of his office but then he stopped and spoke without turning to face Ted.

'In your article you mentioned that Carl and Lana were going on a quest to find Celtic treasure?'

'So they said,' replied Ted, nonchalantly. 'Why, what's the problem?'

The mayor merely shook his head and exited without a further word.

Ted watched him go. Why the hell did he ask me that, he thought? Then a memory sparked to life. It was something about the Celts and their great wealth. He pondered for a long time and decided to look further into the subject. He scribbled down some notes to remind him then leaned back in his seat and sighed. It was a pity the mayor couldn't stay any longer, he thought. He had a whole bunch of replies lined up for him. He loved arguing his point on theocracy. He always felt that religious believers were on a loser every time they opened their mouths because they were willing to pit their mysticism and superstition against logic and reason and that was always going to be a recipe for disaster.

Whilst Ted sat pondering, on the other side of the city, President William McCauley sat in the oval office fuming at his chief of staff. Susan Grey had just informed him that Russia is willing to provide the nuclear bomb that Professor Vinci required to attempt his rescue mission.

'What the fuck are they playing at?' said the president.

'It's unbelievable, Bill,' said Susan, a forty-something career-minded executive, 'but the Russian president, Nicolai Kushnov is believed to have said, and I quote: 'for the first time in history a nuclear weapon will be put to use for peaceful purposes', unquote.'

'We're talking about two American citizens here. It is my duty, as their president, to try and get them back.'

'May I remind you sir, that the official stance from this administration is that Carl Allen and Lana Evans have been murdered.'

The president grimaced. 'This whole story is preposterous anyway. How can anyone believe that two of our citizens have, somehow, ended up back in ancient Rome for Christ's sake?'

'Member states of the UN will be up in arms over the proposed use of a nuclear bomb,' said Susan, as she sat back in her chair looking pensive. 'This could escalate into something really ugly.'

'Those little shits meddling with their science experiments,' said the president. 'It's all a scam to cover up the truth about the death of Carl Allen and Lana... what's her name?'

'Evans,' replied Susan as she took a sip of her black coffee. She placed her cup down upon the desk and sat back looking a little flustered. 'If Ted Brooks is lying to save the skins of Professor Barnes and the other two scientists then he's going to great lengths to hide the truth don't you think?'

'But it can't be true. There' no way anyone can be zapped back in time and then be brought back. It's impossible.' The president ruffled his full head of hair in frustration and stood up from his chair. He was fifty-one years of age, tall and slim and the best looking leader America had had since John F. Kennedy. A democrat through-and-through, he was destined for a second term in office but this news could cause him serious problems at home and abroad.

'I have had Mike Dole look at the National Geographic's claim and he said it's plausible,' said Susan.

'Mike Dole from NASA?' asked the president with a scowl. 'What's he got to say?'

'Quite a lot, actually,' said Susan. 'Why don't you give him a call?'

After President McCauley's phone call to Mike Dole he was immediately on the phone to the United Nations. Dole's argument had been very convincing and the president was determined to take the lead and offer Professor Vinci an American bomb but UN officials flatly refused. They reminded the president that the rules clearly state that no nation is permitted to explode nuclear weapons above ground for testing even though the Russians were insisting that they were not testing their bomb but using it for a life-saving mission. In reply, the UN published their official statement that Professor Vinci's whole project was flawed and utterly ridiculous. They declared him a maverick and ordered that he be given no assistance from any UN member state whatsoever and furthermore, severe sanctions will be imposed on Russia should they explode the bomb. Instantly, the news got out that Russia and America were vying for the right to conduct a dangerous rescue mission using a nuclear bomb. Anti-nuclear protesters took to the streets around the world blaming the politicians and scientists. In order to keep his popularity high, President McCauley went on TV to inform the people that no such proposal was put forward by him. In an effort to calm the global hysteria down, news channels requested that Professor Vinci come on TV to explain to the world just how the rescue mission would work. A few days later, Francesco Vinci went live from his lab in Rome to show just how he planned to bring back Carl and Lana.

Sam sat in his lounge at home watching the live broadcast of Francesco Vinci standing in front of the blackboard in the very same room that he had first met him all those months ago. The Italian physicist looked drawn and tired since the last time Sam had seen him. He had obviously been working tirelessly on the project and it was a credit to his dedication and professionalism that he had come up with a proposed solution. He watched in fascination as Francesco calmly explained his mission with the aid of his drawings upon the blackboard behind him.

'A ten-inch thick stainless steel sphere, which we call the rescue chamber, will be encased within a four-inch layer of lead and buried forty-foot underground at a dedicated site on Severny Island, four-hundred kilometres north of the Russian mainland and within the Arctic circle. The rescue chamber will be big enough to comfortably house two people. It will be cooled from the intense heat given off by the bomb with a constant supply of pressurised liquid nitrogen. The whole apparatus will be housed inside a tank of salt water to absorb the shockwave. The bomb will be directly suspended over the chamber, ten-meters above ground level. Sam Allen's phone will be placed inside the chamber to make the quantum link between Carl and Sam's phones. The nuclear explosion will trigger the opening of a worm hole between the phones which will last a Nano second long. The size of the wormhole is determined by the amount of energy released by the bomb squared by its distance from the rescue chamber. We have calculated that the wormhole will be large enough for two people, give or take a few meters all-round. The explosion should reverse the arrow of time for each phone, respectively, thus swapping the space time continuum between them. If all goes well, we predict that Carl's phone and the immediate space time around it would come to our time and Sam's phone would end up somewhere in the past.'

After Francesco had finished speaking, one of journalists in the room asked the obvious question. Where, in time, will Sam Allen's phone end up?

Francesco admitted that he did not know exactly but he hoped that his team had calculated, correctly, the right distance between the bomb and the sphere which would send it past a time before mankind had evolved so as to rule out any chance of a paradox arising.

The classroom went silent. Francesco's explanation and simple diagrams which he had drawn on the blackboard was plain enough but it was too fantastic to believe. Sam could see that many journalists in the room were left scratching their heads. Francesco quickly excused himself from the stunned audience and exited the room silently.

Sam turned off his TV and immediately felt an overwhelming sense that he should be there at the rescue mission. He picked up his phone and rang his secretary. He was going to Rome on the next available flight.

Malcolm McVie sat opposite Francesco and raised a glass of champagne. He proposed a toast to the Italian physicist and his team for figuring out a way to get Carl and Lana home. Malcolm's contribution was to calculate the amount of nuclear energy needed for the mission to be a success. Thirty-two kilotons was the result – twice the size of the bomb dropped on Hiroshima. All scientists at the table were proud of their achievement, so far, but there was still a nagging doubt that there could be unforeseen problems ahead. One dreaded proposal was that the wormhole could allow ancient bacteria through for which our immune systems would not be able to fight. Another suggestion was that the connection between the two time frames may stay permanently open which would lead to an unimaginably complex situation.

'Now the whole world knows,' said Malcolm to Francesco after a sip of champagne.

'They know that we are all a bunch of lunatics,' replied Francesco who allowed himself a joke at the project's expense. 'But three months from now we may have achieved a rescue mission that will make Apollo 13 look like a walk in the park.'

The atmosphere in the room lifted at once and everyone around the table laughed with relief but they knew that their quest was only just beginning. The work ahead was going to be difficult. The stainless steel sphere had already been ordered and was being built in Poland. The tons of lead required to surround the sphere was being supplied by a firm in China whilst in Russia the ground was being prepared by the authorities for a sixty-thousand gallon tank of salt water to be constructed forty feet below the surface of Severny Island. The price-tag was running at seventy-million dollars and set to rise, but fortunately for the science team, many industrialists and entrepreneurs were willing to fund it. They were all friends of the Russian president Nicolai Kushnov, himself a former industrialist, who had ties with many business executives around the world. Francesco Vinci's project intrigued the president for he was also a learned physicist and an amateur astronomer. But he mainly wanted to use this opportunity to get one over on the Americans.

The media went berserk. Newspaper editorials were written almost daily. Retired scientists and experts in the field of physics were on TV almost continuously; some arguing for and others against. Religious leaders were complaining on theological grounds, phycologists were worried that a doorway to the past could be opened permanently and the paradoxes would be catastrophic. Anti-nuclear campaigners swore they would make their way to Severny Island and disrupt the mission but that was impossible. The Russian army had declared a fifty mile area around the island a military zone.

Unnoticed to the world, Professor Terence Barnes had been quietly released on bail from police custody. From there he went straight to his London home in Kensington. He immediately rang Ted Brooks and thanked him for the publication which helped end his incarceration but Terence Barnes left Ted in no doubt that he was worried about Professor Francesco's rescue plan. Ted did all he could to convince him but the old man was beside himself with guilt. He was most upset about his arrest on suspicion of murder, an act he was incapable of performing. After the phone call to Ted, a tearful Terence Barnes seated himself at his desk in his study and reached out for a picture of his deceased wife, Doris. With tears streaming down his face, he reached inside the top drawer of his desk and pulled out a case similar in size to a cigar box. He opened the lid and took out a Lugar pistol, one that his father had accepted off a surrendering German officer during the Second World War. He put the family heirloom to his temple and pulled the trigger.

23

TWO MONTHS LATER...

FRIDAY, MAY 14ᵀᴴ 80 AD:

The seventeen soldiers sheltered together in the guardhouse for protection against the bitter winds blowing down off the steep slopes of the snow-covered peaks of the Alps. The disgruntled men had been posted here for months under explicit orders of the emperor to cease anyone coming out of the Pass of Juno. To date, all that had come down from the mountains were several highland goats that were forced to lower ground due to hunger. Cursing their luck at being chosen for such a duty, the soldiers hunkered together to stay warm around a pitiful fire that threatened to die on them at any moment. It didn't seem like springtime this far north and this high up but their commander had assured them that the snows will melt soon and it will be like a home-from-home. All of them despaired at his words. They were Mediterranean men, born and bred along the balmy coastlines of the heel of Italy. They were not used to such cold conditions. They had served in Northern Africa and Judea under Vespasian in intense heat. They longed to feel the sun on their backs once more and the waft of the warm, sea air.

'Who is going to fetch fresh wood for the fire?' asked Aquius, the eldest of the soldiers who was feeling the cold the most.

'I will,' said Bruto, 'it's my turn to go.'

Bruto got up and put on his sheepskin cloak. He tied the leather straps tightly around his bulky body and lifted the latch on the door. 'If I'm not back in half an hour you can send out a search party for me.'

'Fuck you,' snapped Aquius, 'you're only walking twenty paces.' The others laughed at Bruto's expense and told him to hurry up.

Bruto returned the laugh then opened the door and left it swinging open as he exited the guardhouse. The men instantly cursed him and slammed it shut.

Bruto quickly made his way towards the pile of logs which were covered with a large tarpaulin. The early morning wind was bitter but not blowing as strongly as previous days. When he reached the pile of logs he undid one of the tie-ropes to the tarpaulin and pulled back the flap. Ice and snow stung his face relentlessly which caused his eyes to stream. He quickly set aside five logs, but as he made ready to re-tie the rope he was distracted by movement up ahead. At the foot of a slope, some fifty feet from him, he thought he had seen an assemblage of human figures, stumbling out of the pass. He quickly wiped his eyes and was surprised to see a group of men who, for all intents and purposes, looked like standing skeletons. They all wore roughly made animal hides that had come off various beasts. He counted eleven men in all. Out of professional habit he withdrew his sword and called out to them in Latin. Upon hearing his voice some of the men in the pass swooned to the ground and cried out for help. Bruto felt confused but then he noticed that there was something odd about them. After a short while it dawned on him that they were missing their right hands. He took a tentative step backwards thinking that they may be lepers from a nearby colony then he turned and ran back to the guardhouse.

Within no time, Bruto's comrades had gathered up their weapons and put on their sheepskins. They followed him out of the guardhouse to the pile of logs and saw the eleven men staggering towards them. They looked weak from exposure and starvation. Their scraggy beards made them look older than they probably were and the look of insanity in their eyes suggested that they had been brutally traumatised. Instantly, the soldiers knew that these pathetic looking bags of bones would offer no threat to them at all.

'What the fuck,' said Aquius?

Bruto turned to Aquius and shook his head in reply. 'Let's go and see,' he said. The others stayed back.

Aquius and Bruto approached the one-handed men and were shocked to see the familiar SPQR (the senate and people of Rome) tattoo imprinted upon their upper right arms. They now knew that they were, in fact, Roman soldiers. Then one of the men approached them and in a forced effort he raised his left arm in salute.

'I am General Catrus Vitrus,' he said in a broken voice that was barely audible above the din of the wind before he collapsed in a heap upon the ground.

Titus dismounted from his horse and entered the barracks at Servinia with little ceremony. He climbed the three wooden steps to the command post and breezed past the saluting soldiers as if they were not there. Upon entering the room he was met by an officer who looked astonished to see his emperor at such a lonely northern outpost. He quickly saluted and welcomed him warmly.

Titus, along with his small entourage, had decided to ride north to oversee proceedings. The lack of news about Paxus and his little army had worn on his mind throughout the winter months but, also, the pressure back in Rome was mounting with every passing day. The republicans were making noises once again on how Rome should be handed back to the people. Domitian was not helping either. Titus' spies had suspected that his brother was forging secret alliances with members of the senate but they could not prove it. Meanwhile, plague had come to the outskirts of Rome and was threatening to spread into the city. To counter the plague, Titus had ordered his soldiers to build a firewall in a thirty mile radius around the city. The wall was to be kept alight both night and day for an entire month. Only supplies from the sea were allowed in under the strictest scrutiny from the Roman navy. The only positive note was that the Coliseum was nearing completion. The Jewish slaves had been driven hard by doubling their workload. Many had died from the effort but for everyone that died there was two to replace them.

Titus saluted the gobsmacked commanding officer half-heartedly and sat down heavily upon a vacant chair. He was glad to be away from Rome, if only for a few weeks. The treasury was running dry and his accountants were at their wits end to come up with a solution. He knew that raising taxes further would end in a revolt. So the urge to get his hands upon the Celtic treasure was more prevalent than ever. He had had a dream that Paxus had been successful in his quest and that the politician's miniature army were now heading through the Alps with at least some, if not all, of the treasure.

'My emperor Titus,' said the officer, 'Welcome to Servinia, Commander Detrinion at your service.' The commander paused in his greetings and then spoke again. 'We have news for you.'

Titus turned from his musings and saw that the officer in command was looking rather perturbed. He was an ageing soldier who looked well past his best days.

'Yes?' asked Titus sensing the comfort of the chair was beginning to make him feel drowsy.

'A rider from an outpost has reported that they apprehended several soldiers at the foot of the Pass of Juno.'

'Soldiers belonging to who?' asked Titus as he yawned aloud.

Commander Detrinion swallowed hard and stared straight ahead. 'Soldiers belonging to you, my emperor,' he said. 'One of them introduced himself as General Catrus Vitrus.'

Titus was up on his feet in one movement.

'Take me to him, now,' he ordered.

'At once,' said Detrinion who snapped his fingers at his guards.

Within minutes, Titus was on the road again. His butt was raw and his back was aching from the long, seven day ride from Rome but his heart was beating fast with anticipation. He hoped that General Vitrus would have good news for him. Detrinion was unable to give him further information but he said that the general and his men were being looked after by the soldiers guarding the Pass of Juno.

Titus and his weary men rode on doggedly. They had travelled from Rome through the countryside to avoid contact with people of the towns and villages that may have the plague though this far north there had been no reports of the terrible affliction which was killing hundreds in their droves further south. Many physicians had argued that the colder climes in the north seemed to slow down the spread of the disease and Titus, for one, agreed.

The two-hour ride passed quickly and Titus soon found himself nearing a guardhouse at the foot of the Alps. The mountains were still covered in snow but he knew the Pass of Juno would be clear enough for a small army to negotiate. Detrinion called a halt outside the guardhouse. One soldier came forward to greet them and led them into the guardhouse which was a rather large wooden building. Immediately upon spotting the emperor the guards stood as one and saluted, though the look upon their faces betrayed their discomfort and surprise.

'Where is General Vitrus?' asked Titus without ceremony.

The guards quickly ushered Titus to the rear of the building where he saw many men huddled closely together around a brazier full of burning logs. They were chewing away hungrily at a few boiled pigs heads. The first thing that struck Titus was the smell. He had endured it before whilst searching for survivors during the aftermath of a battle; shit mixed with vomit. The men's beards and overgrown hair made them appear like wild animals. The guards had provided them with blankets for warmth but the men were still shivering. Then Titus noticed their missing right hands. It was strange to see so many cauterised stumps in one place. They were only half-men now; useless as soldiers, useless for just about everything.

'He's the one you asked for,' said one of the guards as he pointed past Titus at one who had his back to the emperor.

'General Vitrus,' Titus called out. 'You have a report to make?'

The decrepit man stayed with his back turned. Titus knew he had heard him but he refused to acknowledge his emperor.

'Leave me with him,' ordered Titus to the guard. 'And take the others with you.'

The guard did what was ordered and called for assistance to move the others from around the brazier. As they filed past him, Titus was astonished that these bags of bones were still breathing. Their eyes were sunken into their skulls, their lips were blistered and cracked open and their teeth were blackened. He could only guess at what they had been through.

'Catrus,' said Titus as he pulled up a stool and sat down next to the general. 'You look like shit!'

Catrus stopped chewing his food and turned towards his emperor then he turned back to the flaming fire and spoke in a frail tone:

'All my life I wanted to be a soldier; serving Rome as best I could. My finest years were given in the service of your father, a service I am immensely proud of.' He brought up his stump for Titus to see. 'Now look at me. I betrayed you, my emperor. I gave in to greed and this is what I get in return.'

Titus warmed his hands by the fire but said nothing. He watched Catrus sit up painfully as he turned to speak. His features were exaggerated to demon-like proportions from the glow of the flickering fire. The look in his eyes betrayed his emotions. This was a man livid with anger.

'Paxus has found the people who guard the Celtic treasure. They call themselves the Borgoni, but the politician and his friends have been taken prisoner.'

Titus diverted his gaze from the general. His thoughts raced. The secret was lost. He couldn't hide his disappointment whilst he stared hard into the flames.

'Claudius' little secret is out. Now I know why Rome wanted Britannia so much,' said Catrus, triumphantly.

Titus frowned but still kept his tongue.

Catrus placed his good hand upon his emperor's arm and spoke to him like a warrior. 'Give me two legions and I will bring you the treasure. I know where the village is. I will capture their leaders and force them to speak, but we must act fast before the Brits can move the treasure.'

Titus looked the veteran up and down. He knew it would be impossible for the man before him to ride a horse in his present state, never mind lead an army. But the look in Catrus' eyes burned brighter than the fire he was seated by.

'I should have you crucified for betraying my trust,' replied Titus, 'but enough of that. I need that treasure general, and I will send word to muster the forces in Britannia. But you are in no fit state to lead. Instead, I order you to show me the way.'

Catrus looked down at his stump and a flicker of emotion crossed his face. He seemed resigned but undeterred.

'Now tell me what happened to you?' asked Titus as he folded his arms in anticipation.

Catrus spat a piece of gristle into the fire and gulped down a cup of mulled wine. He looked his emperor hard in the eye and proceeded to tell him a horrendous story about how he and his troops had endured the long journey home. After the Borgoni had mutilated the forty-two survivors of the battle they were stripped naked and left to their own devices with no food or water. They were forced to live off the land but their troubles had only just begun. After three days, six of the soldiers died of infection from their wounds. They found it was impossible to make weapons with just one hand so they turned to stealing spears from Brit villages under the cover of darkness. This helped for a short while but one rabbit and a few squirrels could hardly sustain thirty-six men and soon they found themselves facing starvation. As they approached the coast of Britannia another soldier died, the youngest one named Seco. It was then that they took the drastic decision to butcher, cook and eat him.

At this point Catrus made Titus swear he would never tell anyone about it. The emperor nodded, knowing that cannibalism had occurred many times throughout the ranks of the Roman army during stressful times but it was never discussed openly. Catrus continued with his narration:

He told Titus how they managed to steal two fishing boats and set sail across the Britannia Sea. Then, tragically, one of the boats capsized in the heavy swell. On board the sunken vessel was his son, Juna. All the men on that boat drowned. Now they were down to just seventeen. The remaining boat took almost a week to cross, due to their onehandedness and the lack of seafaring knowledge. In that time two more died. They kept the bodies until they reached dry land where, once again, they ate the remains. Then they had a bit of good fortune. A travelling merchant from Rome recognised Catrus and took pity on him and his men. He offered them a horse and cart along with a few days' worth of supplies in return for favours. Catrus accepted the gift and promised he will remember him.

The next few months saw them wind their way through Gaul and eventually onto the foothills of the Alps. All the while, they were, once again, dogged by hunger and the cold. During the trek through the Alps, four more men died leaving the surviving eleven to make it to this point...

'So you see, my emperor,' said Catrus, sounding tired and drawn from his narration, 'we made it back to fight another day.'

Titus felt proud of the soldiery of Rome. He had no fears as to the loyalty and bravery of such men but he needed that gold which now felt so tantalisingly close.

'Do you think the Borgoni people will have executed Paxus?'

'I don't think so,' replied Catrus. 'Paxus had with him a Celtic King; the son of Banax whom they seemed to admire.'

Both men fell silent for a short while then suddenly they heard a shout from outside. It sounded like someone was raising an alarm. Within seconds Titus was out of the door and into the cold, mountain air. He immediately spied four guards waving to a gathering of shadowy figures in the distance. Titus looked beyond and could make out several figures staggering their way out of the pass towards them. He was soon joined by Commander Detrinion and a rather feeble but determined Catrus who had wrapped himself in a sheepskin cloak. He stood shivering next to both men.

'Drop your weapons!' ordered one of the guards to the approaching strangers.

The four men and two women, one of whom was carrying a baby, stopped in their tracks but the men made no attempt to relinquish their weapons.

'Who is your commander?' asked the tallest stranger in the troop.

'By the gods,' gasped Catrus, as his knees buckled from under him with shock, 'it's fucking Paxus! Cease him,' but the soldiers ignored his call.

'Take them', ordered Detrinion, 'and bring them to the garrison at Servinia.'

Servinia garrison was large and comfortable and was gearing up for another spring campaign. The place was a hive of activity. Soldiers and auxiliaries who had sat out the winter months at home were drafted in from all over the north. Paxus and his companions, Drusus and Vaco were bathed, fed and clothed, courtesy of the emperor. Later in the day, they found themselves seated opposite Titus at a large, round table. Paxus felt somewhat perturbed that his emperor had chosen to come to such a lonely outpost but he knew that the promise of riches made men go to extraordinary lengths to achieve that goal and Titus was no different.

'How goes your time in Rome, my emperor?' asked Paxus to break the awkward silence.

Titus did not reply. He sat stone-faced looking the politician up and down with intense curiosity. Paxus evaded his cold stare and glanced around the table at the faces glaring back at him; three soldiers and one decrepit looking, one-handed Catrus Vitrus. A sense of pity for the old general crossed his mind but he quickly dispelled such sentiment. The man had ordered Lana to be raped by his men – a trauma she will never get over. He wanted to crucify Carl and kill the rest to take the treasure for himself and his son. After another long pause, Titus rose from his seat and spread his hands across the table then stared Paxus down.

'You have seen the treasure?' he asked nodding in ascendancy.

'I have,' replied Paxus.

Titus looked to the soldiers seated beside him and grinned, then smiled back at Paxus. 'I will think favourably of you and your companions if you tell me the location of the treasure,' he said as he stood tall to make himself look more intimidating.

'You will have to bring many more men than you think.'

'Ha,' said Titus, 'this tribe you call the Borgoni are a bunch of wild savages. It will take just a few legions to take them down.'

Paxus stirred in his seat and shook his head. 'The Borgoni will not be a problem. The problem is that the Celtic treasure has been melted into a giant, solid pyramid at least two-hundred foot high and very wide at the base. It resides in a deep, cavernous cave system that is dark and damp and is locked away behind a set of monstrous iron gates that look impregnable. It would take months to break through the gates and many years to remove the treasure.'

'Never trust the word of a politician,' said Catrus to his emperor. 'He's lying.'

Paxus looked around the table at the grim faces staring back at him and smiled to himself. He then reached inside his robe and pulled out the skull key, holding it up for all to see. He placed it down upon the table right in front of Titus.

'I give you the key to the gates, my emperor.'

Titus' eyes widened as he reached out to pick up the hefty key. He held it in his hands and grinned back at the politician. Drusus and Vaco looked questioningly at Paxus who merely raised a hand to calm them.

'You give this freely to me?'

'You are a soldier,' replied Paxus. 'If you give me a soldier's word that you will not harm my companions and I, we will show you the way to the treasure.'

'Done,' said Titus without taking eyes off the key.

Paxus leaned back in his chair and sighed. Then he turned to Catrus and looked around the table pretending to be looking for someone who wasn't there. 'Where is your son, Juna?' he asked.

Catrus grimaced back at Paxus. 'He is dead, taken by the Britannic sea. And where is your Celtic king?'

'He was sacrificed by the Druids.'

Titus had heard enough talk. He slammed a fist down upon the table and spoke with all his authority.

'Enough,' he bawled. 'I want that treasure and I will send a hundred-thousand men to get it if need be. The Britannic hordes won't know what has hit them when they see the eagle standard raised above their burnt out villages.' He pointed a finger at the Catrus, Paxus, Drusus and Vaco in turn and spoke with a veiled threat. 'The treasure is mine and you four men will come with me to Rome to help me plan my quest.' Titus rose from his seat and stuffed the key inside his sword belt then left the room with his soldiers in tow.

Paxus swallowed hard. His return to Rome had turned out to be very different to what he had hoped, but at least he was still alive.

24

MONDAY, AUGUST 9ᵀᴴ PRESENT DAY:

The bomb was ready. The rescue chamber beneath it was ready. The area was cleared and ready but the politicians were not.

Squabbles, threats and counter threats ensued all over the planet. Riots in the streets of many capital cities erupted; the lefts against the rights, CND and Greenpeace against 'Friends of Carl and Lana'. Religious leaders and scientists were at each other's throats. Just about everyone was jumping on the bandwagon and Sam was left mesmerised by it all. Even after making a statement on live TV asking for calm and going to great lengths to explain the science behind the rescue mission his words fell upon deaf ears. The press accused him of endangering the planet for the sake of his brother's life. He had been constantly harassed with questions from the media; invites to chat shows, invites to religious seminars and scientific journals. And all the while, he was still weary of the threat of being arrested on suspicion of murder.

The world was going crazy over a scientific endeavour to save lives and Sam was right in the midst of it, so the request from Malcolm McVie for him to go to Severny Island in Russia had been a blessing and he immediately took up the offer. It had been his home now for three weeks. When he arrived, the island was a hive of activity but now, the area around the bomb site was eerily quiet.

Severny Island was no stranger to nuclear experiments. It was the site for nuclear weapons testing by the Soviet Union from 1958 to 1961. On October, 30th 1961 the most powerful nuclear bomb ever detonated, the Tsar Bomba, took place thirty miles up the coast from where he sat. How ironic, thought Sam, Tsar was the Russian word for Caesar.

He sighed with impatience as he sat in the observation shelter looking over the site through the viewfinder. The bomb was five miles to the north, ready and deadly. His impatience was born out of waiting for the politicians to sort out their squabbles. They couldn't wait too long though. The arctic winter comes early this far north and if the snows came whilst they were still deliberating, Carl and Lana's chances of ever returning home could be in jeopardy.

'Coffee for two?' asked a familiar voice from behind. It was Malcolm McVie. He had been on site since the start of the project and he had grown a long beard because, in his eagerness to get to Severny, he had forgotten to pack his shaving gear. Now he vowed not to shave again until Carl and Lana were home.

Sam took the welcome beverage from Malcolm and thanked him warmly. The two men had grown close during the time spent on the Russian army base. The soldiers manning the base were polite but not forthcoming. They stayed aloof and a little wary of civilians in their camp so the two men became friends, more out of need than want.

'Have they decided on a date yet?' asked Sam for something to say, not yet risking a sip from the boiling hot coffee that Malcolm always served up from his flask.

'Francesco wants to go on Friday, despite the politics,' announced Malcolm,'

Deadline days had come and gone and Sam was growing tired of the false promises. 'Friday the thirteenth?' he replied wearily, 'good planning.'

Malcolm laughed at the irony in Sam's comment but Sam could see the young man was troubled. He had worked many hours with Professor Vinci, along with his Russian counterparts who were eager to help.

'Are you worried that the rescue won't work?' asked Sam.

'It should work,' said Malcolm. 'The mathematics is correct. The calculations, predictions, mechanics and software are all in place but...'

'I know,' said Sam sympathetically, 'for all the eventualities you cover there's no way to eliminate human error.'

'It's not just that it's the fear of the unknown.'

'You mean the portal that the bomb may create,' said Sam, 'the one that some scientists are predicting will happen?'

'May happen,' corrected Malcolm. Malcolm frowned and turned to look out at the bomb site through the small window. 'I'm worried that Francesco knows more than he's letting on and that he's going ahead with the mission despite the risks.'

'I'm sure our Italian friend has Carl and Lana's best interests at heart.'

'I know that but there are many eminent scientists who disagree with our formula. Some are even calling us heretics to science and I wonder if they're right.'

Sam placed a calming hand on Malcolm's shoulder and smiled.

'Scientists are people. They have human traits just like everyone else and jealousy seems to be their biggest problem right now.'

Malcolm smiled in reply and looked out over the bomb site. 'How do you think Carl is coping right now?' he asked changing the subject. 'The tracking system is showing that he is back in Rome after his treasure hunt.'

'Well, we can ask him when he gets back,' replied Sam.

Both men fell silent in their own thoughts for a while then Sam spoke up:

'Quite a clever piece of work the tracking system our Russian friends figured out. Triangulation through time by using Carl's phone was a touch of genius, don't you think?'

'Yes. It came like a bolt from the blue; simple and yet brilliant.'

'Tell me again how it works?' asked Sam.

'Carl's phone is linked to yours through space time by quantum physics – the physics of the very small. Particles of energy in this realm come in and out of existence and appear in different places at the same time randomly.'

Sam's brain was beginning to waver slightly. Malcolm continued:

'Valeri Duclov, one of our Russian assistants, cleverly proposed that we can track Carl's phone by scanning a virtual map of Europe into the space time continuum that exists between both phones. And then, by linking your phone to another computer it would form a triangular network which can pick up the footprints of Carl's phone. The supercomputer works out the longitude and latitude of the footprints in a trillionth of a second up to two-hundred thousand times a second thus locating him to within an accuracy of a few miles. It's not sat-nav as we know it but it works.'

Although he didn't understand most of it, it, nevertheless, sounded impressive. 'So long as Carl can keep his phone on him,' pressed Sam.

Malcolm nodded and smiled back. 'Well, your last phone call has hopefully got the message over to him that we are about to go ahead with the mission and that it is imperative the phone stays with him and that Lana doesn't leave his side. The calculations conclude that the portal created by the bomb, centred around Carl's phone, will be about the size of a bus shelter, but if he loses the phone our efforts will have been a waste of time.'

Sam turned and looked forlornly in the direction of the bomb site. His phone was now suspended in a frame inside the rescue chamber. To him, the whole endeavour seemed absurd but the science behind it was real now all he could do was wait.

'What about Professor Ivan Lubic's claim that a permanent worm hole will be opened?' asked Sam, remembering that the Russian theoretical physicist was confident about his prediction. He looked across the room toward Ivan who was busy scribbling down calculations in his notepad. The overly large man seemed always to be perspiring and fidgeting about. He sat with his back to everyone in a world of his own.

Malcolm followed Sam's gaze and smiled ruefully to himself. 'His calculations are wildly optimistic. He has become a pain in the butt for Francesco but he insists on having him on his team, for the sake of international relations.'

'I don't like him, Malcolm,' replied Sam. 'He seems like a bit of shifty character to me.'

'Yeah, but try telling President Kushnov that.'

President McCauley slammed the phone down upon its receiver and swore aloud. The UN was doing next to nothing about the situation. In fact, they were making the matter worse by proclaiming the Russian President a danger to world peace and calling on all nations to sanction him. Kushnov was laughing at the UN. He had just gone on air to proclaim the rescue mission will take place in four days' time, on Friday the thirteenth. The white house had egg on its face. The American people demanded that America should be seen to be bringing back its own whether they believed if Carl and Lana were lost in time or not.

There was no way anyone could stop the mission now. The only hope was for Professor Vinci to have a change of heart but that was never going to happen. The American government had paid a lot of money to scientists to ridicule the mission. They paid philosophers, religious leaders and even ran a TV campaign with children running scared of a mushroom cloud; all to no effect. McCauley now resided himself to the fact. He looked across the oval office table at his advisor, Susan Grey, who shrugged her shoulders back at him and sighed. 'They're going to do it. The motherfuckers are actually going to do it.'

*

Rome was burning under the hot August sun as Titus oversaw final preparations for the opening ceremony of the Flavian Ampitheatre. His organisers stood around the table, smug in the knowledge that they had come up trumps for their emperor. They had ordered one-hundred days of games to help the people forget the ravages of the plague which had now ended. On top of that, the suburbs of Rome had just endured a fire which had killed hundreds but had been put out before it could spread to the more affluent areas, and even better news was that most of the refugees from Campania had been persuaded to return home to make a new life in the devastated land caused by the eruption of Vesuvius. The mountain had been silent for months and it seemed the gods of the underworld had finally been appeased after many weeks of sacrifices. The migrants from the north had long since headed back home and Rome had been given a good clean up in preparation for the games. Even his brother was behaving himself, but the nagging feeling that he was up to no good still persisted.

Even so, the truth of the matter would not go away. The treasury was almost dry. His accountants had calculated that he would be broke by the end of the year. They had called for him to raise taxes or go on another conquest to put the books right. Not having the heart to start a new war in unchartered territory his only hope now rested in the military quest to cease the Celtic gold. The messengers had been sent out to the garrisons all over the southern forts of Britannia to take the villages of the Borgoni tribe and then await further orders.

He dismissed the games masters who quickly gathered up their displays and designs and exited his council chamber. The opening day was to begin in just four days' time, the finest gladiator schools had their contracts and the animal trainers were in town. The city was alive once again. The public loved their emperor once again and Titus loved Rome once again.

'My emperor,' a voice spoke from behind. It was Tulca, the head slave.

'What is it?'

'Paxus Strupalo and his friends, including the two women are here as you requested.'

In the interests of finding the treasure, Titus had kept his word with Paxus, Drusus and Vaco and the man they called Carl and his two women. He made them guests of the palace although they were still, technically, his prisoners. He treated Vaco with extra care, knowing that he was the only person in Rome who could lead them to the exact location. But as for General Vitrus, he allowed him to live but was sent to his barracks to be looked after by his soldiers.

'Greetings Paxus Strupalo,' said Titus warmly, 'I hope you have found your quarters to your liking?'

Paxus, Drusus and Vaco had been rewarded with their own separate quarters befitting of their standing, respectfully, whilst Carl, Lana and Mumi were given a large room with three beds. Civilians of no standing were treated very differently in these times.

Paxus bowed his head in compliance but said nothing in return. Titus immediately ordered food and wine for his guests and asked them to be seated at the table. An awkward silence followed as they sat. Two guards stood ready at the door as all eyes at the table fell upon the Titus who smiled back at them in turn, but then he went straight to the point.

'Orders have been sent to Britannia. As I speak, my soldiers are amassing their forces and will be advancing towards the Borgoni villages. I expect to receive news within the next few weeks of their victory. Once they have secured the area you, Drusus and your guide, Vaco will be escorted to Britannia to lead the commanders to the treasure.'

Paxus said nothing once again. He stared Titus up and down like he was eyeing up a new slave.

'Why do you look at your emperor with such insolence?' asked Titus hiding his displeasure with great restraint.

Paxus finally looked Titus in the eye and spoke:

'We are grateful for the favourable treatment we have received since our arrival in Rome but what becomes of us after we have led you to the treasure?'

'I will grant you all a full pardon with enough money to live out the rest of your lives in comfort but you will be exiled to the east. Where in the east you choose to go is up to you.'

'A soldier's word or an emperor's word?' asked Paxus.

'I am a soldier first,' proclaimed Titus, sounding mightily annoyed at the politician's mocking words. 'In four days from now, the opening ceremony of the Flavian Ampitheatre will begin. Just count yourselves lucky that I don't have you thrown to the lions.'

'If you throw us to the lions you would never find the treasure,' replied Paxus, sarcastically.

Titus stirred uncomfortably in his seat but said nothing.

'Send in the food,' he snapped at the waiting slave with impatience.

Carl, Lana and the others had been back in Rome now for almost a month but they had had not been permitted to leave the palace. Although Titus was at pains to facilitate them they were under armed guard at all times. But thankfully, the time of respite in the palace had allowed Lana's health to improve, although she still looked half the woman she was, she looked healthier and stronger. Carl had finally brought her around to his way of thinking, that they will return home one day. The final phone call from Sam had confirmed that they were going to try a rescue within the next few days but he had insisted that Carl had his phone with him at all times. Once again, the Romans showed no interest in Carl's possessions; even when the phone had rung in his chamber and he answered Sam's call his guards were more concerned with eyeing up the slave girls than the 'weirdos' they were guarding.

Soon, slaves brought in the food and it was good fare; pork, vegetables and fruit but the wine was coarse and heavy. Whilst his guests ate, Titus rose from the table and paced up and down in deep thought. Carl watched as the most powerful man in the ancient world prowled around the room like a predator waiting to pounce. Titus was not a very tall man, about five-foot seven, he guessed, but he was strong looking, stocky and tough. He reckoned that the man was no fool and that he could end his and Lana's life in a split second. But he also seemed to be troubled with many burdens, some of which Carl knew through his knowledge of Roman history. When Titus returned to the table he gripped the back of his chair with both hands and glanced around at his guests.

'How would you all like to be my guests at the opening ceremony?' he asked from out of the blue.

Carl's heart skipped several beats and Lana spat her wine out all over her food.

Titus laughed as he slid his chair aside and sat back down. 'Your table manners leave something to be desired,' he said to Lana.

'We...we are going to the games?' asked Lana, incredulously.

'Why not?' said Titus. 'You are guests here in my palace, so you can be guests at the arena where I can keep my eye on you.'

Carl began shaking visibly whilst Lana was practically falling apart.

'What's wrong with these two?' Titus asked Paxus.

'They are foreigners who are not accustomed to our Roman way of life.'

'Oh. And where do they come from?'

'A place they call America,' butt-in Drusus who was wolfing down the wine as if there was no tomorrow.

Carl and Lana quickly gathered their senses and looked to each other, fearing the worst. It figured, thought Carl. Paxus no longer had any use for either of them. The treasure was found and a bargain had been struck with the emperor. He had gotten away with his life but now he showed no concern for the life of his companions.

'What is this place called America?' asked Titus who stared across table impatiently awaiting an explanation.

Drusus, who was becoming more inebriated with the wine pointed a finger at Carl and Lana and laughed aloud. 'They say they are from the future too.' He giggled to himself and slapped Vaco on the back. Vaco was not amused.

Paxus chipped in some more and spoke up in a cold tone:

'They say, in their time, they have flying machines and they have put men on the moon and ride in ships with no sails.'

Titus rolled his eyes in his head and smiled back at both Carl and Lana in turn. 'You are from the future, you say?'

Carl felt forced to reply and so, once again, he told the truth.

'Lana and I come from a country four-thousand miles to the west of here and we are two-thousand years adrift from the future. We do not know how we managed to end up in these times but we are here nonetheless.'

Silence fell around the table as they waited for a response from Titus but the emperor showed no sign of emotion. His bright blue eyes didn't shift as he stared down Carl with a look, devoid of feeling. Then he suddenly burst into a raucous, overly-loud laugh that echoed around the marbled walls and floor of the room. The guards, hearing their emperor laugh, began laughing along. Carl's tactic had worked once again. The story was too fantastical to believe. He looked to Lana who was staring out Paxus and Drusus knowing that they both had egg on their faces. They would look foolish trying to convince Titus that their story was true.

Titus reached for a goblet of wine and proposed a toast to America then laughed heartily along with his guards.

General Catrus Vitrus felt barely able to hold in the tears as he stared vacantly down at his shrivelled up stump. His pride had been torn to shreds by one single act which had left him a broken man. And his return to Rome had been a tragic mistake. Once, he had command of an entire army, now he couldn't take a piss without messing himself. His left hand had turned out to be as much use as a dead slave. Now he sat with a noose around his neck waiting for the courage to end it. He had paid a local slave boy twenty denarii to set up the noose over a wooden beam in a grain store and the boy had also stacked empty crates high enough for him to slide off. He felt his life was meaningless; a once proud leader of men had been discarded by his own. Upon his arrival back in Rome the emperor had ordered him to go straight to his barracks but the men he once considered to be his brothers shunned him, even berated him for turning up and bringing shame to the army.

The old, worn out rope around his neck, which the boy had provided, stunk of rotting fish. He had obviously cut it off a discarded net next door at the fish market. Fitting, thought Catrus. His passing will go unnoticed. He had no family, no friends and no honour. His estate will be swallowed up by the empire and his slaves sold on. The Celtic gold would have seen him return to Rome in triumph, now that dream was over. His deepest regret was not executing Paxus when he had the chance. The smooth talking politician had tricked him into a fool's errand. He blamed himself for the loss of his men and, ultimately, the death of his son.

'Oh Catrus you fool,' he sighed to himself. 'Greed has tainted you once again.'

Then, from out of the blue, the faces of Carl and Lana came to the fore. The two strangers troubled him. Who were they? What trickery did the man possess with his 'communicator' which enabled him to speak to his gods? And the woman, who was like no other woman he had ever met. He knew he should have executed them along with Paxus and the others and returned to Rome with the skull key for his emperor but that was all gone now.

He took one last look out through a gap in the slats of the store wall and could see the emperor's palace high upon the Palatine Hill lit up by flaming torches. Rome was silent this night, almost eerily so. It was as if the old lady was waiting with bated breath for him to end his life. But instead of jumping he found his mind drifting to happier days when he was Vespasian's right-hand man; a trusted and able soldier, a man who loved conquest and the riches it brought. Oh the memories of those banquets in the palace when women threw themselves at his feet and the wine flowed freely.

Whilst he sat for one last moment before the jump to his death, the doors to the grain store suddenly burst open and in walked four of his one-handed comrades. One of them was holding the whimpering slave boy by the scruff of the neck. The boy struggled violently and was let go to run off into the night.

'General, what are you doing?' asked Tefus, a lowly foot soldier who proved to be a great asset during the long trek home from Britannia.

'What the fuck does it look like?' snapped Catrus, feeling cheated. In a flash, he was airborne, swinging like a sack from the ever-tightening rope around his neck. Immediately, three of the soldiers raced to his side and raised him upwards by the legs. Tefus quickly climbed up the stack of crates as best he could with one hand and withdrew his dagger. Catrus was slowly choking to death. Tefus began cutting away at the rope with his left hand but then, the rotting rope snapped and Catrus, the three soldiers and Tefus all fell in a heap on top of one another.

Moments later, the five men found themselves seated upon the empty crates staring at one another in utter hopelessness.

'I don't want to end up a beggar on the streets,' said Tefus. 'But taking my own life is the last thing I would do.'

'Speak for yourself,' replied Catrus, grumpily.

Tefus shook his head. 'Before I die I want to see the politician and his friends pay for what they did to us.' The other soldiers nodded in agreement. Catrus laughed sarcastically and spat on the ground.

'I hear that one of them,' continued Tefus, 'who whose name is Vaco, is the only man in Rome who knows exactly where the treasure is hidden. He is being kept at Titus' pleasure so he can lead him to the treasure.'

'Then he must die!' said Catrus.

'Hear, hear!' said another in reply.

Tefus leaned forward and stared Catrus in the eye. 'We are soldiers and soldiers can be very good assassins.'

Catrus leaned back in surprise. 'I would give anything to deny the emperor a chance to get his hands on that gold. So what are you saying?'

'You know your way round the emperor's palace, general,' said Tefus. 'I say we sneak in and kill Vaco in his sleep.'

Catrus lowered his head in deep thought. To the men he seemed to be mulling over the proposal. Then he looked up and smiled.

'No, I have a better idea.'

25

The warm air of the late evening wafted through the tall windows of the bedchamber, tousling Lana's hair as she sat upon a stool staring up at the half moon in silent contemplation. It had been almost a year now since that fateful evening when her world was turned on its head. She had come to Carl's tent to get away from the sexual advances of the over-eager students at the dig site but she had no intention of falling asleep. Had she stayed awake and returned to the Coppola Inn she would have been spared this nightmare but fate had dealt her, and Carl, a terrible hand. Now, with Carl's assurances, it seemed they may be going home after all! The miracle of Carl and Sam's phones being linked through time may be a lifeline but what, she thought, had the scientists come up with to get them back and by what mechanism will they do it?

The bed on the other side of the room creaked as Carl shifted his weight onto his side. Lana turned and looked at her sleeping co-worker. He had been asleep now for several hours but Lana could not rest due to her condition. Her aching crotch tormented her at intervals although the severity of the pain had eased over time. Her vagina had never fully healed and leaked blood every now and then. For all her physical frailties the memory of those cocks pounding away inside her remained a mental scar that she would carry with her for the rest of her life. And worse still, she would never forget the faces of the men that perpetrated such a violation.

'Come to bed Lana,' whispered Mumi from the other side of the room.

Lana spun around to see Mumi sitting up, but she was looking in completely the opposite direction. Then she flopped back down on her bed and was out like a light. Lana smiled and felt thankful that Titus had not invited Mumi to the opening ceremony. She was a slave and slaves were excluded from attending the games. In a cradle by her bed, the sleeping Julia didn't stir. The little angel was born only eight weeks ago, high in the Alps. She remembered delivering Julia. The sight of seeing a new-born baby filled Lana with a terrible guilt that she had chosen her career over children. To help her forget that disturbing thought she strolled out onto the marble floored balcony and looked out over the city. She guessed it must be around three o'clock in the morning. Apart from the torches lighting up the palace, Rome was in almost total darkness. The only sounds she could hear were that of a baying donkey somewhere off in the distance and the rustle of the leaves from the many trees in the gardens below. Then, from out of the corner of her eye, Lana sensed a dark shadow detach itself from the wall. She stiffened and froze in fear, but her worries eased when the smiling face of Titus appeared from out of the gloom.

'Can't sleep?' he asked as he approached whilst dressed in a slave's tunic, 'I can't either.'

Lana still had to steal herself that she was actually in the presence of a famous person from history. The madness of it made her shudder. She looked the emperor up and down in the glow of the small lanterns that lit the balcony and felt intimidated by him. This was a man who was responsible for the death of so many Jews; a man with the blood of a nation upon his hands and yet he looked just like your friendly neighbourhood postman or bus driver.

'Do not worry,' said Titus, 'I wasn't prying. I often walk around the grounds of my palace in disguise. It helps me to get away from my guards and it gives me time to think.' He leaned up against the balcony rail and looked up at the half moon. 'The night is fresh and the moon is veiled by the hands of the gods.'

'That is poetic but…' Lana caught her words in her throat and looked away. She was about to tell him that the moon's cycle around the earth causes it to fall in and out of the glare of the sun's rays thus causing it to have phases.

Titus turned towards Lana and pondered for a moment. 'Is it true what Paxus said, that men have walked on the moon?'

Lana cringed and kept her stare fixed upon no particular point. She may as well be honest with him, she thought, the tactic had served Carl so well.

'A man named Neil Armstrong and his colleague Buzz Aldrin stepped out onto the surface of the moon and planted an American flag into the lunar soil. They did it for all mankind.' She left her words hang in the air as she waited for a response from Titus.

'How did they get there?' he asked sounding interested but a little condescending at the same time.

Lana turned and faced the emperor but this time she didn't hold back. As with her lecture at Ducia's villa many months ago, she went through a brief history of mankind, starting with the renaissance and ending with the Apollo mission from take-off to splashdown.

Titus listened with fascination but unlike Ducia, he seemed interested and eager to understand. After her lecture, Lana was surprised to find that she had tears in her eyes born out of a yearning for home. After a long interlude between the two, Titus nodded and let out a long breath through his pursed lips.

'I am speechless,' he said, almost apologetically. 'Your words seem sincere yet, utterly preposterous.'

Lana did not answer. She didn't have the energy to argue her point anymore. She had let it all out to the most powerful man in the world and it was up to him to decide whether to believe her or not. She turned away from him and allowed more lonely teardrops to fall. After several moments, she wiped her eyes and turned back to face the emperor, expecting a barrage of questions to come her way, but she found herself alone. A warm breeze whipped through the rustling leaves of the pines as if to hide the emperor's passing. A moment later, Lana finally succumbed to fatigue and retired to bed. Her last thought before sleep took her was that Titus wanted to believe her but couldn't find the courage to.

At dawn, on the morning of the opening ceremony of the Coliseum, Carl and Lana were taken to the Praetorian guardhouse for a briefing by the games master on how to conduct themselves in the presence of the emperor at public occasions. The games master, a rather dithery and frail looking character, ran through the rules on what to do and what not to do. They were required, at all times, to smile and show joy at being granted a place in the royal box. They were not to speak first and were not to stand up until the emperor stood first. They could not leave the royal box even to relieve themselves. Before entering the box they were to force themselves to vomit and were required to shit and piss at least half an hour beforehand. They were also required to hand out gifts of bread and wine to the poorer people in the crowd. This helped endear the emperor to them. And last but not least, they were not permitted to show any sign of disgust at the deaths of the condemned, the gladiators or the animals slaughtered in the arena. This was considered to be disrespectful to the emperor and was punishable by flogging or even death in the arena itself, depending on the emperor's mood.

After the briefing, they were escorted by slaves to ready them for the games. Lana was taken to a separate area where she was bathed in scented water, had her hair set in the typical Roman fashion and dressed in the finest white robes. Carl was shaven, trimmed and bathed and was given a blue robe to wear. He was also given back his belt containing his phone. The slaves showed no interest in it at all. Once again, Romans from all walks of life raised little curiosity at Carl's belongings because to them, they were not practical objects and he wondered how they would respond if he had a simple device such as a battery operated torch.

When Carl eventually saw Lana, he held his breath at the sight of her. It had been so long since he last saw her looking so resplendent; the bag of bones that she had become over the last twelve months were now but a memory, though she still had a long way to go to match her California girl looks. Nevertheless, the improvement was stunning.

After greetings were exchanged, the two of them were taken to a large waiting room where there was a gathering of many finely dressed people. Paxus, Drusus and Vaco were also present but they stood aside from Carl and Lana determined as they were to distance themselves from them.

'Lana,' said Carl as he looked deep into her eyes.

'What is it Carl?' she asked whilst keeping one eye on the well dressed women in the room.

'In a funny sort of way I hope we don't end up back home today, of all days!'

Lana shrugged her shoulders and looked Carl straight in the eye. 'What do you mean, 'of all days'? You want go home don't you?'

'Yes but we're about to witness the opening ceremony of the Flavian Ampitheatre for Christ's sake!'

'Maybe it would be better if we don't, Carl. The brutality will be worse than you could ever imagine.'

'I know, but from an archaeological perspective this is a good as it gets.'

'Is that all you can think of?' asked Lana, disappointingly. 'What about your thoughts on leaving Julia and Mumi behind to this terrible society?'

Carl looked aghast at Lana's response. He seemed to be struggling with her question and she wasn't ready for a negative reply.

'They were born to these times so they should live in these times,' he finally said, without a hint of emotion in his voice.

Lana suddenly felt angry towards Carl. She turned her back on him out of disgust. She had been disappointed in him since the birth of Julia. He had shown no emotional attachment to her even though the little darling was a joy to behold. Now, all Carl could think about was witnessing the inaugural games, first-hand.

But Lana also found herself with a terrible dilemma on her hands. If Carl was right, the two of them could be home within the next twenty-four hours, without Mumi and Julia. That thought terrified her. Her head was telling her that Carl was right, of course, and that Mumi and Julia were of these times but her heart was telling her otherwise. Then a thought came to her. She could offer to stay and force Carl to bring Julia back with him. The child wouldn't be any the wiser. She will have a better life in the future than here in Rome. But she quickly quashed that idea. She and Carl must go back. There may be unforeseen paradoxes with the whole idea of taking Julia or anyone else from these times back with them. The paradox of Julia's birth was enough. The dilemma was awful whichever way she chose to look at it.

The time was set for three o'clock in the afternoon, Severny time. The bomb, aptly nicknamed 'Titus' was primed and ready. Sam looked at his watch; an hour to go. His heart began to race. His mouth began to dry out and his nerves were shot to pieces. He looked around at the anxious faces in the control room. His eyes finally settled upon Professor Francesco Vinci who was seated next to the Russian president. Francesco looked extremely nervous. He had given Nicolai Kushnov the honour of pressing the red button that will explode the bomb and Sam wondered if Francesco was rueing his decision.

Malcolm McVie was busying himself with final calculations and looking more like a hobo with his overgrown beard than the slick, cool professor that he knew him to be. Other people in the room had one eye on the TV screens showing Sky news which was reporting from around the world, especially from Washington DC where a reporter was stood in front of a crowd waving banners and baying for the rescue attempt to be called off. The atmosphere in the control centre was stifling.

'Still good to go,' announced a voice over the intercom in Russian which was quickly translated by an interpreter into English. The half-hourly message was relayed from the remotely operated advanced observation camera, which was sealed in a bomb casing designed to withstand the blast. The camera was positioned at ground zero only two-hundred feet away from the bomb.

Meanwhile, thousands of miles away in Washington DC, Ted Brooks sat at home glued to his TV watching Sky's coverage of the Russian networks' live broadcast from Severny Island. The Russian president had allowed one camera to monitor the bomb site and through this camera he broadcast the event, live, through Sky news around the world. The camera was fixed to a platform which never moved. Meanwhile, Sky had brought nuclear experts into their studios to comment on the rather mundane picture of a bleak looking landscape which was every so often interrupted by passing birds flying by. Physicists and theorists were also asked to comment but overall, Ted guessed these so-called experts were talking out of their arses and no one really knew what was going to happen.

Every now and then the camera would zoom in and Ted could make out the bomb suspended in the tower. It looked puny and insignificant to the surrounding landscape and he shuddered at the thought that so much power could come from such a small speck upon the horizon.

The doorbell rang making him almost jump out of his skin. He took stock. It's five-thirty in the morning! What does someone want at this hour? Within seconds he was answering his door to a police officer. The man asked him his name. After Ted confirmed his name the officer handed him a large brown envelope then he left in a patrol car without saying another word.

Ted shut the door, made his way back to the TV and stared at the envelope in his hands. It was from the mayor's office. He opened it up and read the letter. It was warning him that if the rescue attempt in Russia failed he would have thirty days to reveal the whereabouts of Carl and Lana, whether they were dead or alive, and that he will be charged accordingly.

Ted crunched the paper up in his fist and threw it to the ground. Then the doorbell rang again.

~ 332 ~

He answered the door to Winifred this time. She immediately showed him a copy of the same letter.

'What the hell is this?' she asked, sounding angered and a little afraid.

'It's the dumbass mayor doing his duty, I suppose,' said Ted as he welcomed Winifred in. 'Come, watch the broadcast with me. I need the company.'

'What if the experiment fails?' asked Win as she sat down on Ted's couch and eyed the TV.

'Then we will be involved in the most extraordinary court case in history and probably the most expensive ever for the tax payer.'

'I need a drink!' she said.

'I think I'll have one too!'

Ted offered her a glass of white wine and poured himself a large glass of Bourbon. She drank her wine down in one gulp and leaned back on the couch. She was dressed in a loose-fitting white blouse and a pair of blue three-quarter length leggings. Her hair had grown long since the last time he saw her and it made her look very alluring but any thoughts of seducing her was out of the question. He had tried that on at the climate summit in Rio many moons ago and she had left him in no uncertain terms where he stood.

'I'm scared, Ted. Anyone whose anyone will want our heads on the block if this doesn't work out.'

Ted couldn't find the words to console her; both fell silent. He gave Win the whole bottle of wine then slumped back into his favourite chair and sipped away at his Bourbon. After several long moments of quiet contemplation, he spoke in a soft tone:

'Well, in half an hours' time we're going to find out.'

At precisely 3pm, Severny time, Titus exploded. The nuclear reaction sent out a shockwave at supersonic speed across the island. Dust, bits of gravel and even rocks were hurled across the barren landscape instantly becoming deadly missiles to anything within a three mile radius. The mushroom cloud rose high above the ground at an astonishing rate. A roiling, boiling cauldron of superheated gasses reached up from ground zero like a clawing monster trying to free itself from the jaws of hell. A second later, the heat blast followed, sizzling and charring everything it touched. The soil around the epicentre of the bomb instantly melted then quickly cooled and turned into a sheet of solid glass. Then, without warning, a secondary explosion occurred within the mushroom cloud. Through their special observation glasses, in the relative safety of the command centre, the onlookers witnessed a flash of white light that suddenly turned into a spinning ball which hovered over the site. Then, from within its centre thousands of bolts of lightning struck the ground right at the point where the rescue chamber was situated. The brilliance of the lightning strikes completely outshone the nuclear blast and penetrated through the onlooker's observation glasses causing them to shy away.

Then, without warning, the spinning ball decreased right down to a singularity which hovered in mid-air for a split second and then vanished. Everyone in the room looked around at each other in astonishment. They hadn't expected this. Now they waited for confirmation from the remote outpost camera to see if the rescue chamber had survived. All the instruments in the room indicated that the experiment had worked but they needed a visual to confirm it.

For Sam, it had been a spectacular demonstration of the awesome power of nuclear physics but he did not have a clue as to what caused the lightning strikes and the spinning ball of light. Then he felt a comforting arm around his shoulder. It was Malcolm.

'Congratulations,' he said warmly.

Sam barely acknowledged Malcolm. His concentration was unbreakable. The camera had obviously survived because it was sending back an image of drifting smoke and dust. The tower, which had held the bomb in place, had been completely vaporised. It was a miracle that the camera casing had survived and now all they could do was wait.

Out of the corner of his eye, Sam could see Nikolai Kushnov shaking hands with Francesco as he prepared to return to Moscow. He had done his job as the first politician to use a nuclear bomb for peaceful purposes. But Sam knew the president couldn't care less if Carl and Lana had survived. As far as Kushnov was concerned, his job was to put two fingers up to the Yanks and the rest of the western world. The president left without much ceremony, followed by his entourage of officials.

Suddenly a red light blinked intermittently on the panel above the monitor. Sam's heart skipped a beat.

'What's that?' he asked Malcolm.

'It indicates that the camera is overheating. Its cooling system is failing.'

Professor Francesco approached the desk. He stared hard at the monitor and shook his head. 'We have to get men on the ground,' he announced. 'We need to know as quickly as possible.'

Within seconds, army helicopters were on their way. Soldiers in protective suits were the first to go, followed by a support group and a medical team. Lastly, the engineers, who were to extract the rescue chamber from the ground, followed at a safe distance behind. Another tense wait ensued as Sam's already shattered nerves were being torn to shreds.

Fifteen agonising minutes later the soldiers had landed their helicopters and entered the blast zone. The dust and smoke had begun to settle but the ground was still hot. The shaky images from the soldiers' headcams showed nothing but a blackened and scarred landscape encircling a large crater. It was almost as if they were cosmonauts reporting from an alien planet.

Then the speaker crackled to life and a Russian soldier spoke. The interpreter quickly relayed the message in English.

'We can see that the rescue chamber is intact but it has been pushed further into the ground by some five meters or so.'

The news was greeted with a sigh of relief but concern that the chamber had moved.

'The lead casing has completely evaporated and so has the surrounding water but it looks like the liquid nitrogen is working fine,' said the soldier.

'It worked. The water and the lead did their job,' said Malcolm.

'Let's get stage two in operation,' announced Francesco, triumphantly.

Sam could sense the atmosphere in the room was lifting with every passing second but he was still concerned for Carl and Lana. The chamber was designed to keep them alive for up to two hours after the blast. He knew that it would be the longest two hours of his life. A camera inside the chamber was a considered option but Francesco objected to putting one in, saying that if the rescue was a failure he did not want to see the bodies of Carl and Lana lying unattended for any length of time. Sam wholeheartedly agreed.

Stage two concerned the recovery of the chamber. The engineers got to work straight away. Firstly, they lowered the chain from their helicopter which was hovering thirty feet above ground. On the end of the chain was a hook which latched onto the large, six-inch thick hoop at the top of the chamber. Using the helicopter to take up the slack they carefully raised it by a few feet. They could see that the outer shell was glowing white hot which meant they had to cool it down rapidly. Quickly, one engineer disconnected the liquid nitrogen hose by a remote switch. Within seconds the chamber was airborne and heading out towards the coast where a sectioned-off area in the sea was waiting. Seven minutes later the chamber was lowered into the freezing cold waters off the Severny coastline and set down upon a sunken framework attached to the sea bed. Powerful magnets on the framework held the chamber in place to stop it from floating away. From Sam's vantage point in the shelter he could see through his viewfinder that the seawater was steaming and boiling upon contact with the glowing chamber.

Stage three had now kicked in. The chamber was to be left in the sea until the thermal imaging cameras on board the helicopter indicated a safe level. The scientists had calculated that it should take at least twenty minutes until the temperature began to fall and that it would be a rapid decline after that. Unnervingly for Sam there was still no indication of life inside the chamber. The torture continued.

'Would you like some coffee?' asked Malcolm, sounding a little nervous.

'Got any Scotch whiskey?' asked Sam knowing that Malcolm didn't touch the stuff.

'If there was any available I wouldn't hesitate in having a wee dram,' he replied with a forced smile.

Sam accepted the coffee and smiled back. Then he burst into floods of tears.

'This is killing me, Malcolm; not knowing if they are alive.'

'It's been a long journey and we're nearly there my friend,' replied Malcolm as he placed a comforting arm around him. Upon hearing Sam's cries, Francesco walked over and placed a hand on Sam's shoulder.

'The moment of truth will be upon us soon. Everything has worked to perfection up to now. I see no reason why it cannot continue to do so.'

Sam nodded and wiped the tears from his eyes. He thanked Francesco for trying his best. The Italian professor looked tired and in need of a good sleep. Dark rings around his eyes suggested he hadn't slept at all in the past twenty-four hours and Sam guessed that he himself must also look like shit.

The longest twenty minutes in Sam's life crawled by at a snail's pace. In all that time he never took his eyes off the monitor. Eventually, the glow from the submerged chamber began to dim. Seated in only fifteen feet of water it suddenly began to change from white to red very quickly. The moment of truth was now a reality and Sam wasn't sure what to think.

Now stage four kicked in. The engineers' helicopter, which had been hovering over the scene all the while and from which the command centre was getting its images, now took up the slack on the chain. A short command from the pilot over the intercom ordered the magnets to be switched off and within seconds the chamber was airborne. This time it was headed straight for the command centre. A few half-hearted claps and a triumphal shout from someone in the room went up but most sat in silence with their mouths open as the chamber swung through the air suspended like a ball on a string. The blackened sphere grew ever bigger on the screen as it came nearer by the second, but soon they realised that it looked slightly misshapen, like a potato. Everyone gasped at the same time but the drill was that all people within the command centre were to remain inside until the chamber was placed safely within the waiting cradle, some five-hundred meters away.

Soldiers in radioactive protective suits were waiting to guide the chamber down. Several fire engines and two ambulances were ready and waiting. Sam couldn't bare the whole scene and automatically reached out for Malcolm's arm, gripping it as tightly as he could. By the look at the state of the chamber, he feared that Carl and Lana were dead.

President McCauley sat in the oval office steaming with anger as he watched the incredible lightning display within the mushroom cloud and then the subsequent arrival of the helicopter which took away a glowing white ball from the epicentre of the explosion. The Russians had let off the bomb in defiance of international law but worse than that, the American people will see it as a failure on his behalf. A brief thought ran through his mind, *'should I resign and leave the vultures to pick over the bones of my office?'* He shook his head dismissing such thoughts and looked around the grand room at the grim faces of his staff. He knew that everyone was thinking the same as him. They now wished the rescue to be a failure; that the chamber was either empty or that Carl and Lana were dead. Either way, he intended to make the most of the opportunity, should it arise.

Before leaving for Moscow, President Kushnov had ordered that cameras were to film the opening of the chamber and had set up links with Sky news to prepare for it. The images were instantly sent around the world. People in many countries were being woken from their sleep whilst others stayed glued to their TV sets way past their bedtime. The world held its breath as the grainy images from Severny Island showed a blackened and charred hulk sitting in a metal framework. Men in protective suits were busy locking down latches whilst two fire engines were hosing down the steaming chamber with water.

TV presenters were second-guessing what was happening in an attempt to try and keep their audiences fixated, but no one was listening. Experts were quick to offer their explanations. Some suggested that it was a cover up; that this was a secondary chamber, prepared off camera to fool the world. Others were worried that if the chamber was opened god knows what might come out but most were simply fascinated and kept an open mind about the whole thing.

The world was waiting.

26

The time had come for the guests of the emperor to make their way from the waiting area to the royal box. Lana wished to be zapped back home and be done with it, even though her heart was breaking with the thought of leaving Mumi and Julia behind.

As she followed the twenty or so guests up the steps her heart began pounding loudly in her chest. The thought of witnessing the Roman arena, first-hand, both thrilled and frightened her at the same time. She had read all the books and been to many lectures but the gory details were always part of her imagination and now she was about to witness the sight for real.

As she ascended the rather long flight of steps she was surprised to notice how little noise there was coming from the arena. Surely fifty-thousand people would be making quite a din, especially as it was the inaugural games, she thought? Several more steps later she entered the royal box and was stunned to see the entire crowd sitting in absolute silence. She turned to Carl who was looking about in wide-eyed wondermnt. She followed his gaze and could see that the Ampitheatre was dripping in marble and gold from top to bottom. The upper rim of the Coliseum encircled a disc of clear blue sky but it was still morning and the sun was yet to rise above the top most edges of the building. Statues of the many gods that the Romans adored were placed at intervals around the rim giving the Coliseum a finished look which was indeed a splendid sight to behold. Then she quickly turned her attention to the arena floor where all the killing will take place. The floor looked bigger than when she saw it two-thousand years in the future. It was quite an impressive sight. Pristine white sand covered the whole arena and she quickly recalled that the word 'arena' was Latin for sand.

'My god,' whispered Carl, 'this is unbelievable.'

She turned back to Carl and saw tears welling in his eyes. She understood how this amazing place could turn an archaeologist to mush but she wished, for Carl's sake, that they would be zapped back right now because when the killing starts his romantic delusions of the Roman games will quickly dissipate.

Suddenly, a blast from a distant trumpet sounded out across the Coliseum, reverberating around the marbled walls loudly. Straight away, the crowd erupted into a cacophony of cheers and calls to their emperor.

'Hail Caesar! Hail Caesar! Hail Caesar!'

Soon, Titus appeared at the front of the royal box from a side door. The emperor looked resplendent in gold and silver armour swathed in a purple cloak and wearing a Laurel leaf crown upon his head. He was carrying a consular which was a small baton; the symbol of Rome that all emperors carried on official duties.

The crowd were on their feet cheering and praising their leader. Lana was struck by the genuine affection shown by everybody. This wasn't like North Korea where you had to applaud and cheer the leader out of fear of reprisals from his henchmen. No. This was up front and honest love for their leader. Both Carl and Lana were taken aback by the adulation that Titus was receiving. It was something akin to The Beatles walking out on stage just as they were about to perform their greatest hits.

Titus took his place at the front and centre of the royal box quite a distance down from Carl and Lana who were stood at the very back just behind Paxus, Drusus and Vaco. He then he raised a hand for silence. The crowd obeyed at once and the arena went still. A light breeze swirled around the Coliseum flapping at the many standards attached to various podiums and high walls.

'Citizens of Rome welcome to the opening games of the Flavian Ampitheatre,' Titus announced. His voice reverberated around the walls sounding as clear as a bell. 'Please enjoy the hospitality of your emperor. I have ordered one-hundred days of festivities for your entertainment.'

The crowd erupted into raptures of applause and cheers. Titus calmed them down once again then raised both arms to the sky. As if on command, a shaft of sunlight fell upon the royal box illuminating the emperor much like a spotlight in a modern day stadium. His gold and silver armour reflected back the light brilliantly, dazzling sections of the crowd. Instantly, they erupted at once and Lana was left shaking her head at the ingenuity of the Romans. She looked to the rim of the building and saw that a strategically placed slit just below the top was allowing the sunlight through right onto the spot where Titus was standing. The effect sent the crowd wild.

'Clever bastards!' whispered Carl beside her.

A soldier guarding the exit prodded Carl in the leg with the butt of his spear reminding him not to speak as Titus continued to wallow in the adoration from the crowd. Carl glanced back at the soldier who, strangely, wore a battle helmet with the visor down and was standing in a most awkward looking posture. The moment was not lost on Paxus who noticed that the soldier was holding the spear in his left hand which was not the traditional stance.

'Hail Caesar! Hail Caesar! Hail Caesar!' the crowd cried out once more and Paxus' attention was quickly drawn towards the spectacle.

Titus calmed the crowd once again. When the euphoria died down he turned to the games master and brought him forward into the light, showing him to the people. It was the same man who had briefed Carl and Lana on games etiquette earlier. Titus grasped the frail man's arm and raised it high into the air. Then he cried out loudly:

'I declare the games open.'

Immediately the sun peaked over the rim of the Coliseum and half the arena was bathed in bright sunlight. The pure white sand reflected the light into the spectator's eyes and they loved it. Titus turned, seated himself down and took in the admiration of the crowd. Carl, Lana and the others in the royal box were then ordered to sit and they sat down upon on cushioned marble benches. Then a fanfare of trumpets and thunderous drumbeats sounded out whilst at the same time, to the left of the royal box, two large, bronze doors slid apart and in entered a parade led by dancing and tumbling acrobats, followed by midgets imitating gladiatorial combats. They looked comical in their completely naked form and Lana couldn't help but chuckle a little under her breath. Next came the animal cages; lions, leopards, wild dogs and bears, respectfully. She could see that the animals looked scared out of their wits and were cowering down in their cages in fear. Her stomach began to churn at the pathetic sight of the poor creatures being submitted to such torment. As quickly as the fanfare began, it ended, as the parade did a complete circuit of the arena and left through the same bronze doors it had entered.

Within seconds a train of wheeled podiums were pulled out into the centre of the arena by a group of labourers. Tied to several posts on each podium were naked children. Lana guessed their ages ranged from about three to twelve. The posts, with the children still tied to them, were removed from the podiums and slotted into prearranged postholes in the floor of the arena. Lana looked to Carl who was already shaking his head at the thought of what was to follow.

The terrified children were arranged in an outward facing circle as the crowd buzzed with anticipation. Lana counted thirty-two of them in all. They looked dirty and malnourished. After the labourers had left the arena, several wooden doors low to the ground, were slid open and out ran forty or so wild dogs of Africa. Immediately, the crowd erupted into a cacophony of noise as the dogs headed straight for the children.

Lana began to baulk in disgust at the sight but then, suddenly, she found that her vision was going out of focus. She rubbed her eyes and blinked rapidly but the fuzziness wouldn't go away. Her view of the arena became blurred and she couldn't make out any details whatsoever. Then she felt a hand gripping her wrist, it was Carl's, he had his phone in his other hand.

'Lana. Oh fuck! It's happening?' he said loudly.

Then suddenly, the guard stepped forward from behind Carl and threw down his spear then he pushed Carl aside and proceeded to pull out a wicked looking dagger, holding it aloft in his left hand.

Lana reached out automatically to Carl in an attempt to save him from the guard but she was taken aback when Carl's phone began transforming into a kaleidoscope of colours and began spiralling down towards a focal point in his palm of his hand followed by a circular wall of darkness that was closing in on all sides.

'Lana,' he cried out in vain but, luckily, there was no sign of the guard; he had disappeared beyond the edges of the circle.

Then, from out of nowhere, the face of Paxus came into focus. He reached out and grabbed a hold of both their arms. He yanked them towards him but Lana could see the circle of darkness was crowding in around her and she suddenly felt herself falling. Paxus was forced to let go of his grip and she saw him and Carl tumbling ahead of her. In the distance, she could hear Carl calling out to her but there was nothing but blackness ahead. A sudden blast of freezing cold air caught her breath for a split second then, after that, she felt nothing at all. There was no falling sensation or any sense of direction and she couldn't hear nor see anything. Strangely, instead of going into a hysterical panic brought on by the total denial of her senses she suddenly felt a kind of serene calmness come over her. It was a peaceful feeling that transcended fear; a kind of dream-state that reminded her of the many drug-induced beach parties back home in California. Then something hit her right leg and bounced away spinning off into the darkness. The impact jolted her back to reality. She screamed out Carl's name but could not hear her own voice nor any reply from him.

She reached out desperately with her hands to try and touch him but there was nothing to touch. She tried kicking out her feet but still found nothing.

Is this it, she thought? Has the rescue attempt failed and we're dead? Is this what death is like?

As she let the maddening thoughts linger in her mind she suddenly became aware of falling once again. Then her shoulder hit something hard with a loud thud and she stopped falling. Sounds of a deep rumbling noise followed by a swinging sensation and then the impossibly loud hissing of steam being let off all around her troubled her mind but she just wanted to sleep and soon enough, she drifted off.

When she woke, she quickly rolled over onto her back and lay still in the dark for long moments, daring not to move for fear of the falling sensation returning. Allowing her senses to take over, the first thing she noticed was an uncomfortable heat similar to a sauna which was causing her to perspire. Good she thought, at least she was still alive. Then she reached out tentatively with her fingertips and could feel a smooth surface that was warm to the touch. It felt metallic and she gave it a light tap to make sure. The familiar sound of an empty metal vessel reverberated all around her and she wondered where the hell she was.

After a few moments, where she was considering whether to chance sitting up, she heard a tap from somewhere above. Was that a reply?

'Hello!' she cried out. Her voice echoed for only a brief moment signifying that she was inside a small hollow container. Then a repeated tapping sound came this time.

She quickly stood up and banged her head on something hard.

'Ow,' cried a voice right next to her ear.

'Carl, is that you?' she cried ignoring the impact that dazed her for a moment.

'Ah, my head,' came the reply.

Lana reached up and immediately grabbed a hold of a hairy leg.

'Hello Lana. Are you all right?' he asked as he pulled his leg away.

They both frantically searched out each other's hands in the dark and held on tightly, determined not to lose each other again.

'Oh, Carl I thought I was dead for a moment,' said Lana.

Suddenly, a loud bang came from above quickly followed by a grating sound.

'I think we're back,' said Carl not sounding too overjoyed at being wrenched away from one of the most famous days in history.

'I think so,' answered Lana.

Without another thought, she banged on the side wall. It was quickly replied to by a return tap. Then she could hear the muffled sounds of voices in a language that she had heard before but could not understand.

'Is that Russian?' asked Carl.

'Sounds like it,' replied Lana without really caring. All she wanted now was to get out of whatever it was they were locked in.

A thin slither of daylight soon appeared above their heads then suddenly the sound of a creaking metal door being wrenched open made them catch their breaths. Immediately, their eyes were filled with blinding sunlight which caused them to shy away.

'Hello,' asked a tinny voice from above, obviously talking through a speaker, 'Carl Allen, Lana Evans?'

The accent sounded Russian.

'Yes,' cried out Carl. 'Where are we?'

'Who is that next to you?' asked the man.

They both turned in surprise and saw Paxus lying unconscious upon the floor, totally naked and curled up in the foetal position.

'Come, come,' said the man from above. 'Wake him up and let's go.'

They both had to squint as they looked up tentatively at the silhouette of a man dressed in what looked like a spacesuit peering down at them from just a few feet above.

'Quick, quick, come with me,' repeated the man who had his hand outstretched to them.

Their eyes soon adjusted to the brightness and a quick glance around confirmed that they were in a misshapen metal ball measuring about eight feet in all directions. Pipes, wires and junction boxes lined the contraption making it look like the insides of an Apollo command module. Then suddenly, they spotted a bright dot hovering in mid-air right in the centre of the metal ball. It was about the size of a grain of rice and was spinning rapidly. They both looked closer at the object and could see light and shades, shifting and changing inside it. It made no sound.

'Come now!' ordered the man who meant what he said this time. They looked up and could see a thin, wiry looking face peering back at them through the open visor of his helmet. He looked strained and anxious as droplets of sweat dotted his half-moon glasses which made him look so unlike an astronaut or a cosmonaut in this case.

Carl and Lana slowly got to their feet and it was only then that they realised that they were both stark naked. They quickly covered their bits up as best they could and looked away from each other out of respect. The next moment, three large military jackets landed next to them from above.

'Quickly, put them on and wake him up!' said the man who was sounding ever more irritated with them as the seconds passed by. 'And please do not touch that!'

After putting on the jackets they glanced back curiously at the spinning object one last time. Then they shook Paxus awake. He stirred as if from a deep slumber then he suddenly sprang into life. He looked around the metal container and scurried backwards from Carl and Lana.

'What witchcraft is this?' he demanded.

'Welcome to our world!' Carl announced, sarcastically as he held out the jacket towards him.

Paxus screamed in terror and swooned to the floor cursing the two before him and ordered them to take him back to Rome.

~ 347 ~

*

Soon, Carl and Lana found themselves being helped out of the hatchway whilst the soldiers had to drag a screaming Paxus out and forcibly dress him in the military jacket. Carl and Lana were amazed to see that they had come out of a blackened and smelly container that was steaming. The three time travellers were aided down spindly metal steps by several men in protective suits and hastily shepherded away across sodden ground into a waiting ambulance. Once they were inside and on the move they were asked to remove their military jackets by the two doctors, one man and one woman who were both dressed in protective suits. Paxus had to be physically restrained by two soldiers all throughout the ordeal as the doctors proceeded with a regulation medical check including a quick scan with a Geiger counter that barely registered a click. The relief upon the doctors' faces was tangible. Carl and Lana immediately bombarded them with questions but they indicated that they did not speak English.

Luckily, the journey in the ambulance was brief and before they knew it, they were being quarantined away inside a military hospital. They were dressed in regulation shawls and told to lie on the beds provided. Paxus had to be forcibly held down to his bed against his will. The confused and terrified Roman was going out of his mind and had to be sedated and was strapped down to his bed for his own protection. Several doctors came and went in the space of ten minutes, all performing different types of inspections. Then finally, a young female doctor approached and spoke to Carl and Lana in English.

'I am doctor, Trudi Mishkov,' she announced with a broad but forced smile. 'Welcome back.'

As one, Carl and Lana looked across at one another and burst into floods of tears.

Doctor Mishkov immediately sedated them both and ordered that they be allowed to sleep undisturbed. Sam, Francesco and Malcolm watched the closed circuit monitor bring them pictures from the hospital of the three travellers. The men were relieved that Carl and Lana had survived but equally shocked at the sight of the other man.

'What the hell have we done?' said Malcolm with a heavy heart.

Whilst feeling ecstatic about the return of Carl and Lana the three men didn't feel much like celebrating with the appearance of the other man. It tainted the success of the greatest rescue of all time. The men could only guess at whom Carl and Lana had brought back with them. But for now, all they could do was wait.

By now, the rescue chamber had cooled enough for the engineers to dismantle it. This was stage five of the operation. It will be done to reassure the watching media that there was no chance of a permanent wormhole being left open. And to make sure, the segments of the chamber were to be sealed in a lead-lined box and buried under thirty tons of concrete.

Meanwhile, inside the chamber, theoretical physicist, Ivan Lubic removed his helmet, wiped his half-moon glasses dry with a handkerchief and stared in wonderment at the object spinning just a few inches in front of his face. This was all that was left of Carl's phone suspended in mid-air just below the empty wire bracket that once held Sam's phone, right where he had calculated it would be. Lubic knew that inside this tiny cloud of pure energy was a very small amount of anti-matter, a singularity that was held in suspended animation for all eternity. He smiled and pondered upon the possibilities that now awaited him.

Without further ado, he reached inside the front pocket of his suit and took out a canister, similar in size to a thermos flask, unscrewed the lid and carefully positioned it right under the spinning ball. Then, with trembling hands, he moved the canister slowly upwards, being very careful not to allow the magnets inside the canister to come into contact with the ball. He watched with relief as it disappeared safely inside and then quickly screwed down the lid.

Professor Ivan Lubic let out a sigh of relief and leaned back against the chamber wall, smiling to himself as he held up the canister. His hypothesis had turned out to be correct. The antimatter was always going to be a 'side-effect' of the rescue mission and no one had seen it coming. The potential for his discovery was limitless and he pondered upon it for a second, secure in the knowledge that this will make him a very rich man. The world will know of him; a Nobel Prize awaited and all the plaudits that will come with it.

A shout from above jolted him back to reality. The engineers wanted to get to work.

'Is your inspection complete, professor?' asked an engineer.

'Yes, thank you,' replied Ivan, as he kept the canister out of view from prying eyes.

'Good. Now we must get on with our job if you don't mind.'

The engineer disappeared down the steps leaving Ivan alone once again. Then, quite suddenly, the canister in his hand began to glow. A blue light extended outwards, filling the chamber and chasing away the sunlight from the hatchway. He gasped when the light suddenly began to change colour from blue to white then red to yellow and back to blue again all in the space of a couple of seconds. To his surprise, a miniature lightning bolt shot from the canister and hit him in the right shoulder, dancing along his suit all the way down the length of his arm. Strangely, there was no feeling of electrocution, only a mild sensation of being gently pricked by hundreds of tiny needles. Ivan began to feel uncomfortable and he called out to the engineers for help but none came. Then, before he knew it, the lightning was all over his body. Now he felt threatened. He made a move to scramble out of the chamber but, as he did so, the canister magically vanished from his grasp which was followed by a violent blast of freezing cold air that forced him to turn away. He closed his eyes tightly from the blast, shunning the bitterly cold air that was almost unbearable to endure. Then it suddenly stopped.

When he eventually opened his eyes he found he was standing in a small, grassless, undulating valley. There were grey clouds above and all around him stood Conifer trees and a variety of Ferns and Cycads backed by rolling hills. He looked behind him and saw an overly large moon, huge and low in the sky. The bright glow from its reflected sunlight lit up the surrounding area which was just as bright as the streetlights of his home city of Moscow. Then he looked down and at his feet and saw that he was standing inside a small crater. And then, hovering just a few feet above his head was the tiny ball of anti-matter which was vibrating wildly. In a flash, it shot down into the ground and vanished.

'No, oh no,' he cried loudly as he remembered that Professor Francesco had predicted that Sam's phone will be sent far back in time.

As his thoughts drifted, a massive beast came ambling towards him from beyond a low rise. Ivan's jaw dropped open in astonishment. He screamed aloud in a maddened rage as he recognised its three horns and hooked beak backed by a broad fan of brightly coloured skin. The Triceratops, three times the size of a Rhinoceros, glanced uninterestingly at him, rumbled a deep sound and then ambled back the way it had come.

For the first time during the Cretaceous epoch, the screams of a human being rang out but there were no other humans around to hear them.

27

In Washington DC, Ted Brooks and Winifred Bainbridge sat staring at the TV screen in dismay as they watched a grainy image of three people being escorted out of the chamber and into a waiting ambulance, but that was all. Had the rescue worked or hadn't it and why were there three people? Neither was willing to comment. Eventually, Winifred mumbled something inaudible and ran off towards the kitchen leaving Ted alone to ponder whether the mayor will come knocking, wanting heads to roll.

It was now 10pm in the evening and the streets in the Washington suburbs were deserted. People were stuck indoors watching the dramatic news reports, fearful that a third world war was about to kick off. Then Ted's mobile phone rang, shaking him awake from his thoughts. Win came running in and stood by the door to the lounge looking pensive as she waited for Ted to answer.

He depressed the talk button on his phone so both could hear.

'Hello,' he asked, tentatively.

'Hello Ted, its Sam Allen here.'

'Sam! What's happened? Has the rescue been a success?'

There was a momentary pause on the line as Ted waited anxiously for a reply.

'They're back,' said Sam in a faint whisper. 'My god Ted, they're back.'

Ted clamped his hands across his mouth and looked to Win, who had made her way across the room to stand next to him. Both looked at each other with an unspoken common understanding; the authorities were never going to believe it; the concocted story, the atomic bomb, the Russian Presidents' involvement and the whole media circus that followed. Tears welled in Win's eyes and Ted reached out to grasp her hand for comfort.

Sam's emotion-filled voice crackled through the speaker once more. 'They are alive but are being kept in quarantine. Don't know how long for though, but we don't know who the other guy is. We fear they brought him with them Ted; someone from the past.'

Ted's mind was frantically searching for a suitable reply when Win spoke up for him.

'Sam, it's Winifred,' she said in a trembling voice. 'How are Carl and Lana doing?'

'Win, they look terrible,' said Sam as he choked back the tears. 'But I think they will be fine after a good spell in hospital. Tell me what's happening back home?'

Ted and Win looked to each other in awkward way.

'Sam, they're not going to believe it,' said Ted without much ceremony. 'The bastards are going to hang us out to dry.'

'But that's ridiculous,' replied Sam. 'You saw the coverage on TV, right? Didn't you see Carl and Lana being taken in the ambulance? Didn't you recognise them?

'We saw three people. That's all Sam. The whole world saw it buddy but they won't believe it. It's like the moon landing conspiracies all over again.'

'Fucking bastards!' cried Sam.

There was a long moment of silence as all three took their own time to divulge the wider implications of their predicament. Then Ted Brooks' front doorbell rang. He excused himself from Sam, placed the phone down on the arm of his chair and slowly rose from his seat to look out of the side window. There was nobody there. Curious, he walked to the door and opened it, expecting the police. Three bullets hit him in the chest and one in the forehead, spattering his brains all over the hallway. Winifred heard him fall and ran to the door only to see Ted's convulsing body laid out on the shag pile carpet in a pool of blood. She gasped in horror and, in a panic, she ran out of the house towards her car, but her handbag was back in the house. As she turned to go back towards

~ 353 ~

the house, a bullet hit her square in the back. Another hit her in the left hand, another in the shoulder and one in neck. She fell, headfirst, into a rose bush and quickly bled to death. No one witnessed the murders. The streets were empty.

On the rooftop of an apartment block, some two hundred yards away, a sniper unscrewed the silencer from her .300 Winchester Magnum rifle and calmly packed it away. Then she texted a message to Cardinal Bell: *The ducks are in the water.*

She turned and made her way through the rooftop door and down the staircase where, outside in the carpark, waited a man on a motorbike. The tall, dark haired athletic woman strode up to the bike and put on a helmet, slung the guitar case containing the rifle over her shoulder and rode pillion away from the scene.

Cardinal Michael Bell read the text message and immediately deleted it then he dropped the phone into a glass jar of sulphuric acid. After screwing down the lid on the jar he placed it behind a brick wall and slotted the two bricks into place. He then made his way back up from the cellar to his first floor office in the Cathedral of Saint Mathew the Apostle where he was to ring his masters in Rome to announce to them a prearranged coded call - *the silence is deafening.*

Cardinal Bell sat in front of his phone readying himself for the call. He did what he had to do, he told himself. The Catholic Church always did what was necessary to keep the secret. Ted Brooks was getting too nosy for his own good and had to be gotten rid of. He had been making calls to the wrong people about the Celtic gold and his enquiries were too near to the bone for the churches liking. The treasure of the Celts belonged to the Holy Roman Catholic Church and has been for two thousand years, stolen from under the Emperor Constantine's nose. The secret had to stay safe at whatever cost.

Sam Allen placed the receiver back down on the phone and frowned. The connection to the USA had been cut. He had heard

Ted excuse himself and then silence. He turned to a now clean-shaven Malcolm who was busy reading an e-mail.

'The fuckers don't believe us,' he said to Malcolm who looked up from the computer and frowned.

'I thought so.'

'You expected this?' asked Sam.

Malcolm turned the monitor around so Sam could see the e-mail he had been reading. It was from a colleague at Edinburgh University which read:

Don't know if you can get media pictures over there but they are refusing to believe the rescue mission was a success. They say it's all been a cover-up by the Russians to spite the west and raise tensions so as to give Nikolai Kushnov an excuse to raise oil and gas prices. All U.N. military bases are on standby around the world. What the hell is going on? Louise McGovern.

'Jesus Malcolm! I didn't expect this,' said Sam looking totally deflated.

'Well, we've got Carl and Lana back. That's all that matters.'

'But they'll be ridiculed and treated as mavericks wherever they go.'

'Worse than that, my friend,' replied Malcolm. 'We'll probably end up in jail, along with Carl, Lana, Francesco and Ted Brooks for wasting time and recourses. And there's the fallout from who the hell other guy is.'

'But we haven't committed a crime,' said an exasperated Sam. 'Shit. What are we going to do now?'

Just then, one of the engineers burst through the doors and went straight to Francesco. He looked agitated and was pointing through the window at the rescue chamber.

'What's happening?' asked Sam to Malcolm.

On impulse, Malcolm looked around the room for Ivan Lubic but he was nowhere to be seen. Both men looked to Francesco who had turned and was waving them over.

When they reached him they saw that his expression was as dark as night.

'Ivan Lubic entered the chamber, now he has disappeared,' said Francesco.

'What?' Malcolm asked.

'Somehow, he managed to get into the chamber and never came out... he's gone.'

A short and awkward silence followed until Sam coughed and spoke up:

'Where the hell has he gone?'

The two scientists turned to him with a look that said it all.

'No,' replied Sam. 'But... but...'

Malcolm turned away and looked down in deep thought. 'It seems that a wormhole had indeed been created by the rescue mission but it was unstable and has gone to wherever... or whenever, taking Ivan Lubic with it.'

'So Ivan was right,' said Francesco. 'He always believed our rescue attempt would create a permanent wormhole.'

'The clever bastard!' replied Malcolm, 'but he has paid the ultimate price. Who gave him clearance to enter the chamber?'

Francesco buried his head in his hands, disappointed in himself for not foreseeing the consequences.

Just then, a clerk from the military came over and turned Sam's head towards a TV screen. He could see that Sky news was broadcasting from a suburban street in America. The clerk turned up the volume and handed Sam the remote.

Sam's jaw dropped open when he saw the photographs of Ted Brooks and Winifred Bainbridge superimposed against a backdrop of ambulances and police cars with their lights flashing. He turned the volume up further and listened to the reporter stating that Ted and Win had both been shot dead at Ted's home in the suburbs of Washington DC. Sam's heart imploded. Then the doors suddenly swung open and in rushed a Doctor Mishkov from the medical team. She raced over to Sam and his two colleagues.

'Come with me, quickly,' she asked sounding most distressed. 'It seems there is a problem with two of our time travellers.'

'What's wrong?' asked Sam.

'They... they seem to be... fading.'

Sam, Malcolm and Francesco were led by Doctor Mishkov to the field hospital. Upon arrival, she took them through two swinging doors and then to a medical room full of the familiar instruments of the trade. At the far end of the room was an open ward where three beds sat side-by-side. The assistant pointed towards the ward and stepped aside.

Three men walked into the ward were they found Carl, Lana and the strange man lying in their respective beds staring silently up at the ceiling.

'Hello Carl.' said an emotional Sam.

Carl turned his head towards his brother and a thin veil of a smile form across his lips. He could see now what the doctor meant by them fading. Carl's lips were almost translucent. His top teeth were faintly visible through his lips and the red of his tongue was showing as if his skin was made of frosted glass. His eyes had a washed-out look to them that Sam had never seen in his brother before. He glanced over at Lana who lay next to the stranger's bed. She looked much worse than Carl. She looked like a ghostly apparition of herself. Sam's eyes strayed over to the other man. He was whole and not fading at all. He looked frozen stiff with fright and kept talking to himself in Latin.

'Hi,' whispered Carl in a faintly audible voice.

Sam made a dash for Carl's bed but the doctor reached out and yanked him back.

'Do not to touch them until we can figure out what is wrong. I'm hoping that maybe you two scientists can help.'

Carl stirred under his bed sheet and made ready to sit himself up. He struggled valiantly against the single sheet which seemed to be weighing him down. When he completed his move he spoke in a very weak voice.

'Everything seems heavy,' he said to Sam in a husky whisper. 'It's like gravity is pulling me down. It's an effort to move or even talk. I can barely breathe because it feels like a grand piano is resting on my chest.' Carl struggled to talk at this point and simply gave up.

Sam smiled reassuringly but failed to hide his obvious distress. Then Lana raised a ghostly arm and pointed to the stranger strapped in the bed next to her. 'Him, him, get him away from us,' was all she could say in a barely audible whisper. Then she dropped her arm to the bed exhausted from the effort.

'The scientists will figure something out,' said Sam to Carl, feeling desperately sad. 'You just hang in there bro' and everything will be all right.'

Carl forced a weak smile back at his brother but Sam could see that he looked very afraid.

Malcolm and Francesco turned to face each other.

'It seems that part of them is in limbo; lost to space time, and that earth's gravity is acting like a wrench, ripping the space time apart,' whispered Malcolm out of earshot. 'I think the man in the other bed has something to do with it, but what? Damn it, my calculations were way out!'

Francesco shook his head in sympathy for his Scottish colleague.

'Don't beat yourself up, my friend. Your calculations were invaluable to the success of the rescue.'

In the next moment, a cry went up from Lana as she forced herself up from her bed and eventually sat upright. Her tremendous struggle against the forces of nature was a sight to behold as she swung her legs off the bed, screaming in agony with the effort. Carl turned to her and called out for her to rest but Lana wasn't listening. She leaned forward and reached out her right hand towards the man in the bed next to her. The man screamed out in fear at Lana's ghostly appearance and tried to move away but his strappings held him firmly in place. Then Lana's fingertips touched the man's left forearm and instantly, his body lit up with a bright light that forced the men to squint. Thousands of tiny bolts of lightning appeared all over his body, shrouding him from view. The walls and beds in the room began to rattle loudly, followed by a blast of freezing cold air that came from the direction of his bed. The three men and the doctor were forced to cover their faces and turn away as the severe wind lasted for several seconds and during that time they could hear what sounded like cheers from a large crowd mixed in with the barking of dogs. Then silence.

When they looked up, Carl and Lana were lying unconscious upon the floor but there was no sign of the stranger. His medical shawl and restraining straps had been torn to shreds and lay scattered in pieces all over his bed. The doctor quickly ordered the men to help her with Carl and Lana.

Upon contact with Carl, Sam immediately noticed that he had returned to his natural form. Both he and Lana were back - in full. Sam watched with relief as two nurses rushed in and helped put them back in bed.

Lana was the first to stir awake. But then Sam noticed something else incredible. Astonishingly, both of them had not only returned in full but they were back to the way they looked before they were lost in time; fully fleshed and in full health. Lana was back to her stunning self. She looked gorgeous with her full head of flowing black hair that fell down the sides of her perfect face. Her fantastic breasts were almost bursting out of the medical shawl which looked as though it could rip apart at any moment.

'Anyone got a cigarette?' she asked, sounding a little drunk and looking acutely aware of the four men staring at her fabulous tits.

Doctor Mishkov immediately reached inside her white medical lab coat and pulled out a packet of Belomorkanal cigarettes. She offered one up to Lana and lit it for her. Lana took a long drag and sighed.

'You like Russian cigarettes, yes?' asked the doctor.

'I've had better,' replied Lana as she puffed out the smoke. 'Now where the fuck am I and what the fuck's happened?'

At that point, Carl woke up. He sat bolt upright and stared around the room in surprise.

'What the hell is going on?' as he glanced at Lana and then at their shawls in total shock. 'Have we been in an accident?'

Sam came up to his bed and spoke. Carl turned in surprise and laughed aloud.

'Fuck's sake Sam, what are you doing here... where the fuck are we?'

Through a blur and a mist that made him feel slightly light headed, Paxus Strupalo suddenly sat bolt upright and found that he had returned to watching a pack of wild dogs devouring little children who were tied to posts in centre of the arena. The spectacle was a gory sight that served only to satisfy the more bloodthirsty amongst the crowd. One dog, in particular, had its head buried deep inside a little girl's stomach and was ripping out her guts. He turned from the primeval scene in disgust. These were the children of condemned criminals, rounded up off the streets in order to keep the city free of unwanted orphans; some were as young as three years of age. But soon, his thoughts were troubled by a sudden sense of the loss of time. He recalled that he had been watching the dogs enter the arena and then in the next moment the dogs had all but finished the children off, all within the blink of an eye.

Then suddenly, his head cleared and he immediately became aware that he was in amongst the aftermath of a fight and somehow he had missed it. Confusion was all around him as he quickly looked down to the spot where the emperor was seated and saw that he was being quietly escorted away through a side entrance. He stepped back in puzzlement and slipped on something under his foot. He automatically looked down to see what it was when to his utter shock and horror the bodies of Drusus and Vaco were lying, face-up in a pool of blood. Each had their throats cut. Next to them lay the body of a one-handed soldier lying face down, cut to pieces by the Praetorian guards. The six guards stood over the three bodies and were busily shepherding away the shocked guests from the royal box.

'Oh no,' cried Paxus to himself. 'Vaco is dead! The only man who could lead Titus to the treasure is dead!'

Paxus' head began to spin until a soldier shoved him in the back and ordered him out. The prompting jolted him back to reality. He watched on in shock as the soldiers turned the body of the one-handed man over and removed his battle helmet. Paxus was shocked to see the blood-spattered face of General Catrus Vitrus. His lifeless eyes glared back up at him as if out of spite.

'What have you done?' he whispered down at the general.

In one, single act the general's sweet revenge had torn Paxus' world apart, fore he knew that this will mean almost certain death for him.

In his mind's eye he thought desperately about what could possibly have transpired as he was ushered down the steps away from the royal box. Then straight away, a memory flashed across his mind. He recalled that he had chanced to glance back at Carl and Lana to see how impressed they might be with the Coliseum when he noticed Carl looking down at the thing he called a communicator. It was glowing with many colours and in response, Carl and Lana began to rise from their seats upon unsteady feet. He remembered reaching out to stop them from toppling forwards when all of a sudden his head began to spin and he felt himself falling. Next thing he knew, he was in a metal chamber, naked and afraid, then he found himself lying upon a bed and staring up at a light that had no flame and then he was back here, in the Coliseum. It all seemed to have happened in a flash.

He quickly scanned the faces of the gathering of startled people from the royal box and noticed that Carl and Lana were missing. But to his surprise, he found that he wasn't shocked at all. Then he became aware of a slight tingling sensation on his left forearm. He looked down and saw four white finger marks, burned into his skin. Immediately, Lana's face came to mind, a ghostly, faded image. Now it all came back to him.

'So they were from the future after all. Oh, Paxus you fool!' he declared to himself as he watched a furious Emperor Titus approach from around a corner with his Praetorian guards in tow.

'I am a dead man!'

*

Cardinal Michael Bell and Mayor John Muldoon stared up at the bust of the Emperor Constantine that was once part of a huge forty-foot seated and enthroned statue of the great man. They were standing in the Palazzo dei Conservatori on the Capitoline Hill in Rome. Next to them stood Archbishop Salvatore Benigni, head of Saint Peter's treasury in the Vatican.

'The church is in debited to many of our patrons throughout its long history but none so much as that man,' the Archbishop said as he pointed a long, bony finger at the white marble effigy.

Cardinal Bell smiled satisfactorily to himself, thankful that the early Christian leaders did a great job in convincing Constantine to hand over the gold of the Celts in return for an eternal life. The egotistical emperor was easy to manipulate during the last few years of his megalomaniacal reign and the church has never looked back since.

The location of the gold had been revealed to Constantine whilst he was the commander of Eboracum (which is now the city of York in northern England) in return for favours which remain unknown to this day. After his father's death, Constantine's soldiers immediately declared him emperor and helped him ship 'the golden mountain', as they called it, piece-by-piece, back to Rome. The church elders at that time were keen to get their hands upon the pagan gold fore they saw it as a divine gift from god so they coerced the fickle-minded emperor into releasing the gold into their trust.

Archbishop Benigni reached inside his jacket pocket and pulled out the skull key. He offered it up to his pay master with a smile.

'Keep this in your safe back in Washington DC. It is part of our great heritage. Remember, *et lapis sanguine,* my friend; our faith is built on 'blood and stone'.'

'Thank you,' replied John Muldoon. 'Let the congregation keep the faith while we keep the money, eh!' And the three men laughed along together.

28

Two years later:

SATURDAY, JULY 20ᵀᴴ PRESENT DAY:

Lana Evans sat upon the warm sands of Malibu beach and watched the waves roll in and out. Today was the tenth anniversary of her marriage to Dennis. Today had also been hot and cloudless just as it was when she had tied the knot on this very spot.

Her memory of that day was as vivid as if it were yesterday but the past few years had been the strangest time of her life. Being told that she had travelled back in time with her colleague, Carl Allen and that they had both been brought back through the use of a nuclear bomb was quite hard to swallow. The endless questions by investigative journalists had worn her out, but she had stayed resolute throughout, claiming that she had no recollection of any such events.

Physical check-ups by eminent doctors revealed that both she and Carl were in excellent health and had suffered no side-effects from the rescue mission. Psychiatrists found no lasting damage other than the natural guarded reaction from the intense celebrity status they had been receiving since returning home.

The suicide of Professor Terence Barnes saddened her terribly. She couldn't believe that he had been accused of their murder and interred without evidence for it. Her anger towards the British Police for such flagrant disregard of a gentle soul, such as his, drove her to consider suing Scotland Yard for second degree murder. And then there were the deaths of Ted Brooks and Winifred Bainbridge; two people whom she liked and admired, both professionally and personally. Who on earth would want to see them dead? What possible motivation would drive someone to shoot them with a high-powered rifle? On top of all that was the tragic death of Carmarello Di Conte, a beautiful student of archaeology, whom Lana remembered as a bright and cheerful soul, murdered by a mugger. The Italian police never found the perpetrator and probably never will.

The political leaders were still at each other's throats over the exploding of the bomb but President Kushnov's popularity was at an all-time high at home. His show of defiance to the west and the United Nations also helped raise his standing amongst international investors who were disillusioned at the crippling interest rates that the western banks had slapped on world trade. Kushnov defied the international bankers and welcomed foreign investors from around the globe with open arms.

In America, President McCauley failed to be re-elected for a second term.

Lana had no doubt that something odd had happened to her and Carl, that night in Rome. The scientist friends of Sam Allen's went to great lengths to explain to both of them that they had travelled back in time. They showed TV evidence of their return and even produced a battered Nikon camera, claiming that it was hers, and also the now famous photo of her and Carl holding up a wooden plaque. She couldn't believe how awful she looked in that picture and, at one point, even considered the woman in the frame to be an actor but she could tell it wasn't.

The evidence was convincing. The pictures of the Coliseum under construction were hard to refute, and recent pictures came to light from the National Geographic laboratories which showed a group of men seated in a cave all dressed up in first century clothing. One of the men was even pointed out as being the stranger they had, allegedly, brought back with them.

The trip to the dig site in Rome did nothing to jog her or Carl's memories. Carl insisted on returning back to archaeology but his licence had been revoked pending an inquiry. Lana had no such desire to return to work for she was a constant source of media attention. Professors Francesco Vinci and Malcolm McVie were hauled before a judicial enquiry at The Hague and charged with reckless practices in the name of science. They were struck from the register and forbidden to work on any science projects for ten years.

It was all too much for Lana. Over the last six months she shunned the publicity and found herself becoming a recluse, staying in the rented beach house, courtesy of National Geographic. She even shunned her friends who had not been very supportive. The over-the-top attention she was getting from the media didn't sit well with them, so, over time her so-called friends drifted from her – excuses, excuses always excuses.

After several moments of contemplation, she rose to her feet and shook the sand from her immaculate body. She felt physically ready for a relationship but not mentally. That small pleasure will have to wait, she thought. The invasion of her privacy over the last few years had left her little time for romance even though her emotions were crying out for company.

She made her way up to the beach house and thought, once again, about Dennis. She had managed to retrieve some of his belongings from his family; clothes, photographs and his old stereo and had spent the last week sifting through his stuff, especially his large collection of books.

She was feeling rather hungry and thought about cooking the T-bone steak she had bought when she heard the house phone ringing. She quickly bounded up the short flight of wooden steps, entered through the sliding doors and reached for the kitchen phone.

'Hello.'

'Hello, Lana, it's Michael Hughes from National Geographic here.'

Lana didn't reply but stayed silent. Michael Hughes was the new chief of Nat Geo. She knew him but not enough to be friendly with.

'We have managed to extract another picture from the SD card of your old camera.'

'Oh,' replied Lana keeping it short. She was really hungry now.

'I'm going to e-mail it to you. Is that all right?'

Michael's voice was beginning to annoy her to the point of screaming. His nasal, high-pitched tone was shredding her already fragile nerves to pieces.

'Go ahead,' she said and immediately hung up.

Ignoring the computer sitting in the corner of the living room, she took off her bikini and strode naked towards the bathroom to take a long, cool shower. After her shower, she dried herself and put on one of Dennis' Star Wars t-shirts and began the process of cooking her supper. She took the T-bone steak out of the fridge and washed it. Then she remembered that she and Dennis always liked to play music whilst cooking so she dried her hands and went over to his old stereo. She turned it on and noticed that there was a CD already in the player so she wacked up the volume control and pressed play.

Returning to the kitchen she picked up a paper bag full of onions. A second later, Creedence Clearwater Revival's song, Travelin' Band blasted out of the fifty-watt speakers. She immediately dropped the bag of onions to the floor, frozen in shock when she realised that her hands had suddenly turned translucent. It was like looking at an x-ray, bones and all. In a panic, she quickly spun on the spot and looked at her reflection in the wall mirror. She could see her tongue and throat right through her skin. A row of perfect teeth looked back at her, even though her mouth was closed. Then suddenly, a searing pain shot through her abdomen as if she had been punched hard by a heavyweight boxer. She fell to the tiled floor of the kitchen, doubled up in agony. The pain was so unbearable that she screamed out loud above the din of the speakers. Then faces, ugly, laughing faces, came into view. Evil, twisted faces full of hate, followed by the sensation of many cocks taking turns to hammer away at her insides. Blood mixed with sweat intertwined with laughter and pain filled her mind until she could no longer stand it. The ramming of her vagina continued until darkness closed in from all sides then she slowly faded into unconsciousness.

The familiar sound of the mellow strum of an acoustic guitar roused her. She lay on her side and listened to the tune coming from the beach. It sounded serene, mixed in with the wash of the waves upon the shore. Then she realised that she was lying on her kitchen floor. She immediately sat up and shook her head.

'What the fuck?' she said to herself as it suddenly dawned on her that it was now dark outside. She looked down at the floor to see a spilled bag of onions lying scattered everywhere. She looked to the stereo; it had run its course. The CD was ejected and sitting in its tray ready to be replaced.

She scanned the beach house. Everything was in its place. Nothing was disturbed.

Rising up from the floor, she felt a little unsteady on her feet but otherwise, all right. The steak was still sitting on the draining board but looking a little dry around the edges.

'I need a drink,' she said to herself. She turned on the lights in the kitchen and quickly poured out a glass of red wine. She moved into the living room and sat on her lounger to contemplate what had happened. After several gulps, she concluded that she must have slipped and banged her head but, strangely, there was no lump on her cranium. Then she remembered Michael Hughes' phone call... the e-mail!

She turned the computer on and went straight to her e-mails. Opening up the message from Michael she sat back and waited for the image to load up. Soon, a grainy picture appeared. Then, slowly, the image grew clearer until she saw it in HD clarity. It showed a smiling black woman dressed in an off-white tunic with a thick cord tied around her waist. The woman was holding up a baby that had lighter skin than hers.

'Mumi,' said Lana aloud, shocking herself in the process.

She put her hand to her mouth and wondered why that word came out.

'Oh my god!' she cried as she dropped her wine glass upon the lounger spilling its contents everywhere. 'It's Mumi and Julia!' She immediately ran to the phone and rang Carl at once.

Walking up the hill towards her former master's villa was a bit of a struggle for Mumi as she carried Julia in her right arm and Carl's sack in the other. The day was hot and the streets of Rome were deserted. It seemed that everyone was attending the second day of the games in the Coliseum. She could hear the roar of the mob baying for blood far off in the distance. When she eventually reached the front door of Fario's home, she turned back the way she had come. There was not a soul about except for few stray dogs sniffing at the dried-out remains of a chicken.

She placed the sack upon the floor and put her hand on the left hand side of the doorframe. With a gentle pull, a wooden slot opened outwards, revealing a key to the door of the villa. She put the key in the lock and turned it. She opened the door and took in a sharp breath at the shocking sight she beheld. The entire place had been trashed; empty crates, broken furniture, litter and shards of glass lay everywhere. Without hesitation, she picked up the sack and went straight downstairs to the cellar.

The cellar door was broken open. She entered quickly leaving the sleeping Julia upon an empty table then lit up a torch and looked around the room. It was empty, except for a few broken bits of furniture. Making her way to the far wall, the mural of familiar faces stared back at her including the image of herself, but she didn't have time to admire the exquisite artwork. Instead, she hastened to the base of the wall and scratched away at the loose soil with her bare hands. When she was satisfied with her labour she opened up the sack and pulled out two wooden boxes and the skull key that she had stolen from Titus' bedroom after he had left for the games. The emperor was in the foulest of moods and wanted blood for the death of Vaco, and in his haste, he had left the key by the side of his bed. Mumi felt it only right to return it to her former master's home. It was the least she could do for Fario.

She quickly placed the boxes, one larger than the other, gently down into the ground and covered them up. Next, she dug another hole, right under the image of Fario and dropped in the skull key then covered that up also, stamping the soil down of both holes with the soles of her bare feet.

Within seconds, she had gathered up Julia and left Fario's home in a hurry knowing that she will never return. She hoped the photograph she took of Julia and herself will be seen by Lana in the future. It would be a small crumb of comfort for her but at least she would have some token to remember them by.

Several hours later, Mumi stood on the bank of the river Tiber holding Julia in her arms. Her beautiful baby looked up at her with big brown eyes, full of innocence and trust. Then Mumi removed Julia's swaddling and threw her into the rushing waters. She watched as her baby's naked body was tossed and turned in the churning water before disappearing below the surface. It was the best thing she could do for her daughter, she thought. Death was welcome at any age for a slave.

After several minutes contemplating upon the disappearance of Lana and Carl, and knowing, in her heart-of hearts, that she will never see Malibu, a tearful Mumi quickly scuttled away, heartbroken and desperate, back into the eternal city and back to an uncertain future.